SHAFTESBURY AVENUE
BOOK X OF
THE PERFORMERS

Shaftesbury Avenue is the tenth novel in Claire
Rayner's sequence *The Performers*, in which she
will follow the fortunes of two families
through succeeding generations from the
beginning of the nineteenth century into the
twentieth. The very different professions of
medicine and the theatre set the background
for this compelling family saga. These are the
paths chosen by Abel Lackland and Lilith
Lucas, the two London waifs who first met in
Gower Street, whose fortunes become
inextricably mingled – and whose children
continue the saga through the later volumes.
Readers who meet Abel and Lilith for the first
time will want to share their earlier
experiences in the other books.

Also in Arrow by Claire Rayner

THE RUNNING YEARS
FAMILY CHORUS

THE PERFORMERS

Shaftesbury Avenue

Book X of

The Performers

Claire Rayner

ARROW BOOKS

Arrow Books Limited
62-65 Chandos Place, London WC2N 4NW

An imprint of Century Hutchinson Limited

London Melbourne Sydney Auckland
Johannesburg and agencies throughout
the world

First published in Great Britain by
Weidenfeld & Nicolson 1983
Arrow edition 1986

Printed and bound in Great Britain by
Anchor Brendon Limited, Tiptree, Essex

ISBN 0 09 941260 8

To Stephen du Sautoy
a publisher and a gentleman

THE LACKLANDS

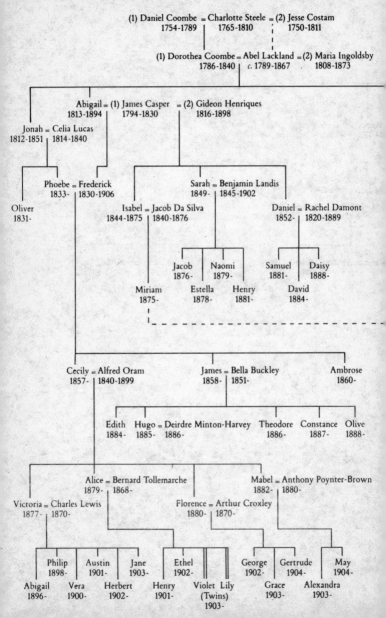

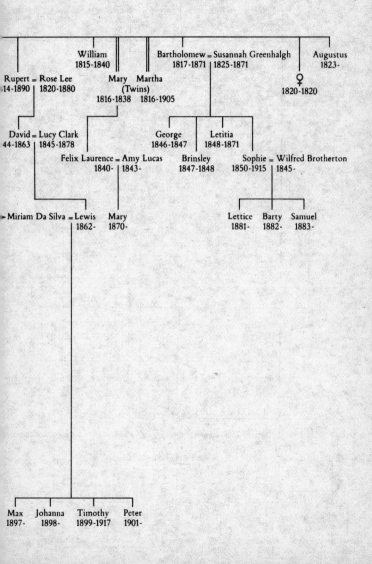

William
1815-1840

Bartholomew = Susannah Greenhalgh
1817-1871 | 1825-1871

Augustus
1823-

Rupert = Rose Lee
14-1890 | 1820-1880

Mary   Martha
(Twins)
1816-1838 1816-1905

♀
1820-1820

David = Lucy Clark
44-1863 | 1845-1878

George
1846-1847

Letitia
1848-1871

Felix Laurence = Amy Lucas
1840- | 1843-

Brinsley
1847-1848

Sophie = Wilfred Brotherton
1850-1915 | 1845-

►Miriam Da Silva = Lewis   Mary
1862-   1870-

Lettice   Barty   Samuel
1881-   1882-   1883-

Max   Johanna   Timothy   Peter
1897-   1898-   1899-1917   1901-

THE LUCASES

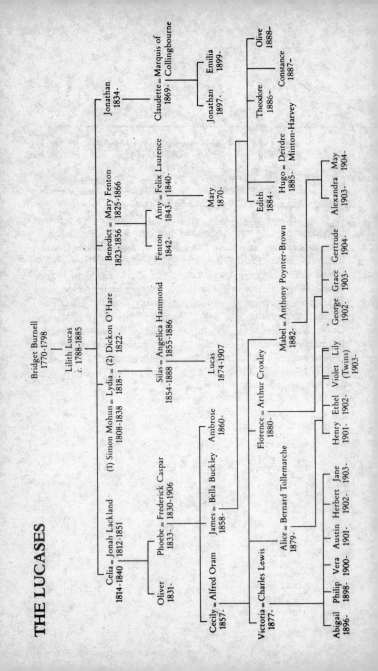

ACKNOWLEDGEMENTS

The Author is grateful for the assistance given with research by the Library of the Royal Society of Medicine, London; Macarthy's Ltd, Surgical Instrument Manufacturers; the London Library; the Royal Borough of Chelsea Libraries; the London Museum; the Victoria and Albert Museum; Leichner Stage Make-Up Ltd; Raymond Mander and Jo Mitcheson, theatrical historians; Miss Geraldine Stephenson, choreographer and dance historian; Mr Brian Coe, Curator of the Kodak Museum, Harrow; Rachael Low, film historian; the General Post Office Archives; the Public Records Office; the Archivist, British Rail; Archives Department of Thomas Cook Ltd; Curator, National Railway Museum, York; British Transport, Historical Records Department; Meteorological Records Office; Archives Department of *The Times*; David Mancur, IPC Archives; and other sources too numerous to mention.

It had started as an ordinary enough sort of Monday in November; grey, raw and cold with the skies gun-metal grey and the roof-tops slicked by the mist to their usual greasy sheen above black pavements and muddy gutters. The traffic had been as it always was in London, a heaving mass of vans and cars and horses and cabs and errand boys twisting and weaving their way through the press. The pavements were as thronged as they usually were, too, in spite of the influenza epidemic, for however much risk there was of picking up germs there was still shopping to be done and anyway, you could always wear a mask.

And then at eleven o'clock, as housewives were thinking about starting to cook midday dinners and schoolchildren were thinking longingly of playtime, the maroons had begun to wail and suddenly the town had run mad. The sound that had once sent people scuttling for cover or staring fearfully upwards for a glimpse of the ominous silvery cigars of the Zeppelins was the signal for a lunatic excitement that was, in its own way, almost as frightening as the threat of air raids had once been.

Men and women climbed on to buses and cars, clinging to the slippery roofs and howling their delight even as they slid off to crash on to the road beneath; vans were rocked on their wheels as terrified drivers tried to keep their balance, and horses, taken totally by surprise, reared and kicked and rolled the whites of their eyes in terror at the sights they saw.

Like the medical students from Nellie's hospital in Covent Garden parading up and down the Strand with a skull reared high on a pole, and chanting 'Hoch der Kaiser' at the tops of their voices, and children scrambling over the rows of captured guns in the Mall, and soldiers on leave swarming up lamp posts in Piccadilly and Trafalgar Square to hang their hats on top and wave and scream at the people beneath them.

From then on, it was anything but an ordinary Monday. The excitement twisted its way through the city, out to the suburbs of Kilburn and Holloway and even as far as Finchley, to Clapham and Peckham and Streatham and on out to Lewisham and Catford to bring hordes more people surging into the West End to join in the fun, not one whit deterred by the drizzle that started at about lunchtime and continued for the rest of the afternoon. Soaked or dry, drunk or sober, it made no difference to them. London was celebrating. The Great War, the War to End All Wars, was over. The Kaiser had been trounced as he deserved. God had been on the side of the Right. Everything was absolutely wonderful.

For some. There were women who stood in the middle of all the hubbub with their faces twisted into carved rock by their tears, making no effort to hide the desolation they felt about the ending of the war that had ended their lives too, when their men were swallowed up in the mud of the trenches. There were men on crutches, or with the blank-eyed stare of the blind or the heavy wheeze of gas-ruined lungs who stood listening to the noise and watching the celebrations and saying nothing with eloquent silence. The roisterers managed not to see them as they jostled past, arms linked, singing 'Tipperary' in hoarse shrieks and staring ahead with their eyes wide and glazed, for who needed such reminders of the hell the past four years had been, this glorious November the eleventh in 1918? It was over, over, *over*. Life was for living again.

Within doors around London, there were people who chose not to rush out into the streets to share the public celebration, people of a more elegant turn of mind and some discrimination. In Vere Street, for example, just down from St Peter's Church at number 4, a party was very rapidly put together that promised to be tremendous fun. Or so Jonty said, as he surveyed the spread laid out in the dining-room and the champagne standing by, beaded and promising, in its ice buckets. He had wanted to have hot food, a delicious curry perhaps, or a few roast birds, but his mother had said, with

2

uncharacteristic concern for her servants, that they deserved to go out and enjoy the celebration in their own fashion, and so a cold collation it had to be, served only by two maids and the elderly butler who had been the only manservant they had been able to hold on to this last four years.

That would be one thing to be put right as soon as possible, Jonty told his mother as the first of their guests came pushing through the crowds in Oxford Street to reach their fashionable front door.

'Some decent service again, Maman, and an end to stupid shortages. Bliss!' He looked around the drawing-room with a considering eye. 'Perhaps some new stuff, too, what d'you say? I saw some positively delicious curtains at Ambrose Heal's t'other day, and there are some rather interesting new paintings at Burlington House –'

Claudette laughed and shook her head at him. She was looking particularly charming tonight with her newly bobbed hair a sleek and shining cap encircled by a silver filigree bandeau with a spray of diamonds rising between her eyebrows. Her dress was silver tissue, cut low and square across her flattened bust and the skirt slender and clinging above her silk clad ankles and narrow kid shoes. It was the very latest mode and only a woman as daring as Claudette, as determinedly fashionable, as youthful in appearance (despite her almost fifty years) and above all as rich could have got away with it.

'My dear boy,' she said, 'I have not the least intention of changing so much as a cushion in this room for at least another six months! There are sure to be all sorts of splendid new ideas available soon, now this stupid fracas is over, and I prefer to wait for them. This all looks tolerable enough at present, and heaven knows it cost enough to do!' And she looked round her drawing-room too, but with satisfaction. The finely turned rosewood tables and brocaded chairs were reflected in the gloss of the polished parquet floor, the heavy Persian rugs glowed with rich reds and greens and blues and the Chinese silk wall-hangings in muted pinks and beiges murmured expensively back at them. The room looked costly without being vulgar, but then, no one would expect otherwise at the

3

Collingbournes' London house which, large as it was (the suite of reception rooms was as handsome as any in all Mayfair, and the seven bedrooms above were as big and airy as they were well appointed) was still regarded by Lady Collingbourne as a mere *pied-à-terre*. The real Collingbourne home was Simister House in Wiltshire, though Claudette would do anything rather than live there. As soon as her dull, although adoring, husband had died, she had with deep relief put Simister under dust-covers and the servants on board-wages and brought her children to London 'to live properly' as she had told Jonty at the time, and to spend the less fashionable months of the year in the South of France or the German spas. The last four years had been tedious indeed to Claudette, locked as she had been in England, and she glittered tonight as she contemplated how much better the future would be now this wretched war was over.

Not that she had suffered much as a direct result of it. There had been shortages, of course, though none that could not be overcome by people with her sort of money, and there had been the boredom of having the best and most interesting of the men in London rushing off to join the army.

That had been dreadfully tedious at first, and one or two of her most interesting friends had even died in France; she had been cast down by that for fully six weeks, and had only been comforted when she had discovered that there were lots of men who wore the splendid uniforms that were so *de rigeur* in one's partners at dinners and theatres, but who would not distress one by going off to fight. Let some of the more heated patriots she met mutter about 'armchair warriors'; for her part they were the only sort worth expending time and energy upon. She wouldn't ever again allow herself to develop a tendre for a fighting man. It just wasn't worth the pain.

Not that she would need to concern herself ever again with so disagreeable a thought, she told herself now as she watched Jonty drift about the big room, rearranging the shaded electric lights a little so that the bronze chrysanthemums in their deep silver and crystal bowls were burnished in their glow. He was looking quite delightful and she felt her customary stab of pleasure at the sight of him.

4

There had been a time, just for a few weeks, when the news from France had been particularly horrendous, when he had actually seemed to be considering joining the army himself. That had been a bad time indeed, she thought now, looking at his straight back and wide shoulders, at the way his neat dark hair shaped his head so beautifully, at his narrow green eyes, and positively sensuous mouth. To have had Jonty a soldier would have been insupportable; thank God he had been so willing to listen to her entreaties and her reminders of his status as Lord Collingbourne. To risk his precious neck before he had produced an heir to the marquisate would have been a positive dereliction of duty, she had told him firmly, and he, blessed boy, had listened and obeyed.

She smiled at him now as he caught her eyes, and he smiled back, and she congratulated herself yet again on his splendid looks. To have so handsome a son was a delight, even though his age did rather point her own. No one could pretend to be as young as she knew she looked with such a son as Jonty!

The door opened behind her and she turned and looked and smiled again, but this time it was a consciously bright and gleaming little grimace rather than the warm regard she had bestowed on Jonty. Dear Emilia! she thought and then sighed. Poor dear, plain Emilia. Such a pity she had to look so ferociously like her poor dear dead papa.

Emilia looked at her and then let her gaze slide away. She knew that look too well to let it hurt her any more. She was no fool, knew to a tee just how plain she was, with her rather long face and her eyes tilted down at the outer corners to give her a somewhat melancholy look. Her hair, thick and healthy enough but a dull mouse was not a patch on the rich dark curliness of her brother's. Her eyes, a rather pale blue, offered no competition to his heavily lashed green ones, and her tall, thin and somewhat drooping shape did not bear thinking about. Although, she now told herself as she stood quietly in her usual place beside the marble fireplace so that the burning logs could cast shadows on her face, this new fashion Maman was so taken with could look good on her too. She wouldn't need the bust bodice Maman required to give herself the flattened boyish look her modiste assured her was the only

5

way fashionable women should look now, and her legs were long and slender and her hips narrow. Perhaps, she thought, if I bobbed my hair and chose some new frocks I could look quite pretty, and maybe Maman would look at me the way she looks at Jonty –

But that was a stupid thought and she knew it as soon as she'd thought it, and pushed it away and let her face sink into its customary sulkiness. Not that anyone noticed or commented. Most of the time, Emilia felt, she might as well not be there for any attention people ever paid to her.

The room was filling up now, many of the men in khaki, with their Sam Brownes gleaming richly with batmen's efforts and their brass buttons winking in the bright lights, and the women as fashionable as Maman, although, Emilia had to admit, rarely as successfully. It was so unfair, she thought again drearily. So unfair that I should look like me and Maman should look like her. She tries, I know she tries, but how can she fail to find me a disappointment? How could anyone fail? Dammit, I'm disappointed in me too –

And she settled herself to thinking her own private thoughts, and dreaming her own private fantasies as her mother's and brother's party – certainly not her own – built up around her. This Armistice was to bring a marvellous new world for everyone; and eventually real Peace; that was what all these people were saying, and she had to believe it. No reason, was there, why it should not be a marvellous new world for her too? I'm only nineteen, she told herself as she watched the dancing begin, saw her mother swept off into a sprightly ragtime cakewalk by a tall man in the uniform of a brigadier. Lots of time to do something better than this. Lots of time. I'll think of something –

A scant mile away, at 17 Leinster Terrace, in Lewis Lackland's big house that was tucked away from the hubbub of the Bayswater Road but near enough to Hyde Park for its occupants to hear the rattling of the branches in the trees in its midst, Max Lackland was doing his best to think of something, too. Something that would help him stop remembering Timothy.

6

If it hadn't happened as it had, just the day after his eighteenth birthday, if it hadn't been so close tonight to the anniversary, for it had been on November the second last year that the telegram had come, it might have been easier, but as it was, it was virtually impossible. His eyes kept filling with tears, and he hated himself for that, because he knew everyone could see them, and he knew how it upset his mother and Johanna and he knew what it did to his father, but how could he help it? He stood there very straight beside the fireplace in the dining-room, as his mother busied herself about the table, unnecessarily rearranging the silver and the crystal, trying to make himself think of – anything. Of the day in Primrose Ward at Nellie's. That had been interesting, now; the child with osteomyelitis, the small boy with the wide puzzled eyes who had been so patient when his painful dressing had to be changed. He had been a delightful child, for all his thinness and his feverishness, chattering on and on about the games he played with his brother at home. Just as Tim and I used to when we were small and shared the big room at the very top of the house and –

Again he wrenched his thoughts away, and back to Nellie's. To the busy wards, so full of gasping wheezing frightened patients now that the second wave of this ghastly flu epidemic was washing over London, and he remembered how he had spent the afternoon helping his father sort out which of them needed to be sent out to the tuberculosis branch hospital, because of the extra risk they were at from the influenza, and which could be safely kept in Covent Garden. Tuberculosis. If I hadn't had it all those years ago I'd have been fit to go to the Front like Timothy. I might have died instead of him. I might have been there with him and saved him. I might have –

No, not to be thought of. Not to be thought of. The woman in Woodbine Ward, think of her instead. The way she had looked at his father and wept her gratitude because he'd cured her pain, because his operation had been so successful. If I'd been at the Front as a doctor maybe I'd have found Tim and cured his pain and brought him home and –

'Max,' Lewis said, and slid one hand into the crook of his son's elbow. 'It's no easier for any of us, you know.'

7

'What did you say, sir?' Max blinked up at him, almost startled. He had been so deep in his own thoughts he hadn't even noticed his father come into the room. 'What did you say?'

'That it's no easier for any of us. Talk about it, if you like. It won't bring Tim back, but saying how bad you feel about him will help –'

Max pulled his arm away, awkward and stiff suddenly. 'I – really, Father, I don't think – I was thinking about that case this afternoon. The boy with the osteomyelitis. Will you be draining that abscess? It looks to be about ready, would you say?'

Lewis stared at him, his face very still. He looked his age now, though he hadn't a year ago. Now the lines that had always been on each side of his wide mouth were set as deep as crevasses, and the untidy dark hair that his wife tried so hard to keep orderly was iron grey. But his face, that square and uncompromisingly heavy face hadn't changed too much even since Tim's death. Lewis still looked solid and sensible and quiet yet friendly, and now he smiled at Max.

'Yes,' he said after a moment. 'It looked about ready. Would you like to open it for me tomorrow?'

'Yes – by all means. Yes, that would be most interesting. He's a good little lad, and should take it easily enough. Or shall I call the ward now and tell them we'll give him a whiff of gas? Might be kinder, don't you think?'

'Yes, kinder,' Lewis said, and sighed a little, but not so that his son could see, and watched him walk a little stiffly from the room to the telephone in the study.

'Will he be all right, Lewis?' Miriam had been standing quietly beside the table, turning a fork over and over in her hand and saying nothing, and Lewis looked at her and again smiled.

She had only just come out of mourning for Timothy now the year was up, and was wearing a dark lilac sheath of plain silk. She had refused to have her thick and heavy hair cut, despite the fashion, knowing how much Lewis loved the way it tumbled about her shoulders when she undressed at night, how much he still delighted in burying his face in its thick

8

curls, and whatever pleased Lewis was her lodestone. Tonight she was wearing it pinned in a heavy bun at the nape of her neck, bound with a string of small pearls, and she looked very good to Lewis. A touch heavy perhaps – she had inherited her long dead grandmother's tendency to *embonpoint* – and the soft flesh around her jaws was a little dependent now, but that didn't matter. To be forty-three and look it was no sin in Lewis's eyes. He would not have had her a moment younger or different in any particular. She was his Miriam and perfect in his view.

He came round the table now and stood behind her, putting his arms about her so that she could rest her head back against his chest, and he could nuzzle the warmth of her neck.

'He'll be all right,' he said, his voice a little muffled. 'Just as we are. Somehow. He'll always be part of us, Timothy. We'll never forget him, but we'll be all right. So will Max. He'll have to be.'

'I wish he'd been as Johanna was,' Miriam said, and went on turning the fork between her fingers, bending her head now to watch her restless movements. 'She wept and wept – I thought she would just – well, she wept.'

'And so did you, and so did I. And Peter. It was right that we did, and yes, I wish Max had wept too. But he will. Eventually. I was watching him tonight and he was starting to cry, I thought, but he wouldn't let himself. I thought if I talked about Tim it would make him – well, you saw. But he will. One day, soon. Maybe even tonight. It's going to be a bad night, Miriam.'

'I know. I wish I'd told them not to come after all.' She began to move round the table again. 'But I suppose it would seem odd to say we didn't want people after all tonight just because of the Armistice –'

'I don't give a damn what it might seem like. They're coming for my own selfish reasons. I want people here because it's better for *us*. We aren't the only family who lost a son, God knows. We have to live the rest of our lives in the world as it is – without Tim. And that means having dinner parties and celebrating the end of the fighting like everyone else. We'll be all right, my love. Never fear, we'll be all right.

9

Won't we Johanna?'

She had come into the room quietly and had been standing at the door and now she came towards them and nodded, smiling as widely as she could, though her eyes were as bright as Max's had been.

'Yes,' she said. 'Somehow. I've said the same to Peter. He didn't want to come down, but he is – and I think they're here. Shall I fetch Max? I think he's in your study.'

'No, he'll come soon,' Lewis said, and squared his shoulders slightly as the bell on the front door pealed, and the sound of the parlourmaid's footsteps could be heard clacking across the black and white marble slabs of the hall floor. 'He'll come when he's ready. Miriam, my dear, it's time we went to the drawing-room. The fighting's over and we're having a dinner party and we're celebrating. Aren't we?'

'Yes,' she said, after a moment and tucked her arm into his elbow as Johanna took his other arm. And the Lewis Lackland family went out to welcome their guests and the start of peacetime.

If noise was any index of the warmth of London's welcome to the Armistice that night there could be little doubt that the most celebratory house in the whole town was in Tavistock Square.

As soon as the news had reached Lady Caspar's ears shortly after noon (for no one ever disturbed her a moment before that) she had sent out her imperious summonses. Everyone, absolutely everyone, was to come to Tavistock Square to dine and welcome the cessation of war. It never occurred to Lady Caspar that anyone would refuse her, and of course no one ever did.

Her brother Oliver, wheezing a little and complaining bitterly as usual about his many assorted symptoms, arrived shortly after six, looking a little more dessicated perhaps than he had at the start of the war, a little more tired, but still remarkably sprightly for his great age ('I'm eighty-seven, you know,' he would tell anyone who would listen, friends and strangers alike. 'Eighty-seven,' and his cracked old voice would wheeze a little more. 'Eighty-*seven*. Ridiculous, ain't it?') with the first of the Oram girls fast on his heels. And then they arrived in a flood, all chattering faster than they could listen, trooping up the steps in their furs and glossy top hats, their children – those deemed old enough to share the evening's excitements – held firmly by the hand and as glad to see each other as though they had not met for months, though in fact the families were all very close and visited each other as often as they could, and Dear Mamma even more often.

It was really absurd the way everyone always called the families of Cecily's daughters the Oram girls, even though they had all been married for many years and had become

Tollemaches and Lewises and Poynter-Browns and Croxleys. Even Cecily herself, the only Oram left among them, thought of her great brood of a family under their umbrella name and was often hard put to it to remember which of her numerous grandchildren was which. Not surprising, really, she would say defensively, seeing there are fifteen of them, but her mother would snort and say loudly, 'Stupid, Cecily, stupid! *I* remember 'em all, and I'm eight-five. You're no more than a gel and you should remember perfectly well!'

And Cecily, not sure whether to be gratified at being labelled a gel at the age of sixty-one, or offended at being labelled stupid would do as everyone did in Phoebe's presence; subside and say nothing. And tonight was no different, Armistice or not.

By eight o'clock the house was alive with bustle and chatter and the sound of silk dresses rustling and stays creaking and the scent of cigars and expensive French perfume and brandy. When Lady Lackland-Caspar gave a party it was done in style, and it said a lot for her strength of will that her servants had obediently worked their fingers raw all day because she had demanded they should, instead of abandoning her in order to rush around the streets like everyone else. But she was strong, and so they had worked and worked extremely well.

James Caspar looked round approvingly and said as much to his cousin Daniel Henriques.

'Not a bad spread, considering, hey? Difficult times we've been through, very difficult times. Glad to see m'mother's as determined as ever to keep things up to snuff –'

'Very nice indeed,' Daniel said, and cocked a knowing eye at the laden table with its rounds of cold roast beef and mutton and vast hams. 'Mind you, dare say there's been a bit of villainy in the kitchen, hey? Not above a bit of food hoarding, Aunt Phoebe, eh, looking at this lot? *We've* been very hard put to it to maintain a decent table this last month or two. Getting nervous, some of the dealers you know, getting nervous.'

James reddened. 'M'mother would never do anything so unpatriotic, Daniel, and well you know it,' he said stiffly. 'I hope I never hear such words from you again –'

'Oh, pooh.' Daniel grinned. 'You can't frighten me, James,

you know! I'm not so dull a dog as I look. My aunt's a stubborn self-willed old villain and we all know it! If she chose to hoard food or buy where she shouldn't, then she'd do it and regard it as her right! And good luck to her, say I. She's someone to be proud of – just look at her sitting there! As straight backed as any sergeant major, and as handsome a woman as can be. Look at those eyes, will you – wouldn't I like to hear what she's saying to that Olive of yours! Looks very put out, don't she?'

'Hmph,' James said, and took a glass from the tray proffered by the sweating parlourmaid. 'In one of your waspish moods, I see, Daniel. Going to miss the profits you've made out of the army, is that it? You've sold a lot of field dressings this past four years, I'll be bound.'

Daniel blew his cheeks out irritably. 'You can stop that at once, James, and you know it. Having a nag at each other is one thing, and we've been doing that these past twenty years, but accusing me of war profiteering is something quite else. I can assure you that Henriques' factories need no special army contracts to keep them in business. Not with two hundred chemists' shops around the country with our name on 'em! I know how it is with you – it still gets your goat that m'father left the business to our side of the family instead of yours. Well, you can forget about it. It's *ours*, and no more to be said, after all these years. Anyway, you're warm enough – must be making a tidy piece out of the old Buckley business – and your wife isn't one to meddle. Not like m'sister and her lot. They never stop nagging me –' And he scowled across the crowded room at the Landis family, clustered around Phoebe and chattering nineteen to the dozen.

'Well, it's their business as much as yours,' James said maliciously, and felt better. As Daniel had said, quarrelling with each other was part of their lives; it wouldn't be a family party if they didn't. Indeed, James would have missed Daniel's sharpness as much as he suspected Daniel would miss his chidings, and he settled to a steady staring round the crowded heavily furnished room, commenting, usually unfavourably, on everyone there. And Daniel, not to be outdone, did the same, and both men enjoyed themselves greatly.

Until Daniel mentioned Theo.

Olive had come to stand beside her father, her round face flushed with annoyance to mutter about her grandmother in very uncomplimentary terms indeed, and Daniel had laughed as James did all he could to soothe her.

'Well, it's none of her affair!' Olive said sulkily. 'To listen to her you'd think I deliberately chose not to be married – it's too cruel!' Her eyes filled with ready tears as she contemplated her grandmother's cruelty. 'For all she knows I might have had a lover killed in the trenches or –'

'She knows,' Daniel said sapiently. 'There's not a thing that happens in this family my aunt doesn't know about. That cat won't jump, m'dear. You'll just have to bite your tongue and let her have her say. She's hungry for more great-grandchildren, that's the thing, and she thinks it's time you did your duty. She knows you turned that young Fletcher chap down, and she knows you're not getting any younger –'

'Be quiet, Daniel!' James said sharply. 'Olive's just a girl, for heaven's sake – barely twenty-five – and she doesn't have to marry anyone she doesn't choose to. No matter what m'mother says. I'll deal with her, my dear. Go and find your Mamma and get yourselves some supper and forget it. She's old and you must indulge her a little.'

Daniel, knowing perfectly well that Olive had passed her thirtieth birthday but for once forbearing to say anything sharp, watched her go and sighed gustily.

'Difficult for these young ones, James,' he said, still in his gentle mood. 'Best of the young men killed, and the rest of 'em damn near ruined by it all – I hope we can mend things a little for your Olive. There's an agreeable chap works for us – cousin of m'wife – about thirty-five, couldn't go to war because of some problems with his chest. Nothing dangerous, you understand, but asthma or something of that sort. Could be a fine match for her. Good family, a tidy sum settled on him – and he's well settled with us. I'll see to it that Rachel arranges a dinner or something of the sort. Poor devils! As I say, they're either dead or damaged – how's your Theo? Getting over it all, is he? Don't see him about –'

At once James stiffened. 'He's not here,' he said shortly.

'Must go and talk to m'mother. Excuse me –' and he moved away through the crowd leaving Daniel staring after him with an uncharacteristically sympathetic expression on his face.

Wretched Theo, thought James furiously. Wretched boy. The day had been bad enough with the way they had argued about it all through lunch and after; James doing his best to make the boy understand that he had a duty to his family, to his grandmother, to all of them, to share this evening's celebration. And what had Theo said?

'Celebrate? *Celebrate*? Celebrate what? Mud and death and stinking corpses? Gas and Big Bertha and men hanging on the wire? I'm damned if I do. Grandmother can go to hell before I go to her bloody party. She's selfish and stupid to even expect it of me.'

And James had exploded with fury, for Theo's mother and sisters had been there to hear the language he had used – and James could not be sure which had horrified him most; Theo's sentiments towards his grandmother, or the terms in which he had expressed them – and had shouted at the boy who had started to shake in that dreadful way of his and had whitened silently and then gone out of the room so stiff-backed and quiet that he might have been an automaton. And Bella had wept as only a mother can and then the girls had joined in, making it altogether a dreadful business, like so many similar scenes in the last few weeks since Theo had come home, finally invalided out of the army.

James should have been able to glow with pride in his son. Had he not been mentioned in dispatches after Passchendaele? Had he not been regarded by his friends as well as his family as a war hero? Why did the boy do all he could in this mulish fashion to upset them all and destroy their satisfaction in him? A father was surely entitled to take joy in his son's achievements. To have had him slam insultingly out of the room the way he had that first time when James had started telling some of their dinner guests what Theo had done that night in the trenches had been the outside of enough. Even now, all this time later, James felt his face redden as he remembered that night and the many other occasions like it when Theo had behaved badly.

He'd never been like it before, that was the thing. A quiet boy, Theo, always, rather in his brother Hugo's shadow. Biddable and courteous, he had worked in his father's office with never a moment's complaint once James had explained to him the wisdom of doing so; not like Hugo who had taken it into his stubborn head to follow his grandfather Freddy into a surgeon's career, even though there was more money in business. Theo had murmured about wanting to travel, to broaden his education and so forth, but he'd agreed quietly enough when his father had firmly pointed out to him the errors of his thinking, and had been an exemplary son, good to his mother, caring to his three sisters, polite to his father. Until this damned war, when he'd taken it into his head to enlist almost at the start, and gone away to be changed into this new difficult sharp-tongued rebellious Theo.

Wretched boy, James thought again miserably, and stumped to his mother's side to stand beside her in a proprietorial fashion. Wretched boy. At his age he should know better than to behave like a spoiled brat. Thirty-two, he should know better by now. *Wretched* boy –

'Stop glowering, James,' Phoebe said sharply. 'You look like a child who's been robbed of a lollipop. We are supposed to be celebrating the end of this horrid war, not looking as though we had lost it! The trouble with you youngsters is you don't know what war is all about. If you'd been with me in Scutari, seen what I saw there with your father and dear old Aunt Martha, why, you'd know what was what! That was a *war*, indeed that was! Why, I remember –' and she was off, chattering on about her days of glory singing to the soldiers at the Inkerman Coffee House in the Crimea more than sixty years ago, while the others clustered around her tried not to look bored at the familiar tale.

'You ought to make one of your films about it, Uncle Oliver,' Daisy Henriques murmured into the old man's ear as Phoebe's voice went rattling on. 'You could make a most exciting thing of it, couldn't you?' She raised her voice a little. 'With Letty to help, of course –' And she shot a spiteful little glance at her great-aunt; the youngest of Daniel's three children had more than a streak of her father's malice in her.

Phoebe, who for all her great age still enjoyed the full use of all her faculties, heard her, as Daisy had fully intended, and responded at once. Her papery cheeks reddened and she swivelled her eyes malevolently towards Oliver. He, woken sharply from the little doze into which he had slipped, and consequently a little less on his guard than he usually was, had heard Daisy's apparently artless remark and responded as she knew he would with instant interest.

'A film about the Crimea? For Letty to make? Now, that *is* an interesting idea – very interesting. Yes. Remember those days well, I do. Could help her a lot, I could. Indeed yes. Splendid notion. I'll talk to Letty about it tonight, see if I don't –'

'Oliver, it is exceedingly vulgar to speak of business matters at a social occasion such as this. Freddy would never have tolerated such behaviour in a gentleman's house,' Phoebe said freezingly. 'Be so good as to hold your tongue.'

'Hold m'tongue? Hold m'tongue?' Oliver said, blinking at her in some agitation. ' 'Pon my soul, Phoebe, you speak to me as though I were one of the children! Hold my tongue indeed –' He blustered on, aware of the solecism he had made in even mentioning Letty's name in Pheobe's hearing. She stared at him for another icy moment and then turned back to James to continue her account of the events in Aunt Martha's hospital in Scutari with magnificent aplomb, leaving Oliver huffed and red and Daisy grinning wickedly at her cousin Jacob Landis who was looking at her with marked disapproval.

'Never mind, Uncle Oliver,' she murmured then, leaning over the old man and keeping her voice low so that Phoebe could not hear this time. 'You're quite right – it *will* make a splendid film and Letty could do it very well. Tell her I said so.'

'Shall, m'dear, indeed I shall,' Oliver said loudly, glowering at his sister, who ignored him with superb blankness, and then, as she got to her feet to move majestically on James' arm to the supper table he relaxed and thought miserably about Letty and how much more agreeable it would be to be with her tonight.

Dear Letty, he thought mistily, as he stared round at the room full of his nieces and nephews and their numerous children. The only one of the whole bunch of 'em worth a row of beans. If only Phoebe hadn't taken against her so unaccountably, how agreeable life would be! He could bring her with him when he came visiting here in Tavistock Square and Phoebe could come to cosy little dinners they would give at Paulton's Square and –

But trying to visualize his formidable sister at the dining-table in the pretty but undoubtedly very small dining-room at his Chelsea house was more than his mind could encompass and he looked at his watch, weary now and thinking most longingly of his bed in that warm room up under the eaves at Paulton's Square where he had lived so comfortably these past ten years or more, ever since that dreadful day when Letty had come to him so white-faced and stricken and told him –

He shook his old head and got to his feet. No time for misery. Bad enough they had this past four years to look back on. No sense in deliberately making yourself miserable thinking of matters that lay even further back. They were comfortable together, he and his Letty. She was the best girl in the world, more to him than any daughter could have been. His lines had fallen in pleasant places, as it turned out, too pleasant to let silly Phoebe tangle them by her sulks. If she wanted to pretend Letty did not exist that was her affair. For Oliver's part, it mattered not tuppence, because Letty did exist and Letty loved him and cared for him and he was going home to find her.

'Going so soon, Uncle Oliver?' Cecily said, coming up behind him as he moved slowly across the big room. 'Can't you stay a little longer? Mamma wants to drink a toast, you know, at midnight, to the first full day of peacetime. She'll be so put out if you leave now.'

She fanned herself gently, puffing a little, and her round face with its dependent chins looked at him lugubriously.

'Not that I wouldn't say no to going quietly home myself, truth to tell. It's been a wearing day, one way and another, and I'll not pretend I'm not tired through and through, what with all the fuss and collecting the girls together and all – still!' She sighed. 'It's an important day, I suppose, and it's miserable in me to want to end it too soon. You too, Uncle Oliver. Do stay a little longer.'

'No thanks, m'dear. And it's not peacetime yet – only an armistice. Got to have conferences and treaties and God knows what before it's peace, you know. M'sister's going up in the air too soon like a balloon, as usual – anyway at my age I can't be too careful, you know, and I'm tired, and I want to go home. So, I shall. And if m'sister doesn't like it, that's too bad.' Standing up to Phoebe was always much easier when she was well out of earshot. 'So, if you please, Cecily, m'dear, send someone to fetch me a cab and I'll be on my way.'

'A cab, Uncle Oliver? But you'll never find one tonight, you know,' someone said behind him.

'What's that? Eh? What's that?' Oliver was thrown at once into a fluster. 'What d'you mean, won't find a cab? Always go everywhere in cabs! Why not tonight?'

'Drivers all out celebrating, Uncle!' Henry Tollemache smiled down at him with all the amiable contempt of the well informed young dealing with their foolish elders. 'Armistice night – haven't you seen what it's like out there? Even here in Tavistock Square, it's a madhouse! Come and see!' And he led the way to the window as his grandmother held out her hand to help her uncle follow him.

Several of the younger members of the party were clustered in the big window embrasure staring down at the street below and laughing and pointing and Oliver stared too and his face lengthened ludicrously. The square was crammed full of people, several having climbed over the railings that enclosed the central gardens, to shin up trees and wave their hats in the air from these vantage points, and someone had lit a bonfire among the fallen leaves which managed to send fitful flames leaping into the air despite the drizzling rain that still shrouded London.

'You see, Uncle!' Henry said. 'Bedlam! I wish I were out in it – such a lark that'd be, wouldn't it? But there won't be any cabs, I'll be bound. No sense of adventure, these drivers, that's the trouble. Not like me – I'd be glad to drive in it if Mamma and Papa would let me go –'

'Drive in it?' Oliver said and cheered at once. 'You have a motor car, m'boy?'

'Do I have a motor?' Henry said and seemed to grow an inch taller. 'I do, as a matter of fact. Just a little tourer, y'know. Nothing particularly grand. Should be getting an Hispano Suiza next year. Now the fighting's over they'll soon be back in production and I'll put my order down as fast as may be, you can be sure. But the one I have now isn't a bad little job, Auto Carrier – cost me five hundred and sixty pounds, you know – eleven point nine horsepower, got a four-cylinder side-valve Anzari engine – a litre and a half capacity, three-speed gear box, lovely finish, nice little goer.' His air of studied nonchalance was magnificent. 'Glad to give you a spin any time you care to try, Uncle.'

'Now,' said Oliver firmly. 'Now, m'boy. Tell your Mamma and Papa, I'm tired and I have to go home and that you're taking me. You tell 'em, Cecily – what's the good of having a great quantity of nephews if you can't get yourself fetched home when you need to be? Yes, fetched home. Time I was there. Tell your Mamma and Papa, Henry. Cecily, find my coat and muffler. Treacherous weather out these nights and me with my lungs so weak, must take care –'

Henry obeyed with great alacrity and despite Phoebe's obvious disapproval Oliver was at last led downstairs, wrapped into his muffler, his gloves, his hat, an extra waistcoat and finally his overcoat, and ensconced in Henry's car which had been brought round to the front door from the mews by dint of much squeezing of the rubber bulb of the horn. He leaned back in the bucket-shaped seat, a little alarmed at the sight of the dancing crowds around him and a little dazed by the noise they were making, as Henry with great pride released the brake and allowed the chugging engine to carry them slowly out into the hubbub of the streets of London.

3

Theo actually saw the car as it moved jerkily along Kingsway towards the river, with Henry pumping noise out of his horn with enormous gusto, and old Uncle Oliver clinging to the seat beside him peering with eyes eloquent of terror and misery over the edge of his heavy muffler, and he stopped in the middle of the hubbub and called out and lifted his arm to wave. And then aware of his own absurdity, shoved his hands back into his overcoat pockets, and bit his lower lip.

As if anyone could see, let alone hear him, in the middle of all this lunacy! He stood uncertainly as the mob eddied good-humouredly around him and watched the car edge its way forwards and at last vanish into the mêlée and tried to think. He had been walking for hours, it seemed, and his legs ached and his head was muzzy, and it was hard to think clearly, but he had to try; he had told them he wasn't going to Grand-mamma's and so he hadn't; that was it. He'd gone walking instead in the middle of all this madness, and then he'd thought he'd been unkind and selfish to refuse to please his family and had set out to go to Tavistock Square after all. But seeing old Uncle Oliver with Henry had somehow changed that plan. No point in going to Tavistock Square now if they're starting to go home, he told himself, and tried to squint at his pocket-watch in the fitful light thrown by the street lamps and the bonfires. Almost eleven. Not so late after all. Or is it really eleven in the morning and they've forgotten to send the sun up? The way it was at Passchendaele the morning after that God-awful bombardment when Peter had lain there beside him so crumpled and quiet and he had turned him over and looked at that face and seen nothing there because it was still so dark outside and because –

No, it's not at all like that. Passchendaele never happened. The war never happened. None of this is happening either. It's just the dreams again. I'm still dreaming the way I used to and I'll wake up soon and it'll just be an ordinary day and I'll get up and shave and have breakfast with Mamma and Father and the girls and go to the City with him and –

It did happen. But not the way you remember it. That's what it is. This isn't a dream. You're awake and this is Armistice Night and you're just tired, that's all, and remembering bad dreams. Yes, that's what it is. Remembering bad dreams, not reality. You never sat in that God-awful trench with that God-awful stink in your nose and you never had your head battered to a jelly by the God-awful noise and saw Peter's God-awful face jellied too and –

God-awful, God-awful, God-awful. He liked the sound of the words, and he turned and began to push his way back along the pavements towards Aldwych and the Strand, repeating the syllables inside his head, because doing that stopped other words getting in, and where there were no words there could be no images. God-awful, God-awful, God-awful –

A couple of girls, arm in arm and wearing sailors' hats rakishly over one eye and giggling as they went jostled him, and he stared at them, his eyes wide, and tried to apologize, but his lips formed the words by themselves; 'God-awful, God-awful, God-awful,' he murmured with an air of great seriousness and courtesy and the girls giggled again, a little uncertainly this time and they stared at him and then went pushing past staring back at him over their shoulders a little nervously. ' 'E's barmy,' one of them said, and nudged her friend. 'Real barmy.'

'Shell-shocked,' the other girl said knowledgeably and again produced her shrill little giggle. 'You got that there shell-shock, mister? Shall I kiss yer better?'

'Garn, 'e ain't a soljer,' the other said and shoved her companion who shoved her back but without any animus. 'Not dressed like that. And only soljers get shell-shock, don't they, eh? You ain't a soljer, mister, are yer? Buy us a drink, eh?'

He doffed his hat, politely, and bent his head in a stiff little bow but he said nothing, not trusting himself, and they stared at him and it was as though he were inside their heads suddenly and could see himself through their eyes; his evening suit a little loose on him now, since he'd lost so much weight, the glossy topper in his hand, the white silk scarf round his neck displaying his high collar and white bow tie, his face thin and pinched and his eyes dark in their shadowed sockets. They gave another of their mechanical little giggles and at last turned and went away, disappearing into the crowds, and he took a deep breath and set his hat on his head again and hunching his shoulders into his overcoat began to walk. This was absurd, it really was. He'd have to do something about it if it went on like this. Something, something, something. Have to do something –

The crowds were showing no sign of thinning, and he had to push and shove to get through, and that was difficult, for every instinct in him made him shrink from such close physical contact and such cavalier behaviour; I must have been mad to come out at all, he thought and then swallowed hard as the word slid into his mind. Were they right, those two girls in Kingsway? Was he a little mad? Were all the things that happened inside his head an indication of insanity? Was that what he really needed, to be locked up in a quiet asylum somewhere to think his dreadful thoughts and remember his dreadful memories and –

'Not mad.' He said it aloud and went on pushing through the crowds. 'Not mad.' Just tired and confused and, perhaps, a little bored. Thinking about his boredom helped a good deal; it got him down the Strand as far as Trafalgar Square, where the light was very bright indeed and the crowds thicker than ever, for someone had lit a huge bonfire on the plinth of Nelson's column and the flames were leaping to a great height and the crowds were delirious with the delight of it and singing several different songs all at the same time. He was able there just to stand and watch and be amused rather than distressed; this was interesting, really it was. It would be something to think about tomorrow morning when the day started and stretched blankly ahead of him.

He'd have to decide soon what to do. Father wasn't pressing

him – he had to be fair about that – had made it quite clear that he knew the family hero needed rest and recovery time, and had no intention of demanding his return to the City office until he had had it. But that didn't help the situation. Sooner or later he'd have either to choose something else to do, or go to the damned City. He couldn't be like his cousin Henry and find all his delight in motor cars, or his brother Hugo who talked only of diseases and operations with as much gusto as if he were talking of food and drink. He needed an occupation, an interest, something to fill his mind so full that the bad dreams and the memories and the images of Peter's face were banished for ever –

He skirted the Square and moved up Cockspur Street towards Pall Mall; perhaps if he went through St James's and up to Piccadilly he could get across to South Audley Street and home and bed without too much difficulty.

Bed. He was tired, but bed wouldn't help much. There, when he was totally alone and silent, the images were even more persistent, the memories even more painful, and he took a deep breath and wondered how long he could stay out in the crowds and not go to bed after all –

It was easier to walk close to the line of the buildings, for the pavements were choc-a-bloc and people were spilling all over the road, but close to the shop windows it was darker and quieter and he could make good progress, and he stepped out a little, became less careful. And nearly went headlong as his foot caught the edge of an obstruction.

The hands that caught him before he hit the ground were thin and bony and as hard as iron nails, and he swore loudly as they gripped his upper arms, for the pain was sharper than that caused by whatever it was had hit him in the shins.

'No need for that sort o' talk, mister,' a hoarse voice said reprovingly. 'Got a lidy 'ere, we 'ave, and it don't do to swear, do it, when we got lidies –'

'Don't be such a damned fool, Alf.' A deep but unmistakably feminine voice came out of the shop doorway, and Theo, rubbing his left arm to ease the lingering pain of Alf's grip, peered in, trying to see, and blinked as a light suddenly blazed. Someone had uncovered a dark lantern and sent a

24

beam shooting across to where he was standing and he lifted one hand to shade his dazzled eyes.

'That was silly, wasn't it?' the deep voice said and there was a scornful note in it that made Theo more aware than ever of the dull ache still afflicting his shins as well as his upper arms.

'Silly?' he said sharply. 'I tripped over something, for heaven's sake! How can that be silly?' He bent his head and narrowed his eyes, trying to see what it was had caused his downfall and saw a wooden strut projecting from the shop doorway and, now his eyes were accustomed to the lantern, also saw that it was attached to a shallow platform on which the woman who had spoken appeared to be standing.

'Look at that!' he said triumphantly, and pointed at it. 'That's what tripped me! It looks as though it's something to do with you, so who's silly? You for making an obstruction or me for being its victim?'

'Pooh,' she said calmly. 'You should have looked where you were going.'

'In this light? What do you think I am? A bat?'

She laughed, and it was an agreeable sound. 'You're squeaking like one.'

'You'd squeak too if you'd been grabbed by that tiger of yours,' he said and again rubbed his upper arm, and turned his head to stare at the scrawny young man now fiddling with a large brown box on a tripod which was beside the woman on the platform. 'What are you doing here, anyway? Planning a robbery? You'd not get much here,' and he peered up at the facade of the shop, which was Jackson's. 'Just a few groceries.'

'If I were a robber I'd be a more efficient one than to be stopped by people falling over their feet,' she said and turned to fiddle with another light set high on a piece of scaffolding beside her. 'You can pack up, Alf. I doubt we'll get much more. The light's hopeless, even with the Kreigs. I've only got about a thousand or so feet left anyway. Can you get the exposed stuff back tonight?'

'Won't even try,' the young man grunted and lifted the box off the tripod and began to fold the metal legs. 'I'll walk it 'ome, get it in early termorrer – ere, Miss Letty, leave that, will yer? – I'll do it – 'ere, you, get aht of it, will yer? Gettin' in the way, you are, and no error –'

Theo had come closer to peer into the doorway, grateful for the diversion and now he lifted his chin sharply and stared at the woman who was still in the shadows and was herself doing something with a mahogany box.

'I know you, don't I?' he said.

'Oh, for heaven's sake!' She sounded disgusted. 'Surely you don't have to waste your time or mine on rubbish like that *tonight*? The town's crawling with available women. Do go away and trip over someone else's work –'

'Filming,' he said and nodded with satisfaction. 'That's what you're doing. I saw cameras like that at the Front. And I do know who you are. You're Uncle Oliver's upstart. Or so my grandmother always calls you.'

She stopped what she was doing at once and moved out of the doorway and its shadows to stand next to him and now he could see her more clearly. A handsome face, square and with a wide mouth and narrow eyes, and hair cut to a modern bob, but curling thickly around her ears. She was tall and sturdily built and she was staring at him with her head cocked slightly to one side.

'Blast,' she said after a moment. 'You're not just a stupid masher on the prowl, then? No – I suppose not. You'd think the odds on meeting someone who knows you in all this row would be ridiculously long, wouldn't you?'

'I'm not a betting man,' he said. 'But, yes, I suppose so.'

'Armistice Night,' Alf said sapiently and slung the now packed-up tripod on his back and picked up the camera by its leather strap. 'Stands to reason, don' it? Everyone's bleedin' well out tonight, so everyone's goin' to meet people they know. I'm goin' 'ome, Miss Letty, if you can manage the rest of it yerself. See yer dahn the Gaff early, then? Get this stuff down the laboratories early as we can – then we can see wot we got, eh? Goo'night –'

'Goodnight, Alf,' she said, and Theo echoed it and they watched him go humping his way through the crowds and then she turned and stared at Theo again, her head again tilted up in that interrogatory fashion.

'Well? And who are you? You have the advantage of me,

26

since you know my name –'

'You're Letty Lackland,' he said. 'Uncle Oliver's –'

'Upstart. Yes.'

'I didn't mean that personally, you know. I was merely quoting my formidable grandmother –'

'Formidable!' Letty made a soft sound halfway between a snort and a laugh. 'Is that all you can say? That old woman is sheer poison, and I don't care who hears me say it! Poison –'

'You could be right,' Theo said equably. 'She can be difficult. I'm Theodore Caspar, by the way. How do you do. I remember seeing you once a long time ago when I was a boy and –' He felt his face redden in the darkness. 'I'm sorry. That sounds appallingly impertinent, doesn't it? I don't mean to be offensive, I promise you.'

She raised her eyebrows at him, and began to fumble in the pocket of her jacket.

'Offensive? Why offensive? Have you a match? I've got a cigarette here somewhere – ah – yes. If you think I'm the sort of woman who takes umbrage at being reminded how old she is, you've another think coming. I'm thirty-seven. Not so old, at that. And you – you're about – let me see –' She took a deep drag on her cigarette, which he had lit for her, and the glow flamed her face to a moment's devilishness. 'You're about five or six years younger than I am, and we last met at Tavistock Square when your grandfather Freddy died. You were down from Oxford at that time, and a very callow youth indeed. And now you're a war hero! Well, well, well!'

He reddened again, this time with anger. 'Stop that!'

'Stop what? Reminding you you were a callow youth? Or that you're a war hero?'

'I'm no hero,' he said harshly and thrust his hands deep into his coat pockets. 'No hero at all.'

She gave a little bark of laughter. 'Oh, but you are! You should hear dear old Oliver talking about you! He's eaten with pride. As far as I can tell, you fought and won the battle of Passchendaele single-handed and –'

'Please stop,' he said and she peered at him in the darkness and after a moment nodded.

'I'm sorry,' she said gruffly. 'Look, are you busy? I have to get this stuff to the car. I left it in St James's Square, and heaven hope it's still there and not hammered into the ground by all these lunatics. There's a good deal of it and –'

'Of course,' he said, eagerly and turned to the doorway. 'What do you want moved? No. Let me do that – it's awkward –'

Getting the wooden platform to the car wasn't difficult at all; it was clear to Theo she could have managed it perfectly well by herself, but that didn't matter. He was enjoying the diversion of this encounter; he felt better than he had all day, and when they had stowed the platform's components in the car – fortunately unscathed by the passers-by – he lingered for a moment as she pulled a woollen hat over her ears, and shrugged on a knitted coat. Used as he was to his sisters' high fashion look, all silk and furs and long-handled umbrellas, her air of studied casualness was very appealing, though he could see she was far from cheaply dressed. She had an air of prosperity about her, that look of richness that despises its own wealth and can afford the luxury of ignoring it.

'Well,' he said uncertainly at the same moment that she said with some decisiveness, 'Well –' and they both laughed.

'I was going to say that the car's going to be stuck here for a long time yet, obviously. These people are out for the night, aren't they? And by the time I drive back through the mobs to Chelsea, I might as well stay put – I mean I've had no supper and I'm hungry, so I shall go and get some. If you'd care to join me you'd be very welcome. And you can tell me more about what that poisonous old wretch of a grandmother of yours says about me.'

He laughed. 'She's not so dreadful, really. Just awfully spoiled. My father and aunt allow her to do precisely as she likes and it's no better for old ladies than it is for children to be given that sort of freedom – thank you, I'd love some supper. Now I come to think of it, I've had none either. Where can I take you?'

'You can take me nowhere,' she said, gruff again. 'I wasn't trying to beg a free meal, you know –'

'Bless my soul, what a very edgy lady you are!' He was feeling more comfortable with this odd woman by the

28

moment. 'Perhaps my grandmamma is right and you *are* no lady! Every lady I ever met takes it for granted I buy her supper or her lunch or anything else she fancies! By all means buy your own supper, or mine, if you like! I don't mind a bit!'

'Thank heavens for that!' she said and her voice was filled with amusement again. 'A man with a bit of commonsense. We'll compromise. You buy me my supper, and I'll buy yours. Come on.'

'Where to?' He fell into step beside her and she strode along with her hands as deep in the pocket of her knitted coat as his own were in his overcoat's.

'Rules,' she said. 'They always find room for me, however busy they are, and everywhere's sure to be jammed tonight. Anyway, I need some good beef. Now I come to think of it I had no lunch either. Can't you walk faster than that?'

Despite the crowds still hell-bent on their noisy celebrations, they made good time as they wove their way back towards Covent Garden, dodging down the side-streets away from the focus of the mobs in Regent Street and Haymarket and Leicester Square, eventually reaching Maiden Lane breathless but not too exhausted by their journey.

His delight in her independence of spirit wavered a little as they stood in the middle of the crowded restaurant, he still neat in his evening clothes and she, now he could see her more clearly, obviously wearing very workaday garments indeed, because of the way people stared at them. One or two women put up their lorgnettes with disapproval as they took in the costume that she revealed when she pulled off her coat and the knitted hat. Another knitted outfit in a deep green with a sailor collar and a woollen tassel in front, surmounting a remarkably short skirt and long black stockinged legs. But then, as he saw the respect with which she was greeted by the head waiter, and the speed with which they found her a table he felt better, and settled himself facing her without any sense of discomfort at all.

'Well!' she said. 'We've made it! Now with your permission, I'll order my own dinner and my own wine, and if you've any sense you'll let me do the same for you. I know the kitchens here better than they do themselves, and I'll see to it that you only get the best. Right? John! A bottle of my usual claret, and oysters and beef – and none of your nasty cuts either. I want the sirloin – and make haste about it. We're both exceedingly hungry. Aren't we?'

4

'You were right,' Theo said almost three quarters of an hour later. 'That was excellent beef. I've had nothing so good since the war started.'

'Of course it was,' she said. 'I'd have thrown it back at them if it hadn't been, and well they know it. And they've been buying where they shouldn't for two years now and well they know that I know *that*! Have you had enough?'

'Ample.'

'Brandy then. No coffee. You look as though you sleep badly at the best of times. Brandy'll see to it you get a better chance of it tonight.'

He frowned sharply. 'Do you always lay down the law to people like this?'

'Only to those worth bothering about. I ignore the rest.'

He grinned at that. 'Should I be complimented?'

'Yes. You should. There aren't many people I meet these days worth laying the law down to, as you put it. Not that I do. I just try to be sensible and not waste time.'

'You certainly don't waste time,' he said, and relaxed his shoulders which had tightened a little. 'I accept the compliment.'

'Good.'

They drank their brandy in companionable silence and she sat and watched him covertly over the edge of her balloon glass. He was swirling the spirit round and round in his own glass and watching the traces it left on the sides, his face shuttered and still, but less guarded now as the claret – they had shared two bottles – and the brandy worked their release on him.

A marvellous face, she thought. An incredible face. Oh, my

God, but I'd like to light that face –

The eyes were long and narrow, a little like her own (and she could see the traces of family resemblance there were between them, distant though their cousinhood was) but set in deep sockets that gave them an extraordinary depth and poignancy of expression. The temples at each side curved into beautiful planes and the hair, short and curly and very dark, met them with a curving line that was just as pleasing. His cheeks were flat and hard under high cheekbones and his nose was fine and narrow, giving him a fragile look that was extremely appealing. And his mouth – an incredible mouth, she thought. Wide, curving, extremely mobile when he spoke, enough to make you shiver –

'What do you do for a living?' she said sharply, and he looked up at her, startled, and now she could see that his lower lashes were the same length as the upper ones, and threw spiders' leg shadows on those high cheek bones. A *superb* face.

'A living?'

'From what I know of the family, you'll not be allowed to sit about doing nothing. Your father, as I recall, has a vast respect for hard work and making money. So, what do you do for a living? Oliver has never told me.'

'He told you,' he said, and looked down again, hooding his eyes. 'War hero, remember?'

'Ah, yes. The subject I wasn't to speak of.'

He was silent for a moment longer and then, still not looking at her, he said, 'It's all such a – it's impossible to talk about something that was so –' Now he did look up at her and that expression in his eyes made her throat tighten. 'I wish I could.'

'Would it make it easier?'

'It might.'

'Then do.'

'I told you, I *can't*.' He said it almost violently and the people at the next table looked across at them and he reddened slightly. 'I wish I could,' he said in a softer tone. 'All I do is remember it, and think about it and dream about it –' He stopped and surveyed his glass and shook his head. 'I think I might be a little drunk.'

32

'Just a little,' she said calmly. 'It'll do you no harm. Have some more and see if you can talk about it.'

'Do you know what shell-shock is?' he said after a moment.

Her face showed no particular expression. 'I've heard some talk of it. Men who were bombarded getting ill –'

'Getting mad. Going up the pole, down the spout, round the bend, up a gum tree, nahpoo –'

'That's stupid,' she said. 'Stop it.'

He grinned at her and she wanted to touch him because his grin was so tragic.

'Sometimes I think I've got a touch of it. Can you have a touch of shell-shock? Like a touch of flu?'

'It's more likely you've got that,' she said prosaically. 'If you're feeling ill. Are you?'

'I'm not sure what feeling ill is. I've no fever, if that's what you mean. No headache. No running nose. Just bad dreams and tired. Oh, God, I must be drunk to be talking like this. I'm going to stop. You talk. What do *you* do for a living?'

'You know the answer to that perfectly well. I make films. Uncle Oliver and I are partners in the Gaff Studios.'

'Partners? I thought you were his heiress or something?'

'I am,' she said and then produced one of her deep chuckles. 'That's what makes your grandmother so furious. Uncle Oliver treats me like his daughter rather than a distant cousin, and it riles her. She wanted Uncle Oliver to leave all his boodle to you. You and your cousins.'

'I don't want it!' Theo said and stared at her with his face twisted with slightly maudlin anxiety. 'I like old Oliver – I don't want him to die and leave me any money.'

'Don't worry, he won't! Leave you any money, that is. He's made up his mind to it that I'm his one and only – even though I'm only a cousin. I think we had a great-great-grandfather or something in common, you and I. Not close enough for your grandmother to feel I'm legitimate for heiress appointment. She thinks I'm a fortune-hunter.'

'Are you?'

She laughed again. 'No. Just a work-hunter. I like what I do and it's Uncle Oliver who makes it possible for me to do it. He's wonderful!'

'He's a nice old buffer,' Theo said and brushed him aside. 'What do you do exactly? I've never really known.'

'I run the Gaff for Oliver and Edwin – he's our other partner. Which means I make films, arrange productions and employ writers and cameramen and actors and all the rest of the hangers-on and see to it they do their jobs and then sell the finished films to the distributors. I organize the extra finance we need for the bigger films and sometimes I share in the distribution arrangements.'

'Is that all?' Theo said and grinned.

She took his comment totally seriously, hearing no hint of the mockery he'd intended. 'I run Uncle Oliver's supper-rooms too, though that's rather small beer these days. It used to be a splendid little place, but now it's little more than a restaurant where we have a bit of cabaret from time to time. But I've a good manager there, so it doesn't take much time. Oh, and sometimes, just to keep my hand in with the live theatre, I'll do a production in the West End. The Gaff – our studios – used to be a theatre, you see. It was founded to be that, but we changed direction a few years ago and –' She stopped. 'Well, I sometimes do a show in town. The Shaftesbury, when I can get it. It's my favourite theatre –'

'Changed direction? Why?' He was leaning his elbows on the table now and staring at her closely and she was very aware of his physical nearness and leaned back in her chair.

'Not so drunk after all,' she said a touch sardonically. 'Was I that transparent?'

'You were bothered.' He nodded, a shade owlishly. 'I thought you were upset when you said it.'

'Someone died,' she said shortly, staring down at her glass and twisting it between her fingers. 'The person who started it.'

'Who was that?'

She was silent for a moment or two. 'His name was Lucas O'Hare,' she said eventually. 'Luke.'

'I'm sorry.'

'Why are you sorry?'

'Because he died. Because talking about him makes you sad.'

'Yes,' she said, and made a little face. 'Sad. But there're worse things than being sad. Like feeling nothing at all. I've taught myself to talk about him. We were to be married, you see. But he died. T.B. He was in Switzerland, supposed to be getting better, but he had a haemorrhage one night and by the time they got to him he was dead.' She looked up at him and her eyes were hard little pebbles, reflecting the light from the glittering restaurant, and he felt a little chilled as he stared at them. 'So there you are. We didn't get married after all.'

There was another little silence between them and he said awkwardly, 'I shouldn't have asked.'

'Why not? I told you – talking about things that make you sad is something you have to learn to do. It wouldn't do *you* any harm.'

'My turn in the confessional?' he said attempting to be light. 'Did you say something about more brandy? Shall we?'

She looked at him consideringly. 'No, I don't think so, after all. You seem rather susceptible to alcohol.'

'An excellent reason to have more,' he said and laughed and lifted his hand to call a waiter. 'Will you have some more?'

'No thank you.' She watched him as the waiter went through the ritual of warming a new glass and pouring in the brandy with great care, and then, as he drank it rather quickly, sighed softly.

'You're a bit of a fool, you know that? I'm disappointed. I thought you weren't.'

'Why a fool?' He didn't seem unduly perturbed by her judgement.

'Using brandy to get rid of your bad dreams, instead of to create good ones. That's what wine's for, you know. To open doors, not to slam them.'

He put his glass down slowly and stared at her.

'How did you know that?'

'What? That you use it to slam doors?'

'Yes.'

'I didn't know. I just thought perhaps you could teach yourself to if you aren't careful. Please don't.'

'Does it matter?'

She looked a little grim for a moment. 'It matters.'

35

'Why?'

'Oh stop fishing! Because you're an interesting-looking man. Because men who drink too much stop being interesting. And because it doesn't work, anyway. I know.'

He was silent again, considering what she had said, and she thought – he does this all the time. He really listens and thinks about what he's heard before he answers.

'Because you tried it yourself,' he said at length and nodded and pushed his glass away. 'After your Luke died.'

'After Luke died. Yes.' She smiled then, and shook her head in some wonderment.

'This is crazy, you know? I hardly know you, collect you from the pavements of Piccadilly because you haven't the wit to look where you're putting your feet and now sit here talking to you as though I've known you for years. You're an interesting person, Mr Theodore Caspar, you really are.'

'Call me Theo. My friends always do.' Again that little silence and then he said, 'There aren't many friends left who do.'

'In the war?' she said and put her hand out and for the first time touched him, closing her fingers round his fist on the table. He sat and looked down at her hand on his and then, awkwardly, pulled it away.

'Who wasn't killed in the war?' he said lightly. 'Wasn't everyone except you and me?'

'Not quite. But a lot were, and it was hell, and you should talk about it. Then you won't need to think of using brandy as a door-slammer.'

'I'll think about it,' he said and leaned back in his chair. 'Now tell me about your film. The one you were making tonight. What was that all about?'

'I'm not sure,' she said, glad to be brought back to commonplaces. To have allowed herself to become quite so intimate in conversation with someone she knew so slightly had been lunacy; it was true she had long ago decided it was necessary to talk about Luke if she was to retain her sanity; it was true that there had been a dreadful three months after the news had come from Switzerland when the only way she had been able to sleep, the only way she had been able to prevent herself seeing the vision of Luke dying alone, drowned in his own blood, had been with brandy. It had been dear old Edwin who had come to her aid then, while all Uncle Oliver had been able to do was weep and wring his hands and shrivel before her eyes at the sight of her distress. But Edwin, foolish, selfish, frivolous Edwin had had the wit to see what was happening and had forced her to talk, made her stop numbing herself with brandy and insisted she start work again. And so it had been this past dozen years or so, pulling herself back to life by the strings of hard work. Strings which had still held firm when the next catastrophe came in 1915 and her mother Sophie had died of typhoid caught from a patient in the Haworth backstreets where she had worn herself to a shred as the only local doctor willing to give care without cash. There had been no one left for her to love, Letty told herself then; Barty gone to America to make his medical fortune, and Samuel deeply embroiled in his life with his mill and his wife and his numerous offspring left neither brother time to concern himself with a spinster sister. So Letty had told herself, and grimly she had slammed the door on her own emotions, refusing to confide her desolation to anyone, not even old Edwin. Until tonight she had never told anyone, as she had told this young man with the incredible face, how deep her pain had gone, and how narrow her escape had been. Now, talking about her work, she watched him and with the back of her mind tried to understand why she had spoken so, what it was about Theo Caspar that had crumbled her defences so swiftly.

'It was just obvious that we had to have some footage,' she was saying, answering his question, even while she was thinking. 'We got a lot of actuality film during the battles of course. Every film company with any sense in their management got a cameraman accredited to the Front, and we were one of the first. Some of it the War Office wanted of course, but we've enough good stuff to make something of it. So Edwin thought, and I agreed, we'd better see if we could get something of tonight to use with it. I knew we'd have the most frightful lighting problems of course, and it's possible we've got no more than a lot of shadows, though I used the best ortho-chromatic stock I could get, and Jackson's let me have access to their electricty supply to rig up a couple of Kreigs for the earlier stuff this evening – well, we'll see when the film comes back from the laboratories –'

'Edwin? Tell me about him,' Theo said, his head cocked to one side in a parody of her own familiar posture.

'Our other partner? He's a good friend, Edwin Zander – an American, though he's lived here for years. You'd like him. Amusing, and not as silly as he seems. You must come to the studios and look at the stuff we got tonight, and some of the battle footage – maybe you could let me have an opinion on its quality as far as accuracy's concerned – and meet him. Friday night, I thought –'

'The studios? I've never seen a film studio – is it as exciting as it sounds?'

'I doubt it. Space. Offices. Lights. Equipment. I'm so used to it I don't know how it looks to other people. I find it exciting, of course. For me it's the most exciting place in the world – but perhaps others mightn't think so.'

'I'll think so,' he said firmly. 'I'll be happy to come. Where, and what time?'

'We're at the foot of Luna Street, at Chelsea Reach. Near Battersea Bridge,' she said. 'I'll start showing at – oh, around nine I suppose. Come at eight, and meet Edwin and you can look round before we begin.'

'I'd like that. Thank you.'

'And now it's time I went. The roads should be clearing a little by now. And I've a lot of work to do tomorrow. I need some sleep. You too. You look tired –'

'Just a little,' he said and smiled. 'I think your brandy will make me sleep, after all. But I'll remember not to use it again.'

She looked uncharacteristically flustered. 'Well, that's your affair, of course. I didn't mean to be –'

'No,' he said. 'I know you didn't. It was kind of you. It's been an odd night altogether tonight, anyway. People say and do things on a night like this that they wouldn't normally. Let's leave it at that. I'll come to your Gaff on Friday and see your films with great interest. Thank you for asking me – now, let me see you back to your car, and on your way. And –

38

er – thank you for leaving that strut jutting out in the dark so that I could fall over it. Being able to be so silly has made my Armistice Night most interesting.'

Long after he had escorted her back through the at last thinning crowds to her car, and she had driven him to South Audley Street before taking herself on her way to Chelsea, long after she had bidden goodnight to an anxious Uncle Oliver, lying awake listening for her safe arrival home, long after she had bathed and tumbled into bed in her neat quiet room overlooking the garden of the house in Paulton's Square, she thought about his face. Not about him as a person – how could she, knowing only who he was, that he had had a bad war and was unhappy? – but about that incredibly beautiful face.

The years of looking through cameras at her world had changed Letty's view of her fellows. She no longer saw them as whole people, but as two dimensional images; she saw planes and hollows, peaks and curves and the effects of lights and shadows, not people, and Theo Caspar's face tonight had seemed to her the most exciting she had ever seen. There were English actors, of course, people who could and did give satisfactory performances in her films, but the real excitement in the industry seemed to be abroad. She had seen films from America with actors and actresses of such incandescence that they had almost seemed to glow on the screen. To find such a personality in England for her own films – now, there would be an achievement! And that face she had stared at over dinner all this evening seemed to promise a very real possibility of just that.

She fell asleep to dream of seeing Theo in a silvery glow, twisting and turning in front of her camera, but looking wrong somehow, even though his face was so perfect for the camera, and then she realized it wasn't a face at all, but a mask, and that behind the mask there was something dreadful. And the worst thing about it was that he wouldn't show her.

5

The four days that elapsed between meeting Letty and visiting her at the studios were among the most agreeable Theo had known since coming home from the Front. He slept as badly as ever, of course, haunted by his dreams – he had come to take that for granted – but his days were less tense, his anxiety less heavy in his head. It was as though having something interesting to look forwards to gave a purpose to the empty days.

Inevitably he fantasized about how the evening would be, and had seen it as a quiet, even cosy occasion. There would be this Edwin Letty had mentioned, but he would probably go away after a while and they could go on talking, she and Theo, as they had done that evening at Rules' restaurant. He'd enjoy that. She was an interesting person to talk to with her abrupt speech and slightly gruff manner, comfortable in her maturity. Not at all like his fashionable sisters and his parents and their friends who persisted in staring at him with that sickening look of mingled pride and anxiety on their silly faces.

So, when he arrived at the Gaff Studios, having managed with great difficulty to find a taxi to bring him from South Audley Street, for taxis were becoming as rare as orchids in the Armistice-mad city, and discovered that the place was humming with people, he was filled with sudden anger. He stood in the lobby of the big building, blinking at the bright lights that came from the space into which it led, staring round at the press of people as a neatly uniformed commissionaire stood waiting to take his coat and hat, and glowered. He was about to turn on his heel and go, when she suddenly appeared, pushing through the crowd to come out to the lobby, and grinned at him.

'Good! You found us! Come and have a drink and meet people.'

He stared at her, and felt his brows crease. The slightly untidy woman in the knitted suit had been replaced by a very elegant and sleek creature indeed; she was wearing a sheath of a gown in some clinging cream coloured fabric, with bands of fur swathing her skirt which reached just half-way down her silk-clad calves, and her hair and forehead bound with a fillet of the same fur. Her ears glittered discreetly with diamonds and her face had the faint blush of expertly applied rouge. She looked to him exotic, very expensive and quite terrifyingly sure of herself.

'I'm not certain that – I didn't expect such a crush,' he began, still holding his hat firmly in his hand, despite the commissionaire's obvious eagerness to remove it from his grasp. 'I had the impression it was just to be –'

She grimaced and suddenly there was a glimpse of the comfortable companion of last Monday night.

'Yes, I'm sorry about that. I'd not intended it to be quite such a big party, but the film we got together really is so good I wanted to show it to a few useful people and –' She moved a little closer and dropped her voice. 'I also have a chance to get a big film together. You'd think a cork had come out of a bottle, the way everyone's suddenly rushing around getting things moving again, now the Armistice is here. But I'm going to need some extra finance and tonight was an obvious time to get some of my possible backers to see what we do. Do stay. I know how it is when you expect a quiet evening and it turns out to be a circus, but I'd like you to stay, really I would.'

'Why?' he asked, bluntly. 'Just to make up the numbers? Are you short of men? That's a common social problem these days.'

'Don't be so damned stupid!' she flashed and again he felt a momentary lift of reassurance and his shoulders relaxed slightly. 'It's because I want *you* –'

She stopped and looked at him consideringly, and he felt that she was reaching some sort of important decision and he stood there and stared at her, turning his hat between his fingers and waited, and then said abruptly, 'Oh, damn, I might as well risk it. You don't have anything much to do, do you? I mean, no work, no plans to do anything in particular, once you're officially demobilized?'

He said nothing, just looking at her, but he made a small gesture with his brows and that wide expressive mouth and the meaning was so abundantly clear that she lifted her chin with a sudden little exultation and nodded with satisfaction.

'I thought so. So I've been thinking – I might be able to suggest something interesting for you. There! That's why I want you to stay. Will you?'

Before he could answer someone else came pushing towards them from the crowded room beyond and cried out, 'Letty, wretched girl, what *are* you doing lolling around out here when I am positively *besieged* by people desperate for talk with you? I really cannot cope another *moment* unless you – oh!'

He peered at Theo, who was now allowing the commissionaire to remove his coat.

'My dear, a newcomer! And I swear a face I never saw before, and wish I had! *Do* introduce, my dear –'

'Edwin Zander, Theo Caspar, Theo Caspar, Edwin Zander,' she said crisply and tucked her hand proprietorially into Theo's elbow. 'And none of your nonsense, Edwin. Theo is a man of action, and not at all likely to be beguiled by your brand of silly chatter. You must talk sensibly to him or not at all.'

Edwin, a small and decidedly plump man with a square face glowing with sweat, brandy and goodwill, beamed at Theo and, totally unabashed, tucked his hand into his other elbow.

'Such a trial to me, my dear Letty!' He sighed with great theatricality. 'I do assure you, dear Theo – I may call you so, mayn't I? Of course I may – no silly formality here, glory be! – I do assure you, my dear Theo, that my talk positively coruscates with good sense. Disdain any calumny she may heap on my poor old head, I do beg of you. She's a good enough girl at heart, but she does have this tiresome blind spot about me. She simply can't tell the difference between wit and nonsense. Never mind. I still love the child, as don't we all.'

'A little less of the child, Edwin,' Letty said. 'I am a deal nearer forty than thirty and it's high time you treated me with the respect I deserve. Ignore his nonsense, Theo, please. He really is quite sensible, when he stops chattering. Now, where shall we start? Ah! Here's someone you know.'

She led Theo towards a little knot of people who were standing in a corner talking to each other quietly. 'Connections of yours, because they're connections of mine too. Miriam, have you met Theo Caspar? Johanna, this is Theo, Max, Theo, Mrs Lewis Lackland, Miss Johanna Lackland, Mr Max Lackland –'

Theo nodded and tried to remember their faces. He had managed to avoid family gatherings for the past four years to such good effect that few of his more distant relations had any place in his recollection, and these three people looked only vaguely familiar.

Mrs Lackland was a small, plump and exceedingly pretty woman dressed in lilac silk and her daughter was a taller, thinner version of her, a grave dark girl with a singularly sweet smile. The young man standing with them did not share their good looks; he had a square face and thick unruly dust-coloured hair and an expression of rather dogged misery that made him seem an uncomfortable companion, for he merely stared at Theo and nodded his head in silent response to the introduction.

His mother, fortunately, was more sociable and immediately began to chatter at great length about the family, asking solicitously after Theo's parents and sisters, and showing she had a firm grasp of the many tangled connections they shared.

'I have not spoken with you for so very many years!' she said, smiling up at him as Letty went away to fetch a drink for Theo, even though he had shaken his head at her when she had offered it. 'Not since dear Freddy died, in fact. Such a sad time that. He was a dear man, your grandfather. I had great affection for him. He treated me so kindly when I was a young girl and before I married Lewis.'

She looked a little misty-eyed for a moment and then sighed softly and smiled brilliantly at Theo. 'But there, that won't interest you! All so much ancient history! Tell me, are you quite recovered from your wounds? I had heard about your great heroism, of course –'

Theo felt the wooden expression settle on his face. He had tried so hard, so often, to find some way to respond to such comments, but still could not. All that happened was the usual wave of anger, and he muttered something about being quite well, thank you –

The young man who had been standing staring rather blankly around him had been aroused by his mother's question, however, and he now focussed his eyes sharply on Theo.

'You were in the war?' he said. He had rather a husky voice which sounded almost as though it had only just left childhood behind and Theo flicked a glance at him and said shortly, 'Yes.'

'Max was at Nellie's branch hospital in Surrey during most of '17 and the beginning of this year,' Miriam said with an odd air of nervousness. 'He is a student at the hospital, you know. I dare say that is why he did not hear the family talk of your – experiences.' She looked up at her tall son with a faintly appealing glance. Theo was puzzled for a moment. 'Theo was at Passchendaele, Max,' she said quietly. 'He was mentioned in dispatches and –'

'Can I fetch you a drink, Mrs Lackland?' Theo said with desperation. 'I'm sure you must be very thirsty – do give me your glass,' and he seized the still half-full glass of wine she was holding in her hand and turned and went plunging away into the crowd. But not fast enough, for when he reached the centre of the room and looked round uncertainly for somewhere to dispose of the glass, he found Max at his elbow.

'What happened at Passchendaele?' he said urgently, and put one hand on Theo's sleeve.

Theo looked down at the hand and said icily, 'I beg your pardon?'

'I have to know from someone who was there. I have to be told,' the boy said and his huskiness was even more accentuated, making him sound even younger suddenly. 'What was it like in the trenches? Really like? What did people do, what

44

did it sound like, the bombardment, I mean – and the food and the water – I have to know – please tell me.'

The anger was bubbling again in Theo, turning to the ice crystals in his throat that were so hatefully familiar. The tremor was starting too, deep in his belly, and there was nothing he could do to stop it.

'Got a taste for ugly details, have you?' he said and the cold sneer in his voice was clear even in his own ears. 'Had a cosy war in your hospital and needing some juicy titbits to throw around when your friends start telling tales of their derring-do?'

Max went so crimson that his face seemed about to catch fire. 'Dammit, no!' he said. 'That's a – I want to know, because of –' He stopped and to Theo's horror his eyes filled with tears. His own emotion, so raw and so near the surface seemed suddenly to threaten to overwhelm him in imitation of the boy, and he said as harshly as he could, 'Stop that, you idiot! I don't know or care why you want to know. I just don't want to talk about it. Now get out of my way –' And he went plunging once more into the crowd of chattering busy people. Only to find himself stopped yet again by a hand on his arm, this time Miriam Lackland's.

'I do hope –' she began and then looked piercingly into his face and took a deep breath and shook her head. 'I can't –' she said then, and, turned to look at her daughter who was just behind her. 'Johanna, can you – please –'

'I hope my brother did not distress you in any way, Mr Caspar,' Johanna said, and her voice was absurdly like her mother's, light and fluting yet with a serious note in it that was appealing. 'He is having great difficulty in coming to any sort of terms with our loss, you see. That is why I expect he wished to speak to you.'

Theo stood very still, his head cocked a little and said nothing, just looking at her with his face very still and she said quietly, 'My brother, Tim. Max and he were very attached and he has taken it hard. Tim died at Verdun.'

'Oh, God dammit,' Theo said with barely restrained violence and then caught himself up and turned to Miriam Lackland. 'My apologies, Cousin Miriam. I meant no disrespect. I didn't realize. I am so sorry, indeed I am.'

'Talk to Max, Theo,' Miriam said, still looking up at him with that air of piteous appeal. 'Please! I'm so worried for him. He seems so determined to suffer all the pain he can. For Tim, you know. If someone could help him, we'd all be so grateful.'

'I'll talk to him,' Theo mumbled after a moment and thrust the glass of wine he was still holding back into Miriam's hand and turned away, looking for the tall boy with the husky voice.

He found him at the far side of the room, where a group of women in very fashionable clothes were clustered round Edwin, who was laughing with enormous gusto, standing quietly and contriving to look as though he were one of the party without actually being so. Theo stood and looked at him for a moment and then moved in more closely.

'I was ill-mannered and I'm sorry,' he said without preamble. 'What do you want to know about the trenches? I'll tell you what I can.'

'Someone's told you about Tim.'

'Yes.'

'Does that make it all right to tell me?'

'Yes.'

'Why?'

Theo thought for a long moment. 'I don't know. It just does. Perhaps it's another way of loving someone, to try to share the bad things? I don't know.'

Max lifted his chin and with a rather childish little gesture rubbed his hand through his already rumpled hair.

'That's exactly it,' he said. 'When we were little, we used to talk a lot, Tim and me. About everything. He was marvellous at explaining – he could tell you what it felt like to be inside him. I used to listen when he told me what he'd had to eat at a party I hadn't gone to and things like that, and, honestly, I could taste the jellies and cake he'd had, and now I've got to be there at Verdun for him. I had T.B. – I couldn't.'

'Don't apologize or excuse yourself for not being there,' Theo said harshly. 'Only fools like me – like I was before – only those sort of fools think there's any glory in a war. It's filth, and it's stinking and it's –'

46

It was starting again. The anger rising in a tide of ice crystals. The tremor in his belly shifting upwards and outwards, slowly and inexorably, taking his guts with it, and he took a deep breath and stared at Max, seeing him through the faint glitter that came with the hateful feelings, trying, helplessly as usual, to control them.

'This way,' Max said suddenly and rather loudly. 'This way, I'll show you – I dare say you left it in your overcoat pocket –' and he took Theo's elbow in a firm grasp and half led, half carried him through the crowded room.

'Just need to find your coat, m'dear chap,' he said even more loudly. 'That's where your cigar case will be, depend upon it –' And then they were in the lobby and out into the darkness of the pavements of Chelsea Reach and Theo could smell the thick mud of the river and hear the soft mournful hooting of the fog-horns downstream towards the Pool of London, for it was a heavy misty night and the lamps on the water's edge could hardly be seen from where they stood.

'That's it,' Max said, in a matter of fact sort of voice that seemed to come from a great distance away. 'Breathe deeply, and let me hold you. Over you go – I want your head downwards – *that's* it –'

Theo found himself bent double over the strong young arm that was across his belly and slowly the tremor eased, almost squeezed out of him by the pressure of Max's arm, and the shimmering before his eyes began to fade and he could look at the soft haloes round the street lights and see them for what they were, instead of as shining crowns of dancing gold splinters.

'Thank you,' he said after a long moment and drew a slightly shaking hand across his face. 'I – it happens sometimes. Thank you –'

'I'm sorry,' Max said. 'I'm truly sorry. It was my fault for asking you to talk about – well, I'm sorry. I shan't bother you again, I promise. Do forgive me.'

'Nothing to forgive,' Theo said and drew a deep breath. 'My fault for being foolish. I'm grateful to you for stopping it that way.'

He straightened and then peered at Max in the dimness and

said, 'How did you? I mean, make it stop? I can't usually stop it like that. It gets worse and worse and I shake and then – it's ghastly. It's been – I've been very frightened of it, to tell the truth.'

'It's the way you treat any sort of vaso-vagal attack,' Max said. 'I mean, whenever you see a patient go white the way you did, you know they're going to faint so you tip them up so their heads are down, to bring the blood back to the brain and make them breathe normally. Sometimes people who are feeling faint breathe too fast and that makes them worse, not better.'

'I'll remember,' Theo said and his voice was a little cracked. 'Treat myself as a fainting woman. Useful, if a little degrading.'

'Nothing degrading about it,' Max said, as Theo turned and went back into the lobby, leaving the raw dankness of the night behind them. 'It's just a physiological reaction –'

Now they were back inside he seemed more like the raw youngster he had been when they were first introduced, the moment of masterful control quite banished. He shivered then and rubbed his face again and looked at his wet hand, for the mist had beaded them both with moisture, and seemed younger than ever.

Theo, feeling better by the moment, smiled at him. 'Well, whatever the cause of it, it's useful to know how to cope. Thank you. And thank you for covering up my lapse. Perhaps I'd better find myself a cigar, to add some verisimilitude to –'

'– an otherwise bald and unconvincing narrative,' Max said and grinned too, and they looked at each other and a strange agreeable companionship hung in the air between them.

There was a flurry of sound from outside, and the lobby door which they had closed behind them flew open and as the commissionaire, who seemed to appear from nowhere, came surging forwards a vision in a white ermine wrap came drifting in with a tall and extremely good-looking boy in the most impeccable of evening clothes at her side, and a rather gawky, tall and plain girl in an equally expensive but much less becoming fur behind her.

'So late, so late, I am quite desperately ashamed!' the vision in white carolled, looking over Theo and Max's shoulders and Theo turned his head to see Letty was there, coming out to welcome the late arrival. 'But we must not be blamed, my dear, for you see it is the fog, so abominable, *so* disgusting, it delays *everything*. But as you see, we are here, at last, and none the worse for a most alarming journey through the wilds of your enchanting Chelsea!'

She had a faintly Gallic accent and certainly her clothes had all the chic of a Paris salon, and Theo caught Max's eye and a spark of amused comment flashed between them. Both obviously found the woman rather absurd in her intense stylishness and both rather despised the exceedingly elegant youth at her side.

'Not late at all,' Letty was saying, and there was a bustle with wraps and hats – the departure of the white ermine displaying a gown glittering with diamonds and quite unbelievably flimsy about the smooth shoulders and splendid bosom – as the woman chattered on and on about the horrors of her journey from Mayfair.

'Theo,' Letty said as soon as the woman stopped to allow breath, and seizing on him as the nearest. 'Please let me introduce you. Lady Collingbourne, Theo Caspar. Lord Collingbourne, Lady Emilia Collingbourne – ah, Max –' She made the round of introductions again and the men bowed and murmured politely and stood back to allow the newcomers access to the big room, but Lady Collingbourne stood still and looked at Max closely.

'Lackland,' she said. 'A connection of our dear Letty, are you? Are you perhaps acquainted with Mr Lewis Lackland, the surgeon?'

'My father, ma'am,' Max said.

'Ah.' She looked at him a little consideringly and then smiled widely. 'Dear me, I should have guessed. His son! Well, well! Are there more of you, perhaps? Are they here tonight? Your *maman*? Your papa?' And she slid her eyes sideways towards the press of people, almost hopefully.

'My mother is here, Lady Collingbourne. And my sister. My father is at the hospital tonight, and could not be here.'

'Then you shall present me to your ladies,' Lady Collingbourne said firmly and held out her hand. 'Come, Emilia. You too. Take her arm, Mr Lackland, if you please. Precisely – now, where is your dear Maman? Miriam, I believe, isn't she? Yes – it will be agreeable to see her again, after all these years!'

And she swept into the party with her head high, clearly taking it for granted that everyone in the room would stare at her, and so everyone did. Except her daughter, Emilia, that is. She was staring at Max.

6

Clearly Letty had been waiting for the Collingbourne party to come before she would start her film show, for almost as soon as they had arrived she hurried away, to return almost at once with Oliver on her arm, looking a little weary but very contented with himself, to settle him in the front row of the small theatre to which the party was now shepherded by Edwin, who emitted little cries and urgings and managed to ensure they all found themselves comfortably seated with the minimum fuss and waste of time.

Theo found a place at the end of one of the empty back rows and so had a clear view of most of the audience, and he watched as Lady Collingbourne talked to Miriam Lackland with great animation, clearly putting herself out a good deal to please her companion, and was both puzzled and amused. Lady Collingbourne did not look the sort of person who would ever bother to enchant any woman and he wondered why she should be doing so now. And indeed why she should be here at all, until he remembered what Letty had said when he had arrived. 'I'm going to need some extra finance –' Was this the finance? Very possibly.

Beside Lady Collingbourne sat Max, and as the audience settled down, Theo watched him a little covertly. He was sitting with his chin down and staring at his hands on his lap and clearly paying no attention at all to the plain girl on his other side, who was talking to him quietly and looking closely at him. An interesting boy with his swoops from boyish distress about his dead brother to capable control of a sick man; that trick he had used of bending Theo double had been wonderful; it had banished that horrible sick glitter and remote feeling so effectively that it had taken the painful anger and the tremor away as well. Theo would have to remember that, he told himself, and as he thought it, Max lifted his head and looked across the theatre directly at him and Theo smiled, widely. At once Max blushed a brick red and looked away again, just as the lights went down.

In front of them the red curtains swished softly and parted to show the silvery glow of a screen and Theo settled more deeply into his chair, to watch what Letty had brought him here to see. Somewhere nearby a small but clearly sprightly little orchestra started to play; Theo could just see them now, in a pit below the screen, and then, as an image was projected on to the screen shifted his attention to it.

He had seen cinema shows before, but not too often; most of those he had seen had been sorry affairs, in his estimation, for he preferred live actors on live stages, so he expected little of interest from what he was watching. But slowly, he found he was being sucked into the action before him and becoming deeply involved in it.

It started with a domestic interior. A man and a woman eating breakfast together, in a pretty room. He watched them as they shared the simple meal, and the music from the orchestra played pleasantly and easily, watched the relish with which the man ate his food, the delight with which the woman watched him, and was comfortable in what he saw. The scene changed to show the man at his office, and then cut to the woman in her kitchen being domestic, then back to the man again, scene intercut with scene to give a brief but very clear picture of simple happy domesticity and good peaceful living.

More scene changes; newspaper headlines as the orchestra swung into martial music; the man's clothes seeming to dissolve on his body to relimn as an infantry uniform – an effect which brought applause from the small audience in the theatre – as war moved into the domestic bliss of the first scenes. There were training sequences – and Theo realized with considerable satisfaction that they had been filmed in real situations. These men weren't actors pretending to train; these were real shopkeepers and clerks and farmers' boys learning to march and swear and kill with guns. He had been through much the same training himself before going on to his training as an officer. From time to time the face of the main actor was shown, but somehow he managed to look like a real soldier too, like all the others and no longer like a mere performer. Theo approved of that.

Picture after picture slid across the gleaming square up there in the darkness. Soldiers embarking on crowded ships, soldiers sharing meals and cigarettes at roadsides, soldiers digging trenches, soldiers laughing, talking, singing. And then the noises started, this time not only from the orchestra. Theo flinched as a sudden crump shook the little theatre and almost jumped to his feet – as did several other people – only subsiding slowly when someone laughed and called out, 'Oh, damned clever! Damned clever – that's a gramophone.' The voices went on as the battle happened up there on the screen in front of him and he felt his breath thicken in his chest as he watched, almost smelled the rich sick sweetness of corpses as an image of men lying draped negligently across the wire and dead horses stretched in the mud appeared. The music as such had stopped now; only a piano note played over and over again, simply and softly and with great dignity, broke the silence. No one in the audience spoke now, not even whispered. They just sat and watched as the images built on each other, each only marginally more ugly than the last, yet showing a picture of horror that Theo knew was only too authentic.

And then, suddenly, more newspaper headlines, more music, triumphant victorious music this time, and now the scene changed for the last time to the streets he had walked in himself only five days ago. People shouting silently with their mouths open hugely wide, drunken girls giggling with thunderous quietness, people pushing and shoving, much as they had pushed and shoved him. And then, in front of them all, in vast size, so that her face almost filled the silver square, the girl from the first scene, watching the celebrations. Standing with her hands in her pockets and with her face quite still, she stared blank-eyed at the crowds and their idiotic excitement, and then turned quietly and walked away off the screen, leaving only the jigging, bobbing, bouncing mob in the street behind her.

The screen darkened, the music stopped and there was a measurable silence in the little theatre.

And then someone shouted, 'Ah, Bravo! Magnificent!' and they were all applauding – all except Theo. He sat and stared at the screen, now covered with its red curtain, and let the people around him surge to their feet and hurry towards the front to speak to Letty, who was immediately surrounded.

It was Edwin again who organized them all, calling out flutingly about the *most* delicious supper that was awaiting them back in the studio where they had been before, and *please* to come and enjoy it before it was *quite* ruined, and at last the audience, chattering and very elevated by the excitement of the film they had seen, moved out of the now darkened little theatre.

Letty came back after she had taken Oliver to sit in the centre of the main room and slid into the seat beside him.

'Well?'

'What do you want me to say?'

She was silent for a moment. 'Authentic?'

'Oh, that. Yes. Very. Well done.'

'Is that all you can say?'

'What do you want me to say? That it's a jolly exciting film and should make a lot of money for you? Is that what you want?'

'No,' she said quietly. 'That it's a terrifying film that will make a lot of people see how stupid wars are. That it's a film about people wanting to live, not about people being forced to die. That it might teach some of the idiots who think war is a great and glorious adventure that it's a sick and miserable distortion of what life is for. That's why I made it, and if I haven't succeeded in making you feel that, then I wasted my time and I might as well set fire to the lot. It's only so much celluloid after all.'

'They don't seem to have heard any of that,' he said after a moment and he jerked his head towards the studio from which loud sounds of merriment were coming as knives and plates clashed and glasses chinked above the laughter and chatter.

'Stop being so insufferably pious! D'you think you're the only person who suffers? D'you think no one but you

54

understands? They heard what I was saying, well enough. Most of the people here tonight are professionals in the same business as me, and they're excited by the techniques I used. They're excited because I could take actuality film that is just five days old and build it into a feature film ready for distribution. They're noisy because they approve of getting films like this out to the idiot public while their memories are fresh.'

He closed his eyes in the dimness, suddenly very tired. 'I'm a fool, aren't I? A selfish fool –'

'There you go again!' she said. 'Wallowing! Self-centred you may be – a fool you're not. I suppose you're entitled to wallow up to a point, though I can't really say, of course. I wasn't there in France and you were and you know what the hell was like. I've no right to tell you to stop thinking about what happened. All I can do is make my films and try to tell people the way *I* see wars, which is as stupid and cruel and wasteful and not great or glorious at all, and hope someone'll listen. I used to fight for votes for women, you know. I thought that might be the road that'd lead the world to a better way. But that's too slow – I know that now. So, instead, I tell my stories on film, trying to convince people of the truth as I see it – the truth about the foulness of war. And I hope somewhere someone'll listen. I hope you'll listen to me too – that you'll believe there can be a worthwhile future for you. That you can forget that war, and all it stood for.'

'It's not just the war, you know.'

'What isn't?'

'The way I am – the way I feel, I mean. I did have a rough time at Passchendaele. Everyone did. That's no secret. It wasn't just that, you see. There were other things –'

'Tell me about them,' she said softly.

He sat for what seemed a long time, staring at her face gleaming a little in the dimness. He was sitting in the shadows, but there was a warm wash of soft light that reached her and he could see, there against her mouth, the fine lines that betrayed her age, and against the corners of her eyes the soft skin that was beginning to pouch and he thought confusedly that she looked exactly the sort of warm caring person he most needed;

like the sister he wished he had instead of the silly gigglers who were Olive and Constance and Edith, and he wanted, quite badly to lean forwards and put his head on her shoulder and tell her everything that was hurting him so dreadfully. About Peter. He needed some sort of absolution, some sort of care, and perhaps she could give it.

'There you are! I've searched for you everywhere, my dear Letty. Such a splendid film – I am sure it will be hugely successful, most hugely – I will of course invest in your new venture. It is clear you are little short of a genius and I'd be mad not to share in your activities! You shall come tomorrow to see me at Vere Street and we shall go to see my man of business in the City – so boring, but it is necessary – and we shall arrange all. Now, however, we must go, I have to go to another party – such a bore, but I promised the Duchess and *que voulez-vous? Bon nuit, ma cherie – à bientôt!*'

Letty put one hand on his as she got swiftly to her feet and then was gone, following Lady Collingbourne, leaving him feeling extraordinarily shaky. That had been a dreadfully near thing. Dreadfully close. He would have to watch himself, indeed he would, and he got to his feet a little wearily and moved into the studio to stand leaning against the jamb of the door and watched them all, eagerly eating and drinking and thoroughly enjoying themselves. An extraordinary woman, Letty Lackland, he was thinking. Quite extraordinary. As long as I take care it could be interesting to hear what it was she had said she wanted to suggest. As long as I'm careful.

Across the room Max sat at one of the small tables which had been spread in the studio by the deft caterers Letty had hired for the evening and watched Theo while his mother beside him chattered and murmured in her soft voice and Johanna on his other side tried to engage Emilia Collingbourne in conversation, though with little success, for she was sitting watching Max as unwinkingly as he was watching Theo. Not that Max noticed for he was too deep in his own thoughts.

He must have suffered quite dreadfully, Max told himself. To have looked like that – so white and taut, just because he was asked about it – the agony of experience that lay behind that reaction must be appalling. Is that how it would have been for Tim if he'd lived to come home and be asked about it? Would Tim have had those dark eyes, so deep set in pain-shadowed sockets? Would his mouth have been so tight with misery? Max tried to see Tim's cheerful round face with its wide grin and eyes glinting with laughter looking as tragic and tortured as Theo's, and quite failed. But at least I've been able to visualize the way Tim had looked, he thought suddenly. For months now it's been getting harder and harder to remember him. And now I've remembered him laughing – that's because of Theo. He helped me, I helped him. I'm awfully glad of that. He said I'd helped him, didn't he? And I did, though I'm not sure it was all that special really, just stopping him from fainting – but he seemed pleased. I do wish I could talk to him some more, I truly do. He's so interesting –

'Mother,' he said abruptly, quite unaware of interrupting her, for she had been talking about the family's plans for Christmas. 'Please, may we invite Theo Caspar to visit?'

'Why yes, of course,' Miriam said and put her plump beringed hand on his. 'Anything you wish, darling. He is charming, isn't he? I recall he was most kind to me when his grandfather died and I became so distressed. He was very young then, of course, but still, very kind – I shall make a plan, I promise you. As soon as I can.'

'Shall I ask him now?' Max said eagerly and Miriam, a little surprised, shook her head.

'Hardly, my dear,' she said with gentle reproof. 'I must decide whom else we should invite – one cannot have a party quite so casually, you know! And we are just out of mourning, after all. Let me speak to your father and –'

'I don't mean a party!' Max said, horrified. 'Just a visit!'

'May I visit too, Mrs Lackland?' They both turned to stare, in almost ludicrous synchrony and Emilia Collingbourne looked tranquilly back at them, her narrow mouth smiling gently.

'Er – why, my dear – er, yes, by all means –' Miriam stammered, a little disconcerted. It was unusual, to say the least, to have young ladies to whom one had only just been introduced proposing themselves as visitors in quite so direct a manner.

'I have so much enjoyed talking to your daughter, Johanna,' Emilia said, in the same calm voice. 'She is charming, isn't she? She's just gone to find me some more lemonade, as I said I was feeling thirsty – so kind. It's not too easy for me to arrange for visits at home – Maman's so busy, you know, and Jonty is somewhat demanding of her time – so I must shift as best I can to meet my own friends. And I'd dearly like to include Johanna among my friends. I do so hope I may.'

Johanna came weaving back through the crowd, a glass of lemonade in either hand, and heard the last comment and smiled a little doubtfully at Emilia.

'Of course. That would be lovely,' she said. 'When we're really back in society, you know. At present it's all a little – difficult –' And she looked at her brother anxiously. But he, to her surprise, was vigorous in his support of the suggestion.

'Of course we shall plan something, Lady Emilia. Perhaps an evening visit, Mother, during the Christmas hols. That would be rather jolly –'

Miriam stopped looking so anxious and again patted his hand. 'Well, I dare say – perhaps I could telephone your mother, Lady Emilia, and make an arrangement? And –' She smiled at Johanna. 'Perhaps your brother could come too. Darling Johanna has seen far too little young life these past months. It will be nice for her if we have a sizeable party –'

At which piece of transparent matching on her mother's part Johanna reddened and promised herself she would do all she could to ensure that Lady Emilia Collingbourne's brother should not be invited to their house. He had looked a most sulky person, and had seemed happy enough to escape with his mother when she had left early to go to another party, leaving her daughter to await the return of the chauffeur with the car to be taken home. The last person Johanna wanted to get to know better was that arrogant young man, marquis or not! But it was good to see Max thinking at last of something other than the loss of his beloved Tim, and she smiled warmly at him as he settled back in his chair and at last began to eat some supper. Maybe Max was getting over it all at last.

'Well, what do you say?' Letty said again, and picked up her wine glass and drank a little, watching him over the rim.

'I don't know,' he said. 'It's so stupid. I'd never have thought of such a thing in a thousand years –'

'Not stupid. Unexpected, maybe, but really very sensible. You've got an incredible face, you see.'

'Incredible? I find it all too believable. It's always there when I look in my shaving mirror in the morning.'

'Remarkable, then. Unusual. Beautiful.' She brushed grammar aside. 'Don't be pedantic. It's a face that will film. You'll do very well.'

'Is that all there is to acting?' he said and laughed. 'And here was I thinking you needed talent and intelligence and a good memory for lines and –'

'Lines, yes – though they don't have to be perfect. Just a way to get the feeling right, for films. No problems of projection, or anything like that,' she said. 'And as for talent – I've got plenty of that. The only talent that matters is the producer's. That's the one who decides what the actors do and how and where they do it. And I could make you look unbelievably talented. Well? What do you say? Have you anything better to do?'

'I suppose not –' he said slowly, a little bemused by it all. 'I can't pretend that the prospect of going to m'father's counting house in the City is so entrancing that it puts this out of court –'

'I'd pay you well, of course,' she said casually. 'I don't know anything about your personal finances, naturally, but I dare say you'd be happy enough to have more of your own. Enough to set up your own establishment, and probably more.'

He lifted his chin at that and stared at her, his eyes a little narrowed as he considered. He had a small private income, inherited from his maternal grandfather, but it was far from munificent. The idea of living in his own establishment and no longer having to tolerate the anxious stare of his family had often come to him, but it had been sent packing for want of the wherewithal. One of the aspects of working for his father that he had found most dispiriting was the fact that doing so would have made it impossible for him ever to leave the family house in South Audley Street. Unless he married, and that was not to be thought of.

'My own establishment,' he said slowly.

'Yes,' she said calmly. 'And probably more –'

'What would I have to do if I agreed?'

'Work with me in the early planning stages. Let me teach you, do some testing, work out the best part for you. And then make the film,' she said promptly.

'Hmm. When would we start?'

She grinned. 'Tomorrow do for you? Or shall we wait till Monday?'

'Monday,' he said after a moment. 'So soon? Dammit, why not? I can't be any worse off than I am – I suppose –'

'Thank you!' she said with a sardonic edge to her voice. 'So graceful an acceptance of an offer is a rare pleasure for me!'

'Sorry!' he said, embarrassed, but she laughed. 'It's all right. I know I caught you by surprise. But the best things always do happen quickly. I'll see you on Monday. And I'll look forward to hearing you've set up your own home – if you can find a flat these overcrowded days, that is. I've got some useful contacts I can try for you – there are a few places available, if you know where to look. It'll be a pleasure to help, if only because I know how infuriated your grandmother will be to hear you've done it, and that working for me made it possible! Catty, aren't I?'

'Yes,' he said and laughed. 'Yes. But at least you're not boring. Monday should be interesting. I'll look forward to it. I think.'

7

'Well?' Edwin said. 'Will he shape up, d'you think?'

'He'll do more than that,' Letty said confidently. 'He's going to be very good indeed. I wanted him because he's got a marvellous face but the man can act too.'

Edwin looked sceptical. 'You've only had him working with us a month! How can you tell so soon? I bow to none in my respect for your judgement, Letty dearest, but really I do think this time you're being beguiled by mere looks –'

She set aside the ledger on which she had been working and reached for another, pushing her glasses up her nose as she did so. Her hair was rumpled and she looked tired, but contented, somehow, and not quite as anxious as she usually was at the start of a project.

'Mere looks, my dear Edwin, are all that matter in this business, and if you don't know that by now, you never will. It's faces, faces, faces – and bodies too, I suppose, but not to the same extent. The Americans are making fortunes for themselves by finding people for the audiences to fall in love with. Your average man or woman wouldn't know good acting if it came wrapped in tinsel. They just respond to personalities. And Theo's dripping with it, and doesn't know, fortunately. That's all any film-maker needs from a performer, and to find one who can act as well is bonus, pure bonus. I'm not saying he's Frank Benson or Lewis Waller – but he could be another Douglas Fairbanks and that's what I'm interested in. D'you know how much that man makes with his films? The return on the investment can be more than five hundred per cent in the first *month* – and the films still go on earning long after. All Fairbanks needs is to smile a bit, and mug a bit, and open his eyes a bit and they swoon over him – and I tell you Theo can do all that and more. And he's got something even better. A natural expression of pain and suffering. Women like that –'

'I'm beginning to think you like it too. Personally I mean,' Edwin said with a malicious little grin and Letty flushed a patchy red.

'Don't be stupid,' she said gruffly. 'I'm a businesswoman first last and in between, and well you know it. So stop being sentimental and trying to meddle in my private life. You've tried it before often enough and look where it got you. I've told you, I'm looking for a draw for this film, and I think this man could be it. That's all about it. Now, if you have nothing better to do than sit here and pester, go and do it somewhere else. I'm busy –'

And Edwin laughed and went, leaving her to her piled desk and the final clearing of the day's work, only stopping at the door to remind her of his party.

'Don't be late,' he said. 'I shall be in *desperate* need of your help, for I've got your new backer coming and truth to tell that woman quite terrifies me. She's too luscious even for my blood –'

'Liar,' Letty said. 'You love her and you know it. She bids fair to outdo your Christmas tree the way she dresses. She's dripping with money and she knows everyone in London. Right up your alley –'

'Well, that's as maybe. But she *will* persist in asking awkward questions about the production and I haven't the least notion what it's all about, so you'd better be early. Anyway, she'll scoop up your Theo if you're not, and *then* what will you do?' And he escaped before she could say anything.

She leaned back in her chair as the distant front door of the studio banged behind Edwin and stretched a little, yawning, and at last allowed herself to think about Theo. Sitting here in the darkened office with just the pool of light spilled on her desk by her table lamp, with the silence of the empty studio all round her, she was comfortable; this was the only place she ever was really at peace, the only place where she could sit and think and not feel threatened by the world outside, the only place that was really hers. Even her house at Paulton's Square didn't have the tranquillity and reassurance of this small cluttered office. For that was Oliver's home too. But here was different.

Ever since the long-gone days when she had been an eager girl, working here at what had been the Gaff Theatre, waiting for her love to come back to her from the depths of his illness, this had been the place where she found solace. And afterwards, in those black and dreadful days after Luke had died, this had been the only place where she could weep and scream at God for treating her so cruelly, where she could allow herself to experience her pain and learn to live with it.

And now it was the only place where she could allow herself to think of what had happened to her since Armistice Night. A man had tripped over her rostrum and in so doing had cracked her carapace, that hard shell of indifference to emotion in which she had wrapped herself for more than ten years. She could see him still, the way he had looked to her in the fitful light of Piccadilly as she stood in the shadows of Jackson's shop, seeing but unseen. The white face with the deep-shadowed eyes, the crisp line of hair against the temples, the shape of the flat cheeks and that twisted unhappy mouth – it had been extraordinary how she had reacted to it all. She had felt a physical response, a tightening of her belly that she had been used to know, long ago when Luke had been alive, but never since. Time and again Edwin and Oliver had tried in their sweet and bumbling ways to get under her guard, bringing her men to talk to, giving parties in order to introduce her with transparent artlessness to one good-looking eligible man after another, but none of them had been of the remotest interest. Until now.

'Stupid,' she muttered aloud, and bent her head again to her ledger. 'Stupid. He's too young anyway –'

'Only five years,' answered a small jeering voice deep inside her head. 'What's five years, after all?'

'Stupid!' This time she shouted it at the ledger, and shook her head irritably, and forced herself to start adding up the columns of figures. Costs of film. Costs of perforation. Costs of development. Costs of editing. Costs of –

'Why shouldn't you?' said the tiny voice inside her head

again. 'Other women love men. Why shouldn't you?'

'Because Luke died,' she thought, answering herself. 'Because Luke died. I can't take the pain again. Not after Luke –'

'Why should it hurt this time? Why not just a sweet and happy love for you this time? It's your turn, you're entitled –'

'Oh, hell!' She got to her feet, slamming the ledger shut. 'I'm tired. Finish this tomorrow –' And she shrugged into her coat and went, methodically locking the doors behind her, and lingering for a moment to stare back at the big central room as she sorted out the final key. They'd have to find some other sites for the interiors, she told herself, struggling to be as matter-of-fact and businesslike as she usually was. We'll never be able to build enough of Cleopatra's palace here – and the exterior locations will have to be sorted out, too. Money, money, money. But all of it would come back, every penny and lots more besides. If I could persuade Theo to play Mark Anthony for me –

'It will be a delightful party,' Edwin said very contentedly. 'You'll see, my dear old friend. Quite, quite delightful.'

'They usually are for you,' Oliver said. 'Spend enough, don't you? Yes. And you usually enjoy yourself well enough, rushing around like a cat on heat. Don't know everyone else finds 'em quite so delightful, mind you –'

'Oh, pooh, you're just getting cantankerous now you're old,' Edwin said and tweaked at a loop of tinsel on the Christmas tree, and then stood back to stare at it judiciously. 'A little more tinsel, do you think, at the top there? No? Well, perhaps you're right. One wouldn't wish to be vulgar – everyone *always* enjoys my parties. There'd be no joy for me in it if they didn't, so the fact that I enjoy 'em proves everyone else does! And this one'll really start up some fun –'

He giggled with great delight and came and sat beside Oliver on the sofa. 'Now, you bad-tempered old wretch, are you comfortable? I want no fussing from you once everyone else gets here. Are you sitting where you'll have the best view of everyone, and they'll all see you, holding court like King Canute? Yes? Good – because there'll be lots to look at tonight. Did you *see* the way that Collingbourne girl was mooning over young Lackland at the studio that night? Too delicious – plain as they come, poor little wretch, and he too lordly to notice she *breathes*, let alone that she's taken with him –'

'And did *you* see Lord Collingbourne staring at the boy's sister? No? There – not nearly as noticin' a chap as you made yourself out to be, are you?' Oliver said and cackled, very pleased with himself. 'Pretended he didn't notice her, o'course – that sort o' young chap always puts on an act of not caring. But I saw, I saw! And I saw that she didn't care for him a bit – thought him too hoity-toity, I'll be bound –' Oliver settled more comfortably into Edwin's sofa. 'Oh, it'll be as good as a show to see 'em all at it again. Glad you asked 'em all. Who else is coming?'

'Most of the studio people – Letty wanted them, likes to make a fuss over her workers at this end of the year, and I grant you it's good business, if a touch tiresome at times – some of them are *too* boring, my dear chap, too boring. Then I thought, those *delicious* little dancers from Charlot's new revue at the Comedy, and darling Delysia said she might just look in, and so did Charles Cochran and –'

'Splendid, splendid,' Oliver said and blinked, his filmy old eyes alight with pleasure. 'Be good to see old Charles. I grant you, Edwin, it should be quite a good party after all – for all your boasting. Get me a brandy, now, before Letty gets here and starts fussin' – go on, now! At least I won't have to see m'sister tonight. Can't ask for more than that, can I? No – not so much soda, Edwin, not so much soda, dammit –'

'Oh, Mother, must I go?' Johanna said, and made a face as her maid began to hook her frock at the back. 'I'd really much rather not –'

'But, dear one, you usually love a party!' Miriam said, her soft voice distressed and her face absurdly anxious. 'Why not this one? I do so want to go, for your poor father has been working so hard and I thought a little entertainment might amuse him and you know he won't go and leave you all alone in the house –'

'Oh, I'd not be alone!' Johanna said. 'The servants would be here, for Mary told me she was staying in, and so was Cook, for the weather's so hateful, and I'd be perfectly happy reading – are you sure Daddy wouldn't go if I didn't?'

'Quite sure,' Miriam said firmly. 'You know how he frets over you all. And I do think it would do him good. They've been dreadfully busy at the hospital with all this awful influenza – and you know how it is if he remains at home in the evening. Sure as eggs someone will call him. If he's not here, then he can't go back to Nellie's, can he?'

'I suppose not –' Johanna said doubtfully and again made a face at herself in the mirror, even though she looked delightful in a green gauze frock with silk ribbons trimming it, and tying her dark hair back behind the inevitable forehead fillet. 'I suppose I'll have to, then –'

'I'm sure you'll enjoy it,' Miriam said firmly. 'If you put your mind to it. Now I must go and see that Max and Peter are quite ready too. It was good of Edwin to ask the dear child as well. He's so excited, bless him. After all, it is quite a fashionable party for a boy of his age –' And she went rustling away leaving Johanna amused as well as irritated. How like Mother to regard Peter as a child when he was fully seventeen!

And how like mother to make sure everyone did what she wanted them to, without making them too aware of how cleverly she was manipulating them. She wanted to go to the party herself and she wanted her husband on her arm; that was really why she was determined Johanna should go as well, for it was true that Daddy wouldn't leave any of them alone if he could help it. There was no one quite as devoted as he was to his children, and all of them knew it. And since Tim had died he had been even more anxious about them all –

No, if Daddy wanted to go – or Mother wanted him to, she corrected herself – she'd have to. And if that meant fending off that tiresome Jonty Collingbourne, so be it. She'd just have to be firm with him. And she looked in the mirror, trying to make herself look firm, but failed and felt worse than ever. Wretched party, she thought.

Max, carefully knotting his white bow tie before his own mirror was feeling anxious about the party too, but not because of any doubts about his own desire to be there. He wanted to be there very much indeed, but the question was, would Theo Caspar be there? He'd been at the last party organized by Letty, so perhaps he'd be at this one too? Max had actually considered telephoning Letty to ask her; after all, he'd known her long enough, ever since his boyhood. There'd been some drama in her life with which his father had been involved which had tied them all close together, but he'd never thought much about that. She'd just been old Letty, his parents' friend as well as some sort of distant cousin, and he'd accepted her as that; now, suddenly, she seemed a worthwhile ally – someone who knew a person he badly wanted to know better, and who might be able to help him do so.

But he'd quailed at the thought of calling her for such a purpose. She might not understand his anxiety; indeed he did not quite understand it himself. All he knew was that this man with the deep dark eyes and the tight controlled face held the key to his own future peace of mind. The only person who could help him recover from Tim's death, he was quite certain, was Theo Caspar. He had to get to know him better, and to spend more time with him. His mother's promise to invite him for Christmas still held, and she had been planning, he knew, a New Year's Eve party, but he really couldn't wait till then. Another ten days, to add to the month since he'd last seen Theo – it was more than he could bear. Please let him be there tonight, he whispered to his mirror image. Please let him be there!

Theo very nearly wasn't. He sat in his snug sitting-room at his hard-won flat at 8 King Edward Mansions, at the top of Shaftesbury Avenue near the Prince's Theatre, and stared at the fire that Mrs MacFarlane, the caretaker who lived in the basement and who 'did' for the various bachelor tenants, had left burning so cosily in the grate, and considered the possibility of telephoning Letty and telling her that he had a slight cold and couldn't attend Edwin's party. He would not be at all concerned about letting down his host; he knew perfectly well that the most important person in the Gaff Studios was Letty, that despite the fact that old Oliver and Edwin were equal partners, it was her moods and her reactions that mattered. And he was beginning to discover, after just a month as an employee of the studios, that her moods and reactions could be mercurial. To upset her could be much more far reaching in its effects than upsetting old Edwin, who might be miffed at an absence from his party, but would hardly make him feel guilty about it.

For Letty could make him feel guilty, and he couldn't quite work out why that should be so. It was nothing she said or did; it was just the way she made him feel. He stared at his fire and then round at his sitting-room and frowned slightly. Maybe it was because it was her doing that he was so comfortable now? Telling his parents that he had decided the time had come to leave their roof had been difficult, had resulted in floods of tears from his mother and sisters and a good deal of blustering from James, but there had been no guilt in him once he had packed his modest bags and taken himself off to the flat her influence had obtained for him, tucked away here at the edge of Covent Garden, hard by Seven Dials. He had felt only relief, and he had rearranged the furniture he had found there together with a few pictures and books bought in the local antiquarian shops and settled in with all the certainty there was in him. This was what he needed, he now knew, and it had been Letty's offer of work, odd work though it was, that had made it all possible, that had helped him sleep better of nights. He still dreamed those awful dreams, but he did sleep between them and that was something for which to be very grateful. Grateful to Letty. That was why he felt guilt, no doubt, when he set his face against her wishes, he told himself now. She had given him what he needed, and what had he to give in return? Only a willingness to please her and his very doubtful skills as a film actor.

Right from that very first day when she had set to work on him, making him posture in front of that horrible camera, while Alf, his cloth cap carefully turned back to front so that the peak did not obscure his view, stood there silently and absorbedly winding the crank handle on its mahogany box, he had felt he had made a dreadful mistake in accepting her offer of this acting work. He'd *never* be able to cope with all this, never be able to feel anything other than a complete fool, grinning like a mad monkey, scowling like a madder one. He'd asked to be allowed to work elsewhere in the studios, to be a cameraman, perhaps, or learn how to run her office for her, but she had been adamant. It was as an actor she wanted him, and an actor he was to be. And no matter how much he had complained, how much he had protested that she was wrong that he could not ever become the performer she wanted, she remained patiently and calmly determined. He could, and he would, she said. Now try anger again. No, not like that. Think of something he hated, something that made fury rise in him and let his face obey the feelings that the thoughts created in him – that's right! Now again. And again –

Looking back over the past month now he marvelled at how patient she had been. In the middle of planning her new production of *Caesar and Cleopatra*, which, he gathered from the snippets of conversation he overheard between herself and other people around the Gaff was to be a very big film, she still worked with him hour after hour, teaching him not only how to allow emotion to show in his face, but how to move easily, how to be aware of that damned camera's baleful glare without showing he was aware of it, how to look into that blank lens that stared back at him so dully and communicate with it as though it were a person. How to breathe, how to relax, how to stand and how to sit –

And as the month had progressed he had become more and more absorbed with his own privacy. The joys of living in a space to which there was just one door, and to which he alone held the key were very new to him. All his life before the war had been spent in his father's house, where everyone was expected to share everything with the family.

Oh, he'd had his own bedroom, of course, but there had been no real privacy there. His sister, his mother, his father, anyone could come and tap on the panels and be amazed and offended if he did not immediately bid them to come in. And even when he'd escaped that claustrophobic atmosphere by joining the army – and he knew now that that had been the prime reason for his eagerness to enlist – he'd been no better off. Sharing a dugout with twenty, thirty, forty other men was hardly conducive to peaceful thought. So, to live as he did now with no one to know where he went or when, no one to care what he did or why, was a joy. Just Mrs MacFarlane to clean the flat once a day and make his bed and deal with his laundry and the rest was blissful, perfect solitude. It was worth acting just to get that.

So, he stirred now and regretfully stood up. To stay here tonight would be eminently better than dressing, struggling to find a taxi or fighting his way through the overcrowded tube trains and making his way across London to Chelsea, but he owed it to Letty to do it. So, he would, not because he wanted to see her but because he valued so highly the gift of freedom she had given him. It was the least he could do for her.

8

'Oh, glory!' Edwin had whispered to Oliver as he went hurrying past on his way to ensure that Alice Delysia had all the champagne she wanted. 'Can't you just *see* all the eddies and currents! I haven't been so enthralled for *years*. Do watch, dear old boy, and tell me all when I come back –' But Oliver was getting sleepy now, and nodded off several times, quite missing the interplay between his guests that Edwin found so enthralling.

It was not surprising he should be tired; the party was quite one of Edwin's best. First, the Waits, all dressed up charmingly in mufflers and David Copperfield caps and carrying lanterns on poles had sung 'Good King Wenceslas' and 'Away in a Manger' in shrill little voices outside the dining-room window, thus making everyone coo and feel excessively Christmassy. And then there had been three white-faced Augustes from the circus who had come tumbling into the room in a whirl of white satin pantaloons and black pom-poms and conical hats, to put on a *killingly* funny performance teasing all the girls who giggled a great deal and paying mock homage to the men who did not. And after that there had been food – vast quantities of it, with whole birds in aspic and stuffed carp specially brought from Schmidt's in Charlotte Street and hot patties filled with the most delectable potted shrimps and marrons glacés and pineapple ices and heaven knows what else besides, an amazing array in these days of rationing and food shortages, and a clear indication of Edwin's total immorality when it came to his pleasures, and gallons and gallons of sweet champagne. And then dancing of the most energetic sort, the newest of new jazz bands with the essential highly fashionable negro musicians playing 'Hitchy

Koo' and 'Everybody's Doing It' and 'Oh, You Beautiful Doll', and all the other of the very latest songs, none of which Oliver really liked. His taste was for sweeter, funnier music than this modern jerky stuff. So, now he sat and nodded on his sofa while around him the party went on and on.

On one side of the room Emilia Collingbourne was sitting very straight on a hassock set near the fire. She was wearing blue silk tonight, which did little for her rather dull complexion, but she looked better than she had the last time she had been in this company, for now her face had lost its sulky expression. She looked calm yet alert and there was a faint smile on her face as she watched Max, who was at the moment dancing with his sister. On the other side of the room, her brother Jonty stood glowering and the sight of his discomfiture, Emilia could not deny, added to her own sense of pleasure. It was exceedingly amusing to see him in the state in which she normally was, standing staring at someone else having fun, someone else enjoying themselves while he hovered on the sidelines alone and lonely. He would have to learn how to school his face better than that, she thought with a stab of glee. He'll make a complete cake of himself if he doesn't –

Not that he hadn't made a fair cake of himself all evening – and Emilia almost hugged herself as she thought of how it had been that Johanna had set him down. The more Emilia saw of Johanna the better she liked her; a quiet girl, not particularly animated but with a pleasant round face with an agreeable expression on it, and very pretty eyes that made her look extremely like her mother, she had made it plain from the start that she was not interested in Jonty's advances. He had done as he usually did when he found a girl interesting to look at; he had lounged across to her and talked to her in a remote rather patronizing fashion, but Johanna, remembered Emilia with relish, had frozen him completely, instead of responding with blushes and giggles as most girls did. That would do him all the good in the world. He would discover what it felt like to want to know someone and to be rebuffed.

She looked now at Max, and thought about how to handle his rebuffs. Not that they were snubs precisely; indeed, he had been courteous and charming to her, when she spoke to him, but there had been none of the response that she really wanted. None of that glitter that was in Jonty's eyes when he looked at Johanna. None of that interest that she knew gleamed in her own expression when she stared at him. She would have to work hard to create that in him, she told herself now, sitting quietly with her hands folded on her pale blue lap. It wouldn't be easy, but it could be done, With Johanna's help. That would have to be the first step, making an even greater ally of Johanna. They were already comfortable acquaintances, thanks to Emilia's determination that they should be so, but she would have to do more –

The music changed and Johanna and Max returned to the hassocks by the fire on which they had been seated earlier when Jonty, coming to ask Johanna to dance, had been forestalled by Max's immediate response to his sister's hasty request to dance with her, and now as they sat there, Johanna fanning herself gently – for the room was very warm – Emilia leaned forwards and said quietly, 'I do hope my brother is not a nuisance to you, Johanna.'

Johanna reddened and glanced at her quickly and then away.

'I'm sure I don't know what you mean, Emilia –'

Emilia laughed gently. 'Oh, my dear, you do! I can quite see he's awfully taken with you, and very naturally too, for you are very pretty. But I know the naughty boy can be absolutely maddening when he takes a liking in this way and can be dreadfully persistent. If you truly don't want his attentions, I can help, perhaps –'

Johanna looked at her uncertainly. 'I'm not sure that I –'

'If you like him, of course, that's quite another matter,' Emilia said smoothly. 'I just thought that –'

'I – it isn't that I dislike him,' Johanna said flushing with embarrassment. 'I mean, I don't know! It's just that he really is so particular in his attention. And a little – well – full of himself. I – he embarrasses me.'

'Then stay with me, and if he embarrasses you again I'll see to it that he stops,' Emilia said promptly. 'I can usually make him do as I say. You know how it is with sisters.'

And Johanna smiled at last and said, 'Well – it's kind of you.

I wouldn't want you to think I don't like him – I mean, I don't especially. But I don't actually not like him either – it's just that –'

'I quite understand,' Emilia said soothingly. 'Really, I do. And if you stay with me, I'll see to it you'll be quite comfortable.'

And Johanna relaxed as Emilia had intended she should. It was true that Johanna had been embarrassed by Jonty's obvious dangling after her, because he'd seemed so intense. Pretty as she was, she was used to boys staring at her and reddening when they spoke to her and generally fussing, but Jonty Collingbourne's cool stares and rather arrogant attitude was something quite new, and it was not a newness she enjoyed. To have his sister as an ally could be very comfortable – not least because she wouldn't choke Jonty off completely. She'd just be able to control him. That was an agreeable thought, after all, Johanna told herself.

And Emilia was content too, for later, when Jonty was watching Johanna disconsolately as she sat with her parents, she was able to tell him quietly that Johanna did like him – a little. That she might be willing to get to know him better – in time. And that, she, Emilia, would gladly advise Jonty on how to approach this girl he so liked the look of – if he would promise to behave as she advised. And Jonty, who for all his surface arrogance and air of self-assurance was genuinely interested in Johanna – perhaps a little because he was so unused to having girls reject him – agreed with almost pathetic willingness to let his dull sister help him in his pursuit of her new and highly desirable friend.

All of which left Emilia feeling better on her own account, for the most important thing she had noticed about the Lackland family was their close involvement with each other. The more she saw of Johanna, Emilia told herself with great satisfaction, the more she would see of Max. And given time, that could lead to considerable benefit for Emilia. She'd see to it that it would.

Max for his part was having a wretched evening. Theo had arrived at the party not long after the Lacklands themselves, to Max's intense delight, and they had talked for a while but in a

74

desultory fashion the way people do when they first arrive at a determinedly festive setting, talking of Edwin's vast and prettily trimmed Christmas tree and the large numbers of glass baubles which he had arranged around the room and the very un-English garland on the front door, *so* American, and *so* charming, and the delightful smell of fresh fir tree, and of nothing at all interesting whatsoever.

Max had ventured to ask Theo how he was, but Theo had chosen to regard the question as a mere social pleasantry and had said formally, 'I am well, thank you. I hope you and your family are well,' and had started to talk about Edwin's handsome Whistler painting over the fireplace and commenting on the quality of the drawing as well as the painting, and Max had had to subside, snubbed.

And then Letty had arrived and annexed Theo and taken him off to the other side of the room to talk to Lady Collingbourne, who had insisted that he sit beside her to talk and he had, leaving Max miserably watching them and feeling desolate.

The room had filled up with people now, all sorts of interesting and pretty people, but all Max wanted was to talk about himself and his dead brother to Theo. And Theo seemed content to talk only to the boring Lady Collingbourne and her boring companions, his own parents.

In fact she was not talking to Theo at all, but over him and through him. As soon as she had seen Lewis and Miriam Lackland on the far side of the room she had planned her tactics. She knew perfectly well that in due course Letty would bring them to her, for she was a careful hostess and always saw to it that all her guests met each other. For Claudette to keep Theo beside her was simple, and very useful when at last Letty did as was expected of her.

'Lady Collingbourne, you met Miriam Lackland, I believe, at our studios. But I don't think you met her husband? He was at the hospital that night. Lewis, this is my good friend and support in my new film, Lady Collingbourne. Without her I couldn't make my *Caesar and Cleopatra* –'

'How do you do,' Lewis said after a moment and then, as Miriam's hand tightened on his arm relaxed a little, said,

'It's been a long time, Claudette.'

'Indeed it has!' She dimpled up at him, all Gallic charm and sparkle. 'An eternity, *mon ami*! And it is so good to see you with your charming Miriam – I remember so well, as I told you when we saw that splendid film of dear Letty's last month, my dear – I remember so well how it was before you were married.' She sighed with a gentle mock melancholy and turned to Theo. 'They were so *charmants*, my dear Theo! She so pretty – not so pretty as now, of course, but still enchanting! – and he so strong and good and quiet –' And she sparkled up at Lewis again, a little wickedly.

'Oh,' said Letty. 'I hadn't realized you knew each other –'

'It was a long time ago, my dear,' Claudette said. 'Such a long time. I am sure we have all almost forgotten. I was just a poor little actress then, with the dear old Guv'nor at the Gaiety, and he was so busy and hard-working a surgeon newly come from Australia. And here we all are now, quite grown-up and married and indeed widowed in my own sad case – well, that is all ancient history. I am sure we should forget all that and start again, and be friends, just as we used to be! *N'est ce pas*, Lewis?'

'Indeed,' Lewis said woodenly and turned to Miriam. 'Would you care to dance, my dear? I seem to remember you like this song –' And he bent his head a little abruptly at Claudette and Theo and Letty and took Miriam away to dance with her, his back very straight and somehow disapproving.

Claudette laughed softly and said under her breath, 'Well, well, well!' and Letty said, 'I beg your pardon?' but Claudette only laughed again and turned to Theo and demanded that he dance with her, for she too quite adored this charming song the band were playing, if she could just recall its title –

Letty watched them as they moved into the middle of the room to join the bobbing swooping couples and found irritation rising in her. Theo was her friend, not Claudette Collingbourne's, dammit. She had no right to take him up like that – especially as it seemed she was more interested in manoeuvring herself so that she was close to Lewis Lackland, rather than in her partner. It was all extremely annoying and she wondered whether after all it mightn't be better to finance

Caesar and Cleopatra herself, rather than to tolerate this meddling and much too handsome woman.

But then her business acumen came back into prime position and she let her tense shoulders relax. To carry all the burden of so costly and ambitious a production would be lunacy. It wasn't that the Gaff Production Company didn't have the money; they did, but they needed it for other purposes. To pour all their resources into just one film which might not recoup all its costs, let alone make a profit, would be stupid. Backers were an essential part of this most modern of modern industries, and she would have to put up with Claudette Collingbourne and her meddling ways with Letty's actors for the sake of her massive bank balance, and that was all about it. But some time, she'd warn Theo about the woman and the reputation she had for swallowing young men whole. For his own sake, of course.

'Why are you so cross, Lewis?' Miriam asked at length, when they had traversed the floor several times and he had still not said a word. 'I thought you'd enjoy a party tonight – you've been working much too hard and –'

'Oh, I'm not cross, my love, of course I'm not.' He hugged her more closely for a brief moment as they turned into a swooping tango step, for the band was now playing old favourites for the benefit of the older guests, instead of the new jazz that was all the rage. 'And you're sweet to worry about me – though it *is* a pleasant party, I can't deny an evening at home with you is the best entertainment I know –'

'Until the hospital rings and you go rushing back,' she said. 'Is it meeting Claudette again that made you angry? I thought you used to be friends. I remember, when I was – well, before we married she did help, didn't she, when I was so stupid?'

'You weren't stupid, my darling,' he said and held her closer again. 'Just very young and ill informed. And yes, she did help in her way, I suppose. No, I'm just a little tired, that's all. Let's not stay too late – unless the children are enjoying themselves? Young Peter seems happy enough talking to that girl there – though Max and Johanna don't seem to be mixing much –'

'They're fine,' Miriam said firmly. 'You must stop being such a father hen! Let's go and have some champagne, and talk to dear old Uncle Oliver for a while and then we'll see about going home. As long as you're not cross, we can stay a little while longer.'

Not cross, thought Lewis, as later they sat on each side of old Uncle Oliver and Miriam talked to him of the things he most enjoyed, like the old days when he had had all the best of the music-hall stars at his supper-rooms in Covent Garden. Not cross, bless her – but I wish we hadn't met Claudette again. It was all so long ago, and it wasn't a chapter of my life I'm very proud of –

Across the room Claudette caught his eyes and smiled at him, a slow, provocative little grin that lifted her cheeks seductively and as though she had actually spoken the words aloud he could hear what she was thinking. Of the times they had shared, many years ago, in her rooms at Vinegar Yard and then, later, at her house in Somerset Street, the richly decorated but oh so squalid house where he had to his own shame worked as a surgeon and where his own beloved Miriam had so very nearly –

He shook his head at himself and turned back determinedly to Oliver and Miriam. He would not let Claudette remind him, he would not. Those days were gone, and therefore not important. But all the same, the less he saw of her the better; to be friends, did she say? On no account, he told himself grimly. On no account at all. There must be a great distance between Lacklands and Collingbournes, that was certain.

9

'Dear one, why so gloomy?' Claudette said and leaned forwards and tapped his hand with one rather sharp fingernail, and he reddened a little and looked up at her. She had always been a doting mother, but there were things that even he dared not do, and paying her too little attention was one of them.

'I'm sorry, Maman,' he said. 'It was just – I was just thinking.'

'Now what can you be thinking about to make you so miserable when you're in so jolly a place!' she said and leaned back in her chair and called a waiter by no more energetic a gesture than a slightly lifted eyebrow.

'Another bottle of champagne,' Jonty said as soon as the man arrived, well-trained to know precisely what his mother wanted and then smiled at her with all the charm he could summon. 'Did you enjoy the play, Maman?'

'Not particularly,' she said. 'I usually quite like Arthur Bourchier but this was rather dull. They have no right to call a play *Scandal* and then have it so very ordinary! I can't think why you wanted to see it.'

'Norah Swinburne,' he said. 'I met her at Peter Stern's, and she said she was in it and I was to come – I'm sorry it was boring.'

'Well, there were some pretty young ones in it, I grant you. Mary Robson, wasn't it? And that boy Coward. But dreary enough, for all that – ah, here we are! Now, dear boy, drink some more of this and do cheer up! I can't abide a miserable companion. I could have stayed at home with Emilia as sit here with you looking like the end of the world!'

'Well, I can't be gay all the time!' he said, with a flash of anger. 'Everyone's entitled to feel low sometimes.'

'Not at the Trocadero,' she said firmly. 'When you order I want smoked salmon and quails' eggs in large quantities and nothing else. I'm sure they've got it if you insist. And send to the band to play "Hitchy Koo" and for heaven's sake, smile! Whatever it is you're thinking about, it can't be that bad.'

He did as he was told and set his mind to being as entertaining as he could, though the glitter in the restaurant around them and the relentless rhythm of the jazz music added to his headache and his depression.

He would not have thought it possible that one girl could make him feel so low; the first time he had seen Johanna Lackland he had thought her pleasant to look at, but not overwhelmingly so. He had met many much prettier and heaven knew more outrageously fashionable girls, and found them good company. But she had been different. She had looked at him with that direct gaze and nodded gravely when they had been introduced and then turned away. And she had gone on being dismissive; not only at Letty's and Edwin's parties, but at her own in the big Lackland house in Leinster Terrace. She had behaved there as though he were just part of the furniture. Her indifference had been irritating at first, but then interesting and he had tried harder to engage her attention, drawling a little more, smiling a little more sardonically – and she had just looked at him in that same dismissive fashion, very coolly, and as though she had said it aloud he had felt her disdain. She had made him feel pushy and boring – he, Jonty Collingbourne! It was a most unusual experience and not one he wanted to have again.

Yet he did! That was what was so very odd. What was it about the girl that made her so enthralling? The quietness? That was at least unusual, for among his acquaintances vivacity was all the rage. A girl who didn't sparkle brilliantly and laugh madly and rush about like a drop of water on a hot plate was regarded as totally out of the swim. Johanna, however, sat still, listened well and spoke little, but with an air of strength about her that was quite remarkable. Perhaps it was that – or maybe –

'Really, I give up!' Claudette said sharply. 'I have said the same thing to you fully three times, Jonty, and you have not heard a word! Now, for heaven's sake, what *is* it? Are you sickening for measles or some other childish ailment? You're certainly behaving like a sulky baby!'

'There is nothing wrong with me,' he said, angry again, and then bit his lip. 'Dammit, Maman, do leave me be! I can't always be jolly – I told you –'

'I don't understand you! It's usually Emilia who sulks, and you who are good company, and now she looks twice the girl she did and you are –'

'Emilia!' he said bitterly. 'Don't speak to me of Emilia. She promised to help me and much she's done to –' He reddened and stopped, and bent his head to his plate.

'Aha!' Claudette said, and pushed her own plate aside so that she could lean over the table closer to him. 'Help you what?'

'Oh, Maman, I wish you would –' He shrugged. 'Well, I suppose you won't be happy till you strip me inside out. It's that Lackland girl. She pays me no attention at all, treats me as though I were a child – and Emilia said if I did as she told me I should do better with her. And all that's happened is that she and Johanna have become fast friends, and I'm still on the outside looking in. It's too bad of Emilia and I really could –'

'You have a *tendresse* for the little Lackland?' Claudette said slowly and leaned back in her chair. 'And you say she does not answer you?'

'You'd think I was a boot-boy, the way she is,' he said bitterly. 'Looks at me as though I weren't there, and then turns to Emilia and – oh, it's too maddening!'

'She must be mad,' Claudette said firmly after a moment and leaned forwards again to take her son's hand in hers. 'Any girl who turns up her nose at you must be completely idiotic, my darling! Quite apart from your title and your income, neither of which are negligible, heaven knows, there is you! You are quite the handsomest boy in the world, and so charming! You must not let yourself be made miserable by a girl who is stupid!'

'But she isn't! She's extremely intelligent, Maman. In fact, she's more intelligent than every other girl I know. Too wise to be beguiled by either my title or my money. And obviously I'm not handsome or charming enough, am I?'

Claudette looked at him, her forehead creased. It would do the boy no harm to be rebuffed; she was a fond mother, but by no means so doting as to want to protect her children from all pain. Indeed, she had long felt that they were damaged by the ease of their lives. Her own childhood had been a dramatic and often painful one, but it had equipped her with the ability to cope with her problems and survive them, and she sometimes feared her children had in a sense been deprived by their very comfort.

So it was not Jonty's distress at his inability to attract a girl he liked that now made her look so intent, and filled her eyes with a faint gleam. It was, rather, the realization that his needs and hers did to an extent march together.

Twenty-five years. A long time, and yet how quickly it had gone! She remembered, sitting there in the noisy Trocadero in 1919, the Lewis Lackland she had known so well in 1893. Such a good friend he had been, so caring in the way he had helped her through those dark and difficult days when Jody had been so ill. Poor old Jody! What would he have thought of his grandson, named after him and yet so very different a person? As good-looking, but so much more fortunate, so much better endowed – although no more witty or charming. Her gaze sharpened as she looked at her son sitting there glooming into his champagne glass; how would he have coped with the life his mother had had to lead so long ago, when she had become a Gaiety Girl in order to support her ailing father? How would he have reacted to the Somerset Street house where –

She shook her head, and drank some more champagne, and stretched her shoulders a little. Time was beginning to tell, she couldn't deny. Almost fifty – me, I'm fifty! I should be relaxing now, not still rattling around the town like a girl. I need a comfortable man at my side to spend my days with. And my nights – and for a fleeting moment she thought with real regret of poor old David. He had been a good husband according to his lights, though dreadfully dull. But he had given her his title and his money and the children and had been complaisant about her naughtinesses all through their years together. It would be agreeable, really, to have him now, to be easy with. No passion there, of course, but a lot of comfort, and that was not to be sneezed at.

Passion, she thought, and again stretched her shoulders. Dammit, there's plenty of that in me yet. Need, even. It used not to matter too much; love was there to take or leave as I chose and I didn't bother much, but now – it matters more than it ever did. And I get tired of finding new men, teaching them my ways –

Lewis, she thought again, and a small smile curved her lips. Those had been happy days – and nights – in her little room at the top of the Somerset Street house. Happy for both of us, not just me. He found satisfaction too, before he married his precious Miriam. Silly woman! Did she really never know what had been between Lewis and me? Or did she choose to forget it all, pretend it never happened? Certainly when they had met again for the first time after so many years she had chatted agreeably enough, saying nothing of their own shared memories. She had behaved as though they had been the most casual of acquaintances, as though she knew nothing more of Lady Collingbourne than her present impeccable social standing, and it had suited Claudette well enough to go along with that.

But Lewis had been different. His chilly response at that Christmas party when he had faced her again for the first time in twenty-five years had been a clear indication of how very important she had once been to him. Perhaps even an indication of the interest that still glimmered there, deep inside him? It could be so diverting, Claudette thought, sitting there at the Trocadero restaurant and staring through the noise and glitter back to those hectic dangerous years of the nineties, to recreate a twentieth-century version of what had once been between them. It would do me all the good in the world. And him. A great deal of good. It is time he was shaken out of that too English-gentleman mould he now occupied and learned something of the French way of life.

And she thought again of Jody, her long dead father, and her years with him in France before coming to England to mend their bedraggled fortunes and this time her lips curved into a wide cat-like smile.

'There's no need to look quite so delighted!' Jonty said, and she blinked and stared at him. He was sitting very upright, looking at her with an expression of great indignation on his flushed face. 'The way I'm feeling is no reason to laugh, you know! I'm very upset about it and that's no laughing matter!'

She leaned forwards at once and set her hands on each side of his face. 'Ah, *cheri*, I was not laughing at you! Of course not! I take *les affaires de coeur* very seriously indeed! No, what I was smiling at was something else. A plan I have to help you!'

'I'm not sure I need any more help,' he said sulkily. 'Bad enough Emilia –'

'Yes, what about Emilia? What is this help she said she could arrange?'

He shrugged. 'Oh, she's very thick with Johanna Lackland. Quite the twin-cherries-on-one-stalk tableau, I promise you. She telephones her every morning and they go about the shops together, and to tea at Gunter's and gossip eternally. But so much for promises to speak for me – as far as I can tell those two girls are too busy with each other to be bothered with me!'

'So that is her new interest!' Claudette said. 'I had not realized – I was just glad she was more contented. Delighted to know she had a new friend to spend her dull times with though I did not know who – but dearest one, do be sensible! A girl may be as close as may be to another girl, but that will never exclude any man in whom she is interested! You must not blame Emilia for your Johanna's coolness. Indeed, their friendship can be of help to us –'

'Us?'

'Of course! For I shall help you, no matter what you say. But because I am so much more experienced in the world, I will be more successful than Emilia. A visit, I think, to Simister. What do you say? An agreeable winter holiday in a week or two's time when you will be able to take Miss Johanna walking into the lanes to seek for primroses and catkins and be very bucolic.'

'She won't come,' he said gloomily. 'Why should she?'

'Because she is Emilia's friend! And because her parents will bring her!' Claudette said, opening her eyes very wide. 'You must not forget they are very old acquaintances of mine. If I invite the whole family, of course Miss Johanna will come. And then I will see to it that Emilia does not monopolize her because she will be too busy helping me, and you shall have your opportunity, Now, stop glowering, dearest one, and dance with me. It will all be delightful, I promise you!'

Lewis was feeling wretched indeed. He had not wanted to come on this visit in the least. He had promised himself that there would be no connection between his family and these Collingbournes, but he had not reckoned with Johanna. He had known of course that she had her own social life; however much she helped her mother run the big Leinster Terrace house, that did not occupy all her time, and of course she spent her afternoons the way all well-brought-up females did, visiting friends, and shopping or whatever it was such girls enjoyed. Johanna, thank heaven, had shown no sign of wanting to be in the least modern, to learn some sort of task that would enable her to take a job, or to be one of these new political women who rushed about to meetings for the General Election and altogether behaved like men rather than nice girls. She had always been content to stay at home, and never before had Lewis had a moment's anxiety about her.

And he did not now, of course – but she had put him in a difficult position. She had been there at the table with them when the morning post had come, sharing their comfortable tea and toast and marmalade in the small breakfast room with its bright fire and the familiar old polished furniture Miriam had inherited from her grandmother, and had gone quite pink with excitement.

'Mother, isn't this nice! Here's a note from Emilia saying there is an invitation coming to us all to spend a long week-end in Wiltshire. Where's your letter – is it there, Daddy? Yes – there's the crest on the back. Do read it!'

And he had, and his chest had contracted with anxiety as he did so. Addressed to them both by their first names, it was written in a breezy informal style that made it very beguiling; certainly it beguiled Miriam.

'Oh, Lewis, that *will* be agreeable – and how charming of her to so carefully ask all of us! That is really unusual thoughtfulness, isn't it? People are not always so caring about one's children. I'm sure Peter will love it – you see she says there is some coarse fishing in the lake in the grounds, and he is quite passionate about that –'

'– and Emilia says there are some interesting ruins and such things to explore in the district and we can go to Avebury and Stonehenge –' chimed in Johanna, skimming the pages of her own letter.

'– and it is for the week-end after this, when you are free from the hospital!' Miriam finished almost triumphantly. 'Shall I tell her we will arrive by the train she suggests? Heavens, it *will* be nice to be out of London for a little clean air. The fogs have been so hateful this past week or two –'

So what could Lewis do but agree? Johanna had looked so eager for the treat, and Miriam too – though he would have found it easier to deny Miriam, for she never complained, always being perfectly content to do as he wanted. Johanna, however, was another matter. Ever since Tim's death he had found himself becoming more and more anxious about the happiness of his three surviving children. Always a devoted father, now he knew himself to be a besotted one. Even if his instincts told him that he was at real risk of spoiling them with too much indulgence he could not help himself. It was as though in giving them whatever they fancied they needed he could in some measure recompense Tim for the loss of all that mattered, his life.

And it seemed that Johanna greatly wanted to go to Wiltshire to visit the Collingbournes. There was an odd little air of suppressed excitement and anxiety about her, though it was mixed with an uncertainty that made him ask her at one point if she was really sure she wanted to accept the invitation, but she had been quite vehement in her insistence that she did. So he had to take her word for it, and glumly agree to go, though watching her covertly he still felt she was seized with doubts from time to time.

Still, she said she wanted to go, so here they sat in great splendour in the Rolls Royce that had been waiting for them at Simister Halt on the branch line from Swindon on a dull Thursday in February. It purred throughout the winter-naked

lanes beneath the tangling branches of the hazels and haw-
thorns on the way to Simister House, as Miriam and Johanna
exclaimed over the glimpses of primroses in the hedgerows,
and Peter examined, for the umpteenth time, the contents of
his tackle box, clearly planning to go fishing as soon as they
arrived and had greeted their hostess. Only Lewis was
miserable, and he hated himself for it.

'Such a pity Max could not be with us!' Miriam said, as the
car left the metalled main road to turn in between lodge gates
to the narrow curving drive that led to the house. 'He would
have so enjoyed the rest. I wish you could have arranged it,
Lewis.'

'I never interfere with the rosters, my dear. You know that.
If he is on duty, then he is on duty. Anyway, he has his final
examinations to work for. He needs all the spare time he has to
devote to his books, not to visits to boring strangers.'

'Oh, not boring, Daddy!' Johanna said, clearly trying to
sound sprightly, but seeming to her father's anxious ears to be
over-bright. 'Emilia is so funny when you once know her.
She's really delightful company. No one could call her
boring.'

'Well, not for you perhaps. But you must agree that she's
your friend, not ours. However, we're here, so we must make
the best of it –'

The car had drawn up in front of the porch of a large and
singularly ugly box of a mansion built in grey stone, and with
no redeeming features about it at all, and Lewis found a certain
grim satisfaction in its dullness. Rich Claudette may be, but to
be forced to live in so dismal a heap could not be enjoyable for
her; and somehow that served her right, a childish thought
which he found embarrassing in himself, and which made him
tighten his jaw as they followed the footman who had opened
the car door for them to make their way into the house.

It was this uncompromising look of harsh disapproval on
his face that was the first thing Claudette saw as she got
gracefully to her feet from the depths of the vast sofa in front of
the wide fireplace in which burned what seemed to be several
sizeable trees. Clearly the desperate shortage of coal that had
made London life such a chilly miserable business since the

Armistice was no problem here in wooded Wiltshire. It was so bitterly cold outside in the February air that here in the warmth his face was lightly beaded with moisture and she stared at him and thought, 'I want him –' and then moved easily forwards with both hands outstretched to welcome him.

'My dears, how sweet of you to be here! I cannot tell you how I have looked forward to this visit! Such weather, is it not – bitterly cold! Never mind. You shall make yourselves comfortable and then we shall all come here and indulge in great quantities of delicious tea and cakes and be cosy together. Jonty, dearest, perhaps you will take Peter and his sister to their rooms, *hein*? And I shall take dear Lewis and Miriam to theirs. No, I insist I take you myself – it is a tradition here at Simister that we look after our guests ourselves as far as we possibly can. Emilia, dear one, please stay here and see to it that William brings tea in half an hour –'

And she laid a soft hand under the elbow of each of her adult guests and led them up the wide staircase with its heavy deep red turkey carpet towards their rooms, as Jonty, with a movement that was absurdly like hers did the same for Peter and Johanna. And which of the Lacklands, father or daughter, was more tense as those hands touched their arms it would have been impossible to say.

10

Max knew that he really had no right to be there. With his finals a bare three weeks away, there was a great deal of work that he still had to do to be ready for them, for although he was a good student and well in control of his work, even the best of students needed to revise.

But he couldn't help it. He had to be here, and after spending half an afternoon at Leinster Terrace with his head bent over his materia medica text books and his gynaecology notes, only to find he had not absorbed a single fact, he had surrendered to the compulsion and shrugged on his coat and hat and pushed his way into the overcrowded tube at Marble Arch to get as far as Sloane Square before walking the rest of the way through the icy, slippery Chelsea streets. He felt guilty about doing so, knowing that if his parents had been at home he would not have dreamed of it, but they weren't at home. They were disporting themselves among the country gentry of Wiltshire. Why should he not, therefore, he asked himself defiantly as his train went swaying along far beneath Hyde Park, visit his own friend? And the thought that his 'friend' had not shown at any point any great interest in his company was one he suppressed. He would, eventually, once he understood how much he, Max, needed to talk to him. And now he stood at the back of the big central area of the Gaff Studios staring round at it all in a faintly bewildered way, and looking for Theo.

Letty hadn't seemed particularly surprised to see him when he had come hesitantly round the big door to stand, blinking, hat in hand, to look round.

'Oh, Mr Lackland,' she'd said vaguely, turning to stare at him. She was wearing a slim knitted suit, her hair was tied back in a bandeau and she had a large block of scribbling paper in one hand with a pencil in the other and a tape measure hanging round her neck. 'I didn't expect to see you here today – did you want me for something?'

'Actually, I was looking for Theo, you know. I thought – I mean, I know he works here now and –'

He faltered as she turned away in response to someone shouting her name from the far side of the big room and he felt more foolish than ever, and would have turned and crept away himself, his tail between his legs, had he not got a glimpse of Theo.

The whole area was alive with light, blazing hot white light, and people were moving about pushing pieces of wood and plaster scenery around or fiddling with the huge lamps on their stands while in the middle a number of people dressed in very exotic costumes stood in small clusters talking desultorily or mouthing to themselves in blank eyed concentration. It all looked very absurd to Max, used as he was to the controlled and obviously purposeful busy-ness of the wards and operating theatres at Nellie's and he stared at them all, his forehead a little creased. Until he saw Theo.

He was wearing a short white tunic, heavily pleated and trimmed in some darker stuff, and his right arm and shoulder were swathed in a short toga-like garment. He had thonged sandals on his bare feet, and heavy leather bracelets on his exposed arm. His hair, now curly and rather wild, was bound with a gold fillet, very similar to those that all the girls were wearing these days for parties, and beneath it his eyes seemed particularly brooding. It was a moment or two before Max realized he was wearing make-up, with his face painted a heavy matt peach, and his eyes strongly outlined in kohl. He looked uneasy and yet so beautiful that he really was breathtaking. Max looked at his muscular legs, at the long curve of his thighs and how neatly they seemed to fit into his trunk beneath the skimpy tunic, at the elegant shapeliness of his bare arm and the crisp lines of his face and jaw and for a moment was confused by the rush of feeling that rose in him. It was as though he was seeing him for the first time, and he thought confusedly, 'He might have been killed, like Tim. All that might have been shot to pieces to rot in the mud like Tim. He might have been killed –' and his throat tightened.

'Miss Letty, for Gawd's sake, will yer tell that silly object down there to 'old on to this bleedin' batten? We'll 'ave the 'ole cock-eyed lot in the bleedin' soup if 'e don't, clumsy great oaf 'e is –'

'All right, Alf, all right!' Letty was calling as she went pushing through the crowd towards the back where Alf could just be seen struggling with a block of plaster which had been painted to look as much like desert stone as possible. 'Kill the lights, Jim, and we'll take ten minutes break, all of you – mind your make-up – no smoking –' and she too disappeared behind the mock rock as the brilliant lights dimmed and left only ordinary electric lamps burning, making the scene seem suddenly dull and depressing.

Theo came moving out of the ruck of the other actors towards the row of chairs in which Max was sitting and he stood up eagerly, thinking that Theo had seen him but then subsided as he realized he had not and wanted only to sit down. He dropped into a chair at the end of the row to sit with both legs outflung and his hands dangling between his knees, his head drooping, and for a moment Max didn't want to disturb him, feeling the need for solitude in him. But he had come so far; he could not just sit silent now.

'Hello Theo,' he said quietly, and Theo jumped with surprise and stared at him with his eyes wide, looking even more startled because of the kohl which made his eyes seem to stare.

'What the hell – oh, it's you, Dr Lackland.'

'I wish you'd call me Max. Anyway, I'm not Dr Lackland yet. Got another month to my finals and even then it's not guaranteed. Though I've been working hard and I shouldn't do too badly – not if I really try –'

He was burbling for the sake of it, and he knew it and he bit hard on his lip, to stop himself chattering and stared at the bent head beside him, for Theo had resumed his defeated posture.

There was a short silence and then Max said softly, 'What is it, Theo? Can I help?'

Theo seemed to make a visible effort. 'Help? Help what?'

'You look – you don't look comfortable.'

'Comfortable? Like this?' He stared down at his costume and pulled at it with slightly shaking fingers. 'I feel an ass.'

'You look marvellous,' Max said simply. 'Really marvellous.'

Theo looked at him for a long moment. 'Are you sure?' he said. 'I mean, I don't look like a stupid child? I feel like one. It's all right for them –' and he jerked his head at the other actors in the middle of the floor. 'They're used to it. But I've never dressed up before and I feel – I can't even remember the damned lines.'

'Lines?' Max said. 'But there are no lines in films, are there?'

'Letty says it's got to be right. If we're doing Caesar and Cleopatra then we can't just chatter what we like the way people usually do. She says you give a better performance if you use good lines, properly written and learned. She's right too.' He lifted his eyebrows almost comically at Max. 'I hate to admit it, but she's right. I've learned a lot this past couple of months. But now, all this – and the make-up – are you sure I look all right?'

'Quite sure,' Max said and relaxed. This was a new Theo. Not the remote rather alarming man he had been trying so hard to get to know, but a younger more tentative person, appealing in his uncertainty.

'I hope you're right,' Theo said gloomily, but he seemed to feel a little better and leaned back in his chair, obviously trying to relax, but not making too good a job of it. Max could see his shoulders still shaking, and his hands were restless against the white pleats of the tunic.

'What are you doing here?' Theo said suddenly, turning his head to look at him. 'You're not usually here, are you? I've never seen you around –'

'No. Not usually.' Max reached into his pocket for his cigarettes and then, remembering Letty's command, pulled his hand out again. 'Actually, I was – er – looking for you.'

'Oh?' The old cool Theo was coming back, covering the more approachable uncertain one.

'It's just that – my parents are away – at a loose end, you know, me, I mean, not them, and I thought I'd like to – oh, dammit. I just thought we could have dinner together or something –'

'You still want to talk about the war,' Theo said after a moment. 'You want to know what it was like. For your brother.'

'Yes,' Max said. He couldn't look at Theo, keeping his head bent low.

'Oh, damn.' Theo almost whispered it, and Max felt his face flame, and got to his feet.

'I'm sorry I bothered you,' he said stiffly. 'I meant no –'

'Oh, sit down, for heaven's sake,' Theo said roughly, and suddenly the lamps came blazing on again and the brilliance of the light had an almost physical effect on Max and he almost fell back into his seat, he sat down so abruptly. 'I suppose –'

'Places everyone! We're ready to go!' Letty's voice came booming at them and Theo took a deep breath and got to his feet, and now the tremor was apparent in him again.

'Wait till we're finished,' he said, and his voice sounded controlled once more. 'I don't suppose we'll be long. We've already done the earlier scenes. Wish me luck – I'll need it –' and he went across to the floor, where actors were now arranging themselves in groups as Letty chivvied and pushed them into position. Max watched him go, straight backed and purposeful and took a deep breath of relief. At least he hadn't sent him away.

Max had thought at first that the film was based on Shakespeare's *Julius Caesar* but as the actors started he realized that it was not, and settled down to enjoy it, for he had never been particularly interested in classical theatre. He had always liked what he could understand easily, and the lines the actors were speaking were clear and unambiguous in the extreme. He could follow it all easily, and watched, enthralled as the actress playing Cleopatra, a singularly handsome girl with very dark eyes beneath extremely straight brows and with a nose of such classic quality that she could have been an image on a Greek coin, went through the ritual of a bath, while her servants talked to her of the beauty of Mark Antony, and she listened, smiling enigmatically.

The camera buzzed and then settled to a steady purr as the

93

handle was turned, and he shifted his gaze from the actors from time to time to watch Letty and Alf dealing with it, for they were as interesting as the action. Letty stood poised behind Alf, watching with her eyes sharply narrowed as each move was made, and whispering to him from time to time so that he moved the camera on its tracks, and sometimes swung it from side to side in a wide arc to increase the scope of the view it could get. The men controlling the lights were watching him too, as they moved the spotlights to give a following beam to the central performers, and to shade out the rear part of the set to give an illusion of greater depth than there really was.

Max was so fascinated by it all that he missed Theo's entrance altogether; but then, suddenly, there he was, standing in the middle of the scene, his legs braced apart, his bare arm hanging relaxed at his side and his swathed one bent, with the fist set arrogantly on his hip. His head was up and his profile in the sea of light looked more beautiful than ever.

He spoke to Cleopatra, though what he actually said Max could not for the life of him have repeated, for it was not the actual words of which Theo made him aware, but the emotion behind them. Here was a man in the grip of an intense physical passion; there could be no doubt of that, and Max watched, his mouth slightly open and his breath held, as Theo moved slowly and with an almost menacing intensity across the great floor towards the girl now lying flung back against a heap of satin cushions on a lavishly decorated couch.

The tension built, step by step, as Theo moved closer and closer, and the following spotlight held him as the camera moved with only the softest of purring as the cranking action Alf was giving it held its rhythm. Max felt his skin crawl beneath his collar as the tension was pulled almost to screaming-point, and then Theo was standing over the girl on the couch who was staring up at him with an expression on her face of mingled fear and delight and triumph and excitement. He stood there and stared down at her and then, very slowly, raised his bare arm towards her, and almost touched her. And as he reached further and his finger-tips brushed the skin, and the girl lay there, her head thrown back with an exultant glare on her face, Letty called sharply, 'Cut,' and the purring of the camera stopped and the lights faded.

There was a short hard silence for just a second of measurable time and then, suddenly, people were clapping, the scene-shifters, the men with the lights and Max too, though he didn't realize at first that he was doing it. He just found his hands were beating together with enormous enthusiasm as Letty almost ran round the camera towards the couch.

'Oh, that was marvellous, absolutely, damned marvellous!' she cried and threw her arms first round the girl, who had jumped to her feet, and then round Theo. 'If we get just a fraction of that feeling in the print, I'll be more than satisifed. That was solid with emotion, absolutely marvellous – Theo – I can't tell you how superb that was – to find an actor who knows when to be still, when to think and when to feel instead of – it's wonderful, couldn't be more pleased –'

'Ta, Theo, ever so,' Cleopatra said, in a tinny little voice. 'You ain't 'arf easy to work with, you know. You make it reely easy – better'n any o' the others wot I've been stuck with. 'Ope we do as well on location, eh?' And she went off towards the dressing-rooms, her arms round the shoulders of an actress who had played one of her servants, chattering busily as she went.

'Really all right?' Theo said, and Max could hear the tension in his voice from where he stood, several feet away.

'Really,' Letty said firmly. 'Come and have a drink in the office – bring you down a bit. And we'll talk about the location scenes and – that'll do for tonight everyone! Many thanks. Nine sharp tomorrow please! Want to use some daylight for the cut-aways – we'll have the stage open – Alf, tell the boys –' And she was gone, leading the way as Theo followed her.

Max stood there in the darkening studio as one after another the lights were doused and the scene-shifters and actors shouted their goodnights at each other, slamming the big doors behind them as they went, and still he waited, confident that Theo would keep his word and come back soon.

But then at last everyone seemed to have gone and there was no one there at all, and Theo still hadn't come, and Max, emboldened by his excitement over the performance he'd seen went across the now empty floor towards the door through which he had seen Letty and Theo vanish.

It had seemed all right, at first. Theo had felt splendid, quite splendid. That scene, the one he'd feared so much, had somehow caught fire for him. The lines he had learned so painfully had slipped out of his mind and on to his tongue with no effort at all on his part, and the emotions he had needed had slipped out with them. He had felt he *was* Mark Antony. He was standing there in an Egyptian palace, under a hot Egyptian sun instead of in a ridiculous mock-up of a set from Aida in a cold Chelsea film studio under a grey London sky. He was a strong man, a passionate man who could hold the world in his hand, and yet hurl it away in exchange for love. It was an unbelievably good feeling.

Which was why, when it started, it was that much more dreadful, that much more disgusting. The bad feeling had started in his belly and come up in a great wave of sick terror as the shaking began. His hands, his shoulders, his legs, his arms, belly, every part of him shook, as wave after wave of the terror crashed over him in ice-cold draughts. He could hardly breathe as first his chest and then his throat went into spasm and his vision broke up into a million shards of spiky light. I'm dying, I'm dying, I'm *dying*, he thought, the words thundering inside his skull. I'm dying, dying, dying, dying, and he could hear behind the words a thin whimpering that went on and on and on –

And then she was there, her face huge and distorted in front of him, shaking him by the shoulder and crying loudly, 'Theo, Theo? For God's sake, man, what is it? Theo –'

The whimpering changed, became a harsh rasping breathiness and he knew he was making these dreadful sounds himself and the shards of light closed up around her face and took away the distortion so that now he could see her more clearly. The waves of fear that had been washing over him slowed, became ripples and then trickles and at last stayed still, and he was lying back against the chair, his face drenched with sweat and his eyes tingling as the kohl got under the lids and irritated them.

'I – what – I –' he began huskily and then blinked and moved experimentally. He was still shaking but it was a different kind of tremor now, a reactionary shaking, the sort that comes after extreme physical effort, and a muscle in his face began to jump, making his lips twitch. He wiped one trembling hand across it and tried to speak again.

'Don't tell anyone,' he managed at last. 'Don't tell anyone –'

Letty had been kneeling beside him, close to him, and now she rested back on her heels and stared at him, frowning. 'What do you mean?'

'I'm all right. I'll be all right,' he said. 'Just don't say anything about it. Please.'

'It's happened before?'

'Yes,' he said. 'Happened before.' He took a deep and slightly shuddering breath. 'It's happened before.' And again he rubbed his face and then looked down at his hand and the streaks of peach make-up on it.

'I must wash,' he said. 'Must wash, get dressed. Must go home. I'll be all right if I go home –'

'But you need help, Theo!' she said, and leaned forwards again. 'My dear, you need a doctor! I can't let you suffer on a rack like that and not know what it is or why –'

At the door Max coughed, gently, and then, as confidence moved into him, more loudly.

'Can I help?' he asked. 'I didn't mean to pry, but I came to find you, Theo and – are you all right now?'

Letty looked up at him very sharply and frowned. 'Really, Mr Lackland –'

Theo laughed then, an odd little choking sound and said, 'Doctor. You said I needed a doctor. Tell her, Max. Almost Doctor Max, tell her what it is –'

There was a little silence and then Max said carefully, 'It's a form of shell-shock, I think. People who were in bombardments, had a lot of responsibility, you know – they sometimes get these symptoms –'

'Are they dangerous?'

'Dangerous? I'm not sure how you mean, dangerous –'

'Did you see what happened to him?' Letty almost shouted

it. 'He was the colour of putty, and when I tried to take his pulse it was like a steam engine, it was so fast. And he was drenched in sweat and he could hardly breathe! It must be a dreadful strain on him, on his heart, his lungs – he needs a doctor, a real doctor and that as soon as possible!'

'No,' Theo said, and tried to stand up, though she put up a hand to stop him. 'No.'

'Don't be absurd,' she said strongly, and scrambled to her feet. 'I'm calling a doctor now and –'

'If you do, I walk out of here and never come back', Theo said. He was sounding better by the moment; still pale and still trembling but his voice was under his control now and his will seemed to have come back completely. 'Never. You'll have to get someone else to make your film.'

She stopped with one hand cradling the mouthpiece of the telephone against her chest as she held the earpiece in the other, almost mechanically, and then as the tinny voice clacked, 'Number, please,' slowly recradled it.

'That's stupid,' she said uncertainly. 'Why should seeing a doctor make you –'

'I don't want to talk about it,' he said, and turned away, tweaking his toga over one shoulder with an oddly petulant gesture. 'I must get out of these damned clothes,' he said fretfully. 'And I want a shower – I mean it, Letty. Call a doctor and I'm finished with this film and any other film. I won't see one.'

'Will I do, Theo?' Max said quietly. 'Not a doctor yet, I know. But I could be useful perhaps. Read up shell-shock, see what the effects are.' He slid a sideways glance at Letty. 'See if there are any dangerous aspects, though I rather doubt it – I've never heard of any, and I think I would have by now if there were.'

'Will you let him, Theo?' Letty said eagerly. However little regard she might have for the skills of a very raw young medical student, at least he was almost a doctor. And better than none. 'Can Max help you? Please let him.'

Theo stood in the doorway, drooping a little now and looking quite desperately tired. 'Max? I suppose so. As long as no one else knows. He already does, so there's no difference, I suppose. But no one else is to know it. Not ever.'

'Did you get my letter?' Jonty asked, standing very straight and looking rather formal by the door.

'Yes,' she said. 'Yes, I did. It was why I came. I wouldn't have done otherwise. But after I read it I thought – well, here I am.'

'Thank you,' he said. 'I knew you were a fair person. That was why I wrote it. Please, after you've washed and we've had tea – I don't think we can get out of that – will you come for a walk with me? So that we can talk properly?'

'It'll be dark, won't it? Too dark. People will think we're very strange if we do that.' She was standing beside the dressing-table in the big handsome bedroom to which he had brought her, staring out beyond it to the window and the darkening sky over the park. 'I don't think I could do anything so – particular. I don't want Mother and Daddy starting to –'

He laughed. 'This house is vast, Johanna. We can walk indoors for hours on end! I'll take you to see the portraits of my far from revered forebears. That won't seem at all particular, I promise you. And I must talk to you. I can't tell you how much I've been longing for this week-end.'

'Yes,' she said quietly. 'I think I – I shall come down to tea as soon as I've washed. Please, don't rush me. I don't think I can cope if you do that.'

'Of course I won't. I'm sorry. I'm being thoughtless, and I'm trying so hard not to be – you've no idea how difficult it is.' He laughed a little awkwardly and then said, 'Ring the bell and the maid will come and unpack for you, and everything. And there's a bathroom through there. Maman put in the most exotic hot-water system – I can't tell you. I'll be waiting for you in the hall. I'm so glad you're here, Johanna.'

'Yes,' she said again and watched him go, standing very still in the middle of the room until the door had closed behind him, and then sitting down rather suddenly and taking a deep and somewhat shaky breath.

It had all been so strange. The letter had come three days before the invitation to the family to come and stay at Simister and she had opened it and started to read it without having the least notion from whom it had come. Perhaps if she had looked at the signature first, as she sometimes did with her letters, she wouldn't have read it at all, would have tossed it into her waste-paper basket. But in the event, she had been half-way down the first page before realizing who her correspondent was, and by then it was too late. She was already caught up not so much in what he was saying, but in how he was saying it.

It had seemed impossible to her that the rather arrogant drawling sneering young man to whom she had taken such a dislike could possibly be the same person as the one who had written those close-packed pages. He stripped himself bare in them. He told her that he was totally bewitched by her. That he dreamed about her all night, and thought about her all day. That he knew he had behaved badly in talking to her in the way he had, but that he had been appallingly badly trained.

'Maman has, frankly, given me quite the wrong view of myself,' he had written with painful candour. 'I've realized that, thinking about how you reacted to me. She has meant well, I know, but she had always had so poor a view of Englishmen, being so very French in so many ways, and has reared me to be like the men she knew as a girl. And so far that hasn't mattered because the only girls I met were silly enough to deserve that sort of treatment. But you're different, Johanna, and you make me want to be different. I've talked to Emilia too, and not as I used to – treating her badly too – but as a friend, and she has told me things about myself that I have not enjoyed hearing. But I'm glad now I have.'

She had put down the letter at that point, unable to read on, confused and a little shaky. It had been so difficult, ever since she had first met him. He had from the start looked to her exciting, interesting, deeply disturbing, but his arrogance and cool effrontery had repelled her. So she had worked hard at resisting his undoubted charm, telling herself that getting to know this young man better would cause her nothing but distress. She had seen enough of her friends moping over men who treated them carelessly; had always been determined never to let herself respond to any man but one as gentle, as thoughtful and as sensitive as her father. Being Lewis Lackland's daughter had in many ways made life difficult for her, for he had shown her standards of male behaviour that were exceedingly high. And now, here was this young man she had found so dangerously exciting and had had to work so hard to keep at arms' length repudiating those very aspects of his character that she had found so unpleasant! If she could really believe that he knew his faults and was willing to change himself in any way he could – she caught her breath then and started to read again.

'So, I am now writing to ask you to let me start again. I don't suppose I've changed completely. No one ever could do that. But, by God, the intention is there, and I know that with your help, I could be a much better person. Certainly a happier one, because until I can convince you you are the woman to whom I have committed my life for always, I won't be happy. I'm not asking you to say you care for me as I do for you. Only that you're willing to try. Please, Johanna, accept my mother's invitation when it comes. I need to know I will see you again, that I will be able to be the person I want to be.'

What else could she have done but respond? When the invitation had arrived she had been ready for it, able to persuade her father to accept it, able to be relaxed and casual, or almost so; though there had been some doubts in her father's mind, she knew. But never mind. Here she was and here he was and perhaps, just perhaps, there was something in the future that would be exciting and wonderful and –

She stood up and moving purposefully went to ring the bell and then to the bathroom to wash. Right now, she had to go back to the hall downstairs and take tea with her hostess and look normal and quiet. First things first, she told herself firmly. First things first.

'It's all rather ugly, Lewis, isn't it?' Miriam said, standing at the window and staring down at the darkening garden below. 'Not a bit like the lovely houses we used to go to, Grand-mamma and Grandpapa and I, when I was a girl. I remember Mentmore and the dear old Sassoon place – they were really beautiful. This one is merely rich –'

And she shook her head regretfully as she considered the dreariness of mere riches, a luxury she could well afford since she had inherited one of the largest fortunes in the country when her grandparents had died. That had been one of the biggest problems of their early married years, but at last Lewis had come to terms with the fact that his wife owned far more than he could actually count, that his own earnings were totally insignificant in their shared lives, and no longer responded to any mention of money with tension and tightly closed lips.

Now he said nothing, continuing to arrange his hair brushes and toilet things on the bathroom shelf, disdaining as he always did the services of a valet, methodical as always and clearly abstracted. Miriam looked at him covertly and then sighed a little. It had never been easy fully to understand her husband's mind. She loved him to the point of distraction, always had, ever since the days when she had been a flighty girl who had caused all sorts of problems for all sorts of people because of her own foolishness. Now, even after twenty-three years of marriage he remained to her something of an enigma. She tried to comprehend the way his mind worked, but she had never succeeded and knew now she never would. But it didn't matter. She loved him and that was enough. He would tell her when he was ready what it was that was clearly worrying him, she told herself confidently as she started to wash, ready for tea downstairs. He always did, sooner or later.

Lewis, however, was not likely ever to tell her how he was feeling at present. The touch of Claudette's hand on his elbow when she had taken them upstairs to their room had been dreadfully disturbing; he would not have thought it possible that it could be so, but there it was. She had touched his arm and his chest had tightened and his breathing had become something he had to think about controlling, rather than something that just happened quietly by itself. Damnable woman! he thought and thumped closed the drawer of the chest in which he had put his clean collars so sharply that Miriam looked up at him with her brows raised in surprise.

'Tea, my love,' he said shortly. 'She said we were expected downstairs to tea. So I suppose we'd better go. I must say I could be as happy without any but –'

'Well, it's been a long time since lunch, after all, so I dare say you'll manage well enough,' Miriam said pacifically. 'And for my part I'm parched. So come along and we'll see how the children have settled in. I'm sure Peter will be enchanted with the place. He's such a country boy at heart, I sometimes feel we have no right to live in London with him.'

Peter was indeed happy and well settled in. Of the four of them he seemed to be the only one now who was really relaxed, for they found him sitting before the huge fire in the great hall with his mouth full of muffins and talking at great length to his hostess about the delights of roach and tench as prey for a fisherman of his high calibre, while she sat and smiled at him, apparently absorbed in every word. But she was clearly thinking her own thoughts, for as Lewis and Miriam appeared at the top of the stairs she turned her head and lifted her chin sharply, and watched them come down, never taking her eyes from Lewis's face.

'Ah, *mes amis*!' she said. 'At last! Now we can be delightfully cosy together in the completely English manner. Here we have muffins and scones and crumpets and jam –'

'Three kinds, Mother!' Peter said, and grinned at her a little wickedly. With her ever-present anxiety about her own *embonpoint*, Miriam had been known to prevent Peter from eating as many sweet and rich foods as he yearned for, and had made no effort to circumvent the still persisting wartime food rationing laws, as so many rich people did, glad to have an excuse to limit Peter's – and her own – appetite.

'– and shortbread and cherry cake and all manner of things. For myself, I cannot eat them, but I know my English guests always adore them! How will you have your tea, dear Miriam? With lemon or a little cream?'

'With lemon please,' Miriam said and settled herself on the

huge sofa beside her hostess. 'And nothing to eat, thank you. I really dare not –'

'Oh, do,' Claudette cooed and gestured at the footman who brought a cake-stand laden with very luscious little cream cakes temptingly near. 'This is a little holiday, after all! You shall not stint yourself while you are with us, I insist!'

'Well –' Miriam said doubtfully and succumbed as Johanna appeared at the top of the stairs and came down decorously to join them. Claudette stood up this time and smiled at her with great brilliance.

'Ah, my dear Johanna – here you are! Emilia will be here directly, I am sure, and longing to chatter with you. You girls are all the same when you are together, are you not? Nothing but gossip and laughter, and how it delights me to hear it! I sent Jonty to fetch you some of our freesias – we have a hot house quite devoted to them – for he noticed there were no flowers in your room, and that would never do! I dare say he will not be long – now, my dear, lemon or milk?'

To anyone coming upon the scene unexpectedly, it would have seemed a charming picture of English country life at its best; a dark and chilly afternoon, a vast wood fire burning merrily and sending its resinous scent and golden light and great distorting shadows dancing over the rich furniture and heavy curtains, the well-dressed and handsome people talking easily and drinking tea from fine Worcestershire china; but beneath the surface feelings were seething.

Claudette, watching Lewis while she talked inconsequentially, was thinking of the sort of lover he had once been, of the way his body had felt against hers, young and hard and urgent. Now he was older but he looked as lean and fit as he ever had; it would not be all that different to make love with him now. Better perhaps, for she was a more experienced person and he – he had had all those years of boring marital fidelity. He must surely be ready for a better, more adventurous love. That he had been faithful to his dull Miriam she did not doubt; he was of that sort – indeed, his depth of sincerity had always been part of his charm. Well, he would soon learn that there was a normal and natural delight to be had in less intense and less virtuous liaisons; she, Claudette, would teach him. And she almost hugged herself with delight as she caught his eye across the tea-table and saw how embarrassed he was. Here indeed was a full-blown rose ripe for the picking, and she would pick it this very week-end, or her name wasn't Claudette Collingbourne.

Jonty, coming in red-cheeked and cold from his run to the great hothouses beyond the kitchen garden with a bunch of freshly cut and very fragrant freesias in his hand, caught that look in her eyes and smiled to himself. Dear old Maman! So pleased with herself, because she was helping him! It would be wonderful to tell her that all was well with Johanna and he. Wonderful. But first, he must make sure it was –

He came and sat down beside Johanna on her sofa, facing the one on which their elders were ensconced, and showed her the freesias.

'Aren't they incredible, Johanna? Our gardener is quite a genius when it comes to these things. I brought him the roots when I was in France a few years ago, before the war, and now we have vast quantities of them growing. Shall we arrange them for you?'

'Thank you,' she said. 'That would be very nice.'

'Now?' he said and started to get up, but she shook her head.

'No, not yet. I haven't seen Emilia yet to speak to properly and I really must – where is she?'

'Oh, I asked her to fetch something for me and I dare say she is having some trouble finding it,' Claudette said lazily. 'No doubt my maid will help her, and she will be here directly. Touch the bell, my dear, will you, and we shall ask for her –'

Johanna did as she was asked and at last Emilia appeared, looking a little flushed and sulky, but clearly pleased to see Johanna and soon the two girls were talking quietly together, leaving Jonty looking rather sulky in his turn; until he caught Johanna's eye. At once he reddened at the clear reproof that he saw there and relaxed into the sofa again, turning to talk to Peter who immediately launched himself into one of his interminable dissertations on the subject of freshwater fish, which at least had the virtue of allowing Jonty to sit and covertly watch Johanna uninterruptedly.

It was almost six o'clock before Claudette at last decided

that they had all talked small talk long enough, and got to her feet.

'Emilia, my dear, I am sure dear Miriam would be most interested to see the collection of antique gowns in the far gallery. You remember I spoke to you of them, Miriam. They were all found in the attics some years ago and my late husband had them arranged as a museum. They are as many as a hundred and fifty years old, some of them, and so interesting. I am sure you will be quite entranced by them.'

Miriam, responding as any well-bred guest should, got to her feet at once and Emilia, after a moment's sharp glance at her mother did so too, turning to Johanna to add her to the expedition. But Jonty was too quick for her.

'And Johanna and I will go and look at the portraits, shall we? I can show you the gowns tomorrow, but I am quite determined that now you shall see my frightful ancestors. Such a ghastly collection, you'll laugh yourself sick. We'll do the flowers first of course –' and he set one hand to her elbow and hurried her away.

'May I go and look at the lake, Lady Collingbourne?' Peter said eagerly. 'I know it's dark, but I'm used to looking at such things at night – I often go into Hyde Park to the Serpentine after dark to see what I can find there, so please may I?'

'By all means,' Claudette said, almost purring. Dear boy! So helpful to his elders, she thought. 'If you bear to the right as you leave the gardens you will find your way with no difficulty at all. The footman will provide you with a lantern, if you wish for one – just touch the bell –'

'I'll come with you –' Lewis said but Peter shook his head at once.

'No need, Dad, really! I'll be fine on my own – you stay here with Lady Collingbourne,' and Lewis had to subside.

The bustle rose to a crescendo as servants came and removed the wreckage of the tea-table, and the various parties broke up and went their different ways and then they were sitting there alone, Lewis on a sofa on one side of the fireplace, she on the other.

'Well, my dear?' she said at length, breaking what had become an uncomfortable silence. 'I never thought to see you here in my house in this way. It is agreeable, is it not?'

'Is it?' he said and his voice was very flat.

'Ah, that is ungracious in you, Lewis! You were never ungracious. Or, perhaps, now I come to recall – well, you were a little, sometimes. It is the honesty in you, I dare say. I always valued that, you know.'

'Then be honest with me now,' he said harshly. 'Why have you asked us here?'

'I could as well ask you why you have accepted!'

'Because of Johanna,' he said immediately. 'She enjoys her friendship with your daughter and wanted to come. And I care too well for my children to put my own wishes in front of theirs. For my part, I would gladly not be here at all.'

She opened her eyes wide at that. 'Oh, my dear Lewis, why? It has been so long – surely there can be nothing between us but the coldest of cold embers? Or – dear me, could it be that there remains glowing in you some sort of tenderness for the old days, some possibility that with a little judicious blowing we could refire them? Is that why you would have preferred not to come?'

'If that is your reason for asking us – to blow on the embers, as you put it – then you can forget it.' He got to his feet to stand staring down at her. 'I am happy as I am, Claudette. Whatever there was between us over twenty years ago is no longer relevant to either of us. I am happily married and intend to stay that way.'

She stretched, catlike, so that the filmy sleeves of her flowered chiffon teagown fell away from her arms. They were very pretty arms, white and rounded and showing only the slightest sagging of age, and she knew they were a feature worth displaying.

'My dearest Lewis, you do me an injustice if you think I'm so stupid as to have any intention of damaging a happy marriage. The last thing I want is to soil my name or my children's with any sordid scandal. Heaven forbid! But I am not averse to a little agreeable and discreet – entertainment with an old friend. And that is what we are, *hein*? Old friends.'

'Not old enough perhaps,' he said. 'I'm going to find Peter. Looking at the cold lake with him and getting thoroughly chilled will be a good deal more pleasant than standing here with you.'

'Now, Lewis, Lewis, do not be so precipitous! After all, if we are to be so close as we are in the future, and all be happy, we must at least be civil to each other! We can't go glowering at each other like tigers or elephants – or in your case kangaroos – and you really do look quite absurdly Australian at the moment my dear, so rough and outlandish –'

'What do you mean, close in the future? I thought I had made myself very clear. I have no intention of ever being close in the future. After this week-end, I doubt you and I will ever meet again. I don't normally interfere in my children's friendships, but this time I feel I must persuade Johanna that she should seek companionship elsewhere, rather than with your daughter –'

'It's not my daughter you need fret about, Lewis,' Claudette said and smiled her slow grin again. 'Not Emilia at all.'

He frowned, staring at her.

'It is Jonty she's here for, foolish man,' she said. 'They are, you know, most taken with each other! So ironic, isn't it? My son and your daughter – it amuses me greatly.'

12

'France looks a lot more like Ancient Gaul than I would have thought possible. It's just like the pictures in my old school-books,' Theo said. 'You'll have the audiences really believing these battles you know!' And reached for the last piece of bread in the basket. He'd eaten more since they'd come to Caen than he'd ever done at home in London, and the effect was beginning to show on his face. He looked sleeker, less haggard than he had, and it was an improvement that Letty greatly approved. Good as he had looked when they had started this film, now he was looking even better – but not so different that it was noticeable on the daily rushes. He simply looked good, and the images of him that appeared on the screen in her jury-rigged office at the farmhouse where they lodged were so superb they made her want to hug herself. The impact this new actor of hers was going to have on the audiences when *Caesar and Cleopatra* was ready for the cinemas was going to be enormous.

'Stupid,' she said now. 'Where the hell was Gaul *but* France? I thought you were an educated man. So much for your old school-books!'

'I am,' he said and laughed. 'But I'm forgetful too. Gaul is divided into three parts – wasn't that it? It's a long time since boyhood Latin. I'll try to remember my Virgil – or do I mean Cicero? I can't even remember who wrote what – a fine Mark Antony I am!'

'Well, it isn't for your Latin scholarship you're here, so I suppose it doesn't matter,' she said and stretched. 'Have you finished your gourmandizing or do you mean to start all over again?'

'I wish I could,' he said regretfully. 'I'd forgotten food could taste this good. Maybe tonight we could have duck, hmm? With Calvados and –'

'Pig. If you go on eating like this, you'll be too fat to get into your costume. Come on. We've got a Roman war to sort out this afternoon, before the light goes. And I've no notion of running overtime for you or anyone else. I've got a reputation for bringing all my films in on budget, and this one'll be no exception. Alf, is Jenny ready? Yes? Then you can get the extras in place and we'll start to shoot in fifteen minutes –'

She hurried away, contented in her busy-ness and Theo watched her disappear into the mêlée of people in the centre of the patch of sand dunes that had been chosen to represent the battleground in which Mark Antony and Caesar were to have a confrontation (Letty and her script writer had taken a considerable dramatic licence with the facts in creating her film) and then stood up and brushed the crumbs of his lunch from his toga. He was wearing a heavy coat over it, to protect him against the undoubted chill of the Norman skies, which though bright with sunshine, even now in late March, were still tinged with winter sharpness. He looked rather absurd, with his bare leather-gartered legs sticking out beneath its Harris tweed skirts, but he no longer had any uncertainty about how he looked in costume, no longer felt foolish or uncomfortable in it. Indeed, in the weeks that had elapsed since the interior work done at the Gaff Studios, and the location work carried out here in Normandy, he had changed a great deal in his attitude towards what he was doing.

He was actually enjoying it now. He had, on that terrifying February evening when he had played that key scene with Cleopatra, unknowingly opened a door deep inside himself. He had found that he had the ability to switch his emotions in directions of his conscious choice, rather than allowing himself to be swept by them along roads he had not wished to travel. He had discovered that there was a real satisfaction in being another person, in experiencing someone else's pains and delights, miseries and satisfactions. Such experience took some of the edge off his own emotions, and for him that could be nothing but good. Those feelings of his had given him a bad time for too long to be missed in any way. If acting could control them, then by God, acting was the life for him.

Not that the bad feelings had gone entirely. There were still nights when he woke sweating with sick terror and guilt and shame, when images of Peter in the trenches at Passchendaele rose in front of his eyes and made him weep into his pillow – but those grim shadows vanished with the darkness instead of lasting all day, as they had been used to do in London. Indeed, he sometimes told himself in the cool light of morning, after such bad nights, falling over Letty's rostrum on Armistice Night had been the best thing he could possibly have done to deal with his blackness. She had given him a new purpose.

And something more. At first he had been unwilling to face the fact, but now he did, and accepted it up to a point, for he could not have admitted it to anyone else. He actually enjoyed the flamboyance of the actor's life. To strut about in costume, knowing he was being gawped at admiringly by the loungers and hangers-on who came flocking out of the French villages and towns nearby to watch the proceedings of the crazy English was enjoyable. To wander into the bars and restaurants of Caen in company with the rest of the exotic company and be looked at with respect and fascination by these dull burghers and peasants was exhilarating. To be one of the band of gorgeous parakeets that was a company of film actors was *fun*. He was more than a little ashamed of himself, to find he had such a taste for admiration, but it remained with him and indeed grew, for all his secret guilt.

So for him the weeks they had spent here getting the rest of the action on to film had been agreeable – not least because it had also enabled him to push to the back of his mind his acquiescence to Letty's demand that he should accept Max Lackland's medical care. He had almost managed to persuade himself that he was cured of his attacks, that the one that had been so severe there at the Gaff that night had been the swansong of his hateful affliction; but he did not quite manage so to convince himself. There were still those dreams, after all; while they remained with him the threat of day-time miseries continued, and he knew it. And that meant that eventually, when he returned to England, he would have to redeem his promise to Letty. But here in France he could be comfortable and refuse to think about that, and go with comparative serenity about his daily activities.

It was a serenity of which Letty was very aware. She could not fail to be so, because she was so aware of everything about him. In the middle of all the work that was going on – and she was as meticulously efficient as she always was in her productions – while she was supervising the placing of the cameras, auditioning extras, ordering supplies, checking the film stock, watching the rushes, paying the bills, arranging for special items to be sent out from London, still she was aware of him. When he was not within sight she felt his absence as though a cold wind had been added to the already chilly weather. When he was there, it was as though the sun had brightened even more. It was marvellous, it was misery, it was never less than exciting.

Because she had to admit the truth to herself now. In just four months the ice that had steadily thickened over her emotions during the past dozen years had cracked and then melted. The feelings that had once belonged solely and wholly to Luke O'Hare, and which she had believed were dead with him, had been released. She was as besotted with her new actor, as starry-eyed and breathless over him as any schoolgirl dealing with her first crush.

Her only comfort was her mature ability to dissimulate. Where a younger woman would have blushed and stammered, she was relaxed and off-hand. Where a younger woman would have shown in every glance the way she felt, she was the gruff self-controlled person she had always been. No one, not even Alf with whom she had worked most closely over the years, ever since he had been a small boy and had helped her film a political riot at the old Gaff when it had been a theatre, had the remotest idea just how much of a turmoil there was inside her.

Sometimes, when at last she fell into bed in the big lavender-scented wooden-beamed room at the top of the old farmhouse where they had set up their headquarters for these days on location, she would stare up into the velvet blackness of the rafters and ask herself despairingly what she was to do. He was not interested in her in the way she was in him; she was quite certain of that. He was friendly, amusing, clearly at ease with her, but still remote, still untouchable. It was as though he were enclosed in a tough glass shell, could see out, and be seen, but could not actually be touched. What was she to *do*, obsessed as she was with him? How was she to contain the physical needs that were rising in her again, freed from their long years of frozen inactivity, if he did not respond to her? How was she to –

And she would turn over, burying her face in the soft feather pillow and curse and then fling herself on to her back again and try to compose herself for sleep. But she often could not and would lie awake long into the night thinking of him, dreaming of him, fantasizing like any girl about how one day he would say this, and she would say that and then he would touch her, and she would touch him and they would be in each other's arms and –

And in the middle of it all was her constant awareness of their age difference. It shouldn't matter, of course. A woman of his age building a love affair with a man of her age would occasion no comment from anyone; but the other way round – that was something else. She was thirty-eight now, with her birthday not long behind her. He would not reach thirty-three until the end of the year. Almost six years between them. It was absurd, it really was. People would laugh if they did manage to –

But we won't, she would tell the blackness above her head. We won't, will we? He's too remote, too cold, too unin-terested in me except as an employer, a friend perhaps. He doesn't see me as a lover. Just as an amusing older woman. That's all. And perhaps that's the charm of him for me? Perhaps it's because he's so cool, so distant while so friendly, that I find him so exciting? If he started to make advances, the way so many men have tried over the years of solitude, I'd despise him the way I despised them? And she thought of the actors she had known who had tried to woo her, of the friends Oliver and Edwin had so assiduously brought to her for approval, and managed to grin at herself. She really was being very inconsistent, not at all herself. Well, I'll get over it eventually, she told herself, but bleakly, unable really to see any prospect of a cure from her affliction.

In London Max was a good deal happier. He still had the same deep need to talk in depth with Theo, to use him as the instrument to release himself from the desolation of his brother's death, but no longer felt quite so desperate about it. Theo's promise to allow him to seek a remedy for his strange attacks was something for him to work on, and work on it he would. He had told Theo that over supper a couple of nights later when he had gone, at Letty's insistence, to Paulton's Square.

Oliver, tired as he often was, had gone to bed early and left the three of them sitting huddled over the meagre fire – for the coal shortage was chilling every household in London – with coffee-cups beside them. They had been silent for some time after Oliver had gone shuffling away clutching his hot-water bottle, and Letty had said abruptly, 'Well, Max, is Theo fit to go to France for the location work or not?'

Max had taken a deep breath, desperately aware of how uninformed he really was, how very new to the business of professional advice-giving, and had said cautiously, 'How do you feel, Theo? You know better than anyone what is possible for you.'

Theo had been quiet for a moment and then had shifted in his chair, and said gruffly, 'I think I'll manage. Dammit, I'm not a cripple. Am I?'

'You're not well,' Letty had said. 'Are you? It's stupid to pretend otherwise.'

'I'm well enough,' Theo had looked angry again. 'Dammit, Letty, you make me sound like a puking invalid, fit only for slops and afternoon naps! I'm *well* – it's just that sometimes –' and his voice dwindled to a silence.

Max had stared at him and tried to organize his thoughts; he still didn't know enough about shell-shock to be able to advise really well; he still had his finals looming ahead and he had to get those out of the way before he could get his head down on the study of this vital new subject, and having Theo in London could get in the way of all that. And, as he said himself, he was physically fit enough. And perhaps the change of scene in

France, a part of France well away from the horror that had been at Flanders, would help him –

'I think you should go,' he said at last, with an authoritative air that sat uneasily on him. 'You'll be busy, you'll have a lot to do and think about – you should be all right. I'll – er – try to get you a mild sedative to use in case you need it.' He had been about to say he would give him a prescription, almost swept by his new role as medical adviser into believing he was already qualified to do so. 'If you come up to Nellie's before you leave, I'll have it for you. And then, when you get back – we'll see how you are –'

So, he had filched a bottle of chloral hydrate from the dispensary and when Theo had come – albeit rather unwillingly – to Nellie's to collect it had given it to him with careful instructions on dosage, and a strong recommendation not to use it unless he felt he really had to.

'If you have any – if you have a bad day, take it that night, to sleep,' he said. 'But don't use it otherwise.' He was uneasily aware of the risk he was taking in handing out dangerous drugs in such a way, and he considered asking his father to prescribe instead, needing the protection of an older and more experienced practitioner. But then he had dismissed the idea. Lewis Lackland was much too good a doctor ever to prescribe for a patient without seeing him, and he knew there were no circumstances whatsoever under which Theo would agree to consult him. So that was that. He had to take the risk. But he was comforted by the look of distaste on Theo's face as he looked at the ribbed green glass bottle with its waxed stopper, and told himself there was no need to worry. He probably wouldn't use the stuff at all. It was just knowing he had it in case he needed it that would help him.

So Theo and Letty and the rest of the Gaff people had gone to Normandy, and Max had settled to his exams. He had feared that he had lost control of his study, that the time he had spent hanging around the Gaff these past weeks and his interest in and anxiety about Theo would make it impossible to get back into the smooth pattern of work that was essential for a successful outcome; but his fears were groundless. When the week of exams started, he threw himself into them with enormous energy and by the end knew perfectly well that he had done satisfactorily. There would be a delay of course, while they waited for the results to be posted, but in the meantime, he could go about his work as a Senior Dresser at Nellie's, serene in the knowledge that he was as near as dammit the doctor he had set out to become so many years ago. And, he could think about the problems of dealing with his first patient's needs.

Like many of his fellow students he had all through his training years been most fascinated by the drama of the surgical wards and departments of the hospital. There, where the blood ran high – sometimes literally so – and life often teetered on the edge of disaster, there was great satisfaction for a young lively mind. The medical wards, with their rows of beds filled with grey-faced, wheezing, often depressed and elderly people, were dull by comparison, and though he had dutifully learned what he should about hearts and lungs and kidneys, he had saved the bulk of his energy for learning about haemorrhage and abdominal pain and fractures and all the other exciting scalpel-centred incidents. And of course, because his much-loved father was a surgeon it was inevitable his tastes should be moulded in that direction.

But now, his interests shifted their focus and he took to volunteering to take over other people's stints of duty on the hitherto despised medical wards. There, maybe, he told himself, there will be other people with problems like Theo's. There, maybe, listening to the consultants I'll find out what I need to know.

And he did. The men's medical wards in particular were filled with ex-soldiers and sailors, and even a few of those particular heroes of the war, airmen. Many of the soldiers were trying to live with the shreds of lungs that German gas attacks had left them; others were showing the signs of kidney failure that had followed long privation in the trenches. But there were some with the haggard looks, the twitching muscles, the intensely anxious expressions that bespoke the aftermath of the horrors they had seen, men whose condition defied firm diagnosis, though their doctors tried all they could to find a way to bring them out of the horrifying past and into a hopeful future.

Late one night, when the men had been settled to sleep by a
stern Sister Spruce before she went rustling off duty to her
bed–sitting-room adjoining her beloved ward, and the serried
rows of beds lay glimmering under their red blankets, and the
night nurse was sitting at the central table with the duster-
draped lamp pulled low over her desk, he came to read the
notes of the various patients. Somewhere, he told himself, in
those close-written pages of medical history and accounts of
examinations and treatments tried and treatments failed there
might be a clue to what he could do for Theo.

And he found it. He sat at the other side of the desk to the
nurse, a cup of cocoa beside him – for he was popular with the
nursing staff, and they were always willing to provide him
with their ministrations when he was, like them, working late
– poring over the case notes of one Samuel Shorter. A man of
thirty-seven, married, with two children, he had been at the
last battle of Verdun. 'Like Tim,' his inner voice whispered to
him, but for once the thought did not linger, nor bring his
grief back into the forefront of his mind, for what he was
reading was too enthralling.

'Complaining of loss of memory, acute breathing difficulties, rapid heart beat, cold sweats, trembling of lower
extremities as well as hands, sleeplessness, poor appetite,
severe constipation –' The list went on and on and then after
the details of the physical examination which had revealed 'no
physical abnormality present' in the neat upright handwriting
of Sir Aaron Aston, the senior physician at Nellie's, the laconic
note, 'Neuresthenia. Prognosis poor. ? consider use of
hypnotism for mental catharsis as recommended by Dr
Kraepelin and Prof. Freud.'

'This patient, Nurse Rogers,' Max said in the obligatory
soft whisper of the night staff, looking up. 'Mr Shorter. What
treatment has he had?'

'Shorter? Oh, bed 17, you mean? Oh, him – a right odd one
that. Used to scream half the night, he did. I mean, I know
they had a bad time, these poor things, but he really was –
well!' She shook her head, quite lost for words. She was a
cheerful round-faced girl with the soft bloom of her country

upbringing still lingering on her cheeks, in spite of her three years in the crowd and bustle and airlessness of Covent Garden.

'Used to scream? Doesn't he any more?'

She settled her elbows on the desk, glad to leave her report writing for a gossip with one of Nellie's nicest medical students.

'Well, that's the thing – he's really done ever so well. They got this doctor from abroad to him, you know – I thought he was German going by his name but they said he wasn't, Austrian, but like I said, there's not much to choose between 'em really, is there? I mean, they haven't finished the Peace Conference yet and already these Germans and that are coming over here and pushing themselves in –'

'What did he do, this Austrian doctor? What was his name?'

'Oh, I can't remember. Some funny sounding thing it was. What did he do? Well, I only heard about it from the day people – I mean nothing much ever happens at night apart from bedpans and bottles –' She giggled softly. 'But the day staff tell me over the report in the evening what was done in the day – so I get to know – anyway, this man, they put him to sleep. Only it wasn't sleep exactly, I mean, he didn't have an anaesthetic or anything. They just talked to him, as far as I can tell. They did it in the side ward which was just as well, because he started screaming and shouting and crying and carrying on no end. They could hear half-way down the corridor, old Copthorne told me. Awful it was for a grown man. Good thing the ward doors are so thick, isn't it? Yes – it would have upset the others no end.'

'You don't know how they put him to sleep?'

'Not me. Told me it was hypnosis, Copthorne did. I've seen that on a stage show once, down at the Finsbury Park Empire when this man used a lamp and made people do the funniest things. There was one that actually took a cigarette and –'

'Did they use a lamp for Mr Shorter?'

'Eh? Oh, I don't know. Copthorne never said. But it was hypnosis all right and like I said he made no end of a noise.'

'And then what?'

'How do you mean, then what? He just woke up, I suppose

– if he'd ever been really asleep which I take leave to doubt, the way Copthorne told me it all was.'

'How has he been since?' Max was doing his best to be patient. Many of the Nellie's nurses were extremely bright and wise women, who understood the work of the consultants better than the medical students did, sometimes. He was just unlucky in drawing one of the less bright ones. He had to take his time, not upset her. 'Is he any better?'

'Well, of course I can't really say, being on nights. Mind you, I can tell you it's quieter in here now. He used to start shouting and screaming regular as clockwork before. Now you can see for yourself how he is.' And she jerked her head at the bed on the right hand side of the ward that bore the number seventeen on the brass plate at its head.

Max got up quietly and went to stand beside it. The man in it was lying on his back, one hand thrown above his head and the other beneath the blankets, and as Max's eyes became accustomed to the reduced light he could see that his face was relaxed and smooth in sleep. There was none of that tension that remained on so many ill people's faces as they made the best they could of what fitful sleep came to them. This man looked as though he had spent a peaceful comfortable day and was now enjoying the slumber of the just.

Slowly Max came back to the table, and stared down at the case notes again as Nurse Rogers went rustling away to the corner of the ward in response to a hoarse call for a bottle. Mental catharsis, Dr Kraepelin, Professor Freud. Well, it was somewhere to begin.

He began to make pencil notes on the hem of his white coat.

13

'Come on, old bean!' Jonty said, rallying her as though she were a sulky child. 'Do join in! Don't sit there looking so gloomy.' And he shot off into the mêlée of whirling arms and legs that was the dance floor, taking Johanna with him, and leaving Emilia with Arnold Eastern sitting blinking beside her.

'Er – yes, topping good idea, what?' Eastern bleated and blinked even more rapidly, if that were possible. 'Bit of the old jazzin', what? Have a little go at it, shall we, and show the blighters how to do it?'

'No, thank you,' Emilia said freezingly, and looked at her wrist-watch with a pointedness that even someone as stupid as Arnold could not fail to recognize and he subsided, rather pink and puffing, to smoke yet another Turkish cigarette and stare gloomily at the dancers.

It had all gone so wrong, and so stupidly wrong. She had been so sure that getting to know Johanna and helping her establish her romance with Jonty would be the way to see more of Max. Although she was not one given to fantasizing – making hard practical plans was far more in Emilia's line – she had visualized the outcome of her friendship with Johanna as cosy foursomes going to dances and parties and theatres with Max making up the quartet. It would have been the most obvious and natural thing in the world, she told herself now, looking sideways at the hapless Arnold with cold dislike, if it hadn't been for Jonty. Damn Jonty! Even though he meant well, and went to considerable trouble to include in their evenings people he thought suitable for her. Still, damn him. The only person with whom she wanted to share an evening was Max Lackland, and since he had shown no sign of realizing this, then it was up to Emilia to ensure that propinquity acted in her favour. Time with him that was all she needed. Then, when they could talk, get to know each other, he'd discover just what it was she had to offer, just how interesting she really could be –

Jonty and Johanna came back from the dance floor, both rather pink and breathless, for the jazz band at Ciro's tonight was a particularly lively one and played everything at twice the normal tempo, and collapsed into their seats to fan themselves with enough vigour to make themselves hotter than ever.

Johanna shot a smile at Emilia of such brilliance that she could not help but smile back. Ever since that weekend at Simister, Johanna had been a different girl. Still her serene and rather grave old-fashioned self in many ways, she nonetheless seemed to have been illuminated from within; her eyes, her face, her very hair seemed to have a new effulgence now and when she looked at Jonty – which she often did – the light glowed even more brightly.

Jonty, too, was different, but in quite another manner. He now seemed smug, with a sleek and self-approving expression on his face which Emilia had found sorely trying. 'You look like the cat that's got the cream,' she had snapped at him one day, driven by her disappointment to a rare display of her own feelings, but he only grinned and said simply, 'That's because I have. She's so wonderful, Emilia! I've never been happier in all my life!'

And Emilia, who did not grudge them their happiness, however desperately she ached for her own, bit her lip and said no more.

That Claudette's plan to help her son by means of the weekend at Simister had worked was very clear. No one would ever know what the two of them had talked about during their long walks through the portrait galleries of the vast house, and later in the park and gardens, but they had emerged from that three days as a fast pair. Emilia had been amused to see it then, not least because she realized that her mother was less pleased than she might be.

Is she regretting helping Jonty find his love? she had asked herself, watching her mother with that apparently casual gaze of hers that missed nothing. Is that why she looks so vexed? But then she perceived, watching more closely, that her mother's vivid chatter and bright insouciance had nothing to do with Jonty, everything to do with her other guests.

They had been odd, all three of them, Emilia had thought. He so dour and quiet, so determinedly dancing attention on his wife, even though they must have been married for centuries and be quite past all that sort of nonsense, and she, his wife, so uneasy while seeming so calm and soft-voiced, while Maman chattered and glittered and glittered and chattered –

And then she had dismissed her boring elders from her mind to concentrate on her own problems. Max. Why she had found him so compelling she couldn't have said. All she knew was that the first time she had seen him there at Letty Lackland's studio she had found him fascinating. His face with its tight unhappy expression; his rough dust-coloured hair, his square very rigidly held shoulders – everything about him spoke to something in her. Maybe it's because he's unhappy in some way, as I am, she had told herself, and then, seeing the comfortable way his parents had with him and the warm affection with which they looked at their children she knew that whatever it was that distressed him, it did not have the same roots as her own unhappiness. He did not feel an exile among his own as she did.

But still there was something, and whatever it was it had set within her a hot core that now glowed in an alternatively agreeable and then uncomfortable way. Sometimes just thinking about him made her spirits soar, filled her with the conviction that she could and she would make with him the relationship she wanted, while at others she was cast into gloom, convinced even more certainly that they would never, never, never, be more than the merest of acquaintances.

Not that anyone observing her would have known of an iota of this inner turmoil. All anyone saw when they looked at Emilia was her quietness, her plainness, her secret eyes. It had taken her many years to learn how to keep her own countenance in this way, but the lesson had paid big dividends. Her secrets were very much her own, quite unlike

Johanna's, whose emotions showed on her face for all to see.

'– So he's going to go on working at Nellie's after the results are out, because he said he's used to hospital work and anyway, it'll cost so much to set up his own practice. Mother's already said she'll gladly arrange it all for him, proper consulting-rooms in Harley Street and so forth, but he's quite determined to do it all himself. He's –'

'Who?' Emilia said, her ears alert to any mention of anything to do with Max. 'What are you talking about?'

'Jonty was asking about my brother,' Johanna almost had to shout it above the screech of the saxophones as the band lifted its corporate voice into a Jerome Kern medley. 'And I was saying his results are due out any minute now. He'll be a doctor – we'll have two in the family! Mother says we'll be like the parson's children who are able to be good for nothing. Only for us it'll be well for nothing –'

'And he'll be staying at Nellie's after that? Not going into his own rooms the way doctors usually do?'

'That's right. I told him I'm sure he'd do awfully well if he did. He's frightfully easy to talk to, isn't he? And people who are ill like that. I wish he would – it's bad enough Daddy has to work as long hours as he does. The hospital never minds calling him out at any time, whenever it suits them. If he had a private practice it'd be different, I dare say. When patients have to pay every time they call the doctor they're more thoughtful. And now they'll do the same to poor old Max, and I'd hate to see him get as tired as Daddy does. Still, he's awfully stubborn –'

'What will he be doing at the hospital, then?'

Johanna shook her head. 'Oh, don't ask me, old thing! I'm just a dim-witted sister – he'll never explain all that to me!' Since her new closeness to Jonty Johanna had started to use the newest slang with an air of great stylishness that Jonty certainly found very beguiling, though Emilia thought it rather silly, and she said now with an edge to her voice, 'Oh! From all you were saying I thought he'd been telling you his plans.'

'Oh, not me, but Mother and Daddy! I just listen, you know and find out that way. He's a darling, old Max, but a bit on the silent side when it comes to me.'

So Emilia had to leave the conversation at that, but it set the germ of an idea in her mind and next morning she went to sit at her mother's bedside while she ate her breakfast from a silver tray, a rather unusual act for Emilia and one which startled Claudette a little.

'Will you have some chocolate, darling? No? Well, there's toast there if you want it – they always send up far too much. What shall you be doing today? Have you any delicious plans with your friend Johanna?'

Emilia seized her opportunity with both hands. 'Well, that's the thing, you see, Maman. Now she and Jonty are such a case –'

'Are they, *ma cherie*?' Claudette cocked a knowing eye at her. She was looking far from the engaging creature she was in company in spite of being swathed in a pink silk nightdress richly trimmed with maribou. Her hair was pinned firmly with flat French curlers under its pink silk bandeau, and her chin and nose shone rather greasily from last night's application of skin food, showing rather too clearly the lines round her eyes and mouth. Seeing her like that helped Emilia to be more comfortable with her and she grinned now, a shade sardonically.

'You know perfectly well they are, Maman. Don't be coy!'

Claudette grinned back at her and for a brief moment there was a companionable little silence between them that made Emilia feel her usual loneliness more sharply than ever. She looked away with a graceless little movement that made Claudette, who meant well enough, however unsuccessful she was in her dealings with her daughter, sigh imperceptibly and pour her second cup of chocolate.

'Well, what of this *case*, then, my dear? Does it mean you and Johanna are no longer friends?'

'Not at all! She's a delightful girl, and will make a most agreeable sister-in-law in due time, I've no doubt –'

Claudette raised her brows at that. 'A little precipitate, aren't you? They're just –'

'Oh, they'll marry, I've no doubt of *that*. You've only to see them together –' Emilia dismissed them. 'The thing is, she's now too busy with Jonty to spend time with me. They spend all day and every day together, and that really does mean – well, I've been thinking, I'd like to do something useful, you know? Take a job, maybe and –'

Claudette set down her cup with a little clatter. 'Oh, no!' she wailed. 'Not you too? Marie Englewood told me her Daphne's taking up photography and wanting to rush around the world taking pictures of Zulus, and Diana Chippenham's gone quite mad and decided she's going to become a nurse for always, because she had such a divine time V.A.D.ing in the War and her father's an *earl* – and now you're doing it too! You'll be telling me you're going into politics next –'

'No fun in that now we've got the vote. Or that most of us have,' Emilia said. 'Anyway I wasn't thinking of anything at all outrageous, so you needn't worry. Though you worked when you were a girl, didn't you?'

'I had to,' Claudette said a little grimly. 'I had a sick father and no money. But it's different for you. We've plenty of money and no one has to look after me! If I hadn't had to work I'd have had a marvellous life shopping for clothes all day and gossiping with friends and – you could too, you know! If you'd go to my lovely Alice she'd make you the most perfect clothes and you'd have such fun. And –'

'You were gay and pretty,' Emilia said flatly. 'I'm not.'

Again there was a silence between them, but this time there was no comfort in it, and after a moment Claudette said with an air of rather false brightness, 'Well? What do you have in mind, then?'

'Well, I think I'd like to learn how to be a typist.'

'A *typist*? But darling, so grey, so boring, so *dismal*!' Claudette looked genuinely horrified. '*Cherie*, I couldn't bear it! Dammit, Emilia, I can't pretend you're one of the everyday sort of beauties – but you've lots of character and such lovely eyes and – and really, you don't have to be one of these pathetic people one sees scuttling about and – a job, I can understand, I suppose, but such a job as that!'

Emilia laughed. 'I didn't say I was going to take a dismal job once I'd learned, you know! Why, there are lots of absolutely marvellous things I could do. Like being amanuensis to a famous writer, or helping the editor of a magazine or' – She stopped momentarily and then went on smoothly – 'or perhaps working in a hospital where they must need their vital information typed out and so forth. They must have to have secretaries – I could be really useful there and it would be frightfully interesting.'

Claudette cocked her head on one side. 'Oh, a hospital? Which hospital?'

'I thought perhaps Queen Eleanor's, Nellie's, you know,' Emilia said with studied nonchalance. 'Johanna's father could perhaps help. It's the only one where I know anyone, so I thought perhaps –'

Claudette was thinking fast, and now her lips curved against the edge of her chocolate cup as she surveyed her daughter over its rim. Emilia ensconced in a cosy office at Nellie's. There was a thought! Not only would it keep the poor child busy and just possibly help her meet other worthy people like herself and maybe make some friends – even meet some sort of man who would care more for goodness and virtue than good looks, though Claudette frankly could not envisage any such odd creature – but it would be the most natural thing in the world for her mother to come and see her from time to time. Collect her to take her out to lunch, to tea or –

Claudette had been slowly but surely becoming more and more obsessed with the idea of ensnaring Lewis Lackland. What had seemed merely a potential source of amusement when she had met him again so many years after their initial entanglement had now become a source of constant annoyance, because of his stuffy reaction to her. She had proposed only a light-hearted flirtation, a game for two rather bored grown-up people to play – and he must surely be bored out of his mind by Miriam by now? – and he had reacted as though she had suggested he hang his grandmother and sell her carcase for meat pies. All the time he had been at Simister he had been so punctilious in his remoteness towards her that you'd have thought he was a tailor's dummy; such a silly man, such an absurd man, such a damnably attractive man. The harder he resisted her, the more determined she was that he should succumb eventually.

Which was why it was that she agreed to her daughter's plan and Miss Emilia Collingbourne (as Emilia insisted she was forthwith to be known, for she could hardly use her title as a *typist*, as she explained very reasonably) neatly dressed in a blue serge business suit with a demure white collar and cuffs and with her notebooks carefully stuffed in a leather bag, reported at the unconscionably early hour of nine in the morning to Pitman's College near the Strand to take her first lesson in the mysteries of typewriting. Emilia had been told that the normal length of training was three months, but she had made up her mind to it that she would complete it much sooner than that. She had already purchased her own handsome Remington machine and set it up in her sitting-room at Vere Street and fully intended to practise every moment she could outside her lesson hours in order to become as proficient as quickly as possible. She had to be ready to start her new job as a secretary at Nellie's very, very soon.

Not that Nellie's knew she was to work for them yet. That was something that still had to be arranged. But with a little quiet guile on her own part, and perhaps a little bit of the help her mother had promised, that should not present any great problems.

She was a very cheerful person that chilly March morning. It might take time to get what she wanted, but she'd get it in the end.

14

One of the major problems James had to face on the rare occasions when his mother consented to be shoe-horned out of Tavistock Square to dine with him at South Audley Street was the matter of seating. His wife, after all, had every right in her own home to expect to sit at the end of the table facing her husband. His mother, however, seemed to regard it as her natural place and had been known to fly into the most monumental of sulks if she was set anywhere else but at the place which indicated she was the queen of the evening. Caught between Mamma's imperiousness and Bella's complaints, James was feeling more than a little flustered.

And even now when they were all settled with Bella sitting only a shade rebelliously beside him while her mother-in-law sat in triumph in her chosen spot, it was no better. Olive was sulking because of something Mamma had said, Daniel was being even more waspish than usual, and Oliver was being deliberately deaf – he could hear perfectly well, of course he could, but it amused the stupid old man to pretend otherwise when he wanted to make mischief – and Theo – Theo didn't bear thinking about!

They had reached the second course, and the talk was lively and general, and James sat and surveyed his guests with his face set in the rather angry grimace which passed for a smile which he always assumed when he was being a host. The table looked good, that was something. The expanse of perfectly white damask, the glitter of crystal and silver and the trailing smilax and fern arrangements; all very tasteful. The food had been tolerably good; adequate without being showy. Of course he could afford to go to the profiteers and buy expensive comestibles in spite of the shortages, but that would be vulgar, he had told Bella firmly when she had suggested that now the Armistice was here it wouldn't be unpatriotic any more to make the most of what was offered. They would have only what was proper and not embarrass anyone with a display of excessive expenditure, he had said firmly. So, it had been a simple consommé or velouté of leeks to start with, and now they were eating a reasonably well-flavoured small piece of Southdown mutton with young vegetables and there was a handsome Brie waiting to be presented after the cabinet pudding and jellies. Theo had brought it home for them from his jaunt to France and that was something for which to be grateful.

But there was nothing else for which to be grateful to him, James thought furiously, looking down the table at his son as he speared the last piece of mutton on his plate and daubed it with redcurrant jelly. Why did he have to answer Mamma so directly when she asked him what he had been doing? He could have been vague, said something that would have turned her attention elsewhere, but not he! He'd had to blurt it all out – and Oliver, damn him, had joined in, deliberately ignoring James' hissed warning across the table; pretending he hadn't heard, and talking at the top of his voice. And now look at Mamma's face!

'Do tell me more,' Daniel was saying now, grinning like the damned monkey he was. 'How do you stop yourself from laughing out loud when you have to make those stupid faces cinema characters make? I'd get the most fearful attack of the whoops if I had to do it –'

'You'd never be asked to do it, Uncle Daniel!' Olive said, vixen-sharp. 'Not with your face – and I'm sure Letty's got more sense than to take on any more family people.'

James closed his eyes in a moment's despair; now Olive joining in! Mamma must be about to explode –

'And what will you do next?' Daniel ignored Olive without any difficulty at all. 'Shall you be investing in a bent malacca cane and a pair of elderly boots and making everyone laugh like jackasses?'

Theo shook his head, and merely smiled thinly, saying nothing. He'd said enough already, James thought. Why *did* he have to answer Mamma so directly? Him and his damned films!

'He don't have to,' Oliver was saying loudly. 'Don't have to, Daniel, m'boy! This young man is much too good to be made into another Chaplin. He's got too much talent to be anything but what he is – hero material, yes, hero material –'

Theo flicked a glance at Oliver this time and James felt a moment of gratification, for he looked thoroughly put out. 'Nothing of the sort, Uncle.' He sounded sharp and it was clear to James that he now regretted being honest with his grandmother as much as James regretted it, and that should have made James feel better, but it didn't; Mamma was looking much too thunderous for that.

'Hero, eh? Is that what they call type-casting? Take a war hero, make him into a film hero? Good thinking, good thinking, Oliver –'

'Oh, pooh!' Oliver had the grace to look uncomfortable, aware now of Theo's tightened jaw. 'Question of looks, that's what it is. Looks. Theo's got great good looks,' and now he glanced at his sister with a propitiatory little smile. 'Takes after his grandmother's side of the family, I dare say. No offence meant, Bella –'

Almost desperate now, with both his wife and his mother looking fit to cut someone's throat, James said loudly, ' 'Strordinary weather we're getting for April, eh? Actually saw a tulip out already in the park this morning, or was it a daffodil? Pretty, anyway, in all that sunshine, very pretty – goin' to Baden Baden this year, Daniel? Missed it badly, haven't you, all through the war? Shows in your figure, you know, shows in your figure –'

But Daniel was not to be deflected. 'So, what's the next film you'll be making with Letty, Theo? More heroics? Or will she just keep pointing her camera at your handsome face and hope for the best?'

'Doin' a play,' Oliver said, seeming to want to make some sort of amends. 'Eh, m'boy? Doin' a play –'

This time Phoebe's lips parted and she turned to stare at Theo, half-way down the table.

'A play?' she said and her voice was remarkably loud for one of her age, and at once everyone stopped respectfully; no one talked while she did, ever. 'A play? And since when, Theo, did *you* have any talent at all in that direction?'

'Well, he's been doin' very well in our film, Phoebe!' Oliver said. 'Didn't you hear what we was sayin'? He's been playin' Mark Antony –'

'Films,' Phoebe said icily, 'are not acting. Acting is a disciplined skill, demanding real talent, not a mere face. As you well know, Oliver. And since I've never heard or seen any hint of such talent in any of the children, I can't see what Theo will be doing in a play. Unless he's stage managing.'

'Don't have to tell me about acting, Phoebe, dammit, don't have to tell me!' Oliver said, blowing out his cheeks furiously. 'Dammit all, m'dear, I've spent more hours dealin' with actors than you have –'

'You were never a performer,' Phoebe said. 'I was, and I know.' And she stared round the table with her chin up, daring anyone to question her omnipotence.

'Only ever sang and danced a bit,' Oliver muttered furiously to his neighbour, Olive. 'Did it on my stage, didn't she? Can't tell me she knows more than I do. An' I say Theo's doin' a play and he's good and –'

'Really Uncle Oliver, there's nothing decided yet.' Theo had been trying very hard to remain out of the argument, but no longer could. 'It's just something that's been suggested and –'

'Ah!' Phoebe said with great satisfaction. 'Knew you couldn't be doing it. Knew you didn't have the right talent. I'm sure it's all very well to play with Oliver's foolish cameras and so forth, but real acting is something else – you could never hope to be of any use at that whatsoever.'

Theo stared at her, his face slowly stiffening. There she sat, immensely sure of herself, immensely smug, totally certain that she was the arbiter of all that happened in her family, telling him that he could not act. He, Theo Caspar! He thought confusedly of the hard work of the past weeks, the effort he had put into learning the skills he needed, the passionate scenes with Cleopatra which the very scene-shifters had applauded, the way people had stood and watched, enthralled, when the rushes appeared on the screen in that Normandy farmhouse, and felt his anger begin to bubble in him. All his own doubts about his ability to sustain a demanding role on a live stage, all the problems of learning a long complete part instead of small sections which could be paraphrased without causing any problems at all for the silence of the screen, all this uncertainty about his ability to push himself over the footlights at an audience, all the arguments he had mustered to fight off Letty's constant coaxing to take the part, were swept away by it. How dare this bullying old harridan tell him how to run his life? He'd watched her ruling his father, his mother, his aunts and uncles and cousins for as long as he could remember. It was high time someone stood up to her.

'It has been a long time, Grandmamma, since you knew as much about the theatre as you seem to think you do. What may have been considered tolerable stage work fifty years ago is no longer regarded by anyone of judgement as anything but exaggerated barnstorming of the most vulgar type. The play I'm doing is a modern one, you must understand. It opens at the Shaftesbury later this year, and I shall be very good in it –'

And he lifted his chin and stared at her challengingly, as James again closed his eyes in despair. There was nothing, nothing at all that could possibly ever go right again with Mamma.

'I still don't think I can do it,' Theo said. 'I still think you're mad even to consider it, but on your own head be it. You said you want me, so I will do it. And when it turns out to be the biggest flop of the season –'

'It won't!' Letty said joyously, and hugged herself with schoolgirlish glee as she leaned back in her armchair. 'I don't know what made you change your mind, but I'm damned glad you did! And you'll be a huge success, you see if you aren't. If we really work at it, we can have *Caesar and Cleopatra* ready for release at the same time as the play opens. I've got the distribution organized already, and they'll see it my way – oh, Theo, you just wait and see what it'll be like! You'll be the biggest name in the theatre before the end of the year –'

'Phoebe!' Oliver said and began to cackle. 'Phoebe did it! If you'd only been there, Letty, you'd have loved it all. There she was, sittin' there bein' more like a duchess than Queen Mary, an' goin' on and on about Theo not havin' any talent and – oh dear – it's enough to make a man burst his breeches!' And he laughed till the tears coursed down his papery old cheeks.

Letty stared at Theo. 'Was that it, Theo? Did the old bat get at you?'

Theo looked mulish. 'I suppose she did. It's so stupid the way everyone gives in to her! My father's the worst – he'll say and do anything to keep her sweet and it's ruined her. I suppose I did lose my temper, and I can't pretend I don't wish I hadn't. I'd made up my mind to it that I couldn't do it, and that I'd make the most awful mess of the whole thing and then –'

'It's not often I have cause to be grateful to Lady Caspar!' Letty said and grinned at Oliver who was recovering from his laughter now and wiping his eyes. 'Eh, Oliver? She's given both of us a bad time over the years – and I've never really understood why –'

'Your mother, m'dear,' Oliver said at once. 'I remember, I remember if no one else does! Dear old Freddy had a soft spot for Sophie, you see, and that made Phoebe mad as a woman could be. Silly, really. Freddy adored m'sister, always did from his childhood. But there it was, Phoebe took a maggot into her silly head –'

'Well, the maggot's worked to our benefit this time,' Letty said, stopping Oliver's reminiscing in full flood. 'And you may as well know I won't let you back off, Theo, no matter how you feel tomorrow, once you think again. I know what'll happen. You'll spend half the night awake changing your mind. So you can sign the contract now –' and she picked up her handbag from the floor beside her armchair and began to rummage in it.

'Contract?' Theo said, and sat up very straight. 'Now? It's midnight – are you mad? Tomorrow will do perfectly well –'

'No it won't,' Letty said and pulled a slightly crumpled sheet of paper from her bag. 'I've been carrying this damned thing around with me for the past fortnight, hoping to get past your guard, and I'm not letting you off now. You'll feel better once you've signed – there'll be no going back, then. It's uncertainty that's the most killing thing – and this'll get rid of it. Come on. Read it carefully – it's a good one, I promise you, and you'll get a lot out of it, and I'm paying you more than any other management would, I'll swear to you. But sign it, and then we can get on to the really interesting things – like getting the character right in your head –'

Theo sat and stared down at the contract she had pushed into his hand and tried to think. Ever since leaving his father's house after the dinner party had degenerated into a hissed but none the less furious argument in the hallway at South Audley Street with his father white with rage and his mother standing weeping as usual beside them, and all through the journey back to Paulton's Square with Uncle Oliver, he had been in a passion of anger. He couldn't have said what it was about his grandmother's behaviour that had so particularly infuriated him. For years she had been a tiresome thorn in his side as she was for virtually all the younger members of the family; Grandmamma says, and Grandmamma wouldn't be pleased and Grandmamma this and Grandmamma that had punctuated his entire childhood and youth. But he had borne her with tolerably well hidden irritation for years, so why tonight had she been so particularly able to set her nails into him, to push him so far that he now sat holding a contract to play a small but decidedly showy part in a London production of a new play? Letty had been urging him more and more strongly for what seemed like an eternity and he had resisted, certain he could not possibly set foot on a stage to give any sort of performance that was not hopelessly amateur. Letty had assured him in every way she could that he had natural talent, that his sense of timing was faultless, and that was something a performer was born with, not something he learned, yet none of her blandishments had worked. Nor had Uncle Oliver's calm insistence that of course he'd change his mind, of course he'd do it, had any effect.

Yet his grandmother's sneers had whirled him around completely and made him lose all his determination. Just one of her acid speeches, and he was driven to do something he had not intended.

'Dammit!' he said aloud. 'I'm as bad as everyone else, aren't I? Just in reverse, that's all. I'm letting her bully me –'

'Stop talking, and sign,' Letty said commandingly. 'It's late and you've got a long ride back to your flat. And I'll be round early in the morning to take you to the theatre and show you what'll be what. Sign.'

He stared at her for another moment, his eyes as opaque as pebbles, and for one awful moment she thought he was going to refuse. But then, he shrugged slightly and took the pen she was holding out and holding the paper a little awkwardly against his knee, signed and dated it, and she relaxed her shoulders and took a deep breath of relief.

'You realize I'm not happy about it,' he said as he gave it to her. 'It's not as though I'd ever even acted at school or university –'

'And thank heaven for that,' Letty said, as she stored the contract safely in her handbag again. 'You'd just have a lot of bad habits to unlearn. We're starting from scratch, and you'll be superb – a real man of the new school. Just relax and leave it to me. You'll be fine –' She looked at him sharply then. 'You're feeling all right?'

He laughed then, a sharp little noise without much mirth in it. 'Beginning to regret your success?' he said. 'Afraid you've signed on a mental cripple? That I'll have attacks in the wings or on the stage and ruin your investment?'

'Don't be stupid,' she said. 'You'll be fine. You promised to see Max Lackland, and –'

'It's time you got Oliver to bed,' Theo said and stood up and moved across the small drawing-room to the chair where Oliver had fallen into the light doze of the very old. 'Do you want any help to get him upstairs?'

'William'll help him,' Letty said. 'Listen, Theo –'

'Eh?' Oliver woke with a start and blinked up at him and then his watery old eyes glinted and he said, 'Signed it, eh, m'boy? Knew you would, told you you would, didn't I? Time I was in bed. Goin' up now. Goo'night, m'boy. Letty, m'dear, good night. Been a good evenin', ain't it? Didn't think much of James' dinner, mind you. A poor spread that was. Got no sense of what's right at all, that one. Miserable bit o' mutton that was –'

He shuffled off to the door and Theo followed him to watch him make his laborious way up the stairs to where his old servant, William, an ex-waiter from the Celia Rooms who had worked for Oliver for years, was patiently waiting for him to help him to bed, and then took his own overcoat and top hat from the stand in the small hallway as Letty stood in the drawing-room doorway and watched him.

'I shan't give up on that either, you know,' she said after a moment, and her voice was gruff.

'On what?'

'You know perfectly well. On your seeing a doctor. I'd rather a real one than young Max, but –'

'I'm not seeing anyone –'

'But Max will do if he's the one you prefer.' She went on as though he'd not spoken at all. 'He's been spending a lot of time at the Gaff lately, since his exams ended and he qualified. Been trying to talk to you for a couple of weeks, you know.'

'I know.' He was standing now with his hand on the knob of the half open front door, staring out into the darkness of the Square. 'He wants to talk to me about his brother. I – I suppose I'll have to, soon. Damn relations! Damn everything and everybody!' And he went plunging out and down the steps leaving Letty standing behind him watching him go.

'I'll collect you at ten o'clock,' she called after him and her voice sounded thin and disembodied in the night air. 'Take you to the theatre –' but he ignored her, not turning his head. She was right, dammit. He was already regretting signing that contract, but he'd done it, and that was that. He was going to be in a West End production of a new play. Mad, quite mad – and he began to laugh helplessly into his upturned collar as he stood in the King's Road looking for a passing taxi that would take him home to his haven in Shaftesbury Avenue.

15

The Founder stared down at the hubbub with the severe bronze frown looking absurd on his dusty face because of the necklace of strung-together enema syringes hung around his neck and the stethoscope wound round his head like a halo. He was wearing a nurse's apron and a sister's cap, and had a flower trimmed bedpan tucked under his bent arm, and a similarly bedecked urinal bottle suspended by a string from the fingers of his other hand. Each year the qualifying students dressed up the statue with all the ingenuity they could muster and everyone agreed that this year they really had outdone themselves. The 1919 class was clearly going out with a flourish.

'Poor old chap,' Aston said, staring up at the statue, and then grinned at Lewis. 'Must be turning in his grave, hey? Remind me – he was your grandfather, wasn't he?'

'Great-grandfather,' Lewis said. 'He died in '67, you know – and I'm not that old.'

Aston laughed. 'Sorry, old man. Meant no offence! And now another generation joining the ranks, hmm? It's quite a record. Don't suppose there's another hospital in all London can claim an unbroken line of so many from the same family. There was that chap Bartholomew Lackland, wasn't there – the one that went off to America? And I believe Hugo Caspar's part of the clan too, isn't he?'

'He's a cousin,' Lewis said, a little abstractedly. He was looking round the crowded entrance hall of the hospital with its confusion of laughing cheering students all with glasses in their hands, trying to see Max. 'He's going to St George's in September. Got a consultancy in dermatology –'

'Cunning devil,' Aston said and emptied his glass at a

draught. 'No one ever gets skin men out of their beds in the middle of the night. Wish I'd done it instead of general medicine. Ah well. Tell your boy I congratulate him, welcome him to the ranks and all that, and if he wants to apply for the junior houseman post on my firm, I'll give him very sympathetic consideration.'

'Very good of you, Aston,' Lewis said, giving up trying to see Max in the crowd. It was an impossible task, anyway. 'But I think, you know, that surgery will be his bent. I certainly planned it that way – though of course it's up to him. But I'll tell him what you say –'

He leaned against the statue after Aston had gone, watching the revels with his face faintly creased with pleasure. He had trained in Australia, the other side of the world, but his own graduation night had been much like this. He remembered how very tipsy he had got, how very noisy they had all been, how very marvellous they had all felt and he smiled a little wider. Whatever had happened to them all? Old Foster, and Comstock, and that incredible chap, what was his name, Bowery – that was it. David Bowery –

'Mr Lackland?' the porter stood there beside him, sweating a little in his heavily buttoned uniform. 'Sorry to take you away from the jollifications, sir, like, but there's a call from Sycamore Ward. Night Sister says as 'ow the 'ernia what you did this afternoon's very restless, needs a bit of sedation, and since all the 'ousemen is horse de combat as you might say, she wondered as 'ow you might –'

'Yes, of course,' Lewis said. 'Would never do to disturb the young men with work tonight, would it? I'll go up. If you see my son, will you tell him where I am? And that I won't come back to the party – I'll see him at home. Not to hurry back though. His mother'll quite understand –'

'Ah, doctors' wives, sir, doctors' wives, they're a special breed, ain't they?' the porter said and shook his three chins in admiration and went back to his lodge to watch the goings on with a benevolent eye, and to tell his junior assistant that none of it was a patch on the qualifying parties they used to have back in the nineties, now they was really parties as you could *call* parties, they was –

Max had managed to wedge himself comfortably on the staircase, five steps up, with his back to the wall. Here he had a good view of all that was going on without being too much in the eye of the storm himself. He'd already seen them debag Davidson, the rather pompous swot who had, of course, topped every list with his superlative marks and who was clearly destined to become a President of the Royal College of Physicians, if not of the Surgeons as well, and had seen them toss in a blanket with great good humour and not-too-obvious care the one and only woman medical student of the year, Lydia Chester, and joined in the cheers for her as she did a lively jazz dance on the top of the piano someone had hauled down from the students' common room. He had a half bottle of good wine tucked beneath his knees where no fellow celebrants could either steal it or spill it, and he felt he could stay where he was for at least another two hours.

He was enjoying it all more than he had dreamed he could. Last year, when the news of Tim's death had reached them he had nearly thrown up his studies altogether. There had seemed little point in going on and it had taken a great deal of parental patience and coaxing to convince him that such a sacrifice, far from underlining the value of Tim's life, would detract in some way from what he had given, so he had stuck to his work, never expecting as the year had ground on its effortful way to find so much ultimate satisfaction from his struggle. 'Doctor Lackland,' he whispered under his breath, now. 'I'm Doctor Lackland.' It felt odd, like being a totally different person, and he contemplated his new status with considerable awe.

But not distress. Even without Tim here to join in the celebration, he felt happy and for a moment as he stared down at his friends' faces, flushed with wine and excitement, he could see Tim's in there too, sharing the fun, grinning from ear to ear, waving his congratulations up at him, and he blinked and shook his head and the vision faded. But he was not unhappy. Regretful, yes, but not filled with that bitter pain and anger that had been his constant companions for so long. They might come back, but at present he was free of them, and he was glad of that. Though he had to admit some

139

of his state of mind could be based on the fact that the rest of that half bottle of wine tucked behind his knees was now reposing inside him.

'Hello.'

He lifted his chin and tried to look back over his shoulder, from where the quiet voice had come, seeming to cut through the noise of the jazz thumping piano with no effort at all. But he could see only the feet and knees of the people who had colonized the upper reaches of the staircase, until they heaved and lifted to make way, and she appeared beside him to wiggle her narrow hips into the tiny space available.

'Oh,' he said blankly. 'Hello.' And for a moment he couldn't think who she was. That he had seen her many times he knew, but she was somehow in the wrong place at the wrong time, and what with the fumes of wine in his eyes and the noise in his ears he just couldn't think. And then she smiled again and this time he knew and said again, but with great surprise, 'Oh! Hello!'

'You remember me now.' It was a statement and not a question and he looked shamefaced for a second.

'I'm awfully sorry, but you know you're sort of in the wrong setting. I mean, I never thought to see you here of all places – why are you here?'

He stared at her, his brows a little creased. She looked the same yet somehow quite different; her eyes had a brightness about them that was very noticeable, even in this light. They were wide eyes, pale blue but very clear and direct and the lashes, soft and pale though they were, were thick and long and gave her an air of rather fragile charm. Her face seemed different too; not pretty, of course; the first thing he'd registered at that party at the Gaff had been how very plain she was, with her narrow cheeks and her rather thin mouth; but agreeable, somehow. Friendly.

Emilia laughed, and hugged her knees so that she could rest her pointed chin on them, but never taking her eyes from his face. 'I'm a secretary here now!'

He blinked. 'Oh! I didn't know there were any! I mean – oh, I'm sorry, I didn't mean to be rude but – I don't get into the office much, you see, but now you mention it I suppose it's obvious. The Bursar and the Secretary and so on – they must have masses of things to be typed. Can you type?'

'Very well indeed. I've just learned how and I'm very fast and very accurate. I'll show you some time if you like.'

'That would be most kind,' he said formally and she laughed again and this time he did too.

'Why are you a secretary here? I mean it's not as though – well, come on, you're not exactly an ordinary working girl, are you? Daughter of a marquis and all that –'

She wrinkled her nose. 'Oh, pooh to that! No one cares these days what your father was – or no one who matters cares! This is the twentieth century, Max, and has been for a long time. And I'm a twentieth-century woman!'

He looked amused. 'And that means being a secretary here at Nellie's?'

'It means being more than just someone who sits about all day bored out of her mind for want of something interesting to do,' she retorted. 'And being a secretary here is a good beginning for me. I might find all sorts of other interesting things to do later –'

'My sister doesn't sit about all day bored out of her mind,' he said with an edge to his voice, and she laughed again, indulgently, like a mother laughing at a child's witticism.

'But she has Jonty,' she said gently. 'Doesn't she?'

He looked blankly at her. 'Jonty?'

'Hadn't you noticed?' she said. 'The way she is now? Ever since the weekend she and your brother and your parents spent at Simister with us she and Jonty – well, they've been very thick.'

'No, I can't say I had noticed,' he said slowly. 'How thick?'

'Very,' Emilia said after a moment during which she stared at him thoughtfully. 'Thick enough to get married eventually, I shouldn't wonder.'

'Good God,' he said and now he looked really amazed. 'Johanna, *married*?'

'Why not? She's a girl isn't she? Girls do get married.' There was another little pause. 'Most of them.'

'But she's just a – oh,' He stopped. 'I suppose she isn't all that young. She's only a year younger than I am. But –

dammit, she's my sister and I never thought she'd, well – well! I must be very stupid not to have noticed anything. And why hasn't anyone told me?'

'Oh, I doubt anyone said anything about it because they don't know!' she said and again hugged her knees and fixed him with that clear blue-eyed gaze. 'But I noticed. And I'm usually right in what I notice.'

He relaxed then and grinned. 'Heavens, you've been getting me all hot under the collar for nothing! I thought I'd been missing something madly important in the family and that no one had told me. If this is just something you've *noticed* I can stop worrying!'

'I told you. I'm usually right,' she said. 'You'll see. If you get to know me better.'

'Well, if they do decide to make a match of it and *they* tell me so I'll agree you're right. But not till then,' he said and turned to look down at the crowded hallway below again as a loud cheer went up. One of the livelier of the young consultants had ventured to join the by now exceedingly elevated students and had been seized and was about to be tossed in their blanket.

'Would you like to?' she said, still not taking her eyes from his face, though now she could only see his profile. It was a strong profile and she liked looking at it.

'Would I like to what?'

'Get to know me better.'

He looked at her, startled, and smiled a shade uncertainly. 'Why, yes, of course – that would be very nice –'

'Especially if we were to be related. By marriage.'

He laughed at her grave expression and relaxed. 'Especially if we're to be related, indeed.'

'Well, no need to wait for that.' She stretched a little and then smiled at him. 'I've got tickets for a play at the New Theatre. There's an American actress in it – she's supposed to be awfully good. Katharine Cornell. Would you like to see it? It's quite a sentimental play, I suppose, but I've always liked the story. It's *Little Women*. Next week, on Friday.'

'Oh!' He was nonplussed. That this hitherto quiet and undoubtedly plain girl should prove to be quite so emancipated as to invite a man to the theatre was exceedingly

142

surprising. 'I – that's very kind of you –'

'My mother gave me the tickets,' she said, still seeming very casual. 'She often doubles her arrangements – she's madly busy and awfully popular so I suppose it's natural enough, and there's a ball she'd rather go to that night. It seems a pity to waste them –'

'Yes. Yes, I suppose so. Friday, you say?'

'Mmm. Curtain goes up at eight o'clock.'

'Er – eight o'clock.' He was temporizing, trying to think of how he felt about the situation; he could never remember any girl he had ever met being quite as direct and – well, un-girl-like as this one. Not that she didn't look feminine enough; her hair had been cut since they had last met, he now realized, and was set in a stylish new bob, and she was wearing – wasn't she? – powder and rouge, and it seemed to suit her. Of course most girls wore it these days; even his sister, he'd noticed lately, had taken to using a little lip rouge. But for all that, the girl behaved as though she were one of his fellow students, asking him to join them for a drink after a lecture or to play a game of billiards in the students' common room.

'Could be quite a jolly evening,' she said then, casually, and he relaxed. Jolly. That was it. Nothing more than a jolly evening with a friendly person. And as she had said, she was a twentieth-century woman. This was the way girls were nowadays. His sister was a bit old-fashioned, and he'd long realized that.

He smiled at her and nodded. 'Yes – that should be fine. Shall I collect you at your house?'

'Er – no – no need for that,' she said and reddened slightly though he didn't notice it in the dim light of the staircase. 'I'll be here working late anyway, I dare say. You'll find me in the Bursar's office. About seven o'clock?'

'Yes. About seven o'clock.'

Another shout went up from the hallway below, and someone peered up at the crowded staircase and called, 'Oy. Lackland, you too –'

'What?' Max called back.

'Photograph, you old ass – come on! We've got to get ourselves recorded for posterity!'

'I suppose I'd better –' Max said and got to his feet awkwardly and swung himself down the stairs by dint of holding on to the banisters and jumping over the heads of the people beneath him, and she sat and watched as the qualifying students were shuffled into position amid much shoving and shouting and the sweating photographer, bobbing in and out of his black clothed camera, tried despairingly to get them to hold still long enough to get a steady picture.

'Friday,' she called after him, and she thought he reddened but she couldn't be sure. But it didn't matter; he'd said he'd come and she knew he would. All she had to do now was make sure she got the tickets from Mamma for next Friday. There shouldn't be too much difficulty; usually she gave such extra treats to Jonty, never thinking that her daughter would go to the theatre unaccompanied, and certainly not that she would find a companion.

But I have, she told herself gleefully. I have. And soon we'll do other things together. He'll see, soon, what a good friend I can be to him. And then, later, maybe, something rather more.

16

'Actually, I'm on holiday,' Max said. 'Qualified, you see. So I'm having a fortnight's break before I go back to the hospital. Or to whatever I'm going to do –'

'Wouldn't it be a better holiday if you went away somewhere? Seaside or something?'

'Bit early in the year for that. Be frightfully cold on a beach in May. Anyway, I prefer staying in London. The essence of a holiday, don't you think, is doing nothing in the surroundings in which you usually work?'

'You don't usually work here, do you?'

'No,' Max said desperately. 'Look, I want to help. I didn't come to – just to make a nuisance of myself, Letty asked me to, so I did. And you did agree that you would let me try –'

Theo leaned back in his seat and tucked his chin into his collar with a mulish expression on his face, never taking his eyes off the stage where Letty was in close colloquy with Alf and the stage designer, a rather intense young man sweating in thick tweeds who was making very heavy weather indeed over planning the simple outdoor set that the play demanded. Around them stretched the vast cavern of the auditorium, the curving rows of red plush seats staring at them with a dumb accusing glare, and the smell of dust and Jeyes Fluid filling the air as the cleaners went lugubriously about their labours.

'Well?' Max said again, lifting his voice a little this time. 'You *did* agree, didn't you?'

'Under duress,' Theo said. 'Under duress.' He took a deep breath as Letty came to the footlights and peered out over them, holding her hand out to shade the glare from her eyes.

'Theo?' she called.

'I'm here.'

'Why don't you join the others at the café over the road? This is going to take longer than I thought. We can have our extra rehearsal tonight. Would that be an awful bore for you, old thing?'

'No,' Theo called back. 'I don't mind – what about your own lunch?'

'Alf's sent out for sandwiches – but you needn't be stuck in here too. I'll see you back here at half-past two, fair enough? Then we can block Act Three properly and get on to some of the detailed work on Act One.'

'Let me buy you lunch,' Max said. 'Please? I do want to talk to you. And I can be awfully persistent, so it'll be easier if you say yes.'

'I had noticed,' Theo said and there was a glint of humour in his eyes for the first time and Max, emboldened, said, 'I've got an idea –' as they got to their feet and began to walk up the central aisle towards the front of the house.

'Oh?'

'There's a super little Italian shop just across the other side by Cambridge Circus. Let's get something there and take it to the churchyard at St Giles'. The sun's out and it could be spiffing!'

'Terribly spiffing,' Theo said and Max reddened at the irony in his voice. 'I suppose we could. I know the shop well enough – I buy my own groceries there. And if it'll shut you up, it's worth it, I suppose.'

Max was too delighted at the success of his ploy to feel insulted at being patronized and as they emerged, blinking, into the bright sunshine of Shaftesbury Avenue, shoved his hands into his trouser-pockets happily and fell into an almost jaunty step beside Theo as he led the way across the road, weaving through the vans and the honking cabs and cars to Greek Street. The Palace Theatre, with its posters screaming its long-running production *Hello, America* which promised the delights of watching Maurice Chevalier and Elsie Janice in the Most Glittering Revue of the Year, loomed threateningly at them from the right and the street was lined with stalls run by bawling costermongers selling everything from apples to chickens, hats to shoes and pots to pans who sent their litter drifting over the greasy tarmac to make the passageway hazardous. The shop on the corner of Romilly Street was festooned with salamis and Parma hams and strings of garlic and onions, and the counter was laden with dishes full of exotic cheeses and strange-looking fish concoctions and pickled peppers. The ten minutes they spent choosing their lunch and waiting for the prosciutto and mortadella to be sliced and olives to be weighed into a little screw of blue paper by the voluble Italian owner seemed to mellow Theo a little, and by the time they'd chosen bread rolls and bought apples at one of the three stalls outside in the street and made their way back to Shaftesbury Avenue and over Cambridge Circus to St Giles' churchyard, he seemed relaxed and comfortable in Max's company.

They chose a bench tucked beneath a dusty laurel bush, deep inside the churchyard where the birds could be heard twittering above the sound of the heavy traffic and old men sat and threw crumbs to vociferously demanding sparrows and pigeons too stupid to prevent their smaller rivals stealing every scrap of food from under their beaks, and unwrapped their packages and ate in companionable silence. Theo had bought a bottle of ginger ale and they shared it, punctiliously wiping the stone lip on their coat cuffs before handing it ceremoniously to the other.

For Max it was a surprisingly agreeable time, and he sat and ate the rather exotic food and stared dreamily at the fresh new green on the bushes and trees beneath the tender blue of the May sky and stopped worrying about why he was there with Theo, or whether Theo would agree to having treatment for his ills; he was content just to be, to feel the sun on his shoulders and the comfortable London smell of petrol fumes and coal smoke from domestic chimneys and moist green earth and the horses that clopped past between the shafts of the myriad vans that thronged the streets beyond the churchyard gates. They were a quiet centre in the bustle that was London, and it was a good way to be.

'My great-great-grandfather was a grave robber here a hundred years ago,' Theo said dreamily after a long silence. 'My grandfather used to tell me about it when I was small. He

147

had been a gutter boy from these slums who started as a resurrection man and ended up founding Queen Eleanor's hospital.'

'I know,' Max said gently. 'He was my great-great-grandfather too. I've heard the tales as well.'

'Yes, I suppose so.' Theo looked at him. 'I tend to forget this cousin thing – not that it makes much difference.'

'No. It doesn't make much difference.'

They were silent again, and Theo leaned forwards and began to throw the remaining crumbs of their bread rolls to the birds, much to the indignation of the neighbouring old man who had been feeding them for some time. 'I'm sorry if I seem difficult sometimes,' he said abruptly, never taking his eyes from the squabbling birds at his feet. 'I don't mean to be disagreeable. It's just that I do feel so – so –'

'Put upon?' Max said softly and now Theo did look at him over his shoulder.

'Yes, just a bit. As though everyone were watching me all the time, and wanting something from me that I haven't got and even if I had wouldn't want to give – it's difficult to explain.'

'And I've been adding to it, wanting you to talk about the war, and wanting you to let me meddle with your – whatever it is. Illness. Problems.'

'Yes. Whatever it is.'

'I mean to help, not to make it worse. I'm sorry if I've been – well, I'm sorry.'

'That's all right. Anyway, I'm cheating really.'

'Cheating?'

Almost viciously Theo pulled another piece of bread from the roll in his hand and flung it to a particularly noisy sparrow. 'I rather like being watched.'

'I'm not sure I understand,' Max said carefully. It was desperately important suddenly to say the right words, not to be crass and stupid and destroy this fragile bubble of communication that hung between them.

'I say I don't want to be watched all the time, but I've discovered I love it, really. I stand up there on the stage and feel the scene-shifters watching, and Letty, and all of the other people in the wings and out in the auditorium and I think – what'll it be like when it's a real audience? When all those rows are full of people and I have to make them all listen to me and pay attention and care and – I like it. I get a great shiver all through me that – it's rather revolting, isn't it?'

'Is it? Frightening, I imagine, but why revolting?'

'People oughn't to be different.' He said it almost savagely and threw the last of the bread at the birds and leaned back against the wooden slats of the bench. 'Being different is hell, you know that? I want to be like everyone else. Grey and dull and – like everyone else. Like that man there.'

And he turned his head and stared at the old man on the next bench along, a bundle of undistinguished shabby clothes and a heavy old face trimmed with ill-cut whiskers and a malevolent and rather watery glare in his eyes.

'Oh, heavens, no!' Max cried, making the old man look up and stare at them and Theo laughed.

'Well, not him precisely. But everyone else. *Ordinary*. It must be marvellous to be like everyone else.'

'I'm not sure I completely understand,' Max said, still being careful, feeling as though he were quite literally sitting on the edge of a rail from which he could tumble at any moment. 'You aren't all that different from other people, you know. I mean, war hero mentioned in dispatches and all that, and frightfully clever and good-looking and so on – but that doesn't mean you're odd or anything, does it? Just lucky. I mean, Tim was fun and frightfully clever and not a bit ordinary and yet he was just like other people, really. The same only a bit more so, if you know what I mean. You're like that, too –'

Theo looked at him and Max felt his face redden under that direct stare, and thought again confusedly of how extra-ordinary his eyes were, with their deep greenness and those lashes and –

'You're a really good egg, you know that?' Theo said and reaching out with his fist lightly closed thumped Max's arm gently. 'Here I sit grizzling when you're dying to talk about your brother and –'

'No,' Max said at once. 'I mean that isn't why I've been –

well, hanging around. I was really wanting to help you. I've done some reading about shell-shock and –'

'But you do want to talk about your brother, don't you? Right from the start that's what you've most wanted of me, wasn't it?'

'Well, yes,' Max said and then looked away, staring at the birds still hunting at their feet for the last remnants of food. 'But not as much as I did. It's not so bad somehow. I mean, I still miss Tim dreadfully. It's still awful when I realize I'll never see him again. It keeps coming over me in great sort of –it's like getting a dreadful fright, somehow. Not at all what I'd have thought being miserable would be. I'd expect to feel sad, you know, but not frightened –'

'Grief is terrifying,' Theo said softly. 'It's the most sickening terror you can know. Except perhaps –' He caught Max's eyes then and managed to grin. 'Well, you're learning, lad, you're learning! You, the doctor, learning from me! Who's going to help who, I wonder?'

Max seized his opportunity. 'Me, helping you. As soon as you'll let me –'

'And if I tell you I'm well now? That I get no more of those – well, episodes? If you go on wanting to treat me now you'll be like those doctors one reads about in the penny papers – the sort who go on dancing attendance on rich old women long after they're well, just to get fees out of them –'

Max sat up very straight. 'I expect no payment from you, dammit! I never said anything *ever* about –'

'I know, I know! I was just making a simile – I'm telling you I'm cured. Quite cured. That I don't need any help, because I don't have a problem any more.'

Max stared at him, startled at the wave of disappointment that rose in him. A doctor should be delighted to hear a patient is well, he told himself, very glad that he has no need of his services, even if he did get better by himself. It's the worst sort of practitioner that gets satisfaction out of a patient's illness –

'I'm pleased to hear it,' he said after a moment. 'If it's true –'

'I don't usually lie. No more than I can help,' Theo said and he sounded amused and Max felt very young again.

'I was not accusing you of mendacity,' he said with a

slightly pompous air. 'I meant only – as long as you're sure you won't – that it won't happen again.'

Theo shrugged. 'How can anyone ever be sure of anything? I can only tell you that I'm feeling fine at the moment. That I've had no – that I haven't had to remember the treatment you give to fainting women for – oh, weeks now. The time we were on location in France seems to have cured me.'

'Then that's splendid,' Max said, trying to keep the flat sound out of his voice, wanting to sound hearty the way his father did when he told a patient he was fit enough to leave Nellie's and go home. 'Splendid –'

'You did help, you know,' Theo said, and leaned forwards and again set his lightly closed fist against Max's sleeve in that friendly gesture. 'I think learning how to control the colly-wobbles when I got them – that head-down trick – gave me confidence. And knowing I could get help if I needed it, that you were willing and ready – it made me feel less scared, you know? So let me thank you and leave it at that, hmm?'

'Yes,' Max said, and tried not to think of the long hours he had spent poring over the books he had collected from Nellie's library learning about catharsis and shell-shock and hypnosis. 'Yes, of course. Delighted to have been of help –'

'Now let me repay you. Not money, you fool! No need to glare at me like that. You wanted to know about the trenches. Do you still?'

Max sat and stared at the patches of sunlight playing on the ground in front of them as the laurel bushes swayed in the light May breeze and sent shadows moving over the rough gravel. 'I'm not sure. Yes, I think I do. He had to – yes.'

'You don't have to. You're entitled to change your mind.'

Max shook his head. 'I don't suppose Tim tried to change his mind when the bullets or whatever it was hit him. So I can't.'

'You can't die someone else's death for them, Max,' Theo said. 'It would be too marvellously easy if you could. The dreadful thing is that you don't die – that you have to go on living.'

'It's worse not knowing what it was, the thing you didn't have to go through. So I have to know. Tell me.'

So Theo told him. They sat on a wooden bench in the tranquil graveyard in the warm sunshine in a city so busy about its commerce, its entertainment and its ceaseless hurry that it seemed to have almost forgotten the four years of bleeding that lay behind it and which had destroyed so many of its young men, and talked of obscenities. Or Theo did, describing in words that were very simple and in tones that were flat and indeed rather dull the way death had come in the trenches of Flanders and France. He talked of greasy mud in which some men drowned. Of the constant mind-numbing bombardment, day and night, that made a man's bones seem pulped to jelly. Of the way bodies hung over the tangled barbed wire like lumps of meat in a butcher's shop, slowly getting more and more stinking as day succeeded day and the struggle to clear the dead and the dying overwhelmed the men pushing their way with their stretchers through the mud and the gunfire and their own fatigue and nausea. He talked of the slow secret gas that crept so silently through dugouts while senior officers sat miles behind the line snugly telling each other that their strategies would work – eventually. Of the way horses screamed in the night and the way men did too, eldritch screeches that seemed to come not from living throats but from the grinding of black rocks in the bowels of the earth. He never raised his voice, he never emphasized any words, he just talked on and on in his quiet way as Max stared unseeingly at the dancing sunshine and shadows on the gravel path of a London churchyard and at last let his brother die.

Max woke early the next morning to lie blinking at the familiar shape of his bedroom window, wondering what had woken him, after a night of wonderfully dreamless sleep of the sort he had not known since his boyhood and certainly not since Tim's death. He realized almost at once what it was, and tumbled out of bed and into his dressing-gown, running for the door and downstairs to where the instrument stood in the hall. His father he knew had been unconscionably late the night before; it was too bad of Nellie's to call him out again so soon. He'd make them wait, if he possibly could –

'Max?' the voice clacked tinnily at him from the ear piece.

'I'm sorry to call you so dreadfully early –'

Max rubbed his tousled head and blinked. 'Eh? Who is that?'

'Theo. I know it's only six o'clock, but suddenly I had to – if I left it any longer I wouldn't – I mean, it seemed all right, but now – dammit, I'm sorry to wake you –'

'What is it – Max?' He looked up to see his father peering down the staircase at him. 'Is that the hospital?'

'No, Dad, it's all right. It's for me. A patient –' Max said and his father lifted his eyebrows and went padding back to bed, leaving Max staring up at the stairs and thinking, my patient – not his, mine – and feeling very odd indeed.

'Well, there it is,' Theo's voice was clacking. 'I couldn't stand it any longer. So, I – I mean last night was hell. It happened again, only worse than it's ever been. Please, Max, whatever you can do, I'll be grateful.'

'Yes, of course,' Max said, almost mechanically, holding the stem of the telephone so tightly that he felt his knuckles whiten. 'Yes, of course. Today?'

'Oh, God, yes. As soon as possible. Please.'

'I'll come to the theatre, then? At about ten? Will that do?'

'Yes. That'll be fine. Ten – or earlier. I'll – thank you.' And the telephone clicked and the earpiece began to buzz as slowly he hung up and set the telephone down tidily again on its small table.

It wasn't until he was shaving that he thought, 'It must have been my fault, making him talk about it all. I felt better, but it made him ill again. It must have been my fault.'

17

Lewis pulled off his rubber gloves and dropped them in the waiting bucket, and then his gown and cap and mask and rubbed the back of his neck with his tired fingers. It had been a long case, a tricky one, but deeply satisfying in its complexity and he'd enjoyed it. The patient looked good, too, nicely pink and breathing easily and should do well. He'd got to her in good time, for the growth had been a small one, well defined and no sign of any pelvic spread beyond the uterus itself. A good morning's work indeed.

'Very pretty, Lackland,' Campion grunted, and stood back to let the porter and the ward nurse push the laden trolley out of the operating theatre on its way back to the ward. 'Those short ligaments couldn't have helped much.'

'You noticed?' Lewis was pleased; it was always a pleasure to work with Campion, an intelligent anaesthetist who took a lively interest in the surgery as well as gas and ether and blood pressure and heart rate. 'It was damnably crowded, wasn't it? And there's a certain amount of rickets in the pelvis which added to the general disorder. But you kept the bleeding down very nicely. Thank you.'

They contemplated each other with the quiet enjoyment that colleagues of equal stature find in sharing a worthwhile task and then went to share the ritual cup of coffee with Sister Theatres, a small and very voluble Welshwoman who fortunately provided excellent coffee. The usual hospital brew was, in Lewis's estimation, virtually undrinkable, but woe betide any surgeon who upset the senior nursing staff by complaining about it. Tradition was a very important part of the life of Nellie's and coffee-drinking and conversation between doctors and senior nursing staff was particularly crusted with tradition.

This morning, fortunately, he did not need to talk much to please Sister Theatres because she was even more than usually loquacious herself. The hospital fête, due to happen in mid July, was in the throes of planning and causing its usual rivalries and sniping as each department and ward set out to outdo all the others with their stalls. The fête raised a good deal of the hospital's essential finance and provided even more innocent pleasure for the hospital staff as for the people of Covent Garden who relied on Nellie's for all their health care, but Lewis had never been able to drum up much interest in it. Fortunately, Campion was enthralled by it all and the two of them sat and gossiped happily over the coffee cups, leaving Lewis free to think his own thoughts.

They were not entirely comfortable thoughts, though some were agreeable enough. He was deeply happy that Max had qualified, and done so with respectable grades in his various examinations. Not so high as to make some people look at him suspiciously as a swot, nor so poorly as to make others sneer at him as the lacklustre sprig of an ancient family tree; just well enough to make it clear that he was genuinely able and a potentially good doctor. It would take a long time yet before he really was a doctor, of course; Max might legally be able to call himself Dr Lackland now, but Lewis knew well – and hoped that Max did – that many years of hard effort and work lay ahead of him before he could be regarded as anything like a really useful practitioner.

But he'd shown no sign yet of being sure of what he wanted to do; but isn't that both a good and a bad thing? Lewis asked himself, staring out of the small window of Sister Theatres' office at the cluster of roof-tops and chimneys that were the upper reaches of Nellie's ever-growing mass of buildings. Good that he had not set his mind on blinkered narrow ways, but bad that he seemed to have no immediate ideas. Lewis had tried to talk to him about an attachment to Aston's firm – and since Aston had offered it, Lewis was punctilious in telling his son so, even though he himself hoped he'd prefer surgery – but the boy had shown no interest in that at all. But then he'd shown no interest in the suggestion that he join Kennedy

Clapham's firm either; he'd benefit from a stint with genital urinary surgery, Lewis had tried to tell him. It was a complex field, one that offered considerable scope to a thoughtful surgeon. But Max had just murmured that he'd think about it and gone back to the books he seemed to be for ever immersed in these days.

That was a disagreeable thought, and he tried to push it away. The fact that Max was reading those rather outré people – Freud and his *Psycho-Pathology of Everyday Life* (as though everyday life could ever be labelled pathological! There was nothing of diseased tissue about it, was there?) and that man Coriat's *Abnormal Psychology* worried him but surely need not make him so uneasy? Lewis had never been a merely technical surgeon; unlike many of his colleagues he was interested in his patients as whole people rather than as collections of interesting organs he could manipulate and slice and rearrange as the fancy took him and the need dictated. He had always paid due attention to the state of a patient's general health and welfare in making decisions about treatment; but wasn't this going rather too far? Lewis had met some of these people who called themselves alienists – a very fancy modern label, in his estimation, for lunatic asylum doctors – and found them far from his taste. Good sensible surgery in which a man dealt with what he could see and what he could do was more valuable, surely, than all this talk about such nebulous matters as complexes and inhibitions and so forth that he'd heard them spouting. Max surely wasn't going to –

No, of course he wasn't. The boy was just recovering from the rigours of the past year, with its huge burden of study and work. He was entitled to amuse himself in any way his intellect took him. Better than rushing about getting drunk and racketing with girls the way some of the new young doctors were doing.

Racketing around with girls. He sighed and drank some more of Sister Theatres' bitter black coffee as she chattered on about the way Sister Buttercup had filched the best site for her stall in the whole of Lincoln's Inn Fields, where the fête was always held, and how Sister Spruce was fit to cut her throat in consequence, and stopped trying to hold the most disturbing of his thoughts at bay. Johanna, oh dear, Johanna.

She seemed to have changed so much, that was the trouble. His sweet and biddable girl, his special companion who had always been so much closer to him than his boys, dearly of course as he loved them all, was no longer his girl. She who had always had time to chatter when he wanted, who knew how to be quiet when he wanted, who was as caring of her mother as she was of him, who knew when they needed to be alone as well as when they would welcome her company, was no longer the way she had been since her babyhood. She was abstracted, somehow, not there when he spoke to her; polite, sweet, of course, but just not there.

He stared down into his coffee cup and remembered how she had been last night. They had been sitting in the drawing-room talking in a comfortable desultory sort of way, while Peter sat and read for the umpteenth time Walton's *Compleat Angler* and Max sat with his nose in one of his big books while Miriam sewed, and the telephone had rung and even before the maid had come to tell them that the call was for Johanna she had gone, her eyes ablaze and her face pink with excitement.

She had been gone a long time, and he had been able to hear the distant murmur of her voice as they sat there in the drawing-room with just the rustle of turning pages and the occasional splutter from the burning coals in the grate to disturb the quietness. He hadn't listened, of course; but he'd not been able to ignore the tone of that muffled voice, the way it seemed to bubble and glow with delight. And then when she had come back to the drawing-room, her eyes brighter than ever, and her lips slightly curved in a remote little smile and he'd asked her very casually of course, who it was and she'd said, 'Oh, just Emilia – and her brother –' and looked away from him, her face very controlled and secret.

That woman's children and his. He wanted no part of it. *None* of it. He hadn't forbidden her to see Jonty, but after that weekend at Simister he'd made it very clear that he was not happy with any association between the families.

'They're really not our sort,' he'd said to Johanna firmly. 'I'd be much happier, my dear, if you saw other friends instead, indeed I would –'

She had said nothing, just looking at him very directly and for a moment he had seen in her not his beloved Johanna, his little girl grown up to a rather big girl, but still his little one, but Abby Henriques, that indomitable and remarkable old lady he had known for so short a time, but had admired so much. Miriam's grandmother had been a powerful woman in many ways, and he had learned a lot about her since their marriage, for Miriam had often talked of her; of her strong will, of how she had determined to live her own life in her own way, and insisted on marrying the man of her own choice – *twice* – and had made a business woman of herself – and a very successful one – all those years ago when Victorian ladies had never done anything so outrageous. She had been quiet and strong, and very stubborn, Miriam had said. And for a moment, looking at his biddable girl Lewis had seen that stubbornness in her. And had felt a sharp coldness rise in his chest.

'Doing your ward rounds now, or after lunch, Lackland?' Campion had obviously asked the question twice for he had raised his voice and Lewis looked at him and blinked.

'Sorry, Campion. Was just thinking – rounds? No, I'll do those this afternoon. I've got to see Bullen about the new instruments we need – you're sure there's nothing else you need to add to the list, Sister?'

'Just a few Allis's, sir, if we can,' Sister said promptly. 'Use a lot of those, we do, it's remarkable. And better to ask when you can get than wait till you need, I always say. So another three dozen Allis's forceps if you please, sir. And perhaps while you're talking to him, a few more trays for the sharps. You'd think I was selling them in Brewer Street market on my own account, the fuss that man makes if I ask him for them –'

'Trays for sharps – yes. And we need some new scalpels too –'.

By the time he made his way down the main staircase from the top of the hospital, taking the stairs his usual two at a time instead of waiting for the lift which was always busy at this time of the hospital day, he was in full command of himself again. He was Lewis Lackland, Queen Eleanor's surgeon first and foremost, no longer Lewis Lackland, worried family man. Which made it all the more of a jolt when, their business completed to their satisfaction – for once Bullen had agreed that the operating theatres could spend a little over their usual budget – the Bursar had said casually, 'I'm glad we were able to be of help in the matter of the job for Lady Emilia – I mean, Miss Collingbourne. Very wise not to use her title. I hope she's as happy as she seems to be? We're certainly more than content with her.'

'Miss Who?' Lewis said blankly.

'Collingbourne. Her mother – Lady Collingbourne – told me that you suggested she talk to the Secretary, and since I need a new lady typist for the Records Department he asked me to help. I wasn't too sure at first, to tell the truth. The young lady had only done a month of her training, but was quite sure that she could manage the necessary speeds, and I had my doubts, I had my doubts! But of course we like to please our surgeons, naturally –' He smiled a little then. 'And as Lady Collingbourne is such a *particular* friend of yours, of course – well, as I say we did what we could. And she really is excellent, excellent – better than we'd expected – as long as she's happy –'

'I expect so,' Lewis said, trying not to let his anger show in his face. 'I hadn't realized in fact that – well, never mind. But another time, Bullen, it might be as well to check with me in such matters. I don't usually ask for such – hum – favours and –'

'Quite,' Bullen said smoothly and opened his eyes wide. 'That was why we were so anxious to be of service to you. Of course, if there is anything *wrong* –'

'Nothing wrong, Bullen, thank you,' Lewis said crisply and got to his feet. 'Just check with me on any similar occasion, that's all. Good afternoon!' And he went to the consultants' dining-room to lunch but ate remarkably little, sitting and staring at his plate as the usual talk went over his head, unheeded.

He waited until dinner was over before saying anything. He had always been able to bite his tongue when necessary, and tonight, angry though he was and concerned though he was, he would wait till everyone had eaten. So he told himself as he came home, taking a taxi as far as Marble Arch and walking the rest of the way through the May dusk so that he could enjoy the smell of fresh greeness from the Park; no point in upsetting everyone's digestion over it. Just be patient, and then be very firm and very direct. The connection between Lacklands and Collingbournes was to cease forthwith. 'Forthwith,' he repeated under his breath as he fumbled for his key. 'Forthwith –'

Dinner was unusually silent, a circumstance he didn't actually notice, for he was so buried in his own thoughts he was less sensitive than he usually was to his family's behaviour. Peter chattered happily enough and ate his usual vast amount before going unwillingly to his room to settle to his evening's preparation for school next day, St Paul's in Hammersmith, where he was due to take his matriculation examination at the end of the summer, and Max, after eating little and spending most of the meal staring at his plate with his mind clearly anywhere but where he was also murmured his excuses early and left. Which left only Miriam and Johanna in the dining-room with Lewis, and that suited him well, for he saw no need to distress Johanna by involving her brothers in the matter. It was clearly mostly Johanna's business and he would keep it that way.

He finished his pudding and pushed his plate away and leaned his elbows on the table, and stared down at the cloth for a moment getting his thoughts together. Should he tell them of Claudette's rubbishy lie to the Bursar as an indication of how encroaching and therefore undesirable she and therefore her family, was? Or should he just tell them, as a father of a family was fully entitled to do, what his decision was, and leave it at that? Miriam and Johanna exchanged a glance, and then, just as Lewis opened his mouth to speak, Miriam too pushed her plate away and leaned on the table.

'Lewis, my dear, we want to talk to you.'

'Eh?' He blinked at her; his own speech had been trembling on the tip of his tongue and he was put out at being stopped. A rare frown creased his forehead and he shot a glance at

Johanna, sitting between them with her head bent as she studied the way her hands were folded on the table before her.

'Johanna and I have something to tell you. It has made me very happy, and of course Johanna is happy too – and now we want to be sure you're pleased. So will you listen to me, please, and not talk till I've finished?'

'What is this?' He was frowning in good earnest now, and Miriam seemed to quail a little; but then she looked at Johanna who gazed back at her with her brows slightly raised and that seemed to give Miriam courage for she took a deep breath and said clearly and in a rather louder than usual voice, 'Johanna, Lewis. Our darling Johanna wishes to be married. Isn't that splendid?'

There was a long silence and then Lewis said carefully, 'Married?'

'Yes, Daddy. It can't be a total surprise, can it? I mean you must have realized –'

'I've realized nothing,' he said harshly. 'Nothing at all. Suppose you tell me what all this nonsense is about?'

'Nonsense, Daddy?' she said, and her own voice hardened. 'To call something important to me *nonsense* is hardly just is it? I'd have expected greater kindness from you than that.'

He closed his eyes for a moment and then nodded with a sharp little gesture. 'Yes, I'm sorry. That was unforgivable of me. Not nonsense, then. But please, you'd better – you must understand you've surprised me. I need time to think. First, who is it you wish to marry?' But he knew with a horrible certainty what she would say.

'Dearest, the Marquis of Collingbourne! Isn't it absurd, our darling falling in love with someone quite as elevated as that? I'm not one of those mothers who go dangling for titles for their daughters to marry, but I must say, to discover that Johanna has fallen in love with someone quite so – well, I can't pretend it didn't make me very happy for her. I hope you are too –'

'Johanna, I told you – a long time ago I told you that – I didn't want you to associate with that family. That they weren't our sort –'

'I know you did, Daddy. But I didn't agree with you. I

wasn't sure what "our sort" was, exactly, anyway. I only know that Jonty loves me and I love him. He wants to marry me, and I've decided I will. He's been asking me for a long time. It's not a sudden whim, you know.'

'A long time? Dammit, Johanna, we only went to that wretched Simister place in February! It's barely three months!'

She blushed suddenly, a charming little flushing of her cheeks. 'Well, I know it doesn't sound long,' she admitted. 'But he's known right from the start it's what he wants and he's been asking and asking – and now I – well, I've said yes.'

Now it was Lewis's turn to flush but it was an ugly reddening that made his eyes seem to bulge a little.

'You had no right to accept! Not before asking me!'

'No right? Why not?' She looked genuinely puzzled.

'Because you are under age. Because I'm your father and you – he – should have spoken to me first. Because –'

She laughed then, a genuinely amused little gurgle that sounded so like the way she had laughed as a baby that his chest tightened even more, if that were possible. 'Daddy, you are sweet and funny! Darling, I'll be twenty-one at the end of this year and it's been for ever since men expected to ask fathers for permission to make love to a girl whatever her age! Actually, he's been madly old-fashioned, the sweet thing, and said he did want to talk to you first, especially as I said you weren't too keen on the whole thing – but I told him not to be a chump and that you were a much more sensible person than he gave you credit for. Of course he'll come and talk to you – I know that's got to be done, and all the boring things about money sorted out – but really, this is 1919 not 1819!'

He sat there with his elbows still on the table staring at her and trying to clear his head and quite failing. She sat very straight, her clear eyes fixed on his and her trust in his concern for her happiness as clearly displayed as if she had written it out in words on a banner to hold over her head, telling him that what he had most feared was true. And he couldn't see what he could do about it. When Claudette had told him that weekend at Simister that her son and his daughter were taken with each other he had stoutly denied it, told her she was just romancing and that he for one would have none of it. He had gone back to

London from Simister, determined to put an end to it all, and heaven knows he had tried. But because he had always been a tender and sensitive father, because he had never forced his children to do anything, always preferring to appeal to their good sense and their affection for him to obtain his own way, he had been hoist with his own petard. Had he been domineering and insisted on severing the friendship between Johanna and the Collingbournes, she would have obeyed him. As it was –

'How much do you care for this young man?' he asked abruptly.

Her face seemed to soften before his eyes. 'Oh, Daddy, so much! I never thought I would, you know. I thought he was horrible when I first met him. All overbearing and arrogant and – I mean, I could see what you meant when you said they weren't our sort. So madly fashionable and everything – but he's changed a lot, you know. He listens to me and realizes when he's being awful and stops it and – I do love him, Daddy. I never thought it would be like this. But now – well, I suppose it's like you and Mother, isn't it? It's the most important thing that's ever happened to me.'

And her eyes filled with tears and she wiped the back of her hand across them unselfconsciously and smiled brilliantly at him and then at her mother and then, suddenly, was weeping in good earnest as Miriam, cooing exactly as she had when the children were small and fell and cut a knee, wrapped her arms about her and stared over her head at her husband. And when Lewis saw that her eyes too were filled with tears, he felt as defeated as he could ever remember feeling. Yet at the same time he was certain that he could not, no matter how much their tears hurt him, he could not give in so easily. To let his beloved Johanna marry Claudette's son without doing all he could to stop it – no. It wasn't to be thought of.

18

Max had thought about wearing his white coat from the hospital, but then dismissed the idea as soon as it came to him. Consultants working in their own rooms didn't wear white coats, and he'd have to learn, sooner or later, to do without the security of wearing a special garment when he was being a doctor. It was odd how naked he felt though, wearing just an ordinary suit, although it was a very neat and respectable one. The trousers with their close sponge-bag checks, the impeccable high collar and white shirt and black cravat under the grey waistcoat, the black jacket; he looked every inch a consultant, and he peered at himself in the mirror over Caplan's wash basin and tweaked his hair tidy again.

Behind his reflection he could see the room stretching beyond to the window and he turned and stared round judiciously, trying to pretend he had never seen it before, wanting to see what sort of effect it would have on a stranger. The desk and chairs looked well polished enough and the carpet underfoot, though cheap, didn't look too shabby. The couch against the far wall was shiny and well stuffed with horsehair and the table alongside with a patella hammer and a stethoscope and sphygmomanometer on it didn't look too rickety. The place was clean and neat without being at all interesting or attractive; probably Theo would find that comforting –

He tugged at his collar again, finding it tight against his larynx and went over to the window to stare down into Harley Street below, keeping himself well hidden behind the net curtains that shaded the rather greasy panes. Would he find the address all right? Would he be on time? Would he come at all? And again he tugged at his collar and thought gloomily of the three crisp pound notes he had given Caplan as his rent for the afternoon.

'I don't mind what you do there, old boy,' Caplan had said cheerfully, stowing the notes in his wallet. 'As long as it's legal. I'm not getting involved in any nasty business with ladies who don't fancy going through with the natural outcome of their adventures –'

Max had glowered at him for that. 'Of course I'm not an abortionist!' he had said furiously. 'And never you dare suggest it! It's just that I've got my own first patient and as I can't persuade him to come to the hospital, I've got to have a quiet consulting-room for him and –'

'That's all right, then,' Caplan said pacifically. 'I meant no harm, you old chump. But a chap can't be too careful, you know! There are some odd characters hanging round Harley Street these days, one way and another, and I've got my future to think of, such as it is. I'll be using the rooms myself again on Friday, thank God, but you're welcome to have them again the week after because I've no appointments, dammit, and frankly, sharing the burden's got a lot going for it.' And he tucked his wallet into his pocket and patted it with a satisfied air. One of last year's Nellie's graduates, he was still struggling to establish his own practice and finding it a great deal more difficult than he had expected. Listening to him talk of how hard it was to develop a private practice had made Max more than a little gloomy. But at least he had one patient, and the sooner he got here and he could start the treatment the better –

He contemplated the street below and bit his lip, feeling the anxiety rise in him again. He wouldn't come, that was it. He'd have got over his misery at that bad night he'd had and he wouldn't come –

But he'd been so very certain he did want help. When Max had arrived at the theatre that morning at ten o'clock, he had found Theo in the lobby, in front of the shuttered box office, and he had come hurrying across towards him with his hands outstetched and his face alight with relief at the sight of him.

It had been a simple enough story. He had gone to bed, tired and comfortable and had fallen asleep normally enough – and then suddenly, had woken in a state of abject terror. He had shivered, he had sweated, he had been cold, he had been certain he was about to die of a heart-attack or a stroke or something equally sudden and had lain there unable to move, unable to get out of bed to seek help, so sick with fright, he had told Max, his face white with the memory of it, that he could hardly breathe.

'And it went on all night,' he said, and his eyes stared at Max with an intensity that made him unable to return their green glare. They looked more deeply sunken into their sockets than ever, hot and glittering and Max had thought uneasily of the other causes of such a symptom and wanted to back away from him, wanted to tell him to go to Nellie's, to see one of the consultants there, a senior man with lots of experience.

'– All *night* – can you imagine what that was like? Hour after hour and it just didn't get any less and the thoughts and pictures that kept coming into my head and – I can't take that, Max. I've got to stop it ever happening again. You've got to stop it ever happening again. You said you could – so do it –'

'Yes, of course,' Max said, trying to sound soothing, the way responsible doctors always sounded. 'Of course. I'll want to do a general physical check, first, of course, but then –'

'Anything you say, anything at all. But *when*? That's the thing I've got to know. When can you start the treatment? I've had as much as I can take. I've told Letty I'm going to see you, and she said that was fine, that I could miss any rehearsal at all as long as I let her know. So, when?' And he had stared at Max again with that intense and desperate stare that he found so alarming that it was impossible to look at him.

'Come to Nellie's. Let me see you there and –'

Theo had shaken his head at once. 'No, please, Max, I couldn't cope with that – hordes of people about and students and – it just wouldn't work, would it? I couldn't cope with that at all. It'll be all I can do to cope with just you –' And he had tried to smile but managed only a tight little grimace.

And Max had to agree that trying to arrange a mental catharsis session at Nellie's would be exceedingly difficult, and to avoid being interrupted by intensely curious fellows, even if he could find a consulting-room he'd be allowed to use all afternoon, would be even more difficult, if not impossible, and unwillingly agreed to arrange for the treatment to be given elsewhere.

'I'll let you know,' he'd promised, hoping fervently it wouldn't take him too long. 'Meanwhile, take it easy, Theo. Try to get as tired as you can before bed so that you're so exhausted you can't help but sleep. I'll arrange it as soon as I humanly can – I promise –'

And he had gone, pushing through the swinging double doors of the theatre into the noise and smells of Shaftesbury Avenue, feeling Theo's anxious eyes on his back and feeling very unsure indeed of his ability to keep his promise.

Thank God for Caplan, he thought now, staring down into the street. To have found him sitting disconsolately in the student's common room at Nellie's bemoaning his lack of patients for his very costly Harley Street rooms had seemed like a gift from the gods and Max had made his arrangements so fast with him that he hadn't had time really to think about what he was letting himself in for.

Until now, and he stiffened as below him he saw Theo's foreshortened figure appear, weaving very purposefully between the passers-by, and staring at the doors he passed looking for the number Max had given him.

I don't know enough, I might make him worse. Maybe it was my fault he had that awful night anyway, making him talk about the trenches, maybe that's what'll happen again. Oh God, I wish Dad were here –

'Mr Caspar.' The extremely elegant and haughty receptionist for the seven doctors who rented rooms in the house stood back at the door and looked with barely disguised curiosity at Theo and then at Max with a slight sneer on her face, and he flushed a little and got up from the desk behind which he had rushed to sit as soon as he had seen Theo hurry up the steps far below.

'Good afternoon, Mr Caspar,' he said very formally. 'Please sit down. Thank you, Miss Burke – I am not to be disturbed on any account, please. You may take telephone messages for me should there be any calls.'

And Miss Burke, who clearly knew perfectly well that there

would not be a telephone call for him in a month of Sundays, went rustling away, disapproval showing in every line of her rigid back.

Max turned back to the desk and settled himself at it, fussing a little with the papers he had set ready in the centre.

'How are you, Theo? Feeling any better?'

'No,' Theo said, and his voice was husky.

'Oh,' Max was nonplussed for a moment. 'Another bad night?'

'No. But the fear of it was almost as bad as if it had happened,' Theo said, and suddenly grinned. 'God, but I'm a wreck, aren't I? As much use as a wet weekend in Margate.'

'Margate?' Max said, and grinned too. 'Can't think a bright weekend'd be any fun there –' and suddenly the atmosphere eased and he felt better. 'Look, Theo, first things first. I want to examine you, make sure you're physically well before we embark on our treatment. History first. Now, tell me, you were a healthy child?'

Working through the familiar pattern of history taking, listing his patient's past illnesses, his present weight and height and such like commonplaces settled him remarkably and by the time he had completed the record and had put his pen down he was fully relaxed.

'Now, would you strip, please, to your underwear? Just a simple examination – on the couch, if you please.'

He waited while Theo retired behind the screen in the corner and then, as he emerged, helped him on to the shiny black couch which he had covered with a red blanket to reduce the chill, and again began a familiar ritual, of observing, measuring, listening. Heart and lung sounds normal. Pulses equal and normal. Neurological reflexes normal, if a touch brisk, but that was to be expected in an anxious man. Eyes normal, and he peered with particular care at the retinae, using his precious Helmholtz opthalmoscope with all the skill he had, desperately needing to make sure there was no evidence of any brain disorder showing there. All was normal, superbly so, and he told Theo as much.

'You really are a remarkably good physical specimen,' he said as he packed away his opthalmoscope. 'It's not often a doctor gets to examine someone in as excellent shape.'

'I suppose that ought to make me feel better,' Theo said. 'It makes me feel worse.'

'It needn't. There's no shame in having an illness like yours, even if you can't see it or touch it or hear it. It's just as important as a cough or a rash and obviously a great deal more painful.'

'Yes,' Theo said, and closed his eyes for a moment. 'It's painful.'

There was a short silence and then Max said, with a bright certainty he was not really feeling, 'Well, I suppose we can settle to our treatment now. I know you're physically fit, so we can start. Would you prefer to dress first?'

'Does it matter?'

'It's up to you. As long as you're not cold. There's another blanket there –' And Max spread the second red blanket over Theo leaving only his bare arms and shoulders showing above its cheerfulness.

'Now,' Max said, as he pulled a chair beside Theo's couch, sitting near the head of it. 'There's nothing very odd about this. I want you to relax, just close your eyes, and let your body go limp. No, that's not enough. Try making your muscles very tight first, and then letting them go. Yes, that's better – relax them now, looser, looser –'

He let his voice drop slightly, and somewhere at the back of his mind a memory emerged of his mother sitting beside his bed in the old night nursery when he first fell ill with those hateful coughs, and murmuring to him to send him to sleep. She had half spoken, half sung sleepy words to him, just sitting quietly beside him, and always he had slept. And he seized now on the memory and added it to the knowledge of how to induce hypnosis which he had culled from his long days and nights of reading the thick books from the psychology section of Nellie's library, and slipped into a gentle repetitive crooning.

'Relax, looser, looser, relax. Your body isn't tight now, it's loose, loose, loose. Your muscles are soft, not hard. Your head is heavy, not light, you're very sleepy. Your eyes are closing, closing, closing –'

And Theo's eyes, which had been fixed with that hard glare of his at the ceiling above did close and Max stared at the still face and almost marvelled at his own skill, but somehow managed to keep talking in that sing-song croon, managed not to let amazement at the results get in the way of maintaining it.

'You're fast asleep now, Theo. Fast, fast asleep. All your muscles are so soft and light that you can't stop me from picking up your arm like this' – and he slid one finger under Theo's bare forearm – 'and lifting it. You're so fast asleep you can't hold your arm in the air. When I take my finger away your arm will float there for a count of three and then it will fall slowly, slowly back on to the couch –'

He held his breath as he slid his finger away and counted the three under his breath and then, slowly, Theo's arm sank and settled again on the couch.

Max sat there for a few seconds contemplating his patient and letting his own very tense shoulders relax. It had worked –and he wasn't sure to whom he owed the greatest debt; the writer of the thick tomes or his mother whose instinctive care of him all those years ago had shown him the way. Whoever it was, he had now induced an hypnotic trance in Theo.

Or appeared to have done so. There was more to be done before he could be sure of that. And he lifted his chin and said softly, 'Theo, can you hear me?'

Theo's lips parted slightly, although his eyelids remained closed and his eyes beneath them motionless and the word came out on a breath. 'Yes.'

'You are going to talk to me, Theo. You're going to tell me about the things that distressed you and made you feel so bad. Do you understand, Theo?'

'Yes.'

'You will experience it all again, Theo, as you tell me about it. Do you understand?'

'Yes.'

Max stopped then, a little nonplussed. Quite where was he to start? He didn't know just what it was that so distressed Theo, where he had been, when –

'Theo. It's the day of the worst battle that you experienced. The one that you dream about. The battle that hurts you most.

What day is it?'

'It's Sunday,' Theo said. 'Sunday morning. The padre comes on Sunday morning –'

'What's the date?'

'September – it's September the thirtieth, isn't it? Yes, September the thirtieth. Peter's birthday tomorrow. Peter's birthday – Golden October. Golden October tomorrow –'

Max wanted to hug himself. Theo lay there, his hands lax on the red blanket, his head still and quiet on the hard white pillow and yet he wasn't there. He was in the middle of a battlefield on a September morning, remembering –

'What can you see, Theo?' he asked. 'Tell me what you see.'

'The padre's coming down the trench. He polished his boots this morning or someone did. So silly – polishing boots where all this mess is. Look at him, all spattered and dirty and trying to pretend he can't smell it all – poor padre –'

'What else can you see?'

'Peter's sitting on the side of his pallet. He's looking at me – dammit. Here's Haddon – he's come back too soon. I want to talk to Peter. Damn Haddon – and the padre. I want to talk to Peter. It's his birthday tomorrow and I want to find a present for him, can't get a present when you're up the lines, can you? I want to –'

He began to roll his head on the pillow and his face creased and now Max could see that beneath his closed lids his eyes were moving, flicking rapidly from side to side as though he were watching a tennis match.

'Easy, easy,' Max said and put his hand out and then at once withdrew it. Perhaps he shouldn't speak now? Perhaps touching Theo would be wrong? All his instincts were to soothe him, to return him to the restful state he had been in to stop this agitated movement, but surely that would be wrong? Talking about it, experiencing it, whatever it was, was the mental catharsis they were seeking. He put his hands in his trouser-pockets, leaning back in his chair.

'What's happening now, Theo?'

'The padre's drinking coffee. Haddon's given the padre coffee. Damn Haddon. Damn him. I want to talk. Does Peter want to talk? I don't know. Why don't they get out of our

171

dugout? Why don't they go and start their damned God-palavering somewhere else? Peter, don't go away –'

His head rolled more frantically on the pillow and his hands came up and began to rub his face. 'Please come back – they'll go in a minute and we'll be able to talk.'

Theo stopped rubbing his face, and held his hands to his cheeks, his fingers digging into them.

'He's come back now – Peter's come back. He's saying something about them beginning – the guns are starting and I haven't got my boots on, it's too early. I haven't got my boots on and the guns are starting – Peter, don't go out there, they'll get you. God dammit, you bloody fool, don't go out there – Haddon – Peter, come here, Peter, I must tell you – Peter – Oh, Christ!'

And Theo threw out his arms and arched his back and stretched his neck so that he seemed to be held to the couch only by his hips and the back of his skull and opened his mouth wide and shrieked with a thin piercing sound that made Max feel the hair on the back of his neck lift against his collar.

'It's all right Theo,' Max said urgently. 'It's all right. Don't shriek – tell me what's happening – it's all right Theo, just talk about it, experience it –'

'Those God damned guns, those God damned guns, I can't hear, I can't think, those guns – oh Christ, the trench, it's gone, the trench has gone – they'll get the dugout next – Peter, where are you? Peter – Oh, Christ the noise – it hurts, the noise, it hurts. Peter! Turn over – it's only the noise, the noise, that's all. Peter, turn over – face, it's gone, it's gone, it's gone. They've battered his face away with the noise – oh God –' And again he arched his back and stretched his neck and then, as suddenly as the storm had started it stopped. Theo was lying collapsed against the red blankets and the hard little pillow and tears were running from beneath his closed eyelids. But he was still.

Max, shaken, put out one hand and set it over Theo's, no longer caring whether he was doing the right thing or not. 'Theo, what's happened?'

'Peter's dead. Peter's dead. His head's gone, shot off his face, the noise shot off his face. Peter's gone. I never talked to him, I never got him a birthday present, Peter is gone –' And the tears slid into the grooves beside his nose and made him look very young indeed.

'Is the battle still going on?'

'The noise is still there. It's worse. I've got to get out of here, got to get back, see if the M.O. can do anything for Peter. Must get someone for Peter – who's that?'

'What's happening now, Theo?'

'It's Haddon, dammit, it's Haddon, he's under the parapet, the mud's collapsed on him. Get him out of the mud, get the M.O. for Peter. Haddon, you fool, told you not to come out here, bloody fool –'

'Was it for rescuing Haddon that you were mentioned in dispatches?'

Theo stopped his head rolling, which had started again and lay very still. 'Mentioned in dispatches. Mentioned in dispatches –' he said, his voice oddly flat, and then he stopped and lay quietly again.

Max could have kicked himself. He'd done it wrong, totally wrong. One of the books he'd read had been quite specific on that point. Don't damage the time scale, the writer had said. If you are taking a patient through an experience remember that for him it is occurring in the present. He is experiencing the now. To shift to a more remote past, or to a time which is, to the patient's understanding, still to come will cause confusion. If this happens inadvertently it is wiser to terminate the session, to return to the matter under review on another occasion if this is required –

'Theo,' Max said softly. 'Theo, the battle is over. Your friends are dead. You must accept this, that they are dead. The battle is over, Theo. Do you understand that?'

'Yes,' Theo said and his face began to smooth out, for it had creased as he wept. 'Yes. The battle is over.'

'Your friends are dead, Theo.' Max said it as gently as he could. 'They are dead but you are alive, Theo. You must learn to live again without remembering what happened.'

'Yes.'

'Soon you'll wake up, Theo. You won't be asleep any more. You'll be awake and remember that we have talked, and you'll remember that now the battle is over and your friends are dead and you must learn to live again without remembering them.'

'Yes.'

'When you wake up, you'll feel very good.'

'Yes.'

'The good way you feel will last and you will be peaceful.'

'Yes.'

'Then,' and Max drew a deep breath. 'Then wake up, Theo. Now.'

Theo opened his eyes and blinked, closed them again and then opened them, much as a child does when leaving sleep behind and yawned and turned his head easily on the pillow.

'Hello there,' he said a little huskily. 'How are we getting on?'

'Very well,' Max said guardedly. 'As far as I can tell. You tell me. How do you feel?'

'Marvellous,' Theo said and stretched again, thrusting his arms so that the blanket fell away and he was half bare. He was sleekly muscled and smooth and his skin was still faintly tanned from his weeks in the convalescent home in which he had spent last summer. Max thought of his own pallid stocky shape and wished he had as good a body.

'I'm not so sure – what did we talk about?' he said and yawned again.

'You can't remember?'

Theo frowned. 'Not entirely. I know we talked, but I'm not sure what I said – I know we talked and that –' He shook his head and Max bit his lip. Dammit, he thought. Damn it all to hell and back. I should have told him to remember what we said, not just that we talked. I've made a mess of this, an awful mess –

'Well, it doesn't matter.' Theo sat up and swung his legs over the side of the couch, making Max move his chair back. 'It doesn't matter. Whatever you did, I feel marvellous, I really do. I haven't felt like this for – oh, I can't remember when.'

He stopped then, sitting on the edge of the couch with his legs dangling over the side and stared at Max with his face set in a solemn expression.

'It seems all wrong. My friends are dead, and I'm alive, But there it is. The battle's over, isn't it? Life has to go on.' He jumped down then and padded over to the screen in the corner. 'It is all right if I dress?'

'Yes,' Max said, staring after him, a little bemused. 'Yes, of course. Come back to my desk here when you're ready.'

He turned his chair to the desk and moving almost automatically folded the blankets neatly and set the pillow straight on the couch before sitting down again, and staring down at his papers. Theo was whistling softly behind the screen as he dressed and Max tilted his head to listen to him. Was it really as easy as this? Was this all there was to curing a man of the sort of misery Theo had been suffering? It was hard to believe, but it seemed to be so. Theo had come in looking as though he'd been hunted for the past weeks by all the hounds of hell, and now he was coming out from behind the screen knotting his tie and whistling contentedly beneath his breath. It seemed incredible, but there it was.

Max's spirits began to rise. 'Well, Theo?'

'Max, I'm very grateful. I wasn't sure you could help, to tell the truth. I was – well, never mind that. But you've been quite marvellous and I couldn't be more grateful. I'll tell Letty – she'll be glad too, that's certain. We open in just a fortnight, you know, and she was getting very anxious about me.' He grinned happily at Max. 'I could kick myself now for not letting you open your bag of tricks sooner. Thanks Max. You'll send me the bill, of course.'

'Good heavens –' Max began but Theo shook his head firmly.

'Of course you will. How else could I live with myself if I didn't pay my way? I can afford it, you know! You don't have to treat me like a charity case at your hospital. I must go, Max. Letty'll want to know how things are. Thanks again. Enormously.'

And as Theo sent the door clicking closed behind him and went whistling down the stairs, Max sat and stared after him, his face blank but his eyes very bright indeed.

19

'It really was quite extraordinary,' Max said. 'I'd read a lot about it of course, but reading doesn't exactly prepare you for the reality, does it?'

'I don't know,' Emilia said. 'I've never had much reality of any sort. It's all been rather dull. I do wish I'd been there.'

He frowned at that. 'Well, of course, any treatment of that sort has to be a matter between patient and doctor. One couldn't have people there just to watch.'

'Oh, of course not.' She opened her eyes wide at him. 'I realize that. But doctors do have help sometimes, don't they? Nurses and so forth?'

'Oh, nurses.' He dismissed them with a wave of his hand. 'Yes, of course. But you're not a nurse. You're a typist. So you could hardly be present when a patient has a treatment.'

'I'm not so sure about that. There's another typist at Nellie's – she works for Sir Aaron, and she always sits in the clinics for his consultations, because he so much hates writing notes that he won't do it. So she sits there, behind the patient where she won't be noticed, and writes down all he says when he takes a history. She told me all about it.'

'I'd forgotten that,' Max admitted. 'Everyone knows he does that of course – but it's not usual, I promise you.'

'But usual or not doesn't matter does it, for a doctor? As far as I can see they can do pretty well what they like, once they're qualified. I listen to the way the Bursar and the Secretary talk and it's obvious they can't do anything they want to do unless the doctors co-operate.'

'Well, yes,' Max said. 'I suppose so – but there are traditions, you see, about what's medically proper and what isn't and –'

She shook her head at that. 'Well, I think it's different. What's done as far as I can tell is what a doctor wants to do. You could do anything you wanted now you're qualified and no one could stop you. As long as you did no harm of course.'

He stared at her for a long moment and then said slowly, 'Well, yes, I suppose so. Up to a point. I *could* do what I want now, couldn't I?'

'You're a doctor. And a good one, obviously. You helped this patient you were talking about didn't you? You must be very good.' And she looked at him with that wide candid gaze that he was now becoming used to from her and he relaxed and even basked in it a little; so much approval couldn't fail to be agreeable and he enjoyed it.

'Er – you realize that you really shouldn't mention that patient to anyone else, don't you? I know you don't know who he is, of course, and I wouldn't dream of saying, but all the same –'

'Oh, of course! I know how important it is to be discreet and I wouldn't say a word to anyone. I've learned a lot since I've been at Nellie's. It isn't long I know, but I'm frightfully quick, and I'm frightfully keen too. That helps, doesn't it? I want to be quick because I want to – well, never mind –'

He smiled then. 'Oh dear, here I've been chattering on and on about my own doings and never asked you about your own! It's very ill-mannered of me and I do apologize. It's just that I got a bit involved with this patient and –'

'I do understand,' she said and leaned forwards and patted his arm. 'I knew you were frightfully busy and concerned about something and that was why I suggested this concert. It's so handy that my mother has so many tickets to so many things, and I thought it would do you good to relax a bit. And you'd seemed quite pleased about going to see that play, so –'

'Oh, I was, I was. It was most interesting.' He had in fact been very bored by *Little Women* but she had been so anxious to please him that he had hidden his *ennui* most carefully. 'And this afternoon's concert was too.' And he bent his head to drink the tea that the waiter had at last brought them, after a half-hour's wait in the busy Lyons' tea shop in Wigmore Street where they had repaired as soon as the music ended.

'Oh dear, I was afraid of that,' she said calmly and poured a cup of tea for herself.

'Afraid of what?'

'That you'd be as bored by the music as you were by *Little Women*. What would you really enjoy most, then?'

He flushed and shook his head and tried to argue with her and then shook his head again and laughed a little ruefully. 'You are an odd girl, Emilia! I never met anyone at all like you. First you ask a fellow to things the way well – you have to admit most girls don't, and then you don't sulk if the fellow didn't really like it as much as you did! Most girls expect you to adore everything they do, and take it as a personal affront if you dare to say you don't.'

'Ah, well, I'm not most girls, am I? I'm me.'

'Yes,' he said. 'You definitely are.'

'Well?'

'Well what?'

'What sort of things do you most enjoy? Not plays and not concerts – what then?'

'I do like plays! Some. There's one that looks awfully interesting that's opening next week. It's fearfully funny and – er – there are some splendid actors in it –'

She raised her eyebrows at that. 'Opening next week! You sound just like my mother – she likes nothing better than to know about everything in advance. If she isn't at the first night of a thing she doesn't think it's worth going at all, and if she doesn't know what's going to happen in the theatre and so forth well before it does she feels a total failure! I never dreamed you were such a fashionable sort of person!'

'I'm not. It's just that this one has Theo in it. You remember him, don't you? He's a cousin of ours – he was at the thing of Letty's where I first met you. And I've been interested in the play for that reason.' He kept his head down, a little alarmed at how much he'd said. A girl as sharp as this one had to be watched. It would never do if she made the jump between mention of Theo and the anonymous patient he had told her about so eagerly. He hadn't meant to pour it all out, but it had been impossible not to. He'd been so full of it all, so amazed at his own success that he had yearned to discuss it with a sympathetic person, and his instinct had warned him not to speak to his father, for quite apart from the forcefully expressed disdain for people he dismissed as 'lunatic-asylum doctors' he had been so abstracted and quiet these past few days that he was totally unapproachable. And the people at Nellie's – no, they too would be most dismissive, he was sure, if not positively disapproving, for it had been a considerable risk he had taken in treating a patient in so advanced a manner on the basis of so little experience. So Emilia's ready interest had been very welcome to him, and he'd been grateful to her for offering her listening ear.

'Oh,' she said now, apparently making no connection at all. 'Yes, I remember. That madly good-looking man Letty put in that film Mother is involved in? I know the one you mean. I believe the film is quite splendid. Mother saw it last week, and it is to be shown in various cinemas very soon, and Mother says everyone will be quite besotted with Theo Caspar once they see it. And you say he's in a play that's opening next week?'

'Mmm. He is rather interesting-looking, isn't he?'

'I can't actually remember,' she said and smiled at him. 'I'm not particularly interested in good looks you know. I've been Jonty's sister too long to notice, really.'

'He is good-looking indeed,' Max said politely and reached for another cream cake.

'They'll make a lovely couple, won't they?' Emilia said. 'Once it's all sorted out.'

'Are you still on about that?' He was amused. 'Still *noticing* things?'

'Oh, I'm right,' she said calmly. 'They've made up their minds to it, Jonty told me. Your father's fussing a bit I gather, but they've made up their minds.'

He put down his cup and stared at her. 'My father is – look, what is this? How is it you know more about what happens in my family than I do?'

'Maybe you've been too busy about your own affairs to pay much attention. I don't have many affairs of my own so I have time to notice.'

'You say that they're going to – but Johanna's said nothing

to me! Though I suppose –' And he remembered how the whole family had been rather abstracted this week, and not just his father. His mother had gone about looking somewhat anxious, but he'd put that down to the sort of things that bothered mothers; maybe the cook had decided to leave or something of that tedious nature. He had all the self-absorption of the greatly loved and was rarely as aware as he might be of the feelings and needs of the rest of his family, and since Tim's death last year he'd probably been more self-centred than ever. So he'd not paid much attention to his mother, or to his sister who, now he came to think of it, had been looking rather peaky.

'You say my father's cutting up a bit?'

'So Jonty says. I gather he doesn't like our family much,' and she giggled, a soft little sound that was very agreeable.

'He said that, of course, but I didn't pay much attention –' Max said and then flushed brick red. 'Heavens, that sounded dreadful! I am sorry, Emilia! It's just that – I believe they knew each other in the dark ages and had some sort of disagreement that – that's why Dad feels that way. It's all boring olden days stuff. I don't suppose he means to be unpleasant –'

She laughed. 'Maybe my mother and your father had a love affair?'

He laughed too, throwing his head back with real gusto. 'My father? My dear girl, don't be ridiculous! He's the most upright man in the world! And he adores my mother beyond anything. That cat won't jump, I promise you –'

'Well, whatever it is I dare say they'll sort it all out –' She pushed the tea-pot to one side and leaned forwards with her elbows on the table and her chin propped on her hands. 'Max, I've been thinking –'

'Mmm?' He was still absorbed in thoughts of the family problems that he seemed not to have noticed.

'This new work you've been doing. It does sound marvellously exciting. Very important, too.'

He was all attention at once. 'Oh, it is, it is. I've read so much that really – well, I'm getting more and more interested. It's becoming more and more clear to me that there are a great many illnesses that people have and which make them feel ill and actually cause symptoms like heart disturbances and breathing difficulties and so forth but which aren't yet fully understood. There's been some excellent work done in Vienna, of course – Professor Freud seems to be a very sound man indeed, very sound – and a good deal of effort's being made to advance this field of study, but it's still very new. I mean a chap could do worse than making a speciality of it, couldn't he?'

He smiled at her, almost shyly. He'd hardly dared to think this himself, and having put it into words this way made it rather alarming. 'Well, maybe,' he finished lamely.

'That's exactly what I was thinking! I was wondering – why just borrow Caplan's rooms when you need them? Why not take proper rooms of your own, and put up your plate and specialize in these problems? I'm sure you'd be awfully successful and –'

He shook his head at her, amazed. 'But my dear Emilia, there's more to it than that! I mean, I'd need to go to lectures, learn more –' The habit of the medical student still hung closely about his shoulders and he could not imagine any other way of being involved in a field of medical endeavour. 'It'd take a long time – and I'm not even sure I'd know how to do that. I mean, go to Vienna, study there? Or go to somewhere like York? The Retreat's a lunatic asylum there that's very modern, I'm told and –'

She shook her head impatiently. 'You're wrong, you know, Max. I've been asking questions at Nellie's, listening – noticing things – and truly you're wrong. You could set up as soon as you like. You're *qualified* now! No one could stop you. That's what I mean about doctors being able to do what they want. You could do it. Of course you could go on learning and studying – but you've done awfully well already for that patient you told me about and that's just from reading about it. With more patients to get experience, and more reading, why you could start tomorrow.'

'Well,' he said uncertainly. 'In principle, I suppose you're right but –'

'I dare say you'd need help, of course. I mean this sort of work isn't like surgery, is it?' Her tone was very casual but there was an air of tension about her. 'It's more like general medicine, but with a lot more talking going on. How long did it take you, did you say, to write down the notes you were making about the things that patient told you?'

'Oh, I was there for ages after he'd gone,' Max said. 'I wanted to get it all down while it was fresh in my memory, and –'

'Exactly!' she said. 'But think how much easier it would be to give people this treatment if you had a secretary sitting out of the patient's view, behind a screen or something so as not to upset them, and writing it all down for you? And then typing it all neatly so you could read it easily and not worry about your handwriting?'

He blinked and stared at her. 'My handwriting's rather frightful,' he said slowly.

'So's Sir Aaron's. I rather think that might be why he has to have a secretary there when he does his clinics. The girl who does it showed me the notes he'd scribbled her once and they were simply ghastly.'

'Yes,' Max said, still staring at her. 'Yes, I've seen them too –'

'The thing is, Max, I've been thinking, as I said. And I wondered – look, if you want to start up your own practice, I'd be a marvellous secretary for you. Simply marvellous. I've told you, I'm quick, and I notice things and my typing's good too. I've practised till my knuckles could hardly move! I wouldn't want any payment either, not till you really got started. I'm madly well off really, you see. My father left me masses, more than I need, because I really don't buy lots of frocks or maquillage like other girls do and – well, it'd be wonderful for me. I do so much want to be *useful*, you see. That's why I'm at Nellie's. And I think I could be ever so useful to you. Wouldn't I?'

It really was quite absurd what a fuss he was making about it all, Lewis told himself. All he had to do was tell Johanna firmly that he couldn't ever be happy about her marriage to a man like Jonty Collingbourne and then go and see Claudette and tell her the same and that would be that. But every time he saw

Johanna's stricken face when she looked so appealingly at him, every time he saw Miriam's puzzlement, he was lost. He'd have to give in –

And then he would visualize a future in which Claudette was a member of his family, his own child's mother-in-law and how that would mean they would meet often. She would be free to visit as frequently as she chose, free to be part of his life for always and always, a joint holder of the future that would exist in his grandchildren. And he would close his eyes at the horror of such a sight and be thrown back into a state of confusion. What was he to *do*?

If it hadn't been for Max he might not have done anything, would have been frozen into inaction by his love for his daughter. He would have gone on allowing his own confusion to run round and round in his mind until at last the sheer passage of time would have resolved it all, one way or the other. But Max came home from the concert he had said he was going to on that warm Sunday afternoon, alight with excitement to throw his father at last into a state of determination. And action.

He had been sitting alone in the drawing-room since six o'clock, when Miriam had pleaded a headache and gone to lie down in her small boudoir, with, unusually for him, the brandy decanter and a glass beside him. He was by no means a drinker, but sometimes enjoyed good vintage brandy when he was quite sure there was no possibility that he would be called upon to see a patient, let alone operate, and this weekend was such a one. Roger Scudder, the other senior surgeon at Nellie's, was on call and he was free to do as he chose.

So, he sat beside the open window that looked down into Leinster Terrace, listening to the faint sound of the rustling from the new leaves on the branches and the cries of the children playing across the Bayswater Road in Hyde Park and tried to relax.

Max's arrival at first seemed welcome; he knew nothing of this wretched business about Jonty Collingbourne, for he and Miriam had reached a tacit agreement to keep it a matter private to Johanna until a decision had been reached, and it would, he felt, be comforting to gossip with his son, perhaps talk of Nellie's affairs, and generally be as comfortable as they used to be, before all this fuss started.

But Max put paid to that at once.

'Dad!' he said, almost before he had come into the room, throwing his soft hat on to the sofa in front of the fireplace before coming across the room to the window embrasure where Lewis was sitting. 'Dad, I must talk to you. I've made a decision, and I want to tell you about it at once. I know you won't be frightfully keen on it, but if you hear me out, I think you'll see it my way. Now –' And he sat down facing his father and grinned at him. 'Listen. You've wanted to know what I intend to do now I'm qualified, right?'

'Indeed I have,' Lewis said, and smiled at him. 'Brandy, m'boy?'

'No thanks. Full of tea. Well, I've decided. You've been a bit rude about it in the past, I know, but I dare say you'll come round. The thing is, I want to be an alienist.'

Lewis stared at him over the rim of his glass and his eyes narrowed.

'What did you say?'

'I knew you wouldn't be too pleased at first, but you'll see. Look, it's an up-and-coming speciality, I'm quite certain. I know up to now it's been just the dustbin for bad doctors – but I don't intend to go and bury myself in some ghastly lunatic asylum and do no more real work for the rest of my life the way some of 'em do. I want to be more like – oh, Tuke, and Maudsley. I read a lot of the things he wrote, and he really was a marvellous doctor. I wish I'd made up my mind earlier than this, because I'd have loved to have talked to him, but he died last year. He was fearfully old, of course, but he was working right up to the end and he'd have been able to tell me a lot – anyway, the thing is, Dad, I've made up my mind. It's what I'm most interested in, and I want to start soon. I'm taking rooms in Harley Street and Emilia Collingbourne says she'll help me with the secretarial side and so forth – and that'll be very useful, of course, because there're reams of notes for these nerve cases, far more than there ever are for surgical ones, and even ordinary medical ones and – actually, she's been really encouraging about it all –'

'Emilia Collingbourne?'

'Yes.' Max reddened a little. 'I know you said you aren't too keen on that family, Dad, but really, that is a bit silly, isn't it? I mean she's a spiffing girl. Frightfully plain and all that, but so sensible, as good as any of the fellows in our year. We've been talking and talking about this, and she's shown me that there's really no reason why I shouldn't try. She's awfully level-headed. It makes a change from some of the girls you meet, even the nurses at Nellie's and –'

He faltered as his father stared at him silently. 'Look, Dad, I know you aren't keen on my being an alienist,' he went on almost desperately. 'But really, it's all I'm interested in. And I've definitely decided. So please, wish me well, and don't try to stop me. Because it won't make any difference. I'll still do it. I'm qualified now, after all –'

But still Lewis said nothing. He emptied his glass and filled it again and drained it as Max stared at him, his eyes wide, and then, without a word, got to his feet and walked out of the drawing-room leaving Max sitting alone in the window seat. He heard the door slam and felt the silence come surging back into the house as his father's footsteps went clattering down the front steps on to the street.

20

Claudette had had a most boring afternoon. All the people with whom she might have spent the day were otherwise engaged, out of town or occupied with their tedious family affairs, like David Lazar, her current favourite companion, who had gone off to some ghastly family wedding (and how strange these Jewish families were, having their weddings on Sundays) and her dear old friend Marie Reid, who had gone down to the country to see her grandchild christened. (Marie with a grandchild! It was impossible that we should be that old. She's a year younger than I am, damn her!) Even Jonty had taken it into his head to spend the day elsewhere, no doubt with his precious Johanna (and Claudette had to admit she was getting more than a shade bored with his total preoccupation with her) and Emilia, whose company would have been better than nothing, had come in late from some afternoon jaunt and then had gone straight to her room murmuring about the need to practise her typing.

So Claudette sat before the small fire in her drawing-room wearing one of last year's tea gowns (for there was little point in dressing up when there was no one about to see her) and desultorily reading a dull book and feeling thoroughly sorry for herself.

Which was why, when she heard the doorbell ring below she sat up with great alacrity and hopefulness, and then ran to lean over the upper banisters to hiss at the footman that she was at home to whoever it was, however dull, and then went back to the drawing-room to smooth her hair before the mirror and straighten her gown and wait for whoever it might be.

When she saw Lewis standing there at the door she couldn't

help it. The smile of welcome that spread over her face was a wide one, not in the least coquettish, and she held out her arms to him in a spontaneous gesture of welcome that made the chiffon sleeves of her rose-coloured frock fall to reveal her round white arms in a most beguiling way. She looked as she felt; extremely happy to see him.

He had meant, of course, to be very hard indeed, right from the start, and had she been as he would have expected her to be from their previous meetings over the past few months, which was fashionably bright and mocking, it would have been easy. But she was so like the old Claudette had been long ago before her father had died, before she had become the flippant Gaiety Girl whose only interest was her own well-being, before she had revolted him by so brazenly marrying for money, that he forgot for a second why he was there and said, 'Hello Claudette,' as though there were only the most amiable of relationships between them.

'Lewis, my dear old friend,' she cried. 'You are precisely who I most needed to see this afternoon! I've been so lonely and miserable here on my own. Do come and sit down and we shall have a cosy prose. I'll ring for some tea – or would you prefer something a little better than that?'

He collected himself, furiously aware that he had lost the first move in what he had known all through the hard twenty minute walk from Leinster Terrace to Vere Street would be a difficult encounter. 'Nothing. Thank you,' he said shortly, making his voice as crisp as he could and she stood there and stared at him for a moment and then, with a small sigh, sat down again on her sofa, setting her arms spread wide along the back in a posture which she knew showed her to advantage, minimizing as it did the slight sag that had appeared in her figure.

'Dear me!' she said. 'So cross? And here was I hoping you'd realized how very dismal you'd been when we were at Simister, and come to make amends!'

'Amends!' he said and came in to stand on the hearth-rug in front of her. 'If anyone has to make any amends, it's you, not me!'

'Why?' She tilted her chin to look up at him, and at once the commanding position he thought he'd taken became less commanding, so that he felt more like a humble suppliant than the determined adversary he meant to be. 'Whatever have I done to upset you, my dear man, apart from being an old friend who has always held you in the highest esteem, and a –'

'Look, Claudette,' he said, and thrust his slightly shaking hands into his pockets. 'Can we get something clear? I have been married to a woman I love very dearly for twenty-three years. Whatever there may have been between us before that time is – is nothing. You understand me? It's as though it never happened and –'

'Oh, Lewis, Lewis, you're so wrong, so very wrong, you know! Why be ashamed of what you were, of what we shared? If it had been after you met and loved your precious Miriam I could perhaps understand it – well, perhaps, though I do think you are absurdly punctilious in these matters. Much too English! But you actually take punctiliousness to the point of – of idiocy! In the days when we were so – close' – and she allowed her eyes to open slightly wider so that she gave him a provocative little glance – 'Miriam had no place in your life. So how can there be any disloyalty to her in recalling what we shared? None at all! Indeed you must agree that it contributed to your later happiness. You cannot deny you learned much from me of the art of love, Lewis, my dearest. That some of that education benefited your Miriam and –'

'Stop that at once!' he said harshly. 'It's because of this sort of – of nonsense from you that I don't want to see you again. Why I don't want my children seeing yours. I know all the way through to the middle of my being that any connection between your family and mine is bound to cause problems. That there can be no happiness for them or for me and surely you too if it isn't nipped in the bud now.'

'Nipped in the bud? D'you mean my Jonty and your girl?' She laughed and abandoned her pose on the sofa and stood up to go to the mantleshelf to find her cigarettes and light one with a practised flick of her wrist. 'You're more than foolish if you think you can do that, Lewis! These two are totally besotted with each other, and that's all about it. You can't nip in the bud a flower as full-blown as that one is! I'm already bored out of my mind by the way he goes on and on about her –'

'You've encouraged them!' he said accusingly, still standing there with his hands pushed hard into his trouser-pockets as though he were afraid to take them out, lest he might hit out at her if he didn't maintain constant control. 'You set about captivating her just to amuse yourself and to – to anger me and –'

She frowned then and stared at him with her head on one side. 'You know, Lewis,' she said softly. 'I'm beginning to revise my ideas about you. For many years I thought you had forgotten me entirely. That I had been to you just some little fly-by-night you'd enjoyed and then abandoned without a second thought. That once you'd found your passion for your Miriam it was as though I'd never existed. But now, all this fuss you're making, why, it makes me suspect that in fact you were more attached to me than you ever let me know. That you've nursed a *tendresse* for me for all these years that, now we've met again, has been woken up again. That you actually have an affection for me that goes beyond anything I feel for you. To tell the truth, *mon ami*, all I feel is the sentimentality that always attaches to the associations of one's youth, and the challenge, shall we say, of captivating a man who is, on the surface, so determined not to be captivated. But for you it's different, isn't it? You really *care* about me.' And she lifted her chin and stared at him with a look of pure triumph on her face and then laughed at him, staring into his eyes mockingly and laughing aloud.

It was more than he could bear; more than any man could bear, he told himself confusedly, and he stepped towards her, pulling his hands out of his pockets as he did so, not sure what he meant to do but driven beyond his own control. He lifted one hand as though to strike her, though it was so totally against his nature ever to strike any person, and she flinched for a moment and then set her lips tightly closed and lifted her chin even higher and put up one hand to seize his wrist. They stood there for what seemed to be a second so elongated, so stretched that they could hear the time tramping past and then she smiled, very slowly letting her lips open so that her teeth, small and white as sea-washed pebbles showed clearly and her tongue tip appeared neatly between them. She moved with what seemed to him to be the same measured slowness, but what was in reality great swiftness, pushing his wrist up and backwards so that her hand was behind his head, and then let go, sliding her hand on to the crown of his head and pulling it forwards inexorably.

His own hands behaved as though they were creatures with their own volition, moving forward, curving round to take her in the small of the back, pulling her towards his body, and it was as though the memory of how she had felt all those years ago was still in them more vividly than it had ever been in his mind. They held her, those hands, digging in their fingers with an intensity that made her whimper – and it was the whimper so close to his own lips that he could have made the sound himself that made him realize that their mouths had met, that she was kissing him with all the old skill and all the old passion.

'No.' He tried to say it, but all that emerged was a muffled sound that could have been ecstasy rather than the distress and rage it was and she clung on even harder, holding his head against hers with a barnacle grip, and again he tried to pull back and couldn't.

It was, he thought later when he was fit to think at all, like something out of one of the old Lyceum melodramas, it all happened so pat. They had been so completely alone, so buried in their own miniature maelstrom that they had heard nothing, been aware of nothing apart from themselves and then, as they parted because Claudette at last let go and stepped back, he felt rather than saw them behind him, and whirled to see Jonty standing in the doorway with Johanna a step behind him, staring at them with her face as grey as putty and looking so appalled that it was almost funny.

'Johanna –' he said huskily and coughed and tried again, and knew he sounded stupid, apologetic, craven, sickeningly trite. 'My dear, I didn't know you were there –'

'Evidently,' Jonty said, and turned to look at Johanna, a mocking glint in his eyes but she just glanced at him, then at her father again, and then shook her head and turned as though to go. Jonty put out his hand and said in what was no doubt meant to be a reassuring tone but which came out merely jocular, 'Oh, Jo, my love, don't fuss! I dare say there's a perfectly good explanation and anyway, one mustn't be too censorious these days –'

She shook her head at him, and then looked at Claudette, and Lewis said loudly, 'Johanna, I have to explain –' just as Claudette said easily, 'My dears, *quel brouhaha*! So inopportune, *n'est ce pas*? Well, no need to –' And Johanna put her hands up to her ears and once more shook her head.

'Johanna –' Lewis said again but she would not listen to him, and turned and this time unhindered by Jonty ran out of the room and down the stairs and Jonty said hastily, 'Don't fret, sir, I'll deal with it all –' and went plunging after her, leaving Lewis and Claudette standing side by side on the hearth-rug.

'For pity's sake, my love, do be reasonable!' Jonty said again, and tried to put his arm about her shoulders. 'You're really making far too much of this, you know! So he kissed her! Dammit all, what does a kiss matter?'

She turned a face blazing with anger at him, shaking off his arm. 'Is that all it means to you when we – when it's me? Something that doesn't matter?'

'Of course not, you little goose. It's different when it's us, of course it is. We're young and in love and they're old and – well, it's different for us! But to carry on like this just because you saw your father – dammit, you'd think I'd have more reason to fuss than you. My Maman's a widow, defenceles and all that apart from me, and your father's a respectable married man and so forth. And do you see me throwing conniption fits and –'

'You ought to!' she cried furiously. 'You ought to! You should be as sick as I am, as revolted as – oh, why can't you understand? How she could – how he – and you, that you can sit there and –' she bit her lip and shook her head and opened her mouth to speak again and then burst into tears, covering her face with both hands as she flung herself into an ecstasy of weeping.

There was a muffled slam as the front door closed and Jonty got to his feet and went to peer through the window of the small morning-room to which he had taken her when he had caught up with her trying to open the front door to go rushing out, and saw Lewis go hurtling down the steps and along the road in the direction of Oxford Street and watched him through the net curtains until he was out of sight. And then sighed and came back to the armchair where Johanna was sitting in a crumpled heap weeping as though her heart would break there and then with a resounding crack.

'Darling,' he said and knelt in front of her, 'Look, darling, he's gone. Back home, I imagine, and no harm done. Let's leave it at that, hmm? Pretend we never saw that bit of hugging and so forth and say no more? It's none of our affair, after all. My Maman is a grown-up lady, perfectly well able to take care of herself, and I dare say your father is just as sensible. Leave it at that and –'

'Your mother is a – a – she's no better than a – I can't even say it!' she blazed at him and began to weep again, wiping the tears from her blotched face with the back of her hand.

His face tightened and he sat back on his heels. 'Now look, Johanna, I know how you feel. Or I suppose I do. But I don't think that gives you leave to slang my mother. I said it before and I'll say it again, it's none of our business! I don't give a damn what they get up to – it's boring! But let's be fair, for pity's sake, and agree that no one person is to blame for –'

'She is, she is, she *is*,' Johanna cried passionately, sitting up now and glaring at him. 'She *is* and if you don't see that she – she must have tormented my father and forced him to –'

Jonty tried to laugh then, but his face was still tight and anger was increasing in him. 'Look Jo, I know you've had a very sheltered life and so forth but this is too much! To suggest your father is a total innocent abroad is to make a fool of him, and to suggest my mother's some sort of – Mata Hari is to make her – well! Never mind. But do be sensible, for heaven's sake and –'

'If being sensible means being as wicked as you, then I won't be sensible,' she cried passionately. 'How can you be so – so casual, so ordinary about it? It's dreadful, dreadful and –'

'Now you're really annoying me,' he said sharply. 'I love you, Johanna. I've changed in a million ways to please you, but I'm damned if I'm going down this road with you. You sound like a grandmother prosing on and on about morality and how people used to be, and how they ought to be – it's perfectly ridiculous to make such a drama out of something so very minor. For heaven's sake, Jo, people are kissing and more all the time these days. The war changed everything! Maybe in the old days there was something in it, all this faithfulness and so forth, but not any more. Your father's no worse than a million other people, and nor is my Maman. That's the way people are these days and –'

She was sitting very straight now, staring at him and her face, which had begun to regain its colour, was white once more.

'Do you really believe that?' she asked and her voice was very quiet, the note of hysteria that had been there quite gone.

'Of course I do,' he said, not seeing the pit that yawned beneath his feet. 'I see more of the world than you do, my darling, and I know. Of course it is.'

'Then you'd better call a cab so that I can go home,' she said in a tight little voice and shrank back against the armchair as he tried to reach out and take her in his arms. 'No! Don't touch me, don't you dare touch me! I'm going home at once.'

'But what –' he began, bewildered. 'I don't –'

'And I never want to see you again,' she went on and her voice began to rise. 'Do you understand? Never again.'

'But why? Because of that stupid business upstairs? What the hell does that have to do with you and me? Nothing, nothing at all!'

'No. Not because of upstairs. Because of *you*.'

'But what have I done?'

'If you really believe that faithfulness doesn't matter, that it's all right for married people, whatever their ages, to go about kissing other married people and – and – well, then there's nothing we have to say to each other any more. Nothing at all. Goodbye, Jonty. I'm going home. And don't ever speak to me again.'

21

May blurred into a damp June as London filled up with American visitors bent on escaping the threat of Prohibition at home and eager to share the tennis at Wimbledon and the Peace Celebrations being arranged for July, and the Lackland family slowly found a routine of life within which they could appear to be tolerably comfortable. To outside eyes, that is. For themselves they knew that for every one of them something had changed; that they had been driven apart in a way that even Tim's death had not driven them. Indeed, that tragedy had drawn them closer together, made them an even tighter unit, so much that other members of the clan, notably the Oram girls, had become quite waspish about them and their aloofness from family affairs.

But now it was all different. Johanna went about looking white and pinched, and seemed to have aged five years overnight. She looked thinner and stopped paying much attention to how she looked, only putting on a pretty frock when her mother chose one for her and insisted she wore it, and completely stopping her use of maquillage. Miriam watched her and grieved, but said nothing; over the years she had come to curb her original youthful ebullience, for she had learned from Lewis how necessary it was sometimes to say nothing. He had often needed to be quiet, to be left to think his own thoughts in his own time without prying from her, and she passed on what she had been taught by him to her dealings with her children. So, she said nothing to Johanna about why she was so desolate, simply waiting for her to speak and reveal the source of her unhappiness.

But Johanna said nothing, and neither did Lewis. He went about the house – when he was there – with his face as still and tight as his daughter's but spent more and more time at Nellie's so that the family saw little of him. Peter was groaning over the efforts demanded of him by his matriculation examinations – something that at least gave Miriam the chance to be a helpful mother – and Max was so totally absorbed in his own doings that he hardly noticed that anything was amiss at home at all.

Or seemed not to do so, certainly showing no signs of awareness of problems when he was at Leinster Terrace. He would sit at the breakfast-table chattering cheerfully of the day's news, of the way Suzanne Lenglen was dominating the first post-war tennis tournament at the All England Club, of the chances of the very topically named 'Grand Parade' winning the Derby, of the doings of Clemenceau and Woodrow Wilson and the Fourteen Points of the Peace Plan, of Alcock and Brown and their incredible flight over the Atlantic, of anything but personal matters. He said nothing about how he was spending his days, of his own busy plans, of the reasons for the many telephone calls that came for him, because he felt it would be easier that way. He knew his father was displeased by his plans, but though that saddened him, it did not deter him. He would go his own way, but do so silently. He was well aware of the tension in his home, but put it down to his father's anger at him, and grimly refused to show any response to it. So, he would just fold the newspaper after his breakfast peroration and kiss his mother and sister and ruffle his young brother's hair and go, following his silent father down the steps outside the front door on his way to Nellie's.

Once there after their equally silent journey they would part, Lewis to immerse himself in the operating theatres and clinics and wards, and Max to go through the day's work demanded of a senior dresser, which was the status of the newly qualified doctor, as fast as he could. His heart, his mind, every atom of his interest was elsewhere, in his own plans.

Each lunchtime he would meet Emilia at the Lyons' tea shop in the Strand, a few minutes walk away from the hospital, to eat poached eggs on toast and drink stewed tea and talk and plan interminably. He had at first suggested that she share his lunch in the medical common room, but she had demurred at that.

'I'm just a secretary, Max,' she had said earnestly. 'Making too much of a point of our – er – professional connection wouldn't be wise and if we lunch together, well, you know how people talk here at Nellie's! It's a positive hotbed of gossip –'

So he had agreed and Lyons' anonymous tea-shop it was, and Emilia relaxed. She knew perfectly well that a great chasm now yawned between her family and Max's. Jonty in his misery had poured out all his woes to her, almost in tears as he told her how Johanna refused to speak to him or to come to the telephone when he called, and returned all his letters unopened. Her mother had been terse in the extreme when Emilia had asked her, as innocently as she could, what the problem was with the Lacklands, so she had wisely bitten her tongue and said no more. The less either family knew of how involved she and Max had become over their plan to set him up in practice the better. She had worked hard, heaven knew she had worked hard, to reach this stage of friendship with him. It had been a battle all the way, and she was not going to lose her trophy to some stupid family argument. What happened between Lewis and Claudette interested her not a whit, and what happened between Jonty and Johanna even less. She cared only for one thing; her friendship with Max. It was a thriving young shoot at the moment, a mainly businesslike relationship, but it would change, it would grow, it would ripen into what she really wanted – as long as she was given time and propinquity. And that demanded a certain amount of subterfuge; eating lunch in the view of curious eyes which might communicate what they had noticed to Max's father was the last thing that would help.

So each lunchtime there they sat at the little marble-topped table in the corner as the frilly capped and aproned nippies bustled about among the tea and toast and cream cakes and the little string quartet in the corner scraped away at their eternal selection from "Chu Chin Chow", still playing to packed houses at His Majesty's, and talked and talked and talked.

They pored over descriptions of the available rooms in

Harley Street and Wimpole Street, comparing the virtues of consulting-room plus dressing-room and small office against consulting-room with no dressing-room and shared office accommodation at half the rent and doing interminable sums on the backs of old envelopes which Max kept in every pocket. She had done all she could to persuade him to allow her to use some of her money to start the practice off but he had been adamant about that. It would all have to come out of his own pocket, or not at all. Bad enough she was to work for no salary to start with; he would not, could not, allow her to be more financially damaged than that.

Wisely, she had said no more. To push too hard on that would have been to destroy the whole hopeful plan, and it was too precious to risk. She could always spend money once they had taken the rooms, quietly making them look handsome with good furniture and pictures and plants in pots. Manlike, she told herself, he wouldn't realize such things cost as much as they did. And meanwhile it was heaven to sit there each day from half-past twelve to one o'clock with their heads together.

He had, tentatively, talked to some of his friends about what he was doing, choosing only those he knew would have the sense to keep their mouths shut, and who would be adventurous enough to approve, without making long faces at the unorthodoxy of setting up as a consultant before the ink on one's graduation diploma was dry. Two of them, Caplan and Forster, had been enthusiastic and had promised they would send him any nerve cases they might have as long as he promised to send suitable cases to them; and he began to realize, listening to them and talking to other more senior men who were already in practices of their own just how inter-locked the whole of the Harley Street consulting system was. Colleagues looked out for each other on the understanding they would share fees when relevant. It was a system that made him feel uneasy, but it existed and there it was; who was he to try and change it? And anyway, he had to establish himself before he could enjoy the luxury of becoming any sort of reformer.

Slowly, then, his plans took shape with Emilia doing most of the hard work of letter-writing to estate agents and the bank and the landlords, as he read more and more about his new speciality, and made copious notes about the sorts of treatments he would use on his patients once he had any. And he rewrote and embellished the notes he had made about his one and only patient so far, spending long hours every evening – often missing dinner, to his mother's unspoken distress – in his room reading and re-reading them.

He would have much preferred to see the patient himself rather than his notes, but that became less and less possible. He had of course tried to see Theo several times since their afternoon in Caplan's rooms, but somehow Theo had always been too busy.

'Can't manage it, old bean' he would clack cheerfully down the telephone at Max when he tried to talk to him. 'Never been so busy in my life! Rehearsing all the hours the good God sends, and several more besides, positively exhausted, and that's the truth of it. We're at the Shaftesbury all day and when I get away at night I simply fall into bed and descend into the most swinish of slumber. Sleeping like a baby these nights, Max, and I do thank you for that. That treatment of yours – really remarkable, what? Remarkable –'

And Max would stand there after he had hung up, holding the earpiece to his head still and listening to the faint burr and feeling uneasy. It shouldn't have been so easy, should it? Was mental catharsis really such a miracle cure? He had been well trained at Nellie's by very experienced and learned doctors. They had told him over and over again that only quacks would promise spectacular cures and immediate relief of symptoms. Real medicine was painstaking and slow. Miracles were rare in hospital wards and consulting-rooms, however common in the shadier purlieus of Harley Street, to which the quacks had penetrated. Don't seek them, don't offer them, he had been taught.

Yet here now was a patient telling him he had in fact wrought such a remarkable thing; and he could not believe it. There had to be more to it than this, didn't there? But deep beneath his doubts, he was full of exultation. He had found a way to help people with severe shell-shock. He would become a byword among the unhappy wreckage of the past four years, they would come to him in droves and he would cure them all as he had cured Theo, and Tim, wherever he was, would know and grin and nod his head in warm approval. Max was indeed a very confused and eager and self-absorbed young man that summer of 1919.

It was at the end of June when everyone in London was talking about the way the German fleet had been scuppered at Scapa Flow and was on tenterhooks waiting for the Germans to sign the Peace Treaty at last when he saw Theo again. Early in the month the film of *Caesar and Cleopatra* had opened at a cinema near Leicester Square and though the critics had been scornful – especially *Punch* and the *Illustrated London News* – the audiences had been enthusiastic about the actor who made his début in it.

Max had gone to see the film by himself and though he did not find it as dramatically satisfying as some films he had seen, still he was fascinated by Theo's performance. It seemed to him that the screen glowed with a special light when he appeared on it, and he had wondered at first if that was simply because it was so very odd to be sitting here in the stuffy red plush dark, breathing in the scent of dust and not humanity and Jeyes Fluid and watching a person he actually knew performing in that patch of silver.

But then he had decided that it wasn't that at all. Theo really could act, and that was, in fact, the cause of the film's overall disappointment. He was so very powerful as Mark Antony that he made the rest of the cast seem wooden and that gave the film a lopsided air. Max had emerged blinking into the light of the early evening, having crept away early from Nellie's in order to see the film, and stood staring up at the plane trees in their soft new green helmets and marvelled at the way Theo had managed to make him feel as though he really had been in ancient Egypt –

The film had been on now for three weeks when the notices about the opening of *Never Kiss and Tell*, the new farce at the Shaftesbury, went up. Letty, shrewd as ever when it came to publicity had all the posters clearly marked with Theo's name and the fact that he was currently appearing in *Caesar and Cleopatra* and several of the newspapers published squibs about the "new star in the West End" some making sardonic points about his inexperience, but others biding their time and their gibes till after the first night.

Max had decided of course that he was to see the play and had, in a moment of enthusiasm, bought five seats for the first night, only telling his family of his plans for a shared night out after he had done so. At first Miriam had clapped her hands softly and said eagerly, 'Oh, Max, yes, how lovely! I should like that above all things! I haven't been to the first night of a play for so long. They tell me it's all very exciting these days –'

But then she had seen the blank looks on her husband's and daughter's faces and subsided and, for a moment, it looked as though Max were to be left with four very expensive tickets on his hands. But happily Peter joined in, and cried eagerly, 'Perfect! I need to celebrate the end of those hateful exams – do let's, Dad –'

Lewis had looked up and had opened his mouth to speak and then closed it again as he caught sight of Miriam's face. She didn't look precisely upset, but that she wasn't happy was clear, and his guilt filled him with an even greater surge than those he had suffered this past month, if that were possible. He had behaved appallingly and he knew it, and had excoriated himself over and over again because of it but he had no right to distress his Miriam any more than he had already by being so tense and silent. She had been sinned against enough and he must stop heaping pain on her, he must – and somehow find a way to make his peace with Johanna who had treated him with the most remotely cool of attitudes ever since that ghastly Sunday.

So he managed to smile and said as amiably as he could. 'That's very good of you, Max. I'm sure we'll all enjoy it. Tomorrow, you say? Yes. I'll be sure to be home early –'

So the Lacklands had set out in the clear light of the late June evening to walk, as they usually preferred to do, to Marble Arch tube station to travel to Piccadilly Circus. The trains were always crowded these days, but that was very much better than struggling to find a cab at the end of an evening's entertainment, and while they were travelling in trains, of course they didn't have to talk much. The activities of ticket-buying and escalator-walking and strap-hanging were enough to occupy them till they reached the theatre.

And once they did the bustle of fashionable people was equally protective. Johanna stood silently beside her parents, sunk as usual in her own unhappiness while Lewis stood on Miriam's other side listening to her chatter eagerly about the fashions and the famous faces they saw ('that was, wasn't it, Patterson, the man who won the Men's title at Wimbledon? And wasn't that the newly married Princess Patricia over there with her dashing husband Admiral Ramsay, and *didn't* she look divine in that frock?') and Peter stared about with his young face rather overawed and saying nothing.

Max too was unusually quiet. He was to his own amazement filled with a great deal of apprehension, and he couldn't quite understand why. This was not a play in which he had any special interest, apart of course from Theo. He had no investment in it, as clearly some of the people standing near them had, for they were talking loudly about percentages and the chances of a long run, nor had he worked on it in any way unlike the droopy young man now standing on the far side of the foyer and talking even more loudly about the work he had put into the set designs. He simply had a cousin in the cast, that was all. A cousin who was also a patient, of course, but that was all. Why be so anxious that his hands were damp with sweat and his shoulders shook slightly under his dinner jacket? It really was very odd.

Once the play started his apprehension vanished, however, for the audience were clearly enchanted with the piece and it was undoubtedly a good one. The lines were funny, the actors lively and well rehearsed and Theo – Theo was quite magical, Max decided. He moved about the stage with a relaxed and easy air that sometimes was so relaxed he bumped into furniture and so easy he clearly got his lines a little tangled on occasion. But he did it all with such easy charm and looked so devastatingly handsome in the costumes devised for him – the play was one of the many that tried to make the most of the taste for Chinoiserie engendered by the eternal *Chu Chin Chow* and was set in some vaguely Chinese venue – that it was impossible not to enjoy him.

And Max did, and realized his anxiety had been entirely for Theo. He had been as nervous as if he himself had been about to step on to a West End stage for a first night.

They decided to remain in their seats for both the intervals, not wanting to join the fashionable throng in the foyers and bars, and read their programmes and listen to the entr'acte music and thought their own thoughts, all of them grateful to Miriam for her unending cheerful talk. She could speak so much and say so little that required any response – it was very comforting.

Johanna sat and thought of how much she hated Jonty. Of how much she never wanted to speak to him again, to think of him again, or to hear his name spoken again. Of how he was to be expunged from her mind and heart for always, and never be considered again. Since this dreary litany had been running through her mind almost ceaselessly for the past month, she found no comfort in it, and Lewis, looking at her covertly and noticing her violet-shadowed eyes and the droop of her pale mouth was smitten yet again with an awareness of his own hatefulness. To have allowed his beloved daughter to suffer so, to see her so heartbroken by his revolting behaviour – he deserved to be whipped at the stake, burnt alive, stripped of all he held dear and left to rot for ever, he told himself passionately, and then hated himself even more for being so exaggerated in his thinking. Dammit, it wasn't his fault! It was Claudette, Claudette, Claudette, not him! She had been the one who had behaved disgustingly, she had been the one who had displayed to this vulnerable child of his the sickening reality of the world she inhabited and always had –

And he moved in his seat roughly and asked himself again how long he could go on being so silent. He would have to talk to Johanna, explain, ask her to understand, beg her to forgive him and try to be her happy self again sooner or later. He couldn't go on like this. Could he? And what about Miriam? Didn't she deserve to be given an explanation for the surliness he had shown these past weeks, some recompense for the way he had withdrawn from her, some reason for the nights when in spite of the warmth of her arms about his neck and her body against his in the big double bed they had always shared, he had feigned sleep and rejected that rich love she offered him. But he couldn't tell her, not ever. He couldn't tell Miriam that he had allowed Claudette to – no. That wasn't to be thought of. It was Johanna he had to talk to eventually. Somehow he would have to talk to Johanna. That would set it all out. But not yet. Not yet – and he buried his head once again in the programme to read it for the tenth time.

And Miriam sat between them and chattered and chattered till even her own head swam, and wondered miserably how much longer it would be before these people she so loved and who could be so foolish would come to their senses and talk about whatever it all was. Lewis would tell her in his own good time she knew, and any attempt to push him would make matters worse. That had happened in the past, for he could be for all his tenderness and lovingness the most stubborn of men. And she sighed and squeezed Johanna's hand as the lights went down and the curtain rose again and tried to concentrate on the action on the stage.

The play ended to the most rapturous applause, with several people standing up in order to clap more loudly, and Max was one of them, his face crimson with pleasure as he stood applauding wildly and never taking his eyes from the line of actors bowing on the stage between their frames of red velvet tableau curtains, their faces glowing damply in the footlights.

When at last the audience let the actors go and the curtains closed for the last time and the orchestra began playing its sprightly time-to-leave music Max turned to his family with his face still glowing and cried, 'Oh, do let's go backstage and tell Theo how good he was! Shall we! I'm sure he'd love to see us – there can't be anyone who enjoyed it more than we did, can there? And he'll want to be told – please let's –'

Lewis looked at Miriam again and at the expression on her face managed a smile. 'Of course,' he said with as hearty an air as he could manage. 'Of course. Which way do we go?' and took Miriam's elbow as she looked at him with her eyes wide with pleasure.

'Oh, that will be exciting!' she said. 'Won't it Johanna? It all feels so terribly modern to be doing this. Like the things one reads about in magazines –'

They had to push a good deal to get through the hubbub that poured out into Shaftesbury Avenue and then on round the corner into Nassau Street on the way to the stage door in Gerrard Street. It seemed to Max that the entire audience was on its way there too, but that just added to his own determination to get through and he shouldered his way forwards against the mob, a little surprised that it was so thick – did the theatre really hold so many people? – and also that it consisted of so many young women, all giggling and shoving at each other and crying out in shrill tones, with his chin down and his mother held firmly by the hand.

They were almost at the stage door, which was barricaded by a large and very truculent-looking stage doorkeeper when Miriam's name was called by a high pitched cry and she turned her head and peered and then cried delightedly, 'Why, Bella! How lovely to see you here! What are you doing in – oh, I am a fool aren't I? Of course you'd be here! I'd be so excited if Theo were one of my boys – didn't he do it frightfully well? I did think he was lovely! Where's James?'

'Well, he's in a stupid wax about Theo acting at all. So he wouldn't come and see the darling boy tonight. But I'm sure he'll come round in time. Oh, isn't this a dreadful crush! Who *are* all these awful people?' And she looked fretfully about her as though she were in her own drawing-room, and all these strangers had come pelting in uninvited.

'Why, hello, everyone!' The new voice was not raised but was crystal clear for all that, and they all turned their heads, almost like clockwork toys and stared at its owner.

'Are you all coming to see dear Theo?' Claudette said sweetly. 'Do follow me, my dears! I've special entry, you see – since I've backed the play rather handsomely. This way, now. Thank you, Swift – yes, they're all with me! Every one of them –' And she hustled them all before her into the cramped passageway inside the theatre, and they all stood and stared at each other in the glare of the naked bulb that dangled from the middle of the grimy ceiling and were silent.

22

'There now, isn't this cosy!' Claudette said after a moment and beamed at them all. 'Such an age since I've seen you, Miriam, darling! Not since that weekend you came to us at Simister. And Lewis, my dear, so nice –' She smiled brilliantly at them all and turned to Max. 'Did you enjoy the play? Wasn't dear Theo too marvellous? I told my darling Emilia here that I thought he was quite the divinest man I've ever seen this year or any other and asked her if she didn't agree, but you know my dear girl – never one to say much –' And she looked at Max knowingly and then at Emilia.

But Emilia simply looked blank and said nothing and Max merely smiled and murmured, 'Indeed? Perhaps Emilia doesn't like the play too well.'

They had never discussed with each other whether or not to let Claudette become aware of the friendship between them, but had nonetheless reached a tacit agreement to keep their own counsel. Lewis's dislike of the Collingbournes and Claudette's malicious curiosity were enough to make both of them feel discretion was much to be valued. And it seemed now to have been a wise agreement, for Claudette relaxed, clearly losing interest in them.

'Where is Theo?' Bella said sharply, and pulled her sable stole more closely about her ears, for all the stuffiness of the passageway and the warmth of the June night. 'I really can't stand here chatting all evening – I must get back –'

'Of course, of course,' Claudette said smoothly. 'Well, I dare say he's changed by now – shall we all go to see him? Lewis, my dear man, your arm.' And she tilted her chin at him with a brazen little glint in her eyes and raised her brows at him insolently.

'I don't think I want to stay after all,' Johanna said in a strangled little voice. 'Dad, will you take me home please –' and she turned and made her way blindly back to the doorway. Lewis moved at once, following her. 'Of course. Miriam? Peter? Do you wish to stay – or shall we all –'

'Oh, Dad, I thought we were to see –' Peter began but his mother took his arm and said soothingly, 'Perhaps it is rather late, and such a crowd. I think after all we'd better go – it took longer to get here than I expected and – goodnight, Claudette. Jonty and Emilia, so nice to see you. Bella, shall we meet for tea tomorrow? That would be nice, wouldn't it? Then you can tell me all the family news – Max, are you coming too?'

Max, a little bemused by the sudden mass exodus shook his head and opened his mouth to speak, but was spared the trouble, for Jonty, who had been standing in the shadows behind his mother, stepped forward.

'Johanna –' he began but she ignored him and smiled brilliantly at her mother. 'Are we going, Mother? It really is so frightfully late and I'm madly tired – goodnight everyone –' And she went plunging out of the door, her parents and younger brother, he looking somewhat sulky, following her.

Claudette's eyes were glittering as she watched them go and Max was puzzled. He knew his father objected to Lady Collingbourne, but that there should be so much tension between them was really very odd –

'Maman, I think I'm going too. I can't face all that dressing-room chatter after all. Emilia, I'll take you home,' Jonty said loudly and made for the door too, and Emilia with one conspiratorial glance at Max followed him meekly.

'Dear me, but darling Theo will feel neglected!' Claudette said and laughed, a brittle little sound that echoed against the grimy cream and green paint of the passageway. 'Won't someone introduce me?' And she looked at Bella with her head on one side.

Max, a little flustered at the reminder of his social ineptitude repaired the omission and then stoood uncertainly as Claudette, murmuring ecstatically in Bella's ear about how superb her son was, went away down the corridor towards the dressing-rooms. Should he stay, and try to see Theo in the middle of everyone else – for there were many other people hurrying along the passageway – or hang about and try to talk to him on his own, later? That he didn't want to be just one of a party with Cousin Bella and Lady Collingbourne was certain, and after a moment he turned to ask Swift, the stage doorkeeper, where he could find Letty.

She was standing in the wings checking a lighting cue sheet and as he appeared she looked irritably over her shoulder, but then grinned with real welcome on her face.

'Why, Max, how spiffing to see you! You really are a wonder-worker, aren't you? The difference in Theo's really something to see – I'm so grateful to you. How do you think he was tonight?'

'Marvellous,' Max said truthfully. 'Quite marvellous. Is he still all right, then?'

She lifted her brows at that. 'All right? My dear old bean, don't you know? Surely you've seen him since you did that treatment thing of yours?'

'Well, no, actually. He's been too busy rehearsing and all that so –'

'He's a wretch! He knows perfectly well I'd have changed the rehearsal schedule for him if he'd asked me. And he should keep in touch with his doctor, for heaven's sake! I'll speak to him. Since you ask – he seems well enough. But sometimes –' She frowned and turned back to the cue sheet. 'Well, I do wonder a little sometimes. He looks a bit – well, strained, if he thinks no one's looking at him –'

'He said he was sleeping well. When I spoke to him on the phone.'

'Oh, perhaps he is. Actually I'm sure he is, because he says the same to me, but I don't know – sometimes –'

She shrugged and said no more. It had been a difficult few weeks, what with the première of the film, and the bad notices it had had (though those had been more than compensated by the extremely good box-office receipts as the film became popular by word of mouth) and with the play to rehearse too. She had had little time to think of her own feelings in consequence. And that had been a sort of comfort. Bad enough she had fallen as head over heels in love with her leading actor as any silly schoolgirl; at least she didn't have to compound her idiocy by mooning over him for lack of something else to think about.

But even so, she had noticed his changed behaviour. At first she had been enormously relieved at the change in him after his session with Max. He had been as bubbly as a glass of champagne, his laughter the loudest, his speech the quickest, his jokes the funniest when they all sat and relaxed over mugs of tea or coffee during rehearsal breaks, but then she had begun to wonder. Wasn't he a bit too effervescent? Wasn't he a bit over-excited? The gloom in which he had seemed to be permanently sunk had gone, but she wasn't sure she enjoyed the edgy sparkling gaiety that had taken its place. The contrast was too great.

But she had pushed away her doubts and tried to believe that he was well again. No more of those dreadful attacks, that was the most important thing. No more of those dreadful shaking sweating glassy-eyed attacks. He was cured of his shell-shock, if that had been the problem, and from now on was to be the most glorious gem in the Gaff Studios' diadem. But then, as she had told Max, there were times when he looked so strained that she felt the anxiety rise in her again, together with the need to take his head in her arms and soothe him like a baby. A need which had to be put down with a very firm hand indeed.

Now she smiled at Max and said brightly, 'Well, my dear old chap, shall we go and find him so that you can tell him how marvellous he was? If those damned critics don't praise him to the skies for this, I swear I'll shoot the lot of 'em. I'll never send any one of them another stall for any show I do. Did you see what the wrteched creatures said about my *Caesar*? Stupid ignorant asses –'

'I thought Theo was awfully good as Mark Antony,' Max said tactfully, and she looked sideways at him and grinned a sharp little grimace. 'Oh, damn, you too? It wasn't all that marvellous, was it? I got it wrong, that one. Mind you, it's getting Collingbourne her money back, so no one need complain. But no one likes doing a bad job –'

'It wasn't bad,' Max said. 'Just not as good as Theo was, if you see what I mean.'

'I see what you mean,' she said and laughed. 'Out of the mouths of babes, hmm? In theatrical terms, that is. I'm sure in your own field you're one of the whizz-bangs. But in the theatre –'

'Oh, I know less than nothing,' Max said cheerfully. 'I'm the first to admit it. Just one of those who likes a good laugh, you know, something to admire. And I must say tonight I got that.'

'Good.'

'And – er – may I go and see him? Or will there be too many people there at present?' And he thought of Claudette and felt uncomfortable again.

'Lady Collingbourne, is it?' Letty said sharply. 'She's a bit of a mouthful for anyone with a tendency to indigestion, isn't she? No need to look like that. I've had her hanging about my heels for months. We pay hard for our money in the film business, my dear Max, and never let anyone tell you otherwise. I'll get rid of her. You stay here and I'll get Theo out and you can ask him for yourself how he is. And see perhaps –' And she hesitated as though she were about to say more and then shrugged slightly and reached in her inevitable knitted jacket for a cigarette and lit it and went away, leaving him standing quietly in the wings.

Around him the theatre stretched, cavernous yet somehow cosy, for it was filled with heat and distant muffled sound and vagrant smells and was, for all its size, of very human dimensions. The great stage itself with its gold and white set and pagoda-like structures glowed softly in the light of a single flood that had been left burning high above, and on each side of him the great canvas flats of painted scenery stretched away. The air smelled of fish glue and Leichner's grease-paint and stewed tea and kippers and beer, and he took a deep breath of it and for a moment, remembering the excitement of the evening on the other side of the great wall of iron-studded material that was the curtain now shrouding the front of the stage, understood what it might be like to be an actor. He almost felt the exalted, exultant loneliness of the centre of the spotlight, surrounded by faceless people demanding love and laughter and delight and happiness from you, almost felt the barely controlled envy and hate that lay behind their adulation, knew how easily the roars of love could turn to roars of fury, and shook inside. To be a doctor was frightening enough, for people demanded more than love and laughter of you; they demanded life. But to be an actor must be infinitely harder –

There was a clatter of sound from the distant corridor that led to the dressing-rooms and he shrank back against the spurious security of a canvas flat and wanted to run away. The high emotion of the evening had evaporated and he was left with a sense of dreariness that made him want to crawl into bed, to sleep and dream of being a child again instead of having to cope with all these complex adult emotions. It wasn't that long since he'd been a child, after all; it took a lot of getting used to, all this reponsibility.

'There he is!' Letty's voice was so close that he jumped, for he hadn't realized she had come across the wings, so quietly had she trodden. 'Theo – come here! I want to check some cues with you –'

'I'll have to go.' Theo's voice came easily across the wide space and Max stepped forwards to see him. He was standing with Claudette very close beside him and looking up into his face with an air of ownership that suddenly made Max very angry and he moved closer to Letty, aware that she was feeling the same.

'It's getting late, Theo,' she called sharply, this time. 'The stage staff'll want to be getting away. Good night, Lady Collingbourne – so good of you to come round like this –'

Claudette lifted her head and tried to peer into the darkness to see Letty, but she stood close beside Max in the shadows and after a moment Claudette smiled and said loudly, 'Well, I dare say we shall see you all at the party, soon, then? I've arranged all sorts of delights for you all, so don't be long –'

'Of course,' they heard Theo say. 'That'll be lovely. As soon as we can, then –' and he watched her as she went unwillingly away, and then came across the spread of dusty wooden floor, his head set inquiringly on one side.

'Letty? Where are you?' he called softly and after a moment, when they had heard the distant stage door slam she relaxed her shoulders and said quietly, 'I'm here.'

Max stood there beside her, aware of the tenuous link that bound them together; both disliking Claudette Collingbourne and her encroaching ways, both seeing her as a threat, both not wanting to admit they were allies in their concern and care for Theo –

'Hateful woman,' Theo murmured as he came up to her and grinned in the dimness. 'Such a creepy-crawly. She'd eat you alive if she could. As long as you're some sort of fashionable type,' and he made an odd little sound, half grunt, half retch and at once Letty relaxed even more and moved away from Max's side. The link between them stretched, frayed and finally parted and he felt the old dreariness again. He should never have come backstage. He should have wrapped up the magic of the evening, put it in his mind's pocket and gone home. He should have –

'Hello Max!' Theo said, sounding cheerful and loud in the dimness. 'I didn't realize you were there! How nice of you to come round. Did you see the show? What did you think? Did you notice the way I fluffed those lines in the second act? Wasn't it frightful?'

'It was tremendous,' Max said. 'I didn't notice anything except that it was tremendous. I did enjoy it. I thought – I just wanted to come round to see how you are and say – well, thanks for a spiffing evening. I did love it so – laughed all the time –'

He felt a little shy suddenly and Theo seemed to realize it and tucked one hand into his elbow and grinned even more widely.

'Well, that's all right then! Isn't it, Letty?'

'Yes,' she said and sounded wooden now, and Max felt a difference in her. Not only had the link between them gone; now there was a faint hostility in her. 'Look, Theo, it's been a long day, and it's time you went home. To hell with parties. Let that woman feed and water half of London if she likes – you go home to bed – I'll see you back if you like –'

'It's all right,' Max said. 'I will. I mean, I'm walking home anyway, and it's no trouble.'

Theo looked from one to the other and laughed, still

sounding relaxed and easy and Max wished he could see his face for he needed to know if he really was as well as he seemed. But his voice gave nothing away. 'Heavens,' he said. 'What a brace of nursemaids! We'll *all* go back to my flat, that's what we'll do. I've got some rather good champagne there, in a bucket of ice I got from old Luigi, if it hasn't melted by now, and we'll all three share it. What do you say? Come on!' And he set his other elbow akimbo so that she too was invited to link with him and after a moment Letty laughed, and set her hand in its crook.

'All right,' she said. 'Come on, Max. We'll go and celebrate the third of London's plays with a kiss in the title and drink damnation to *Kiss Call* and *Kissing Time* and may the Gaiety and the Winter Garden rot while *Never Kiss and Tell* packs the Shaftesbury for the next ten years!'

'Heaven forbid,' Theo said fervently. 'Do this for ten years? You must be mad! Ten months'll kill me! You'd better make sure the understudy's in good voice if you get a run that long –'

'Well, he's not bad,' Letty said as they made their way towards the stage door. She sounded cheerful now, not at all the tense and strained woman she had been just a few moments earlier, quite skittish, Max thought and wondered not for the first time at the odd ways of women. 'He could take over at a pinch tomorrow – but he wouldn't be you, and that's what'll keep this play on the boards. You're incredible, Theo Caspar, and I must be a mad manager to tell you so, but there it is. You're the biggest thing to arrive in the theatre this side of Henry Irving –'

They pushed the stage door open, Theo leading the way and it was suddenly as though he had stepped into a new world, a mad and dreadful world full of noise and heat and the weight of bodies, for outside the girls Max had noticed earlier were still waiting, and their numbers seemed to have increased. There must have been hundreds of them there, all shoving and pushing and waving autograph books and pieces of paper and at the sight of Theo a great shriek went up and they surged forwards, almost pressing him flat against Max and Letty who were immediately behind him.

'What the bloody hell –' Theo began and then was submerged as the phalanx of girls seemed to fall over him, seemed to be climbing over each other to get at him and Max heard himself roaring at them, felt his hands pushing and scrabbling at soft hot human flesh as he tried to pull Theo out of the mêlée.

'Oh, my *God*,' Letty was shouting behind him as though she were both praying and swearing, and Max realized that she was pushing at the bodies too, while trying to get Theo to his feet.

Behind them the door which had been smartly closed by Swift the stage doorkeeper when they went out, burst open again as the noise of thumping on it called him from whatever fastness he had disappeared to, and they half fell, half jumped through as Swift, his face solid with disapproval, pushed away the girls who tried to follow them in. And then they were standing there, the three of them, as Swift locked the door noisily and swearing beneath his breath went away to check that the other doors that gave entrance to the rear section of the theatre were safely bolted too.

'Ye gods, Theo, that was the most –' Letty began shakily, and rubbed her hands through her hair. 'Did you *hear* them? Some of them were calling you Mark Antony – it must be the film. I've heard of this sort of thing happening to film actors, but I've never actually seen it like that before – Theo? – Theo!'

He was standing very still and straight, his hands held awkwardly at his sides and Max, who had been straightening his jacket and tie, both of which had been almost torn from him during the miniature battle they had fought, looked up sharply at the note in her voice.

'Oh God,' Theo said softly and then said it again, louder, and then louder still. 'Oh God. Oh God –' And the shaking began, first his head and then his arms and his shoulders until his whole body developed a tremor so violent it seemed he would shake himself apart. His face glistened as the sweating began and his skin whitened and then turned grey until at last, almost to their relief, his eyes turned upwards beneath his open lids and he slid slowly down the wall in a dead faint.

23

'And what the hell else am I supposed to do?' Letty said savagely. 'Of course I've got to put the understudy in –'

'You told me last night that I'm the one who'll keep the play running and –'

'That was before,' she said firmly. 'Now I know you're ill and –'

'I'm not ill!' he began hotly, but she rode over him.

'You are. You're as ill as if one of those damned girls last night had jumped on you and broken your leg. If I let you go on performing after what happened to you then I'd not only be a bad friend to you – I'd be a lousy management. I can't risk my lead actor getting ill in the middle of a performance, can I? Even on stage, maybe. I'd have to be out of my mind not to insist you stay off till you're well again. Really well. So I'm going to insist. You've got to get well, got to get away for a rest, and that's all about it.'

There was a short silence and then he sat up more stiffly against his pillows and looked at Max. 'Tell her she's wrong, Max, will you? That it's the first time it's happened since – for ages. It was just bad luck, that's all. They caught me unawares, those women. Christ, did you see them? They'd be enough to make anyone get a bit upset. Tell her, Max.'

'I can't,' Max said, and shook his head, sitting very straight on the edge of the bed with his hand on Theo's wrist as he felt the pulse racing thinly and urgently beneath his fingertips. 'And I won't. Last night you actually passed out, and you've not done that before, have you? Right now you've got a pulse rate of over a hundred and twenty and you're sweating and you're tremulous. When you've had these attacks before you've got over them fairly quickly, but this one's different, isn't it?'

'No!' Theo said, but there was a defeated note in his voice and he tried to pull his wrist away from Max, but failed, for there was no strength in him.

'It is,' Max said firmly. 'More severe than any of the others. I'm quite sure it's essentially the same, so you needn't worry about that. It's not an indication of any physical disease, that is. It's still the sort of panic attack you used to get, but it is a more severe one.' He sounded confident, he knew, and that in itself helped feed his self assurance. 'I've learned a great deal about cases like yours, Theo, even since I last treated you, and I'm quite certain now that the answer for you has to be more treatment and –'

'Another of your hypnotisms?' Theo said and laughed, a harsh little sound in the quiet bedroom. 'Doesn't seem to have done me much good at that, does it? Not if this attack is supposed to be so dreadful –'

Max reddened a little. 'That's hardly just, Theo,' he said stiffly. 'You said yourself that you felt a great deal better and –'

'And you also looked it and behaved it,' Letty said, and got up from the other side of the bed where she had been sitting and went to the window to stare down into Shaftesbury Avenue, bustling and bright in the June sunshine. 'I think the best thing I can do is make a virtue out of a necessity. I'll publicize the fact that you were so popular that you were mobbed by your admirers outside the theatre and were so shaken that you've had to go away for a rest to recover. That'll help the film takings a good deal – I might even manage to get it booked into a couple more cinemas on the strength of it. It won't help the play, of course. I doubt the understudy'll keep that going all that long. Peter's a good lad but –'

'For God's sake, Letty, how long do you think I'm going to be off? A couple of days at the outside! I'll be back soon and then –'

'No,' she said flatly. 'I'm not prepared to sacrifice your health for a play. Plays can always be done again – or different ones done. You're too valuable in the long run to be wasted on just one production. There's a film future for you, my boy, and I'm going to make sure we get it right. We've invested a good deal in you – the Gaff Studios have – and it's my responsibility to see we get a proper return on our investment.'

She could feel the chill in the room behind her, but didn't turn her head. She wanted, quite desperately she wanted, to turn and throw herself at him, to hold him close, and stroke that rumpled dark head and soothe the tension out of that strained white face with her finger-tips, but that of course was unthinkable. But he had to rest, of that she was certain. She felt almost sick with guilt as she realized just how far she had pushed him, how much she had driven him; maybe it's my fault he's looking so dreadful, my fault he's so ill now? But there was no point in wasting energy on self-recrimination. What she had to do was find a way to convince Theo that he had to leave the play and get well, and if the only way she could do that was by making him think she was more concerned with the financial implications of the situation than she actually was, then that was what she would have to do.

'I see,' he said now. 'Of course, I mustn't do anything to stop the books balancing, must I?'

'No,' she said and still didn't turn round.

'So what do you propose I do? Give up the flat here and go home to my parents' house? Sit around all day doing nothing the way I did before? I can quite see that would make me feel quite splendid!'

'Oh, don't be a fool, Theo! Of course the Gaff will go on paying your salary while you're ill! We insure all our players, whatever they're doing, so we can afford that. So as for giving up the flat – nonsense! Unless you refuse to go away for a rest, that is. I wouldn't hear of you being alone here –'

'I was last night!' Theo said. 'And –'

'Actually, you weren't,' Max said a little diffidently. 'After I'd got you to bed, given you that sleeping draught, I didn't feel comfortable about leaving you. So I stayed after Letty went –'

Letty turned then and stared at him, just as Theo was doing. 'I see!' she said. 'That's why you were here so early! I thought when I got here at eight you must have got up at the crack of dawn but –'

'I slept on the living-room sofa,' Max said, a little pink now. 'Just to keep an eye on you, Theo. It seemed to me that I should –'

'I suppose so,' Theo said gruffly after a moment and then moved awkwardly in bed and picked at the covers. 'Then at least you must know I slept like a baby and I'm more than fit to get up now –'

'Of course you slept,' Max said. 'I gave you a considerable dose of chloral. I found that bottle I'd given you in the bathroom cabinet. If you'd ever taken any after I'd given it to you, you'd have realized how helpful it can be. Used in the right way.'

'So can I get up now?'

'How is it you could just stay here like that?' Letty said abruptly. 'I mean, shouldn't you be at the hospital?'

'No,' Max said. 'I mean yes, but it's not essential. I'm qualified now, remember. I haven't got a full job anywhere at Nellie's. I haven't applied – so I'm just filling in as senior dresser. But I don't have to. There're the new final-year people on the wards to do all that now. So, I'm pretty well as free as I want to be. Actually, I've been busy making plans to set up in my own practice – I'll be leaving Nellie's soon.' He tried to sound casual, very much the senior professional man, but he knew he sounded merely awkward. But he took a deep breath and went on as coolly as he could. 'So, I'm far more my own master than you seem to think, Letty!'

'And what about your family? Weren't they worried when you didn't go home last night? You're a close lot, aren't you? I'd have thought they'd –'

Max shook his head. 'I told them I had a patient I didn't want to leave,' he said. 'They understand that. We're a medical family, you know, even if we are close, as you put it.'

'Then you can take care of Theo for me when he has had his rest,' she said after a moment, and moved purposefully across the room towards the door. 'I'll phone Edwin at the office now, and get him to organize it. Where do you want to go?'

'Go?' They said it together, and she laughed shortly.

'You sound like a bad music hall act, you two! G.O., go, go, I said. Theo's got to have a rest. He won't go to his parents' home and I can't blame him. He can't stay here, because I won't let him. He needs a proper holiday. I'd worry myself stupid if he went anywhere on his own – and you're the best person to take him. You're his doctor. And you say you're free. So, where do you want to go?'

The water purled greyly beneath them and Max watched the bow-wave open, widen and curve smoothly away into the swell and felt his own spirits curve and swell to match.

'It's lovely, isn't it?' he said after a moment and turned his head to look at Theo leaning over the rail of the SS *Invicta* beside him. 'There are so many different colours in the water.'

Theo said nothing, still staring down at the movement far below.

'I mean, most people like it best when it's brilliant sunshine and blueness, but for my part this is much more interesting. More subtle –'

'You don't have to make conversation,' Theo snapped. 'It's bad enough you've got to play bear-leader to an invalid. You don't have to wear yourself out with sprightly conversation as well.'

Max bit his lip and took a deep breath. 'Theo, I'm not putting myself out,' he said as patiently as he could. 'I've told you before. It's a pleasure to be doing this. Ye gods, old man, how often does a person get the chance of a totally free tour to Rome like this? If you'd said you wanted to go to Timbuktu, Letty'd have sent us there. I'm glad to be here, well on my way. It's a marvellous chance to see a city I've never seen, and a marvellous chance for you too, to see Rome, I mean, and get a good rest and –'

'I don't want to see Rome. I don't need a rest and I'm sick of being treated like a child,' Theo cried and hunched his shoulders in his overcoat, for the wind was sharp for all it was midsummer.

Max stared at him, feeling the anger rise in him and decided, suddenly, to let himself enjoy the luxury of losing his patience. Ever since Letty had made up her mind to it they were going to go away together for a rest, Theo had been impossible. He had complained, he had sulked, he had railed, but she had been adamant. When he had flatly refused to choose a place he wanted to go to, she had chosen for him. Rome, she had said, was the only place she could be sure to get him and his companion good accommodation at present because this first post-war summer had sent thousands of English families to the Continent to resume their old pattern of foreign holidays, and so Rome it had been. When he had just as flatly refused to take any part in the organizing of the holiday she had arranged for Edwin to book them on to the boat-train from Victoria and on to the newest of the fast steamships from Dover to Calais, and the Rome Express from Paris thereafter. No matter what Theo said – and all through the long arrangements and confused planning he had fussed and generally made life difficult – she had gone ahead as inexorably as the SS *Invicta* was now cutting through the waters of the Channel on its way to the French coast. And Max, delighted both to have the opportunity to go to a place he had never visited and always been fascinated by, and eager to help his one and only patient get well again, had been as emollient and as calm and as reassuring as he had known how to be. He had talked to Theo, coaxed and cajoled him, modelling his care on the sort of behaviour he had seen the sisters and nurses at Nellie's use on recalcitrant patients.

But now he had had enough. Perhaps it was the fact that they were now on board the ship, and safely on the way and it was therefore too late for Theo to dig in his toes and refuse to travel further – for he could hardly swim back to Dover from mid channel – that gave him the impetus. Whatever it was he let the words come ripping from him and enjoyed them.

'Theo, you're behaving like a child! And a thoroughly hateful spoiled brat at that! No one can blame you for being ill. You had a dreadful time in the trenches – I know that perfectly well, because you told me more than you might have realized when I hypnotised you. No one can blame you for hating the effect it's had on you. But you can be blamed for all this stupid performance you've given ever since! You're as ridiculous as a man who's told he needs a splint for a broken leg and refuses to have it, and goes marching about making his injury worse. You're being thoroughly selfish too, because you're upsetting a great many people by all this stubbornness. Cousin Bella looked positively sick with misery at Victoria this morning and you were as cold as – you'd have thought you were made of ice, you were so harsh to her, and she's your *mother*. And Letty's doing all she can to help, and you treat her appallingly. Well, you needn't think I'm going to put up with it, because I'm not. You can stop this stupidity right now, do you understand me? Right *now*. Because I'm your doctor and I won't put up with it!'

One or two other people walking about the deck looked at them curiously as they passed, the two young men standing at the furthest point they could in the bow of the sleek steamship and looking so intently at each other and one of them speaking so vehemently, if in decently lowered tones, but Max was totally unaware of them. He could see only Theo's pale face framed in the high collar of his coat and the heavy scudding grey clouds above them and the restless grey water beneath and feel his own pulses thick in his throat. He wanted to help this man; he cared a great deal for his welfare, needed to help him just as he would have helped Tim, but there were limits, there had to be limits, to his tolerance.

And when he'd finished what he had to say he set his lips grimly and stared at Theo and waited, not sure what he would do if Theo still refused to see reason.

There was a long silence and then Theo frowned slightly and looked away from Max's very direct gaze, and then flicked his eyes back. And after a moment he managed to grin. It wasn't an easy smile. There was little of pleasure in it, but it was there for all that, and he bobbed his head, almost as a child would after being reprimanded, and turned back to the rail to lean over it.

'Look,' he said after a long pause. Max still stood there, not sure what to say next. 'Isn't that a gull? I thought they didn't fly this far from the coast? We must be about midway, mustn't we?'

'I imagine they come with the ships,' Max said. 'I'm not an experienced seafarer, so I can't be sure, but there's lots more up there in the rigging, see?'

'Yes,' Theo said. 'I dare say you're right. Begging a ride, as you might say.'

'Yes,' Max said, and then couldn't resist it, and gave him a little sideways grin. 'Like us.'

And after one terrifying moment when Max feared he'd gone a step too far, Theo laughed and said, 'Yes. Like us.'

24

It was as though a great weight had been lifted from Max's shoulders. From that moment on the holiday became one in real earnest. The cold angry ice-cold Theo disappeared and was replaced by a companion as cheerful, as garrulous and as amusing as anyone could wish. At Calais he chattered teasingly with the blue-overalled porters who carried their luggage, reeling out his stock of wartime French until they guffawed and chattered back at him and showed him the best place to have a decent *déjeuner*. In the restaurant he joked hilariously about the eating of snails – a new experience for Max – and showed him how to manipulate the special tongs and the long fork to extricate them amid much encouragement from the other lunchers. On the train to Paris he regaled Max with tales of the funnier doings of soldiers and villagers – for not all the war days had been fighting ones – and once arrived in Paris took a real delight in using the day that elapsed between that arrival and the departure of the Rome Express from the Gare de Lyon to show him the sights of the city. They wandered round Montparnasse, they climbed to Sacré Coeur and walked the Champs-Elysées; they crossed the Seine to the Ile de la Cité and Notre Dame, and rattled around the Metro like seasoned travellers.

And even after they had ensconced themselves in the lush splendours of the Rome Express and duly admired the red plush and gilded fittings of the dining car, the snug and marvellously designed accommodation of the Pullman sleepers with their cosy bunks and individual washbasins and cupboards, the magic was still there. Theo tucked himself in a corner of the carriage that had been reserved for them and as the train pulled majestically out of the Gare de Lyon and started its twenty-four hour journey south talked easily and comfortably of books and music and plays, making Max feel, for the first time for a very long time that he had a really close friend. In his boyhood he had been content enough to share all his free time with Tim. The age gap between them had never worried him for Tim had been so witty, so sympathetic, so irresistibly interesting that it hadn't mattered. And now it was almost the same. Theo was dark and Tim had been fair. Theo was often serious and Tim had rarely been so, but it was somehow the same for Max. A sense of camaraderie filled him, a peacefulness he had forgotten could exist, and he relaxed and basked in it.

Chambéry, Mondane, Turin and Genoa, Pisa and Livorno, and the heat rose steadily and the light brightened as they left the north behind and the passing landscape showed less green and more yellow as the water-levels in the hot summer earth dwindled. And still they talked, sitting over their meals in the dining-car long after all the other passengers had returned to their seats to sleep the hot racketing hours away, their elbows on the table and a bottle of Chianti between them as the fields and houses of Northern Italy fled past the unheeded windows.

Viminale railway station at Rome was a maelstrom of shouting, gesticulating porters and reeked of hot engines and bad tobacco and garlic and Max wilted a little under the hubbub as they tried to explain in their halting Italian that they wanted a porter to carry them to the nearest taxi-driver, but as they emerged, feet rattling on the marble floor, blinking into the blazing heat of the huge Piazza del Cinquecento his spirits rose. Rome; this was *Rome*, and he caught Theo's glance and produced a great wide schoolboyish grin of delight and Theo grinned back. It was a wonderful moment.

Max had told Edwin during all the fuss of plan-making in London that he personally would rather not stay in too large or sophisticated an hotel. He wanted very much to ensure that Theo rested and he doubted that would happen anywhere too grand. And Edwin had listened and nodded and assured him that he would choose well. And he had.

The driver took them to a small and impeccably neat *pensione* at the top of the Spanish Steps and when they ducked

223

out of the sun into its shaded and cool interior, Max breathed a deep sigh of relief. The proprietor, a large very cheerful Swiss, greeted them as though they were his long-lost children and bustled them into their room, a big one that overlooked the gardens of the Villa Borghese at the rear of the *pensione*, and brought them a tray of iced tea 'Until you should eat the proper meal' and left them to recover from the rigours of their long journey.

And they dropped on to the beds – twin couches set neatly side by side and covered with demure white linen covers – and slept until the sound of a distant gong roused them.

They ate vast quantities of Signor Hassler's excellent fettucine and veal cutlets and melon and a bottle of good Lacrimi Cristi wine and then, leaving Signorina Hassler to unpack for them, went walking. The worn stones of the Spanish Steps, with groups of young Romans sprawled on them, stretched below into the golden dusk, and ahead of them the sky glowed deep orange with the setting sun. There were sleepy horses drooping between the shafts of their traps as their drivers stood and gossiped in a haze of reeking pipe-smoke, and the fountain in the middle of the Piazza Espagna tinkled in a desultory fashion far below them. There were a few tubs of geraniums set about the steps too, making a splash of blood red against the old grey of the stones and Max stood there, feeling tears of some unexplained emotion pricking his eyelids.

'It's beautiful,' he said huskily as he stared down the steps and beside him Theo laughed.

'Isn't it? And did you ever see such beautiful people, either? Look at those boys. They're like models for da Vinci.'

'Mmm? I hadn't noticed. Yes, I suppose so – very Roman, I imagine. Look Theo, can you see the colour of that sky? It's like eggshells –'

'I prefer people,' Theo said and then, with a sudden surge of energy cried, 'Come on! Let's run!' And run he did, leaping down the steps like a puppy newly off the leash, and Max perforce had to follow him.

They walked it seemed for miles, through narrow sometimes malodorous streets and alleys as the Roman darkness deepened and the sound of clopping horses' hooves became less common as the drivers went home and the streets emptied, and at last they returned to climb the Spanish Steps again, exhausted but happy. Max in particular felt wonderful. He had not realized how tired he was, how hard he had worked for his finals, and now he was here in this ancient and to his English eyes exotic city he felt the fatigue and strain of the last years begin to fade away from him. London and grief for Tim and the diseases that stalked the wards at Nellie's seemed as remote as the butter-yellow Roman moon now lying low in the indigo sky above them.

They slept, both of them, like babies, although Max had looked at the ribbed green glass bottle of chloral he had long ago given Theo and considered giving him some; but he had decided not to, discreetly tucking the bottle away in one of the drawers of the carved oak chest against the wall, and he had been right. Almost as soon as Theo had fallen into the welcoming bed, now waiting with its covers turned invitingly down, he was asleep. And to the best of Max's knowledge didn't stir until the next morning when Signor Hassler came panting up his well polished stairs to bring them bowls of creamy coffee and fragrant hot bread and butter for their breakfast.

The magic lasted for day after day, pleating into weeks. They went to the Colosseum and Arch of Constantine and tried to imagine the ancient stones thronged with Christian slaves and lions. They climbed Capitol Hill and walked down the Via dei Fori Imperiali, pretending they were Caesars. They went to the Baths of Caracalla and were suitably overawed by its size and tried to admire the vast monument to Victor Emmanuel in the Piazza Venezia. They drank tea at Babington's English tea-rooms in the Piazza Espagna and giggled at the several American ladies who sat there poring over their Baedeckers, and wandered from one incense-shadowed and scented church to another. They put their hands in the Mouth of Truth and prayed at St Peter's. They strolled along miles of Lungotevere watching the ochre river move sluggishly alongside them and talked and laughed and talked again. They marvelled at the Sistine Chapel and blinked at the glories of the statues that were everywhere, and picked the oleander blossoms and threw crumbs to the squabbling birds whenever they sat – as they often did – to drink cold beer and eat cake at the roadside cafés. And Max watched Theo and listened to him and felt happy for him, for his face lost its pasty sickness and glowed under a newly developing golden wash of tan, and his eyes lost their strained look and his hands stopped shaking.

But he did not talk to him of another treatment. He had thought a good deal about the possibility of trying hypnosis once more. After all it had helped. Admittedly it had not been the total answer. Theo's problem had returned with greater severity. But it had been banished for a while and that was an important step. Surely, if he tried again he could banish it for even longer? And then next time perhaps it would be even more effective until eventually – and, after all, he had argued with himself, watching Theo clambering up the crumbling walls of the Colosseum while he preferred to sit below in the shade and watch him, fanning himself with his hat – after all, I'd been worried about the speed with which the hypnosis had seemed to work. The fact that the problem isn't completely cured is a form of reassurance, isn't it? It shows that the treatment needs repeating, that it's a real long term method and not just some mumbo-jumbo nonsense –

So he would argue with himself, but he said not a word of these private colloquies to Theo. He felt obscurely that this was not the time or place. They would return to London and then he would talk about the possibility. When Theo was really rested, really comfortable again, no longer in a state of blind panic as he had been last time, they would go back to the consulting-room couch and try again.

And though Max would not, could not have admitted it to himself, part of the charm of that idea was the use of his own consulting-rooms. A letter from Emilia had told him that his ambitions were almost on the point of realization. She had found the ideal set of rooms, had haggled for a reasonable rent and had taken the liberty of signing an agreement. In her own name of course! He could settle the finances on his return, naturally –

Until the bubble burst. It had been a day of oppressive heat, the very stones seeming to bake browner, and they sat in the Pensione Hassler's small roof-top garden in the shade of the bay tree Signora Hassler cossetted there, drinking quantities of soda-water and waiting for the heat to end, for even they could not walk in it. The change in the weather when it came was spectacular, with great clouds rolling ominously from the north to swell over sweating Rome and finally explode in the most stunningly noisy thunderstorm they had ever seen, either of them, in all their lives.

The roar of the thunder and the terrifying crash of the sheets of lightning took them unawares, for they had been dozing a little in their long deck chairs. The water came in hot and stinging attacks, forming heavy drops that became needles of rain that grew colder and colder until the gutters were awash and the house fronts streamed and windows everywhere slammed as prudent housewives ran to protect their curtains and floors.

'Come on!' Max cried, running for the door that led into the *pensione,* but Theo stood still, his face turned to the sky and his eyes wide with pleasure as his soft shirt and flannel trousers crumpled into a sodden mass that clung to him, outlining every muscle. 'Come on!' Max shouted again, but Theo shook his head, turning to laugh at him.

'Run where? Why? This is heaven – come and get wet! It's better than swimming – come and get wet with me!' And he pulled off his shirt and then his trousers so that he stood in just his soaking wet vest and drawers, letting the still pouring rain wash him like a shower bath.

'You're mad! Max cried, but none the less did as he was bid, first prudently taking off his own shirt and trousers in the doorway, and leaving them safe inside. Bad enough he'd have to get his underwear dried out –

He splashed his way back across the paving stones of the roof garden, blinking as the water stung his eyes and sent locks of his hair dripping into them, feeling considerable self-consciousness, but Theo reached out for him and pulled him into the centre of the open area and shouted, 'Lift your chin!' just as another great crash of thunder made his ears ring.

It was as though they were completely alone in the world. There was just the drumming of falling water and the streaming ancient stones of Rome shaded below and ahead of them by the seething mist of the falling rain. There was the reverberation of the thunder and the crashing blinding screams of the lightning and their own breath noisy in their chests and no other persons anywhere at all. Two wet young men standing on the roof of a small *pensione* at the top of the Spanish Steps wearing just soaked rags of underwear.

And as though it were some sort of insult to be so absurdly draped, Theo suddenly began to pull at his vest and then at his drawers, hauling them off and shouting as he waved them round his head, one garment in each hand, and roared back at the thunder as it cracked again.

Quite why he followed suit, Max didn't know and was never to know. He just saw Theo's taut body gleaming richly in the now lurid light thrown by the still thickening clouds, saw how his flat belly curved into a concavity as he stretched upwards to wave his garments even more widly, saw the way his buttocks tightened and made the most elegant of outlines as he lifted on to his toes and found himself pulling his own underwear from his own soaking body and then standing with a garment hanging limply in each hand, watching Theo.

He was capering now, kicking up first one leg and then the other as the rain became even more violent and the heat and dust and sweat and langour of the past few days were washed away in the great torrents that were being hurled at them from the livid skies.

'Theo!' Max shouted but the noise of the thunder snatched the words from his mouth, tossed them in the air and hurled them back at him, so that Theo didn't hear him, but he seemed to realize that Max was trying to call him and came capering closer, still dancing like some sort of mad creature of fantasy, and for one crazy moment Max believed he was in fact dreaming.

But he wasn't, for Theo dropped his wet clothes and seized Max by the upper arms so tightly that he winced, but Theo, now in almost a frenzy of simple physical experience pulled even harder at him so that he dropped his own garments and went, will-he, nill-he, capering after Theo to the middle of the roof garden which was now awash with half an inch of water.

'Heaven, it's heaven, It's wonderful!' Theo was shouting. 'Feel it, Peter, feel it, love it, let it touch every inch of you, Peter – love it!' And he pulled on Max again and that made him feel angry, for Theo's nails were sharp, painfully so, and he tried to pull away, pettishly.

'No!' he roared back against the din of the battering rain. 'I don't want to – don't be such an ass, Theo –'

'Live it, Peter, live it!' Theo was shouting again, still holding on to Max's arms and dancing. 'Live it –'

'I'm Max, dammit, and I'm living all I want!' Max shouted. 'Let go, you ass –' And he tried to prise Theo's fingers open with one hand, even though that hurt his biceps even more.

'We'll dance and we'll laugh and we'll walk the freedom way!' Theo seemed to be singing now, and his eyes were glittering under the tangle of wet hair on his forehead as he stared at Max and there was a feverishness about him that made Max frightened suddenly and he put out his now free hand to push the wet hair out of Theo's eyes and making the most of a temporary and blessed lull from the roar of the thunder said gently, 'Theo, my dear chap, do come in, and –'

It was as though he had whipped him, for Theo jerked his head back so sharply that Max felt his own neck crack in sympathy and then, as another roar of thunder split the sky at the seams at the same moment that the lightning blazed the light into a golden impossibly vivid glow – for now the storm was directly overhead – Theo reached out and with arms as hard as his hands had been took hold of Max's bare and streaming wet body and pulled him close.

For Max it was a fraction of a second that seemed to last a life time. His face was so close to Theo's that he could feel his breath hot on his cheeks, could recognize the scent of basil and garlic from the lunch they had shared an hour before. The taut muscles of Theo's spare frame were tight against his own and the hair on Theo's belly and across his groins was harsh against his skin. He was aware of every aspect of this male body straining so tightly to him in a way that was so vivid it was as though it was his own and he tried to pull away. But it was too late for that, for suddenly, the light disappeared as Theo's head came down and he was kissing him. Not the sort of kiss that Max had shared with his brothers and his father, the sort of salute that was a part of every man's life, but an experience of the sort he had never known before. Max's mouth was pushed open by the urgency of Theo's lips, his tongue was attacked by the darting shape of Theo's and his eyes closed almost involuntarily as the sensations filtered his body as though he were a great glass jug and water was rising in him from the very depths of his being.

Cold, sickening water, for he felt his gorge rise even as the sensations did, and he pulled his head back, dragging against Theo's desperate hold and managed to slide his wet arms out of that intense grip and pull back and hit out and as his fingers met Theo's wet cheek with a resounding slap the thunder crashed yet again like a burst of applause and he wanted to laugh, it was so absurdly well timed.

But Theo didn't laugh. He was sitting on the wet ground to which he had lurched as Max's blow upset his balance, staring up at him with his eyes wide with shock, and his face slowly reddening where Max's fingers had hit it. And he was beginning to shake in the same way that he had at the theatre that night, only now the shaking was so violent it seemed he would disintegrate.

25

The clean freshness of the air that came after the storm had spent itself helped Max a good deal. It made him feel so different, after the long days of langorous heat, that he could almost persuade himself that he wasn't here in this Roman *pensione* at all, but at home in London, at Nellie's, looking after a sick man there, could almost persuade himself that he was just a doctor caring for a patient who had suffered a shocking experience, rather than the person who had been most closely involved in that experience. Almost, but not quite.

He had half dragged, half carried, Theo into the bedroom, and got him on to the bed and under the white linen cover, not attempting to dry him. He'll cool down, he'd thought as he pulled up the cover. It'll be as though he's had a cool sponging, he's feverish, got sunstroke, needs to cool down – not daring to admit to himself that it was important to him to cover Theo's nakedness in decency as fast as he could. He dressed himself as quickly as he could too, dragging fresh underwear from his chest of drawers, throwing on trousers and shirt before turning to look at Theo.

He was lying very still under the covers, staring up at the ceiling with his head so tightly controlled that even lying down against the pillow his neck tendons were as taut as wires.

'I – I –' Theo began and then as though opening his mouth had released a spring action somewhere deep inside him began to shake again and he closed his eyes and let out a strangled little wail that was so piteous that Max lost the lingering disgust that had filled him and went over to the bed to sit beside him. He put his hands on each of Theo's shoulders and pressed down hard, as he'd once seen Sir Aaron do at Nellie's with a patient who was reacting to treatment with terror and said loudly, 'This has got to stop. Right now. It's got to stop!'

And amazingly Theo began to relax, rolling his eyes towards Max with an anxious glare and then beginning to sweat as he struggled to control his trembling muscles.

'I'll give you something to help,' Max said, suddenly remembering the ribbed green bottle he'd hidden away, and he went and fetched it and poured a small dose into a tooth glass. 'Drink that. No, don't look at me like that. It's just a sedative. Now drink it and do as you're told.'

From where he was getting his authoritative air Max didn't know. He just knew that somehow he had to make Theo lose his terror so that he could talk. For of that he was certain; not just for Theo's sake, but for his own, there had to be talk, and explanation, and –

The room slid into silence as slowly the chloral began to work in Theo and Max pulled a chair to the bedside and sat down, feeling the fatigue in his own bones. What had happened out there on the roof? Had anything happened at all, in fact? Had he just dozed, been disturbed by the coming storm and dreamed that mad scene in the flash of a second before he woke up? But if that were the case, wouldn't it be worse than if it had been true? Max had read enough of Professor Freud's work now to pay close attention to dreams, and the thought that he could dream such an experience –

He moved roughly in his chair and Theo shifted his gaze and stared at him and said in a husky voice, 'Max? Sorry, Max. Sorry –'

'Be quiet,' Max said, trying to sound like a cool detached doctor. 'I've given you a sedative. You need to relax.'

'I'm beginning to feel better. Not so – the shaking's easier,' Theo said, and his voice had indeed lost that tremor that was so much a part of the attacks when they came. 'Max, I've got to tell you. Before I fall asleep – got to tell you –'

Max stared at the dark glow of his face against the white pillow, for his tan hid any pallor that might be there, and tried to think. Talk – he wanted to talk, too. I need to talk. I don't want to talk. I need to bury the whole stupid episode –

'Why did you call me Peter?' he said abruptly and was startled to hear the words come out of his mouth, for he hadn't

232

thought about the question of Peter at all.

'That's what I've got to tell you,' Theo said, and there was a querulous note in his voice now. 'I can't stand it any longer and I've got to tell someone and it's got to be you, now, hasn't it?'

'Why?'

'Because I called you Peter. Because of what I – because you're my doctor. Because I've got to tell someone –' He began to roll his head against the pillow and Max said loudly, 'Stop that,' and at once Theo obeyed, holding his head rigid and staring up at the ceiling. The light was beginning to fade now, as the dusk moved in from the eastern sky and there were shadows in the corners of the small room.

'Peter – he was my friend. He died in the battle. The one I talked about when I came to your rooms. The one you hypnotized me about.'

Max frowned sharply. 'But you didn't remember what you'd said that day. You forgot it all. Just felt better, you said –'

'I know. I did forget. For a while. And then it came back, bit by bit. I remembered what I'd told you. It all came back bit by bit because I hadn't told you properly – I told you it was Peter's birthday, didn't I?'

'Yes.'

'The next day, I said, was Peter's birthday?'

'Yes.'

'But I didn't tell you of us together, the night before, did I? Didn't tell you what we did?'

'No.'

And I don't want you to tell me, Max thought passionately. I don't want to know, not now or ever –

'Shall I tell you now? Please, shall I tell you now?' And Theo again swivelled his eyes sideways at Max and produced that appealing look and Max stared back, feeling the need in the man reaching out to him.

'Yes,' he said after a long moment. 'Yes. Tell me now.'

Theo licked his lips and then lifted one hand from beneath the covers and rubbed his mouth. 'I'm getting dry,' he said and there was a complaining note in his voice again. 'It's that damned stuff you gave me. It's making me dry and tingling – don't like it much.'

'I'll give you some water,' Max said, and did, moving slowly, for he was getting more and more tired, feeling more and more drained by Theo and his needs. Theo drank, lifting his head awkwardly as Max slid his hand beneath it to help him and then took a noisy little breath.

'Tell you,' he said drowsily and closed his eyes. 'Tell you –'

For a while it seemed that he'd gone to sleep and Max felt a wave of relief rise in him and then of anger. Anger at himself for his lack of professionalism, for surely what mattered was not his own feelings in this matter, but his patient's? And he tried to remember the words that he'd read in one of the many books with which he had filled his days in London.

'The patient's demands may feel onerous to the clinician,' Dr Kraepelin had written. 'He may shift his dependence from others to the doctor he comes to regard as the fount of his well-being. This situation of transference requires great care on the part of the practitioner, if it is not to be allowed to become too major a factor in the patient's life –'

It was as though the words had opened a door in his mind, and suddenly he leaned forwards and touched Theo's shoulder. 'Theo you were going to tell me,' he said, speaking gently now. 'About Peter. Tell me now. You'll feel better when you do –'

'Hm?' Theo opened his eyes drowsily, and then blinked, opened them widely again as though in an attempt to force them to stay open. 'Yes, tell you –'

'Well?' It's all right, Max was thinking. It's all right. It was nothing to do with me. It's a transference, it's because I'm his doctor, that's all it is, it's because I helped him, and he needed someone to lean on and who better than me? It's all right – 'Theo?' he said aloud, more sharply 'Tell me –'

And at last Theo began to talk, dragging the words out of himself at first, but then more easily until he was fluent if a little slurred in his speech by the chloral. And it was a sad little tale, Max thought, sitting in the dwindling light of the rain-washed afternoon and watching him. A sad little story, which once it was stripped of the disdainful opinions he had heard so

234

often expressed by others about men like Theo bore the seeds of tragedy in it.

It was as though he could see him change from a child to an adult before his eyes. Theo talked of his loneliness when he had been at school and his growing awareness that he wasn't like the other boys. They talked often of the girls they saw, of the buxom maids who made their dormitory beds and served their meals, of the chances of catching one in a quiet school corridor and kissing and touching her, while the young Theo had listened and been revolted. For he wasn't like them. He felt differently –

The long lonely years of working with his father, pretending to be as interested as the other clerks were in the lady typists, but becoming more and more shut away, more and more isolated. Until the war and officer-training college and Peter.

It had taken a long time, Theo murmured, a long time, and again he rolled his head on the pillow in that restless anxious way and Max reached out and touched his shoulder and at once he was still again. But he went on talking, talking, talking.

It must have been like a sledgehammer, Max thought, listening, and felt an odd pang of sympathy. He had himself never yet fallen in love. Like the boys at Theo's school he'd been fascinated by the plump maids at his own, had enjoyed his share of grapples in the shadowy corners, had dreamed of having his arms filled with warm femininity, but he had been too occupied always with his studies, and the life of a busy student to give much attention to such physical affairs. They had never yet loomed large in his own life. But listening now to Theo he began to have a glimmering idea of what it might be like to be completely physically enslaved. To see another person and to feel your belly crawl with need, to be terrified of touching that person, yet even more terrified of being parted –

'And I didn't know,' Theo mumbled. 'You see? I didn't know. He was just one of the others – never showed what he was like to any of us. Was just himself, so marvellously himself. And I wanted him so badly and he never showed what he was like – and then they sent us to the same section of the Front and we were together all the time, in that damned dugout, sharing everything, going everywhere together because we were duty officers together – and it got worse and worse –'

Until the night before the battle which was to kill Peter. They had been alone in the dugout because one of the other men had gone sick and been taken away behind the lines and outside it had been a black calico night as dark and moonless and blessedly silent as only a night in those trenches could be, and they had talked. At last they had talked – or Theo had. And Peter had not argued or said anything when Theo trembling with excitement had crossed the packed earth floor and stood beside his camp bed, and then moving stiffly with the tension of his own need, slipped into bed with him –

'It was beautiful. It was right and it was beautiful and I'd never known it could be so – it was right – but in the morning when I woke he'd gone to the trench and when he came back the others were there, he wouldn't talk, he just wouldn't talk to me – and then the battle started and I never did talk, I never did, I never did –'

There were tears running down his face now and Max leaned forwards and touched him, putting his hand on his bare shoulder and Theo turned his now bleary eyes on him, and said piteously, 'You see? I'll never know now. He died and I'll never know what it was for him. I loved him so, and I'll never know. I tried to die too, I tried so hard but all that happened was bloody hero, lousy stinking bloody hero, and I'll never know –'

He drew a shuddering little breath and closed his eyes and after a moment, his lips parted slightly and be began to snore gently and Max wanted to laugh, for it was so anticlimactic that it was ridiculous. But however ridiculous, the tragedy was still there, hanging in the air like a mist of tears. And somewhere behind his need to laugh was a need to weep, too.

The journey home was a very different one from the journey out. They packed in the morning as soon as Theo had emerged from the bathroom looking a little dazed with the aftermath of his chloral-induced sleep, but calm and collected without being unduly controlled, not discussing the matter at all. The decision had been made for them, in a sense, and they paid their bill to the lamenting Signor Hassler, who 'had persuaded himself the young chentlemen would stay and sample the Roman vay a leetle more' and found a cab to take them to the Piazza del Cinquecento to check on the availability of seats on the London leg of the Rome Express.

It took a sizeable bribe to get them on it, for the Thursday journey was the most popular of the weekly departures, but they managed it, and after sending a terse cable to Letty to say they were on their way back and would reach Victoria on Saturday ('She's paying the bill, she's entitled to know,' Max said crisply when Theo had protested at bothering her) settled in their corner seats well before the train was due to steam slowly out of Viminal Hill.

It was not the fact that they did not talk to each other on the journey that made it so dismal an experience. Indeed, they talked a great deal, seeming to be full of bright conversation on every subject from the passing scenery to the behaviour of their fellow passengers, but it was hollow echoing empty talk. The delight they had found in each other's jokes and laughter on the way to Rome had been left far behind them in a roof garden at the top of the Spanish Steps.

The crossing from Calais was smooth and the passage through the customs sheds at Dover trouble-free but all the same by the time the Victoria train pulled in Max was exhausted, as much by the emotional strain of trying to keep up a front of friendliness as by the rigours of the journey itself. He was white with weariness and moved sluggishly as the train pulled in to the accompaniment of great gouts of steam puffing up under the roof as the engine let go of the last shreds of its power, and it was Theo who stepped down on the platform first.

Max could hear it as soon as he was standing on the grey concrete, swaying a little as he set down his suitcase. Beyond the barrier at the far side they were screaming and waving again, and for a moment he experienced a stab of *déjà vu*. He was outside the theatre again after the opening of *Never Kiss and Tell* and the frantic admirers were shrieking for 'Mark

237

Antony, Mark Antony —'

He blinked and shook his head and stared and there they were in their hundreds; eager girls with bobbed hair and girls with long hair, girls fashionable and girls plain, girls young and girls extremely young and not a few older women as well, of the sort he was used to seeing sitting patiently waiting for attention at Nellie's out-patient department. And he stared again as Letty appeared, hurrying along the platform from the barrier with a flustered sweating station master in tow.

'It's unbelievable!' she said. 'I'd never have let Edwin do it, if I'd known it would happen this way. How are you, my dears? You look superb —' and she gave Theo a judicious stare and nodded in approval. 'That tan suits you. Better see to it we make sure you keep it. Look, we can talk later. Right now, we've got to get you out of here. Mr Lewis here says he can sneak you out through the side way. I'm truly sorry, Theo, but as soon as the notice went into the society columns — that you'd be back today — it started. They've gone mad over you, my dear. I do apologize.' But she looked as pleased with herself as a woman could, and Theo laughed.

'My dear Letty, you're not a bit sorry. That's money in the bank, isn't it?' And he lifted his chin with an oddly exultant little air and stared down the platform at the ticket-collector struggling to let out their fellow passengers while preventing the passage of the pushing screaming fanatics shouting for their beloved Mark Antony.

'Well, yes,' she said. 'But we'll have to talk about how to make the best of it. Right now, we'll go the side way with Mr Lewis here and you'll be safe —' And the sweating station master huffed a little and tried to lead Theo away to the other side of the platform.

'No,' Theo said and pulled away from him. 'I want to go the proper way. Through the barrier — are you ready, Letty? Can you cope?'

She stared at him and then slowly a grin split her face.

'Can I? Try me! Come on —' And she pulled her coat more closely round her and turned to march along the platform. 'Coming, Max?'

'No,' he said. 'No. I'll wait till the fuss dies down. I imagine it will, once you've gone.' And he shot a sardonic little glance at Theo who stared back coolly and then smiled.

'I told you Max, once, didn't I, that I'd discovered I liked being looked at? Well, I've discovered something else. That you are what you are and you might as well roll with it as fight it. Don't you think I'm right?'

'I don't know. You may be.'

'I've tried it the other way. Fighting it. Now I'm going to walk right into it. This and – everything. It's the only answer, isn't it? Wish me well, Max.'

'What is all this?' Letty said sharply, looking from one to the other and Max felt the old hostility in her and wanted to reassure her, wanted to tell her she had nothing to fear from him. It's different now, Letty, he heard himself shouting inside his head. It's all different now – be warned, Letty. It's different –

But he just shook his head at her and said nothing, looking at Theo who lifted his brows again and said quietly, 'Won't you wish me well? I shan't be seeing much of you in the future, I suspect –'

'Of course,' Max said and was surprised at how tight his lips felt. 'Of course I wish you well – and of course we'll see each other again –' But Theo shook his head and turned to walk away down the platform and the shrieks of the waiting girls lifted to a crescendo as he reached the barrier and made his way through to them, closely followed by Letty and the station master.

The last Max saw of him as he stood there on the now empty station platform was Theo's head above the mêlée as the girls all round him pushed and shoved and wept their delight at having him with them. And suddenly perceiving the irony of their adoration, Max began to laugh.

26

'But how can you possibly imagine you can be an alienist, my boy, if you can't even talk about your own anxieties?' Lewis said, pushing down his exasperation as best he could. 'As I understand it a great deal of the care these chaps give involves getting the patients to talk. Well, surely that means you need to do so as well? You've heard me say it many times – the best physicians have had pneumonia, the best surgeons have been under the knife. So I can't see how a silent alienist is going to be of much value to anyone.'

Max stirred in his seat and then leaned forwards and set his elbows on the table. His mother and sister had been delighted to see him (though Johanna was still rather more quiet than she'd used to be) and he to see them, but he'd been grateful when, dinner at last over and the interminable questions about Rome answered until he felt like a walking Baedeker, they had retired to the drawing-room leaving him alone with his father. His young brother was away on a school visit and now there were just the two of them lingering over the port and walnuts in the cool dining-room. The windows were open to the summer evening air and it was very peaceful with just the sleepy twittering of the birds' evening chorus from the garden disturbing the silence.

'Does that mean you're willing to approve of my taking up the speciality?' he said. 'When I went away you were very opposed, weren't you? I'd told you what I was going to do and you – well, you weren't precisely pleased.'

'I know.' Lewis looked down into the depths of ruby in his glass. 'I had my own reasons for that.'

'And I've my own reasons for being quiet now, Dad,' Max said gently.

Lewis lifted his chin and looked at his son, at the squareness of his face in the lamplight and he frowned slightly. 'I know I'm right,' he said and he sounded almost petulant. 'There's something wrong. You keep dodging when I ask you, but there's something wrong. Something different, I mean. Not Tim. Something else.'

Max was silent for a moment and then he said in a very level voice, 'No. Not Tim. I'll never forget him, but that's over now. Tim's dead and I know it, and there's nothing I could have done to stop that and there's nothing I can do now to help Tim's yesterday. But I can be glad he lived now that I know he's dead.'

'That's what I meant,' Lewis said. 'It's something different. Why won't you tell me?'

Max leaned back in his chair again and frowned. 'This is a new thing in you, Dad. You've never been a – well, the other chaps have their fathers never leaving them alone. Nagging and – but you've never been that way. But now you're as bad as any of 'em. Why?'

Lewis bit his lip and looked down and then back at Max. 'You're getting exceedingly sharp!' he said and managed a laugh, but it was a strained one and Max said nothing, just staring at him interrogatingly.

The silence between them lengthened and then Lewis began to crack walnuts, twisting the shells between his strong surgery-trained fingers and peeling the kernels with finicky attention to detail.

'I need to know what's worrying you, Max,' he said at length. 'Before I can talk to you about – well, before I can talk. As soon as you walked in this afternoon I knew something was upsetting you, and that worried me for selfish reasons.' And he gave Max a crooked little grimace of a grin. 'I'd decided, you see, while you were away – I've been thinking a lot while you were away – that I'd ask your advice. No, don't look like that! You're an adult now, remember. I know you're my boy, I know that whenever I look at you I see a sort of shadow of the baby you used to be standing there in your shoes, but I'm ignoring that! You're a doctor now. One of my own profession. And while I was trying to think who I could talk to, knowing I needed someone's advice, someone I could trust, I thought of you. Who better could I go to? But I can't till you talk to me. Can I?'

Max shook his head, bewildered. 'You want my advice? Are you ill? You look well –' His voice sharpened with sudden anxiety. 'Are you having symptoms that –'

Lewis laughed. 'No, you foolish boy! Of course not. If I were I'd go to the most senior man in the relevant speciality, you can be sure. I've more sense than to do otherwise! No, it's nothing like that. I'm as merry as a grig in my body. It's – I have a personal anxiety, and I can't talk to anyone but you. Even at the risk of making you despise me.'

'I can't imagine ever feeling that,' Max said and smiled across the expanse of polished wood at his father, aware suddenly of how much he cared for him. His heavy greyish head, the lined face, the way the polish on the table reflected the whiteness of his hands as they rested on its surface; it was all inexpressibly dear, and impulsively he leaned forward and set his own hands over his father's and said, 'I'm damned lucky to have you, you know!'

'And I to have you,' Lewis said gravely. 'What is it, Max? You can tell me.'

And Max told him. As easily as if he'd been discussing the content of an examination question, and how he had dealt with it. He told his father what had happened in Rome, of the explosion of feeling in the middle of that explosive thunderstorm; and all through it Lewis listened, watching his son's face and making no attempt to interrupt.

'The problem now is,' Max said at length, a little hoarse with fatigue and so much talking, 'to understand myself. Was it something I did? Did I make him feel I was like him? *Am* I like him? I – it's not something I've ever thought about much, to tell the truth. I've heard the sort of stupid jokes the others tell, you know, but it was always something remote. Nothing to do with me. And now it is.'

Lewis shook his head. 'No, it isn't,' he said. 'You're not effeminate in any way.'

'How can you be so sure? Couldn't that be the fond father speaking, not wanting to think ill of his son? I dare say Cousin

James would deny that Theo is effeminate. Anyway, he isn't. He's every inch a man and you know it. The way he acted at Passchendaele was enormously brave. No one could see him as anything but a strong man. I simply don't understand.'

'Black and white. Black and white,' Lewis murmured.

'Eh? How do you mean? What's that to do with –'

'I'm sorry. It was just that – it's a risk being too cut and dried in your ideas. I rather suspect I've been thinking that way lately myself. But seeing things in black and white can be a disaster. Life isn't as easy as that.' He leaned forwards then and poured himself some more port. 'I wish it were.'

'You still haven't answered my question. How can you be so sure I'm not – that I'm all right?'

'You'd have known long before this if you weren't,' Lewis said. 'When he told you of himself, didn't Theo say as much? Or did he tell you what happened with this Peter of his was some sort of sudden revelation?'

'No,' Max said slowly. 'No, he didn't. He said he'd always known. At school and – he'd always known he was different. He said that another time too – about the hell of being different.'

'Have you ever felt different?'

'Not really. At least I don't think so –'

'What about girls, then? Have you ever felt towards the men you meet the same way as you do about girls?'

'I've never bothered with girls much. The nurses at Nellie's – well, you know how it is there –'

Lewis grinned. 'Indeed I do. If you don't duck you're likely to be hooked in a matter of weeks after getting there. Many a fine medical career's been deflected into the backwater of general practice by an eager nurse getting her matrimonial trap set first.'

'You told me that before I started training – so I kept out of the way. Besides, I've never been –' He flushed and looked away. 'Well, some of the chaps seem to find all their pleasure below their waists. For my part, I've never been all that concerned –'

'No need to apologize,' Lewis said, and smiled. 'There's no law that says you must. I started late too –' and suddenly his

243

face shadowed.

Max didn't notice, still absorbed in his own affairs. 'So you think that what happened was because – well, it just happened? That I did nothing to encourage it?'

'I'm sure of it,' Lewis said. 'And I dare say you found you quite liked the sensation to start with, I mean a kiss is a kiss, whoever gives it – it's only when you realize it's the wrong person that it stops feeling as good –'

He stopped suddenly and stared at Max. 'Good God!' he said very loudly. 'Good God Almighty!'

'Eh?' Max was startled, for his father was staring at him with his eyes wide. 'What's the matter?'

'What did I just say?'

'About what?'

Lewis shook his head, his eyes wider than ever. 'The last words I said. Repeat them back to me exactly.'

'I'm not sure,' Max said uncertainly. 'Something about a kiss being a kiss whoever gives it –'

'Yes. Go on – go on!'

'That it's only when you realize that it's the wrong person that you stop feeling good.'

'I said that? I did, didn't I?'

Max laughed a little uneasily. 'Dad, what is all this? Of course you did! And I'm glad you did. It makes sense and it helps me – a lot, I think.'

'It does make sense, doesn't it?' Lewis said with sudden great enthusiasm. 'It's the best bit of sense you'll hear this week! I'll tell you something – it's the best bit of sense I've heard myself for a long time. Any kiss feels good because it's a natural neurological response. But as soon as a thinking person realizes it's the wrong person giving it it stops feeling good. Yes – but that doesn't mean that the sensation that came with the kiss in the first place meant anything significant. Right?'

And Max grinned. 'Right,' he said. 'I think –'

'Think?' Lewis said with great vigour. 'Dammit, boy, I know! So take my word for it. You don't have to worry about the sort of person you are, when it comes to such things. One of these days when you're ready you'll meet a pretty lady and fall in love with her, and make children with her. And if you're lucky, you'll be half as happy as I've been with your mother these many years. And if you're touched by magic as we were, you'll be exactly as happy as we've been, your mother and I, and will, God willing, go on being so for many years yet.'

Max stared at him, his face still doubtful.

'If you're sure, then I – well, yes, I dare say you're right. It was just that I was so confused –'

'I know, my boy. I know all about confusion,' Lewis said, and now there was an earnestness in his tone. 'I've been bedevilled by it. Ambiguous feelings, you see. They bedevil every one of us. You feel one thing and then damn me if you don't go and feel the precise opposite and act accordingly and hate yourself for the confusion and the conflict! It's enough to make a man spin on his heels –'

'Or make him ill.'

'Indeed, yes, I dare say it could.'

A slow smile moved across Max's face. 'Dad, you're talking like an alienist,' he said softly and began to laugh. 'You're sounding like one of Professor Freud's books. Maybe you're discovering that being an alienist wouldn't be such a terrible thing for me after all?'

Lewis took a deep breath and shook his head then. 'Now, wait a minute, Max, wait a minute. Let's not rush into this. I know there's something in this business of nerve afflictions, of course there is, but I'm not sure these Viennese chaps have got it precisely right –'

'There're plenty of good English practitioners, Dad. You mustn't be a xenophobic, you know. That's a sort of nerve affliction in itself.'

'Hmph. That's as may be. It's the – oh, it's the unscientific nature of it all that I can't swallow. These days we've got science tethered to medicine's apron-strings. We don't just bleed 'em and purge 'em and leech 'em the way our grandfathers did! We really look and listen and understand and act accordingly –'

'So do alienists, Dad.'

'But where are the schools of the speciality? Where do these people really do their clinical work? Where can you demonstrate in the anatomy room the processes involved in it all? How can you trust a so-called speciality that has no structure?'

'I dare say surgery didn't have it when it started. When they were barbers,' Max said. 'And wasn't your great-grandfather who started Nellie's a mere apothecary? Everything has to start somewhere.'

'He was a surgeon, studied properly. Robbed graves to do it,' Lewis said and gave a crack of laughter. 'How's that for the scientific method? He'd have had no truck with all this alienist stuff.'

'I suspect he might, if he were here now. It's time that makes the difference. The more we find out, the more we realize we have to learn. I want to do it, Dad. This first case of mine mayn't have been a successful one – well, so far that is. He might get better yet, to spite me – but I still want to go on. Learn more –'

'How?'

'What?'

'How will you learn more?'

'Read. Listen to lectures –'

'Where?' Lewis sounded triumphant. 'That's precisely my point. Where are you to get the training you need?'

'I can go to Vienna,' Max said after a moment. 'Or somewhere like that. It can't be impossible.'

'You've made up your mind to it then?'

'Pretty well,' Max said gently. 'I told you that before, Dad. I know what I want. And now you've helped me feel better about – well, feel better, I'm still determined. There's a lot to be learned about that particular affliction, isn't there? Why some men have such a strange need. It is strange, isn't it?'

Lewis laughed then and got up from the table. 'More things in heaven and earth Horatio –' he said. 'More things – I can't say whether it's strange or not. Nor can you.'

'But I can try to find out. And I shall.'

They'd reached the door now. 'Will you wish me well, Dad. Or prevent me?'

Lewis stood with his hand on the doorknob, staring at his son, seeing as he always did the face of the small boy with the eager wide eyes and the soft mouth which could collapse into a pout at the sight of his father's slightest frown, and tried to smile. 'I shan't prevent you, Max. If you're so determined. As long as you do it well, how can I? Just let me share whatever it is you do and what you plan and we'll be good enough friends, I'm sure.'

They were half-way up the stairs to the drawing-room when Max remembered and stopped.

'You wanted to ask me something.'

'Hmm?'

'You said you wanted my advice. What was it?'

Lewis smiled and began to climb the stairs again. 'No need my boy, after all. Listening to you talking helped me sort it out on my own. There's no need to bother you after all.'

27

Letty had kept herself very busy all morning, checking the highly gratifying box-office takings from *Caesar and Cleopatra* and arranging for extra prints to be made of the film so that it could be shown at out-of-London cinemas, as well as doing the accounts to see if it would be possible to resurrect the takings on *Never Kiss and Tell* now that her star performer was back and apparently in good health. But all the time her own needs and feelings were nagging at the back of her mind and making her miserable.

Edwin put up with her snappiness until eleven and then took his hat and stick and told her silkily that he was off to the Burlington Arcade to get a new hat, quietly telling Alf on the way out to Chelsea Reach that he'd better watch his Ps and Qs or he'd have his nose bitten off, and Alf, agreeing with him, found the day a good one to take himself off to the scene dock at the Shaftesbury to check the set. The Gaff Studios were not a comfortable place to be that blazing July morning.

By lunchtime Letty herself was aware of the tension she had created and decided that if she stayed there any longer she'd get in the way of essential work – the studios were currently making a series of comedy one-reelers to fill out the pro-grammes at the chain of provincial cinemas with which Letty had recently signed a lucrative contract – and she tugged on her straw hat and went out into the hot street to walk away her anxiety.

Not that walking helped that much. She went swinging along Luna Street, making a fast time and attracting not a few glances from passers by who were startled by seeing so determined a woman in an area of London more noted for fashionable loungers than determined workers, and made her way to the King's Road, on her way to Sloane Square station. She'd have to see him, that was the thing. She couldn't go on as she'd been these past weeks since the first night of *Never Kiss and Tell*. It was getting perfectly ridiculous, spending night after night lying awake, day after day having to make an almost physical effort to keep her mind clear of anything but work. There was only one person who could help her, and somehow he'd have to be made to do so.

Not that it was going to be easy. It was all very well to be a modern independent woman, all very well to tell yourself that you could do anything any man could, even prove it by running a business of great complexity virtually single-handed, but the hard fact was that when it came to matters to do with love, a woman was at a dreadful disadvantage.

Love, she thought and made a grimace as she passed the Pheasantry, still striding along at a rate that threatened the equilibrium of everyone she passed. Such slush, such senti-mental sick-making slush! Love was what she made films about, love was what brought the money into the box office, love was what those damned screaming women at the stage door that night and at Victoria Station yesterday were on about. Love wasn't for her, Letty Lackland, the sensible, controlled Letty Lackland who had left such emotions behind her when Luke O'Hare had died in Switzerland –

But you didn't, did you? Her secret voice jeered at her from somewhere deep inside her. You didn't leave it behind, for why else are you marching down the King's Road like some damned centurion looking for an army to destroy, if you aren't eaten up with it? Love, love, love – you're eaten up with it –

And I'll have to deal with it, she told the jeering little voice as she bought her ticket at Sloane Square station and went down to wait on the platform for a train to take her to Piccadilly Circus from where she could walk up Shaftesbury Avenue. I'll have to deal with it. That's why I'm here now, why I'm going off to behave like a brazen self-indulgent hussy instead of a well-ordered female, and sort it all out, one way or the other.

When she reached the doorway of King Edward's Mansions

she almost quailed, for all her earlier determination. The building stretched above her, red-bricked anonymity in the vivid sunshine, its windows staring blindly back at her, and she thought, almost in a panic – I'm mad! I must be mad to be here like this – in the middle of a working day at that – but then the main door opened and a large woman wrapped in a voluminous flowered apron and with a man's flat cap firmly skewered on to her sparse grey hair came out with the bucket and a mop to clean the front steps.

'Can I 'elp yer?' she asked suspiciously and stared at Letty's neat green linen frock and shady cream straw hat as though they were the cloak and dagger of a wartime spy. ' 'Oo was yer wantin'?'

'Mr Caspar,' Letty said, trying to sound as crisp as she could, and at once the suspicion vanished as the flabby face split into a wide gap-toothed grin.

'Ow, our Mr Caspar – yers, luv, 'e's in, and a real treat it is to 'ave 'im back all safe and that. Would you be a relation like?'

'I'm from the film studios,' Letty said sharply, hating the woman for her immediate warmth at the mention of Theo's name, hating herself for the craven need to display her special connection to him, and the woman at once wiped her vast red hand on her overall and pushed the front door open for her.

'You go right on up, ducks, an' tell 'im as I sent yer. No need to ring 'is bell, like, on account I opened the door fer you. Mrs McFarlane, tell 'im –'

The staircase was cool and echoing and she marched up the linoleumed treads trying to control the rate at which her pulse was beating by breathing deeply, and knowing how absurd she was being. But knowing didn't help much.

The door of number 8 was ajar and she tapped on it and waited but there was no response and after another moment she pushed it wider and went in. The tiny hallway was empty and beyond it the sitting-room was, too, and she went in and looked about and then called in as casual a voice as she could conjure up. 'Theo!'

'I'm in here, Mrs Mac!' his voice came muffled from the other side of the hallway and she tipped her head and listened and now could hear the splash of water.

'Not Mrs Mac,' she called. 'Letty. I'll wait here for you,' and she sat down, smoothing the green linen over her lap and then edgily taking a cigarette from the pocket in the skirt. She was leaning back with a fine air of insouciance when he came in, cigarette smoke curling round her head, and he stood in the doorway, tying the cord of his dressing-gown and grinned at her.

'Well, there's a surprise! Sorry I thought you were Mrs Mac. Anyone less like that rather unfortunate heap I never saw!'

'Thank you,' she said dryly. 'I've met the lady.'

'Then you see what I mean. But she's a good soul, keeps this place as neat as a pin for me and makes perfectly delectable breakfasts.'

He looks well, she thought, staring at the way his neck, brown and muscular, rose from the cream silk collar of his pyjama jacket. I mustn't look at him. I mustn't.

'This is a hell of a time to be thinking of breakfast. D'you realize it's almost one o'clock?'

'So? I've nowhere special to go at present.' He sat down, perching on the arm of a chair and grinned at her, and she smiled back, but it was a strained smile. The way his hair's rumpled is very appealing. Makes him look vulnerable and – mustn't look.

'Forget breakfast. Let's have lunch,' she said abruptly. 'Go down to Rosa's at the other end of Shaftesbury Avenue. I've got to go to the Film Censor's office later this afternoon and it's just a few doors down on the corner of Dean Street. It'll be convenient to go there.' And inside her head the little voice jeered; what the hell's the matter with you, woman? Why are you twittering in this stupid fashion?

'That'd be delightful,' he said and looked at her sharply. 'You all right, Letty? You look a bit –'

'I'm fine. Fine. What about you?'

He stretched with catlike satisfaction. 'I feel wonderful,' he said and smiled again. 'Quite wonderful.'

'Then your holiday did you good?'

'Indeed it did. In more ways than one. Thank you for arranging it.'

She shrugged that off. 'Then you've had no more attacks?'

He was silent for a moment and then stood up. 'Nothing that need worry you.' He went to the door and stood there for a moment. 'I'll dress then. Shan't be long. I'm glad you came, Letty. I've got to talk to you.'

'Oh? Anything important?'

'It is to me.' He stopped then and stared at her and she felt a stab of – what? Anxiety? Hope? She couldn't be sure. 'I don't know how you'll see it. But I want to talk to you and then – well, I'll get dressed. I won't be long.'

They walked along Shaftesbury Avenue in silence, until they passed the Shaftesbury Theatre. Theo made a face at the facade and the pictures of the understudy in his role that adorned it, and she grinned at that.

'Annoys you, does it?'

'I never thought it'd matter that much, but dammit, it does! It's my part, and I want to see my face up there on the hoardings. Disgusting, isn't it?'

'Not at all. It's just professional. Every actor feels that way.'

'But I'm so damned new at it! Not a year old, this acting business with me! and here I am already as vain as a peacock –'

'No,' she said again. 'Just professional. Are you ready to go back into the play?'

He flicked a glance at her. 'I haven't thought about it,' he said and she heard the evasion in his voice and the stab she had felt before came back but now she knew it was anxiety.

The small restaurant was busy, but Rosa Scheggia, who knew Letty well, found a table in the corner for her and settled them there with an agreeable little flurry that helped Letty at least feel less self-conscious and they ordered the *plats du jour* and settled to the glass of wine fat cheerful Rosa hurried to bring them.

But the self-consciousness returned and she spoke after a while with a gruff sharpness she hadn't meant. 'Well, what was it you wanted to talk to me about?'

'It can wait. Let's eat first. Tell me what's been happening here while I was away.'

She shrugged. 'What could happen? The film's been taking a lot of money, the play's been taking less though we've had a lot of box-office inquiry about when you'll be back in the cast and I'm thinking hard about the next film for you. What about you? You still haven't told me properly how it was in Rome. You said a little last night, but what with the hubbub with your adorers and getting you safe home –'

'It wasn't easy, was it?' His lips curled with obviously agreeable recollection. 'They really were excited, weren't they?'

'You liked it?'

There was a little silence and he drank more of his wine.

'Yes,' he said then, and lifted his chin with an oddly obstinate air. 'Is that so dreadful? Yes I did.'

'You want more of it?'

'Yes.'

'Then we'll make good films together,' she said and felt the old familiar satisfaction come bubbling up in her, the satisfaction that she had learned to enjoy so much in her business dealings. To get an actor with the appeal that Theo so obviously enjoyed firmly attached to the Gaff Studios would bring nothing but future benefit to the business and that was something to be glad of, whatever happened to her personally.

'That's one of the things I wanted –' Theo began but their food arrived with much flurry on Rosa's part and he had to stop. They ate in slience for a while, Letty picking at her salad with ill-disguised uninterest, though Theo seemed to be hungry enough. It wasn't until the main course had come and gone and they were sitting with cups of coffee in front of them that she felt able to come to the point.

'Theo,' she said abruptly. 'There're things I have to say to you that – they have nothing to do with the films I want us to make in the future. Well, they have in a way, but –' And she stopped and stared down at the tablecloth in front of her, wanting to find elegant words to say it with, and not being able to.

'Me too,' Theo said quickly. 'I've been thinking a lot and it's important that –'

'I'm probably mad to insist on saying what I want to say first.' Her voice was rather loud now. 'But I've got to. I ought to wait and be the way other women are, eyelashes fluttering and – well, I'm not. I can only say what I have to say. And it's been driving me mad this last – I don't know how long.'

And now she lifted her head and looked at him very directly. Curiously, it was easier now that she'd started; the words were at last there ready to come out and the fear that had been thickening in her chest all morning had melted. She felt strong and capable again and it was a good way to feel.

'Theo, as you said, it's been less than a year since we met. But it's been long enough for me to know that in spite of myself I've developed a great deal of affection for you. More than that. I love you. I love you and I want you and I hope very much you can find the same sort of feeling for me. I don't ask you to marry me. I know I ought to care about things like that, but I don't give a damn, frankly, I do as I like. And if you prefer not to marry me, that's fine with me. But I want you as a lover on any terms you like. There! I've said it. I love you, and what are you going to do about it?'

He stared at her with what she first hoped was simply amazement but then as the silence went on realized with a sense of real physical sickness was not. It was horror.

'Oh, my God,' he said softly. 'I never thought – oh, my God –'

'If I've made a fool of myself say so.' Letty's voice was still rather loud and clear and with a small part of her mind she was glad that the restaurant was almost empty now. Not that it would have made much difference if it had been solid with eager listeners. She had started now and she had to finish. 'It won't kill me to be told. It's much more painful not to know where I stand.'

'I'd hoped I wouldn't have to tell you,' he said, never taking his eyes from her face. 'I thought I'd be able just to explain my plans and then – I didn't think I'd have to tell you why. But now I must, mustn't I?'

She shrugged, and her shoulders ached and her mouth felt so stiff she could only just form the words. 'If there's someone else in your life I don't know about of course that's different. I'm not a special bargain of a woman, I know that. It wouldn't surprise me to know you loved someone else.'

'There's no other woman,' he said gently. 'I can promise

you that. Does that help?'

'Not much,' she said and tried to smile, but it was almost impossible. 'Well, yes, perhaps a little. Maybe it means that one day you might change your mind – when you get used to having me around. I've no pride, have I? I'm willing to wait while you work at it. If you're willing to work at it, that is.'

Please say you will, please don't tell me it's impossible. I couldn't stand it. Please don't say it.

'No,' he said. 'That's not the answer. I'll have to tell you, won't I?'

'Tell me what?' and now there was a spark of anger in her, and she blew on it, nurturing it, needing it to replace the sick desolation that was slowly filling her. 'I don't know what the hell you're talking about.'

'I made a decision. Last night. I sat up for a long time, thinking, and I made a decision. I'm going away, Letty. I'm grateful to you for opening the doors for me, and now I'm walking through them and I'm going away.'

'Where to?' The words came out clipped and tight but inside her head they made a great wail of misery. 'Where to?'

He grinned a little sheepishly. 'Well, America, actually. I want to go and make films in America, in Hollywood. They may tell me to run away and play and not waste their time, but it ought to be possible to try. And after *Caesar and Cleopatra* – well, I'm going. And – there're personal reasons too –'

'Personal reasons.'

'Family. And now you – I didn't want anyone to know but –well, my family never will, that's certain. But you're different. You've been so honest that I've got to be as honest with you. I think it might help you to understand, too. To feel better about yourself.'

'You don't have to worry about how I feel,' she said harshly. 'I'm a grown woman. I can take care of myself.'

'But you hate yourself right now. You feel you've thrown yourself at a man's head and been rejected. Well, I want you to know you haven't.'

'I see. Then all this has just been you being coy, pretending you didn't –'

'No!' he said. 'Listen, for God's sake. This is harder for me than it is for you, believe it or not.' And as she stared at him, her mouth open to expostulate, his face seemed to harden, to become older and more tired, and for just a second she feared he was about to have another of his attacks.

'The thing is, Letty, I can't love you. I can't ever love any woman.'

She frowned, not understanding. 'But –'

'Don't be obtuse, for God's sake. Listen to what I say. *I can never love any woman*! It's no fault in women, not you or the Venus de Milo herself. Not any woman. I'm not made that way.'

'Not made that way,' she said blankly and then slowly her own face began to redden and she looked away, as embarrassed as if he had suddenly taken off all his clothes and begun to caper naked about the little restaurant with its now empty marble tables and tired hot air.

'I – do you mean that – that you –' She stopped and shook her head. 'I'm sorry, I can't quite –'

'I found out years ago. I've been trying to deny it ever since, and it's made me ill. That's been the cause of the hell I've been through all these months. It wasn't just what happened at Passchendaele. It was because of Peter. My –' He stopped and took a deep breath. 'My lover. He died there. And I couldn't let myself grieve for him until I admitted what I am. That's what I have to do. And because of my family I can't do it here. I'm going to America. There it won't matter so much, will it? If people jeer there I'll be the only one to be humiliated. My family won't.'

'You don't have to go,' she said desperately. 'They needn't know and it won't matter to me. I can help you. I love you, Theo. I can make you well again –'

'I'm not ill,' he said gently. 'You have to understand that, Letty. I'm not ill. I'm the man I am, and I won't change. I don't *want* to change. I'm grateful to you, my dear, deeply grateful. You've given me back my life. The best thing I ever did was falling over you in that doorway last November. But now you've given me my life and my whole new future, you've got to let me go to live it. Goodbye, my dear. I don't think, do you, that I ought to go back into *Never Kiss and Tell*?' He laughed then. 'What a damnably apposite title that turned out to be!'

He was at the door of the little restaurant now, his hand on the knob. 'I'm sorry, Letty. Truly, truly sorry. To have made you sad, that is. But for myself –' And he lifted his chin exultantly. 'For myself I'm not a bit sorry. I feel marvellous. I've made a decision and I can stick to it. I feel *marvellous*. Goodbye Letty. *Bon chance!*'

And he was gone, leaving the door swinging behind him as Rosa came padding out of her kitchen with the bill for their lunch.

28

'Damn stupid time of year for a wedding,' grunted Oliver and he pulled his Ulster more firmly about his ears. 'Why couldn't they wait till spring like any other well-conducted people? Draggin' a man from a decent fireside on such a day – ain't reasonable.'

'Probably thought they'd better hurry it up to make sure you hadn't turned up your toes before they tied the knot,' Edwin said and giggled his malicious little giggle. 'After all, my dear chap, you're the most important member of the whole family aren't you? And I dare say they were thinking of you and only you when they made their plans!'

'Hmph,' Oliver said and glared at him. 'You'll turn your toes up sooner than I will, the way you racket about. Drinking your damn-fool head off and –'

'Pooh,' said Edwin calmly. 'I don't drink half what you do, you old reprobate, for all your complaints about your indigestion, and don't you try to pretend otherwise! My dear chap, will you just *look* at those Caspar girls. Olive, isn't it? Dressed up like the proverbial lamb –'

'Pity she didn't inherit her looks from me the way her brother did,' Oliver said and again tweaked his coat irritably. 'Ain't they got any heating in this church? Maybe it's fashionable, but damme, it's as cold as charity – when will they begin? If they don't get on with it, I shall thank you to get me to m'feet and back to the house for a restorative. Much more of this ice and I really will turn up my toes and then won't you be tickled –'

'Oh, pooh,' Edwin said again. 'They'll start soon enough. The groom's there at any rate. Good looking enough lad, I must say. I imagine dear Lewis and Miriam are delighted. It's not every day a Lackland marries into the peerage.'

'Hah, well, you're wrong there!' Oliver said and swivelled his watery old eyes at his companion. 'Because they wasn't above half pleased at that. Been a sorry drama there, there has.'

'Really?' Edwin settled more cosily into his pew. 'Do tell, my dear old chap, do tell.'

'Not that much to tell *you* – stranger an' all that you are. Keep it in the family,' mumbled Oliver and then went on, hardly taking a breath. 'Lewis was very waxy over it all. Didn't want the boy at all I'm told, made a great to do over it, and only gave way because the girl was pinin' away. Nice child, Johanna, always liked her, really saddened me to see the way she got so peaky. Told her once – you go on this way and you'll be as bad as those foolish Oram girls. But then Miriam put an end to the fuss. Told Letty all about it, she did, and Letty told me. Said it'd all been ridiculous and went to see young Jonty Collingbourne and put him right. And put her girl right too. Took him a long time though, Miriam said. They'd had some silly tiff, she never knew what it was, but some silly tiff or other, and young Johanna wasn't goin' to forget it. And I couldn't find out more from Letty, she being in Scotland with that *Ivanhoe* film. But she did in the end, so there you are. You can never –'

'Sh! Here she is – come on, old man. Up we get – that's it –'

'Daddy! I'm frightened.'

'Of course you are. Every bride is. You'll be fine, my darling. Just relax and hold on to me. Once the music starts you'll be fine.'

'I shouldn't have let him persuade me. I shouldn't –'

'You said you loved him –'

'I do, Daddy, I do. That's why – but maybe he doesn't love me enough? Maybe he'll just go off with someone else and stop loving me and then – ?' And she looked at him piteously through the folds of her veil and her fingers dug more deeply into his arm.

'It's still not too late,' he whispered. 'If you don't want to marry him, we can turn round right now and go home and forget it all. But you've got to be sure. Don't just panic. And remember what we said about it all. What happened with Claudette and me doesn't matter to you. It never did – all ancient unimportant history. It's how you two are together that matters. How you feel about being without him –'

She turned her head again to stare down the church at the rows of backs that awaited them and at the tall distant shape of Jonty standing beside the altar rail. 'Being – what did you say?'

'It's not whether you can be happy with him, my darling. The question is could you be happy without him?'

The first chords came crashing from the organ, and she took a deep breath. 'No,' she whispered and it was almost impossible to hear her. 'No. Whatever happens, whatever he does, I know that now. I'll just have to take a chance. Right foot first, Daddy – here we go.'

'Well, they've not stinted on the champagne, have they?' Daniel said and neatly fielded another glass from the tray of a passing footman. 'This is the Widow, I'll take my oath. Never thought old Lewis'd push the boat out with this much style. Always thought him a dull stick, to tell the truth – but he's come up handsome. Handsome. And everybody here, right enough. Look at your mother, will you! Bullying poor old Cecily again – don't know where she gets the strength from. There, you see! Y'sister's in tears again – she'll be along any moment wanting you to sort it all out. Where's your boy, then, isn't he here to help his aunt?'

'In America, as I've told you often enough. You're getting a good deal older a good deal faster than you might, Daniel. Got no memory at all, have you? I told you he's making those films of his in America. Tells me he's collecting money as fast as they can print it! Can't say it's my cup of tea precisely, but there you are, suits the boy well enough, and he's no sort of burden on me. How's your Samuel gettin' on then, in his little business?'

And Daniel reddened and sniffed and went in search of yet another glass of champagne, leaving James in triumphant control of the field. It would be a long time before the family would forget the embarrassment of having one of its members declared a bankrupt, and a somewhat dubious one at that.

Theo hadn't turned out to be as satisfactory a son as he might have done, but at least the boy was doing well. And he settled to telling his cousin Estella a highly embroidered account of just how well Theo was doing in that outlandish Hollywood place he'd buried himself in.

'My dear, I do feel so sorry for you! I mean I'm sure the child is enchanting to Jonty in her own way, and madly pretty and so forth, but really the *family*! So upright and proper. They must be a fearful bore!'

'Mamie, you're being fearfully catty!' Claudette smiled brilliantly across the flower-scented drawing-room at the tall man standing near the door with a glass of champagne in his hand. 'They're well enough, though for my part I hardly speak to them apart from commonplaces. So I suppose I can't deny they are ghastly boring – but, thank God, they're Jonty's affair, and not mine. And of course you must remember that Johanna's mother inherited the whole of the Gideon Henriques fortune. Useful with Simister to keep up and eating its head off, don't you know, and I've no intention of letting go of a penny more of my own jointure than I have to. Collingbourne left me well enough off, of course, but a bride can come expensive to a young man. Not that the dear girl seems to have enough of her wits about her to be much interested in the things one can do with money. However, that's by the by, as I say, since her mother's so – Mamie, my dear, I have to ask right now – who *is* that man over there? The tall one by the door? Too too divine. It's so ridiculous when one doesn't know who one's fellow guests are – have you any notion?'

'Eh? Who? Oh, him. My dear, that's David Henriques. His mother was a Damont – brother went wildly bankrupt a few months ago, caused an enormous *brouhaha*. He's a cousin of the bride, umpteen times removed.'

'Is he bankrupt?'

'Not that I've heard of. He's something to do with the diamond bourse through his mother's family. Claudette, my dear, do come back. I wanted to ask you –'

'Do you mind not being there?' Emilia asked. 'I mean, for yourself? I know your mother does, of course, but mothers always do, don't they? Mine was livid, but there it was. I told her I couldn't and from this distance what could she do? But you and your parents – it's different for you.'

'I suppose it is,' Max said and stared up at the naked trees above their heads as they strolled through the Prater looking for the first greening branches. It was February, after all. It couldn't be long now. 'But they understood. They know I've got an exam in a fortnight and I can't possibly cope with it if I'm racketing about in trains going to a wedding. Even Johanna's. I promised 'em I'd drink a toast though, at the same time. So we shall. Where shall it be?'

Emilia laughed. 'Where could it be but Sacher's? I don't know anywhere else you can get champagne and chocolate cake at the same time. Do you?'

'In Vienna you can get anything anywhere,' he said. 'Come on. Because we've both got work to do tonight, Saturday or not. Did you get all your translation finished?'

'Every bit,' she said and hugged herself. 'Max, I'm awfully glad we're related now. Aren't you?'

'Related? Are we?' They were coming out of the park now, into the wide square where the trams clanged their way towards the Ringstrasse. 'I suppose so. Am I your brother-in-law or what?'

'Something like that,' Emilia said, and pulled her coat up as the wind nipped viciously across the Square. And one day, she thought dreamily, we'll be more than that. One day. I managed to get myself here to study with him and I'll manage to get myself home to love him and live with him. You see if I don't. 'Something like that.' And she tucked her hand into his elbow and swung into a matching step as they went across the square head down towards Sacher's to drink a toast to the pair getting married in London, almost eight hundred miles away.